THE PANDORA QUEST

ISBN number is 978-0-244-45725-9.

Cover artwork by: The Author

Chapters

FOREWORD

Dear Reader,

Thank you for opening - and hopefully, for continuing to read through this book! Because I have written it - *for you...!*

I have to tell you as well, that in addition to opening your book, you have also just opened a portal! - *But please don't worry! - It's not to another World - in a galaxy far, far away!* It's actually to the World - *you are on right now...!*

Soon - and it shouldn't take *too long* to happen after you have taken your initial steps through the portal, and then walked along the sands of the revealed pathway - *where at first it all seems to be really quite familiar,* so, reassured, you journey on, by continuing to read. But you will, now *very* soon, *start to see this World you are on, and all that is around you,* from a 'different' perspective, with a 'different' awareness, and so, I venture to suggest, it may well turn out not to be *quite the same old World* you always 'saw' before...

Especially when, at first, you start to only glimpse - *then properly see what is really going on all around you.* Because then - *perhaps,* you might even decide to go on research Journeys of your own to learn and understand much more about all the things that have been revealed, and *you* can see now...*But they remain hidden, un-seen, and un-known about, by most people*...unless, of course! - *You Go Out And Tell Them!*

There are quite a lot of Chapters along the pathway from the portal you have just opened, which will take you to many different places, *(where many things are revealed - and there are many more to discover...!)* Some will take you a while to pass through. Some won't. But they all flow together in this Journey's account - as the storying of it should do. However, each Chapter does, I hope, 'stand alone' as well, as a place - 'in its own right' - for you to quickly portal back to, and then spend some time there once again, just to enjoy being in that place, and with the people there.

And when you do *eventually* come back – *and from having*

travelled far and wide on research Journeys of your own as well, you will, *like a pilgrim, have left only your footprints in the sand, and have taken, only your memories…*

…So Go Out And Tell People About Them…! Because The Real And Current Danger is That:

"Nothing Strengthens Authority so much as…*Silence*"
Leonardo da Vinci

So…I hope you enjoy this story, *and all your Journeys.*

Temet Nosce…Namaste…In Lak'ech
(please do look up the meanings of these Great and Powerful Words…)

yours sincerely,
I.A.M.

Chapter 1: The Whitby Road

70 mph...**80...90...100...120mph! Whoooooaaa!** Jake's mind shouted out to him. *Come down, come down! - Wi' these raised up 'ape-hanger' type 'andlebars any faster an' y'll need arms stronger than Tarzan's to hold on to 'em!*

...Ease off the throttle...just a touch o'brakes...get back down to 70mph...*Phewww! That's better! - Any faster an' I'd abin blown off back'ards!*

He was immensely relieved though that the bike was now accelerating smoothly when in high revs and firing properly on all cylinders at last - after stripping down and reassembling the engine several times over the past week to try and find out why it hadn't been. The last time was a couple of days ago. But that had involved doing a partial re-wire as well with the all new electrical system components he'd ordered - and had painstakingly tested *each one of* this time to make sure that they *all worked when having to operate under their maximum load first–* and they all had - unlike the previous lot he'd originally fitted straight out of their packs, without testing them, and it turned out through a slow and tedious process of elimination that two of them had been intermittently faulty when under high revs, and were the hidden culprits causing him so much frustration and days of wasted time stripping the engine down time and again trying to work out what was wrong!

*Still...*he thought...if they'd all worked first time I mebbe wouldn't'a gone down to the harbour for a stroll last Monday lunch-time to have a break from it - *before I pulled all me hair out!* - and then seen Sophie sittin' there...and then bin involved with everythin' that lead to when we went to the Fair together that evenin'!...*An'...now, well, bein' proper involved wi' Sophie an'all...! - So I reckon it's true that there's always a silver linin' in ev'ry dark cloud!*

His thoughts then returned to fully concentrating on riding as he put the big powerful bike through its paces, constantly monitoring the way it was handling, whilst ticking off a mental check list of every aspect of its performance.

This 40 mile return route along the scenic, often winding, but with long up and down straight stretches, 'moors' road' to Whitby from Scarborough and then back again was ideal for very early morning – when he often had the road to himself more or less, as any later it was usually packed with tourist traffic - test riding of the custom bikes he designed and put together.

This bike project had been a bit more challenging than some – and not just due to all the hassles with the electrics. *But Finally! Here we are! An early sunny morning, the road to meself, and we're motoring along nicely. What more could y' want?* Well he knew exactly what more - and it suddenly appeared about a quarter of a mile straight ahead as he came out of that last corner 'Like A Bat Out Of Hell', as the song goes…

A few seconds later he pulled in to the lay-by where a ramshackled old catering van was parked up. It had a big, amateurishly hand painted sign on its side that read: *'Big Sammy's Sarnies 'n' Breakfast Baps'*, and he strolled over to it, taking his helmet off.

"…*Bloody 'Ell Jake! - I put y'bacon int' fryin' pan when y'left Scarborough! – I 'eard y'set off…!*" A loud growly voice shouted out to him from inside the van.

Jake grinned as he approached the serving hatch. "Aye! *Bet y'could an'all Sammy!* Client wanted 'straight through' exhausts on it, no silencers, he said he, *'…wanted to drown out all the Yankee Harley Davidsons on't road!'* They do mek it roar a bit like!"

"*- Bloody Right They Do An'All!* Crikey me! – *Ee'll 'ave every traffic cop in't county pesterin' 'im every time 'e gus out wi' them noisy things on it!*"

Jake laughed and said, "Aye! 'Appen he will! But…*'straight throughs' are what he said he wanted!* - Thought I might get pulled over by 'em meself on't way up 'ere, or 'appen I will yet on't way back - but I 'aven't seen 'em so far."

"Nah, y'll be alreight mate - theys 'ad a bacon sarny each 'ere abaht 'alf 'an hour back, then went back down into Whitby. I 'eard 'em sayin' there's only them two on today, bit short staffed, 'oliday season or summat, an' they're gonna be around Whitby all day."

Big Sammy then leaned out over the serving hatch to get a better look at the bike. *"Very nice Jake! Y'know what? – It reminds me...it looks like...that bike in the seventies film...'Easy Rider'* – weren't it? *The one that Pete Fonda rode?"*

"Aye! Well spotted mate! *That's the one!* Wanted me to mek 'im a replica of it, but wi'a Triumph Daytona twelve 'undred engine and a St. George's flag painted on't tank 'stead o' Stars an' Stripes. Primer an' undercoats are all done, as y'can see, I'm startin' on doin' the final paint job when I get back this mornin'. Ol'Billy's lettin' me use 'is spray booth at the garage."

"Y'll be wantin' y'usual Big Breakfast Bap, coffee an' cake, afore y'start on that job o' work then?!"

"Errr...Nah...think I'll 'ave lentil soup an' a cucumber salad, wi'a cup o' green tea mate...!" His face didn't betray a sign of anything other than being totally earnest. Which wasn't easy, as he was splitting with laughter inside, waiting to see Sammy's predictable reaction, and he wasn't disappointed....!

"EH?! Y'What?! Bloody 'Ell! - Not 'ere y'wont! - Y'll 'ave a 'Big Sammy Special': bacon, sausage, black puddin', tomato an' three fried egg King Size Big Breakfast Bap mate, an' chocolate cake fer afters wi'a big cracked mug of old engin' oil coffee...! - *Just like y'normally do ev'ry Sat'day mornin'...!"*

He turned back into his mobile kitchen and started to noisily rattle culinary implements around. Jake heard him muttering about...*'Bloody Lentils!'...Windy enough up 'ere as it is!'*, and grinned, he always enjoyed having a good crack with Big Sammy. The sizzlings and aromas of frying bacon and sausages soon wafted out over the lay-by.

They bantered back and forth with each other whilst Jake's food was being fried up, although being partially cremated would be a more accurate description. Then he took his huge breakfast bap, not

7

far off the size of an old fashioned galvanised bin lid, on a giant sized cardboard plate, over to one of the white plastic picnic tables and chairs.

The views from up here in the lay-by were superb. On one side, below, in the distance, he could see the picturesque harbour at Whitby, and the headland at the side of it where the old, mysterious looking Abbey ruins were lit up in the sunshine, the sea behind them glinting brightly all the way to the horizon.

On the other side of the road the endless multi hued green moors rolled out to another far horizon. I'll 'ave to bring Dave The Artist up 'ere one mornin' he thought, he'd do a great paintin' of it all - even wi' Big Sammy's ancient ol' van belchin' out clouds o' burnt bacon an' sausage - bein' a blot on the landscape, he grinned to himself.

"Give us a shout when y'want yer coffee mate – an' I'll put t'kettle on! Oh, *'Ey up!* 'Ere come more 'ungry bikers…!"* Big Sammy called out. Jake had also heard the approaching sounds of several motorbikes revving loudly towards the lay-by, having raced up from Whitby.

He knew it would be the Whitby MC (Motorcycle Club), as they usually called in at Big Sammy's about this time early on a Saturday morning before going off on a day's ride, to fuel up on his infamous and *locally named*: 'Big, But Burnt, Breakfast Baps!' A dozen bikes, some with pillion riders on them pulled in noisily and parked up.

A parade-ground-loud voice suddenly shouted out to Big Sammy, it came from an imposing, bald headed but long bearded figure walking with a slight limp, in the front rank of the black leather clad gang of bikers now rapidly approaching his van on foot.

"'Ey up Big Sammy! 'As tha gorr 'owt left?! - As I see our Jake gorr 'ere first!

"Oh Aye! - *But only just enough tho' fer yous lot!* Ee's left y'a few odds an' ends! - *Any later an' y'd all abin back on't army ration packs agin Simmo!"* Sammy shouted back.

"Cheeky sods! *Talk about 'Pots callin' Kettles!'"* Jake shouted back at them, then laughed, calling out, *"Y'alright then Simmo?!"*

8

"*Aye!* Magic, cheers! An' ow's you then Jake? *Good to see y'mate!*" he boomed loudly, shaking Jake's hand in a comradely hand clasp. "An' that! – *That is summat else mate...!*" The biker called Simmo, who was the Club's 'President' said as he looked over and saw Jake's bike.

Well that was it for the next half hour or so. The 'Easy Rider' look-a-like chopper bike and the film it had featured in was then the main centre of conversation amongst them all as they munched on their fry-up breakfasts.

The Whitby MC riders were going down to Lincoln for the day to visit a Classic and Custom Bike Show. Jake had had a text about it from Simmo earlier in the week, but he'd had to reply saying that he couldn't go to it today, due to working on the bike's paint job this morning.

As they were finishing their breakfasts, Jake told Simmo that after the morning's paint job he was picking up Sophie from the Estate Agent's office in town, where she worked a half-day on Saturdays, and then going over to Filey with her to see their new mates, Dave and Melanie, in their new place in the afternoon. Then after that he was taking Sophie to meet his Mum for the first time, and have their teas with her, before going off to the last night of the Scarborough Fair. So all in all it was going to be a busy day for him as well!

Through a mouthful of Breakfast Bap, with egg yolk dripping down his beard, Simmo said,

"Oh good...we're all goin' to Fair tonight an'all mate, on't way back, as it's its last night, so we'll 'appen meet up with y'all there then."

Another of Jake's mates in the Whitby M.C., Reg, then told him about a garage find of an old, 'sixties Norton Commando bike he'd come across when he'd done a house clearance a couple of days ago. He outlined the ideas he'd got, that he wanted to run past Jake, for him to renovate and re-style it as a classic cafe racer. But with time moving on, and the others having finished their breakfasts, and now making moves to get back on their bikes, they agreed to get in touch again over the next couple of days to discuss it in more detail.

Jake rode back amongst the pack of riders, thoroughly enjoying the exhilaration of being out on the open road again, tearing along with his biker mates. He veered off at Scarborough to much horn blasting and good natured two fingered gestures from them all.

Ol'Billy, the owner of the back street garage near the centre of town, was just starting to open up the shutters when Jake noisily arrived.

"*'Ey up!* Mornin' Jake! - I 'eard y'cumin' when y'were about five mile away! I'll get us a brew on in a minute an' then give y'hand clearin' out the spray booth, it's all yours fer this mornin' an' Monday mornin' then." He shouted out over his shoulder, fiddling with an awkward padlock on the main entrance's big pull-down shutter. Jake switched the very loud engine off so they could talk at normal volume as Ol'Billy finally got the padlock off and opened up the shutter.

"Oh cheers Billy. I did all the wet n' dry rubbin' down o' the tank, side panels' an' mudguards' under coats last night, so I should get a coupla top coats an' the flag paint all done this mornin', an' then the clear lacquer finish'll be on Monday, and I'm aimin' to 'ave it all finished by the end o' play on Tuesday. Client's cumin' fer it late Wednesday afternoon."

All that said whilst grunting at the same time with the effort of pushing the big, long and heavy bike up the steepish ramp into the cavernous garage. Once inside and resting on its chromed side stand he then walked back over to Ol'Billy.

"...Just rode back with the Whitby lads from up at Big Sammy's – he asked me to say *'Ello'* to you - an' so did Simmo. *An' it looks like I've gotta 'nother job an'all!* Y'know Reg – he was there, well...he wants me to make 'im a classic style cafe racer from an ol' sixties Norton Commando he's now got that's all in bits – some bits are missin' like, but that's not a problem – an' can y'believe it! - Lucky sod said he found it all under a great load o' junk in a big double garage that 'e was doin' an 'ouse clearance on in Pickerin'! - Told 'im it were nearly as good a find as that couple o' ex-army World War Two despatch bikes I got that turned up in that farmer's barn in Bridlington a couple o' weeks back!"

"*By Gum!* Nice find that 'eh! *An' ol' Norton Commando!* I 'ad one o' them back in the day! *Eeee - reight machine it were an'all!* 'Ey - y'll 'ave a waitin' list soon! *An' so y'should!* - Y've done a bloody great job wi' this latest one Jake - as y'did wi' all t'others before an'all. *An' a paint job'll really put The Top Hat on it!*

"Always said y'could tek any ol' wreck, some odds an' ends from outta metal skip, add a splash o' paint an' end up mekin' summat knockout! Y'Dad were same...but some of 'is other inventions I never did unnerstand! - 'Ow's he doin' these days mate, y'll 'ave bin to see 'im this week ah tek it?"

"Aye, we went round last Thursday night, me an' Mum. We could see he's well looked after and in good 'ands at that nursin' 'ome, them nurses an' staff are brilliant, don't know 'ow they do it...Least he recognised us fer some o' the time...*that bloody Alzheimers is just a bloody rotten thing to 'appen to 'im, to anyone, it's not right...*

"...Anyways...she's puttin' a brave face on, but she's in a right state really...Glad I'm back livin' at 'ome now so I can be with 'er an' 'elp 'er out a bit, otherwise she'd be 'avin to cope all on 'er own..."

Recalling his visit with his Mum to see his Dad suddenly saddened Jake, bringing him down from the high after his ride back. Gone, yet still there, was the Dad he remembered from his childhood, his teenage years, and upto the recent times of his mid twenties.

For the past few years his Dad had always seemed to have been even busier than usual with something he was working on in the big workshop sheds he'd built in the large back garden at home that he'd mostly paved over. Those sheds had always fascinated Jake - from as far back into his childhood as he could remember. Because in them, amongst all the weird and wonderful clutter, the man he remembered was always making and inventing amazing and sometimes, more often than not, to the young Jake, unfathomable things for purposes he hadn't understood.

His Dad had always been so patient, talking and explaining to him all about what he was doing, even though a lot of it went over the young Jake's head at the time. He'd always taken pleasure in showing and demonstrating to Jake how to use his vast array of tools, machines and specialist equipment. Often then giving Jake 'special projects', as he had called them, for him to practice using them, and helped him to design and make things with them, before moving on, as the years went by, to teaching him how to renovate old motorbikes.

Jake gave out a long deep and sad sigh, his head down, as images from these reminiscences had flitted in front of his mind's eye like a scratchy old cine film. Seeing Jake suddenly upset Ol'Billy reached up with one hand and squeezed his shoulder, his face grim in sympathy with him, nodding silently.

"Blimey Jake! If y'carry on growin' I'll 'ave to get me steps out to reach up t'you! - Time was I remember 'avin *to reach down* to you! *Don't seem that long back either mate!"* He said with forced joviality. *"C'mon*...if you finish openin' up rest o' shutters I'll go an' put kettle on. Then we'll get crackin', 'fore rest o' lads get 'ere."

"Aye...cheers Billy...I've a lot to get done before I pick up Sophie at lunchtime..."

"Oh I see! *Gettin' a bit fond o' that nice lass are we then, eh...?!"*

"Aye! I am, she's...*reckon she's the one for me…!"*

"Good on yer Jake! I'm right pleased for yers, an' I mean that. Mind yer - *if I were fifty years younger yer wouldn't 'ave 'ad a look in like!"*

Jake grinned affectionately at him, his mood now lightened.

"Oh aye?! I hear y'don't do too badly with 'The Ladies' as y'are Billy! - *Rumour round 'ere 'as it that they're all linin' up for you - on your long waitin' list!"* He turned away with the big bunch of keys that he'd just been given to open up the rest of the shutters, and muttered just loud enough for Ol'Billy to hear him say, *"...Can't see what they all see in y' meself though!"*

"...Still a cheeky little bugga!" Ol'Billy muttered back with a grin, shaking his head as he walked off to go and put the kettle on.

Chapter 2: Filey Brigg

Jake roared up the hill of the new wide bypass out of Scarborough with Sophie holding on tightly to him, her arms wrapped around his waist. He was back on his own bike now, having picked Sophie up on it outside the Estate Agents in the town centre.

Saturday was a half day in the office there for her, and they'd both been looking forward to going over to Filey this afternoon to see Dave and Mel's new home - which was the large static caravan owned by Dave's parents they used to use for family holidays.

Mel had said when they'd all been in Gypsy Magda Leah Rose's Romany caravan at the Scarborough Fair last Monday night that she, *'...loved her caravan! - and would much prefer to live in something like this...!'* So, in the space of four hectic days they had given notice to the Letting Agent of the flat, and forsaking the month's rent in advance they'd already paid – they'd moved out! *'How about that for a quickly created manifestation!'* Mel had texted Sophie! They could live there now because recently the caravan site had had a licence granted by the Council for all year round occupancy.   Previously it had been for only nine months of the year. So the young couple had met with Dave's parents who had agreed to let them move in and live there.

Compared to the poky and damp flat in a not-so-good area of town that they had been living in it was a great move for them, plus the site's ground rent was a lot less than the monthly rent they'd been paying for the flat.

Judging from the many photos that Mel had sent to both Sophie and Jake it looked idyllic - sited as it was near the cliff tops overlooking Filey Bay, with Filey Brigg, a narrow rocky promontory nearly a mile long that jutted out into the sea more or less in front of them. Archaeological excavations on 'The Brigg' in recent decades had revealed the foundations of a fourth century Roman watch tower, and 'The Brigg' had many mysterious legends about it, as fishermen and townsfolk over the centuries have claimed to have seen strange creatures on it, or in the sea near to it…

As they passed through the entrance to the caravan site Jake slowed his powerful bike down to a jogging pace and Sophie called out the directions to the caravan she'd memorised from the text message Mel had sent her that morning.

"There it is! And Look! There's Mel and Dave!" Sophie called out to Jake excitedly. The young couple were standing on the timber decked patio along the front side of a huge static caravan and were waving to them. Parking right outside it Jake put both his large booted feet on the ground as Sophie dismounted. With loud exclamations of delight and excitement Mel rushed over to them, jiggling up and down as she hugged Sophie before she'd even had time to take her white open face helmet off!

"Oh it's so great to see you both!...So much to tell you!...Did you find it okay…? What d you think…?!...Wh…?!"

"Hah Ha Ha! Give them a minute! - *Let them arrive first luv!"* Dave interrupted her with a laugh, moving in and putting an arm around her shoulders and bear hugging her close to him.

"- But she's dead right! – It is great to see you both and we do have lots to tell you! But first, I thought you'd both want coffee...and...*well, I'm not quite so sure about this though*...but would a local Filey delicacy called...oh - *what was it...?* Oh yeah! – *'chocolate fudge cream cake'* - be of any interest…?!"

"Hah! *Certainly would!* Now y're talkin'! - 'Ey Soph' – *I'm glad we came now…!"* Jake said with his usual deadpan humour, amused at Dave's similar delivery.

"Well come on in then! - You'll have to excuse all the clutter, we're still living out of boxes and bags!" Dave laughed as he shook Jake's hand.

"Eeee – Y're lucky! - *I used to dreeeam o' livin' in boxes and bags…when I lived in't middle o't'main road wi' just a few ol' ripped an' soggy newspapers fer a blanket...!"* Jake said, shaking his head, sounding just like John Cleese in the famous: 'Four Yorkshiremen', Monty Python comedy sketch; as they all went into the caravan.

14

Mel and Dave had certainly been busy! Even in just a few days they had already made great inroads to make the large caravan into a cosy home. There were three bedrooms, a double and two big singles, both of those were piled up nearly to the ceilings with still unopened boxes and black bin bags full of clothes and all sorts of other stuff spilling out into the corridor.

"There's still *loads of stuff* back at the flat, we keep going back and forth and piling our little car up with it, but it takes ages, and we need to move the furniture out as well, we just don't need it all now...it's crazy just how much stuff you gather *and don't really need*." Mel said.

"Yes, I think the word of the week for all this we're doing is - *'cathartic'* – sorting and purging out all the clutter and baggage we've gathered as Mel says - so we can have a new and fresh start here – so we're downsizing to just the essentials! Just not really sure how, and what to do, with everything we don't need now though!" Dave said, obviously frustrated at all these domestic practicalities.

Sophie said, "Well...my friend Michelle is the manageress of the Age UK charity shops in Scarborough...I'm sure she'd really appreciate anything you want to donate, furniture as well, so you could have it all gone in one go! Trouble is though she told me on Thursday when I saw her that their big van's off the road for about a week being fixed up for its MOT..."

Jake said, "Er...*if y'want*...I'll 'ave a word with me mate Reg, actually I saw 'im this mornin' at Big Sammy's, he's got a big Luton van for removals an' house clearances, he'd geddit all in for yous in one load, he'd do a drop off at the charity shop an'all, so then you'd 'ave the flat emptied an' then that'd be it, job done. In fact he'll be at the Fair tonight – we could sort it then with 'im, prob'ly do it all tomorrow, as I know he's busy all next week, an' tell y'what – it won't cost y'anythin'! I can knock 'is bill off the cost of doin' a bike renovation job 'e wants me to do for 'im – a Norton Cafe Racer!"

Jake's spontaneous words of kind generosity silenced Mel and Dave for a moment, then Dave grasped Jake's hand firmly saying, "*Oh Jake*

15

man...that's really brilliant of you, thank you mate!"

Mel stepped in and gave Jake a big hug, her spiky blond hair only reaching halfway up his big leather jacketed chest, saying, *"Oh bless you!* Thank you *so* much! It is starting to get a bit overwhelming now for us…especially as Dave's old car has started to play up a bit now as well, it keeps stopping and it's difficult to start up again. But between you two you've solved it! *Thank you! Thank you both!"*

"Oh, er, no worries – glad to 'elp y'out! But we 'ave got summat else as a house – *caravan* – warmin' present! – Well, I say *'we'* it were Soph who eventually found it! Think she searched every antique and charity shop in town on 'er day off last Thursday before she found one in't Market Vaults! I 'ad to re-frame an' re-glaze it tho' as it were cracked...y'got it there Soph?"

Sophie opened up her large shoulder bag and took out a gaily wrapped parcel the size of a paperback book and gave it with a big grin to Mel.

"I finally got this - *in the last place I went to!* The crazy thing is though is that it was actually *in the first place* I went to! - But the Market Vault's shop hadn't opened when I went round there in the morning! So I tried again – last thing, after going everywhere else, just on the off chance - and I couldn't believe it! *There it was all along!* It's the same, I think, as Magda had inside, above the door in hers…!" Sophie said.

"Oh Wow! It's Fantastic! *Oh thank you so much!* Look Dave! It is as well! *It's the same!"* Mel exclaimed, showing Dave the small antique looking hand embroidered tapestry sign in an ornate gold coloured frame saying: 'Home Sweet Home'.

"Awesome! *Thank you both!* It's going straight up above *our* door now!" He said.

One demolished chocolate fudge cream cake and several mugs of coffee with general catching up conversation later, Sophie asked, "Well...what can I do now Mel? What do you want me to help you unpack and sort out first? I think if just us two get on with it - *without Jake and Dave getting under our feet I'm sure us girls can get loads*

16

done!"

" - Err... *'Ow could I ever get under anyone's feet?!"* Jake asked her as he shuffled his huge body along the fitted sofa, nearly pushing Sophie off its edge.

"I'm dainty an' careful me!"

Sophie squeaked, grabbing hold of Jakes arm to stop herself from slipping off, and then gave him a mock stern glare for a moment before she couldn't help herself from giggling at him.

Dave grinned, "I think Sophie's right mate – we might be best leaving them to it! We'll take a walk down the Brigg, tide's out - *and there's somethings I want to tell you about and show you."*

"Oh, *o-kaaay then, huh,* an' I was all set to hem the curtains and then do all the dustin' an' polishin' as well, ah well, *neverrr mind...!"* Jake replied with a loud *'tut'* and comically dead-panned disappointment. Then with exaggerated clumsiness he stood up, disrupting the table and nearly knocking over their mugs.

They were both volubly shooed outside by the two girls.

" - Nicely done mate! – *You got us out of all that unpacking and sorting out carry on!"* Dave said.

"Well, I'm findin' out that with women it's best to let 'em think it's their idea – *what y'wanted to do in't first place!*...I think!"

"We Heard That...!" Sophie called out from inside the caravan, "...And it's Not Allowed! – *It's What We Do!"*

"Oh 'eck! Right - c'mon then mate – we'd best be off! - *While the goin''s good!* - Where we off to?!" Jake asked him.

"Yeah I think you're right! - We'll go across the field to the cliff top and then along the path and go down it onto the Brigg right to the end, if y'fancy that? - It's a great walk!"

"Aye! I do! *Sounds good!* Not been down onto the Brigg for years. Think I'll leave me jacket 'ere tho', it's a warm one today!" He slipped off his big heavy black leather bike jacket and folded it up, putting it way under the caravan safely out of sight. Dave couldn't help noticing the powerful and well defined musculature of Jake's arms and upper body now revealed in a sleeve cut off black T shirt. After a few minutes walking they stopped at the cliff top to take in the magnificent view across Filey Bay.

"It's a lot bigger than you think it is, Filey Bay, when y' see it all from 'ere, in't it mate." Jake said.

"It is, you're right...Y'know, I think I've always wanted to live here – ever since coming on holidays as a kid, and now I am - *we are!* Feels just like one of those long childhood summer holidays - but you don't have to go away and leave it at the end of a couple o' weeks!"

"Last time I was 'ere were years ago, think I were only twelve or thirteen, summat like that, came with me Dad an' 'is mates, we went just a bit further along the cliff path towards Cayton Bay, it were night time, middle o' winter it was, snow on't ground, an' I remember it were bloody cold! Used to come 'ere – an' all over, with the UFO Spotters Club he'd 'elped to start up, before I were born. We all saw a lot o' very strange things over the years in't night skies an' out at sea..."

"Well well well – you've started off on something I was going to tell you about!"

"Oh aye?! Sounds interestin'!"

"It is mate! - And it sounds like you'll know a lot more about it than I do! - But I'll get to it in a minute. First I've got a long story but I'll cut it short: last Tuesday morning, we drove over to my Mum and Dad's to borrow the keys for the caravan. Y'know Mel had never been in one before! Well – apart from Magda's that is last Monday evening! So anyway, she wanted to see it - kept me up most of the night talking about it! – And about everything else that had happened last Monday night!

"Soon as she got here, went inside, had a good look round – that was it! She loved it! - Never had occurred to me to think about moving here to live in it instead of that damp, poky flat! Well you couldn't anyway, as the site didn't have an all year round licence then for that.

"Anyway, we went back to have a long chat with my Mum and Dad, and they thought it was a great idea for us to live in it, as long as we thought we'd be okay in it. The past few years they've only used it for a day out or a picnic now and then, didn't want to sell it as they said it had too many nice memories for them. But now they're retired they prefer the guaranteed Spanish sunshine and luxury hotels for their holidays!"

"Aye, I know what they mean – well, not the luxury 'otel bit – I've never been in one o' them! I mean that Spanish sun - it's summat else! But I still say y'can't beat a good English Summer! 'Avin' said that I did right enjoy it tourin' an' campin' round Spain a couple o' summers back on't bike, me, Simmo – he's a good ol' mate - an' a couple o' the Whitby lads – in fact Reg were one of 'em, just before he started 'is removals business - *even us bikes got suntans!* But anyway...it were good o' y'Mum an' Dad to 'elp y'both out like they did weren't it?!"

"Yes, it was, I think they *finally* realised that Mel and I were seriously together and I was set on doing my own thing, going my own way, as we both were, are, after they were against all that at first – like I was saying at Magda's last Monday...So they'd obviously decided to support instead of oppose...But that's not all of it....and I haven't even told Mel about this next bit yet…!"

"Oh 'eck mate – sounds a bit ominous…!"

"No! – *no, it's incredible…!* Dad rang me this morning, when I was out shopping – getting that chocolate fudge cream cake! - And there's another one in the fridge for when we get back...*Oh!* - *It was* supposed to have been a surprise for later!"

"Oh Brilliant! - *Now I Am Definitely* glad I came!" Jake laughed along with Dave.

"So...he rang me to tell me that he and Mum had thought about it and decided to sign the caravan over to me! They've made a gift of it to me! So it's now mine! I own it!"

"*Bloody 'ell mate! That's brilliant!* No wonder y're made up! *But – y' 'aven't told Mel yet?!*"

"No I haven't, and the reason why is – *because when it's all finally sorted* – when all the moving in hassle and everything *is all done and finished with* – which'll only be a few days now I think, thanks to your kind offer with your mate Reg's van, and Sophie suggesting her friend's charity shop for all the stuff to go to, so, when all that's done - I'm going to tell her then!   Over a Romantic Kebab Takeaway Candlelit Dinner in the caravan!"

"Hah Ha ha! Fantastic! 'A Romantic Kebab Takeaway'! I'll 'ave to tell Big Sammy about them!   Might put 'em on 'is menu! *Nice one mate!"*

"Cheers!   Can't wait to see Mel's face when I tell her! So...one evening next week, the day after we're all done and I've told her, if you and Sophie are up for it we can have another do – how about a mega barbecue?!"

"Awesome! *Definitely* mate!"

"Great! - And after...we could all go down the Brigg - *and see if it comes back again...at night...*"

"What's that? – *See if 'what' comes back...?"*

"Well that's the next thing I want to tell you about...I've saved the best till last! Well...no, not *'the best'* I don't mean it like that - because everything else that's happened this week, since last Monday evening when we went to the Fair, has made it *'the best' week I've ever had!* No, I mean, I think...well...let's go down the path a bit and sit on those rocks over there - it's where I saw...*'it'*...from, and I'll tell you everything, won't take too long, and then we'll see what you make of it..."

He'd pointed to a cluster of jutting rocks just off to one side of the narrow path. Jake was highly intrigued, what was Dave going to tell him? And what was this 'it' he'd just said he'd seen…?

When they had both sat themselves down on the rocks, their backs resting against the cliff, and facing out to sea, their feet dangling over a steep gully in the cliff face, Dave, hesitantly at first, started talking again.

"Right...well...here we go...I came down to this exact spot yesterday morning, very early, it was still a bit dark, to watch the sun rise. I'd just woken up suddenly and felt an inner urge to come here. Sounds a bit daft I suppose, but I just did. Mel was fast asleep and I didn't want to disturb her, so I just crept out quietly from the caravan and came right here! I sat down, just like we are now, and relaxed, gazing out to the horizon and started to drift into a meditation...which since last Tuesday I've started doing again...*needed to with all the stress and hassle of moving!* – Anyway - after a while the sun started to come up, the tide was in, no one else was around, it was just me, the Brigg, the sea, the rising sun...and..."

He took a deep breath, "and *'it'*...out there...!" He pointed out to sea.

" *'It'?* " Jake couldn't help himself from quietly asking Dave.

"Yes...*'It'*...At first I thought I was probably dreaming...but I wasn't. What I was seeing looked like a, well, I thought then, trying to make sense of what I was seeing, was that it must be a massive, freak shoal of jellyfish floating on the surface of the sea, because it was all sort of translucent like jellyfish are.

"But it seemed to be going in and out of focus, *an' jellyfish don't do that do they?!*...There was a top, long curved part that was floating just above the waves and it shimmered reflecting the sun's rays off it. And it was big! And I mean big!" He stretched his right arm out straight in front of him and made a fist, "it was a bit bigger than my fist and just under half way to the horizon."

Jake stretched his long right arm out as well, made a fist, squinted his eyes and looked along his arm, out to sea. "Blimey, then y're talkin' about summat getting' on fer the size of a football pitch, or even bigger mate - an' that'd be a lot o' jellyfish!"

"Yeah, y're right - it would be, but then...my mind finally realised, or it came to terms with the fact...*that it wasn't jellyfish*...Because then, after twenty, thirty seconds or so, it seemed to...well, the best way I can describe it is - it seemed to go into sharp focus and *solidify*, because I couldn't see through it then. And then it slowly rose up so all of it was just above the waves...the sea was just pouring off it. As it slowly went up my stomach felt like it was rapidly going down with my heart pounding frantically as it followed it!

"I'd only seen a small part of it that was visible on the surface before – and now I could see it all, and it was huge, a deep, long oval like shape...and metallic, shiny like chrome, it hovered for a few seconds in plain sight then it silently shot off just above the waves, right along the sun's rays on the water, before it gradually submerged again just before the horizon, and disappeared into the sea completely...!

"I just sat here then for ages as my mind, stomach, heart – everything! Slowly got back to normal, calmed down and got over the shock...*of what I'd just seen...it was just incredible mate...!*"

"*Wowww!*" Jake said, "you must've thought then...what I'm thinkin' now Dave?!"

"Well, if you're thinking *it was obviously a UFO!* – Then yes, I was, and you are...!"

"Aye! I am! But they're called 'USO's' – Unidentified Submersible Objects. When I used to go out a lot with the Spotter's Club - before I discovered motorbike's – we saw quick glimpses an' flashes o'coloured lights from more than a few o' them along these coastlines, 'specially further along down at Bempton cliffs. Some came out o' the sea like y'saw, an' some came down from the sky and went in to it...

"But none of us ever saw anythin' as big an' as clear an' for as long as you did in full daylight mate! - That is...though...apart from what just one of us saw one mornin'...*an' that were more or less right 'ere as well...!*" He then added, with noticeable concern as he quickly looked at Dave, "Oh - I tek it then that *I'm the only one y've told this to – y've kept it to yerself so far...?*"

"Oh yeah, I haven't said anything about it to anyone. But *Woww! – Didn't any of that – everything you all in the club saw - ever get in the local papers or the news back then? –* I don't remember ever reading much - if anything, to be honest, about all that going on locally – and I didn't even know of there being a UFO Spotter's Club round here?!"

Jake had nodded his head in relief at Dave's assuring him that he was the only one he'd spoken to about it. Then he said, "Nah, it didn't - *it weren't for lack o' tryin' tho'!* At first the club always reported all its sightings to a reporter at the Scarborough Newspaper me Dad knew, he were called Dave an'all, an' he were dead interested in it all, he even went out wi' 'em some nights when t'club first got started up, a lot o'folk did. Some nights there'd be more than a coupla dozen spotters spread out in groups o' twos or threes 'alf a mile or so apart all along these cliff tops..!

"It were all really well organised. Me Dad 'ad repaired an' tweaked up a load o' ex-army surplus radio walkie-talkies an' a base transmitter for 'em he got from a government auction down South. He worked on 'em in't sheds at home, fixed 'em up good as...well...*better than new*! An' he showed me 'ow to do it wi' him.

"So all the spotter groups were then in contact wi' each other, all the time, an' they all 'ad powerful binos', telescopes, cameras an' even some ol'cine cameras they 'ad in them days an'all.

"But after a while that reporter just went cold on it all, an' then he suddenly moved away, left the area, an' after that the club got no more coverage or even any interest from the local press..."

Jake looked out to sea, pausing for a moment with a far away look in his eyes, as he recalled these memories from years ago.

"Me Dad said to me, when I were a bit older an' I started goin' out at night wi' 'em, and I asked 'im the same question - about why the newspaper's were ignorin' the club's activities, I remember he said: *'that it were as if the reporter that used to cover their sightings, an' all of 'em at that paper, an' t'other papers in the area, 'ad all been suddenly told to say we were just fakin' our photos an' stories, an' then make a joke of it an' take the piss out of us...then eventually they just completely ignored us...'*

"I'm goin' back now to the very early days o' the actual Spotter's Club like, about thirty odd years or so ago, when it were at first just me Dad an' a few of his local mates goin' out at night once a week, or now an' then, in the eighties. But some o'the blokes that went out wi' 'em were ol'boys who'd been spottin' 'em since the fifties an' sixties! It were made into a 'proper club' in the late eighties by me Dad as a lot o' folk, some from the big cities miles away, 'ad got interested, an' they were all goin' out together more regular. All that were well before I were born like!

"At first the membership grew quick, partly I s'ppose 'cause then folk could read a sensible an' serious weekly article in't local paper – an' sometimes in one o' national papers - detailin' all the strange sightin's an' that, so it generated a lot of local – an' sometimes, national interest.

"There were even talk o'Yorkshire Television doin' a programme about the club! Other affiliated groups got started up an'all, up an' down t'coast, from Hull upto Staithes. Eventually they were all in radio contact wi' each other when they were out, thanks to me Dad sortin' that out for 'em, an' as I said, I learned a lot about electronics, radios, transmitters an'all that from 'elpin' him.

"Ol'Billy from the garage where I do a bit o' mechanicing work – I was there this mornin' - were one o' me Dad's mates that 'elped get it all started up proper in Scarborough. They'd all meet at his garage an' then pile into an old ex-army four ton Bedford truck he'd done up 'imself at the garage, so he could drop off an' pick up our local groups, 'cos as the membership grew y'couldn't 'ave a dozen or so cars all parkin' up in a field or blockin' up narrow country lanes!

"There'd been a few run-ins before wi't Police about that. Their top brass were obviously dead against the club...an' then they found out that some o'their local Bobbies were interested an' were goin' out wi' 'em an'all! – on their days off like - but then one week those blokes told me Dad that their Inspector 'ad told 'em all that they 'ad a new policy come from County HQ an' they were all banned from gettin' involved wi' club an' goin' out spottin' in future!

"Me Dad reckoned it were because the top brass realised that if a Policeman stated he'd definitely seen summat strange in't sky, an' described it, he'd be much more of a credible witness – which is the last thing the Authorities'd want...!

"Anyway...Hah! That old ex-army Bedford truck! Ol'Billy 'ad it fer years! I spent many a night huddled up next to a paraffin heater tryin' to keep warm in't back of it when I started goin' out wi' 'em as a lad! It were dead excitin' pilin' into it an' goin' off into the night wi'a load o' blokes!

"Me Dad taught me an' a lad called Simmo who was a fair bit older than me, but he became a good mate, how to operate the big radio transmitter he'd set up in't back of it, like a military command post, an' how to keep a proper report log of everythin' that 'appened an' came to us on't radio from the spotter groups an'all that. Simmo eventually went off an' joined the Army, he got in the Paras, he's out now like, an' y'll meet 'im at the Fair tonight. Bit larger than life is ol'Simmo! But he's a great bloke, been a bit like an older brother to me…

"Anyway – I'm goin' on a bit aren't I! But nowadays o' course wi' t'interweb in full swing everywhere there's folk all over the world communicatin' an' puttin' their photos, videos an' that up all the time now, but the mainstream press still seem to ridicule an' deny 'em all don't they?!"

"Yes, they do...And no – you haven't gone on at all mate! That was fascinating! Thanks for telling me about it all! I wish I'd had all the excitement of doing something like that as a young lad! Most exciting thing me and my mates got up to was going apple scrumping!

"But when we get our internet sorted in the caravan I'm going to look into all this much more and try and do the same. I think I'll try and put up some video and photos as proof of what I see out there...if I see it again...What you said ties in exactly with what Anders and Magda were saying last week, that things like this are, *'deliberately suppressed by 'the authorities',* to keep us in ignorance, dumbed down' - and all the rest of it..."

"Oh aye, *that's exactly what they do,* without a doubt, no question about it now. As I said in 'The Trocadero Cafe' last Monday: 'I always knew summat weren't tickin' over right in't world…!'"

Jake then lowered his head with a big sigh and said, "If that's what y'thinkin' o'doin...well, I 'ave to tell you, to warn you, about this next part as well mate..."

"Ah…! Now it's my turn to say...*'that sounds a bit ominous.*"

"Aye...it is a bit, well, more than a bit...anyway...y'remember

25

Ander's sayin' - *'that 'they' suppress by brutal an' by subtle means...'*? Well, there was one incident that 'appened, a good few years back, that sort o' made everyone involved in the Spotters' Club avoid contacting any so called 'authorities' ever again after it 'appened. An' they went sort o' underground after it, them that stayed...as a lot left...'cause what 'appened were at the brutal end o' that 'suppression scale'..."

"Crikey mate – what happened?!"

"Well...I said before that only one other in the Club actually saw summat as clear as you did – an' funny enough it were just 'ere near the Brigg as well...he was o' me Dad's mates in the Club, bloke called Tony – 'Taxi Tony' – 'cause he drove a taxi.

"He were parked up in the caravan car-park here after gettin' back from an early hours run to Leed's airport. He told us that he'd wanted a leg stretch an' a bit o' fresh air before gettin' back to Scarborough an' goin' on other jobs. So he 'ad a stroll up 'ere; an' he said he was just goin' back to the car, 'avin watched the sun come up, when he saw this thing, this big shiny circular craft come straight down from the sky, about a mile or so out to sea, and just stop dead, an' hover over the water…

"...Well, Tony 'ad a mate in the Coastguard that was 'ere at the time – funny 'ow they've all gone now – p'rob'ly because if any o' them saw one or more of 'em, they'd be more credible witnesses - like the Bobbies who used to go out with us woulda bin...Anyway...this mate o'Tony's 'ad always joked with 'im sayin', *'next time he saw any little green men in a flyin' saucer to give 'im a ring - an' they'd go out an' introduce themselves wi' a flyin' cup o' green tea to go wi' their saucer...!'* - Just tekin' the piss like."

Dave shifted his position slightly to look at Jake, enthralled again by his story telling.

"So anyway, Tony rings 'im. Turns out 'is mate were still on duty and just about to finish 'is night shift. Anyway Tony tells 'is mate what he can see right in front of 'im out at sea, an' exactly where it is an'all that. After a bit 'is mate realises he's not tryin' to just wind 'im up an' tells 'im to calm down an' hold on a minute as he needs to transfer 'is call – so he waits, then this other posh voice comes on an' tells Tony that they're lookin' at the radar screen an' there's nothin' there, nothin', must be a trick o' the light, sun reflecting off the sea an' all that...!

"Well Tony then 'ad a right go at 'im apparently, made a right fuss – an' he were well known for gettin' right stroppy an' really flyin' off the handle at times - everyone always said that he must o' been the one that invented 'road rage'...even though he were a Taxi driver! Anyway he tells this other bloke wi' a posh voice like some Army officer's who's on't 'phone, summat like: *that whatever it is it's still there out at sea just hoverin' in plain sight so he's obviously lying to 'im - as he must be able to see it!'*

"Not 'avin' a camera in his phone - them days they didn't all 'ave 'em did they, but then he tells this bloke: *I've got a top o' the range Pentax camera wi' a big telephoto lens in the taxi's boot, so I'll get it and photo this craft to prove it to ev'ry manjack on't planet!'* Then as he's runnin' back to the car to get 'is camera - the call gets cut off...

"So did he take some photos as proof then?"

"Aye! He Did! *'Just in time an'all'*, he said to us, as he'd quickly banged off one reel o' film, then when he was puttin' a second one in – the craft just went silently down into the sea an' that were it, it'd gone. An' then he drove straight round to our house to tell me Dad all about it...

"He didn't 'alf bang on our front door! Woke us all up! Dead excited he were an' in a right state, shoutin' to open up and let 'im in!" Jake shook his head at the memory of that morning.

"Me Dad an' 'im went straight into the kitchen. I got up an' went down in me pyjamas an' I listened to Tony tell 'im all about it an' ev'ry thin' he'd said on't phone to this other officer type bloke!

"He'd teken a full reel o' thirty five mill' colour film of it, thirty six shots, an' he was goin' to tek it in for the rapid same day developin' an' print service as soon as the shop in the town centre opened...Well, when he finally left...that was the last time we saw 'im...alive...and we never got to see all the photos he'd taken..."

"Oh no mate...w,what happened...?!"

"Well...later that mornin'...'is car ran off the road into a dry stone wall at high speed...an' apparently his neck got broke...killin' 'im...The Police said, *'he must've fallen asleep at the wheel an' speeded up'*, which were rubbish, he'd been taxiing for years, must 'o done a million miles goin' on early mornin' runs to airports, comin' back an' then doin' a few more jobs after.

"An' as: *'there were no evidence of any other car being involved'* – so *they* said - that's what got recorded when they did the inquest.

"But none of it stacked up! Both his camera bag *an' his ticket to collect the prints* 'ad somehow disappeared! – Police said they didn't know owt about 'em – said they weren't in the taxi or in his possession when they went through everythin' at the scene, but he *always* 'ad that camera in't car with 'im, in case he saw 'owt in the skies on 'is travels...

"Me Dad went to the photo shop to enquire about gettin' the prints later that day – it were just before they closed - *but it turned out they'd bin collected earlier!* – An' when he asked 'em what time it was when they were collected – turned out that it was at a time that *were after t'crash!* - 'Cause the print shop kept a deposit an' collection log! *One o' staff 'ad obviously slipped up and registered them on their system as being teken! Not who by, but just the ticket number, date an' time!*

"The shop staff did admit they *remembered 'im tekin' them in* 'cause he were their first customer that day – *he were waitin' outside for 'em t'open up!* - an' he were a bit of a regular anyway! So he 'ad a numbered collection ticket with his name on it when he left the shop, and they had a deposit ticket on their system log with the same info'. *But no one in the shop said they remembered who later on came an' took 'em!*

"The manager said to me Dad, *'they 'ad scores o' folk in that day, lot's o' folk on their 'olidays an' that, they couldn't be expected to remember 'em all! - If you show up with a ticket – you get a paper wallet full o' photos – simple as that!'*

"An' o' course in them days there weren't CCTV cameras everywhere watchin' everyone - tho' even if there 'ad abin I bet they'd o'bin somehow not workin' at the time...So somebody else who knew about all the photos, an' 'ad the ticket for 'em – 'cos it weren't in 'is wallet, or in 'is pocket, at the, the crash scene, obviously must'a been and got 'em...!

"An' mebbe whoever went to get 'em 'ad a word in private with the manager, prob'ly flashin' some official ID at 'im, and told 'im to tell the shop staff not to say owt to anyone either...scared em' off wi' threats o' losin' their jobs, *or worse,* like...*I dunno...I just dunno...*

"...but me Dad said they all acted a bit strange, *seemed a bit cagey,* so he went straight up to the Police station an' told 'em what 'ad 'appened. But they just weren't interested, he were furious with 'em but they just fobbed 'im off an' did nowt about it...even threatened *to arrest him* if he didn't stop shoutin' and calm down!"

"*Kerrrist Jake!   That's all...horrendous, poor, poor bloke...Taxi Tony.*"

"Aye, it were, shocked all of us. *But that's not quite all of it mate... not by a long chalk...*

"Turned out that a farmer, nice old bloke called Gerry, who still lives right near to where Tony 'ad is crash, 'ad been on the roof of 'is farmhouse all mornin' fixin' some loose slates, an' he were climbing down the ladders when 'e 'eard car *engines* revvin' up real loud, a screech o' tyres and then the thuddin' bang o' the crash an' a long rumble o'rocks an' stones collapsin' from a wall cumin' down...!

"...So he got off the ladders sharpish an' legged it the few yards out on't t'road along the front o'the farmhouse, but he couldn't see 'owt down the road, past the bend, so he then went quick as he could back up the ladders, which were at the rear of the farmhouse on't back slope o' the roof, to try an' get a better view from up there past the bend, to see what 'ad 'appened.

"He crawled up the roof again, an' stood up holdin' onto the chimney stack to see if he could see owt. An' he did see it then. The crash were on the next bend further down the road an' he saw a good length o'the dry stone wall down and the front o' Tony's car all crunched up an' covered in't wall stones an' rocks. It were a bit less than an 'undred yards or so away from 'im - *but this is the thing…*

"*…when he were climbin' back up he'd heard two other diesel engines revvin' loud again, then as he got on't roof he saw two black land-rovers, that looked like they were new-ish, one going off fast right in the distance on the same straight road back towards Scarborough, an' the other had passed the farm yard and was drivin' away, 'like hell-fer-leather', he said, round the next bend…!*

"It were farmer Gerry who'd rung the Police about the crash, told 'em where it were an'all that, an' they said they'd get the Traffic section an' Fire Brigade out there straight away an' call the ambulance as well. He told 'em about the two black land-rovers an'all - but they ignored that then an' even tho' it were in 'is statement later it were completely ignored again, an' it never really came up much later at the so-called 'inquest'.

"It was only when Gerry, who'd known both Tony and me Dad for years, 'cause they often went on 'is land at night spottin' wi't Club, came an' knocked on our front door that afternoon, and me Mum sat 'im in kitchen and called me Dad out o'sheds to come in quick, that we first 'eard about the crash and about 'em...I'd just got back from school an' 'eard everythin' he said as well.

"These days y'd know just about straight away what wi' everyone 'avin' mobiles an' social media an' all that. But it were different then, an' Gerry only 'ad 'is land-line to telephone from.

"Anyway, he came to our 'ouse because he 'adn't wanted to risk talkin' about it all to me Dad on't phone…He said he'd tried to ring the taxi firm to let them know, as he'd recognised Tony's car, an' anyway it 'ad the taxi company's sign stuck on't back doors, and then he'd tried to ring me Dad – but his phone had strangely gone dead when he'd tried to mek both o'them calls - straight after he'd rung the Police to report there'd been a crash! But it 'ad come back on again a few hours later...!

"So...by the time he'd legged it back out the farmhouse after callin' the Police, an' quickly tryin' to mek them two calls, an' got about halfway to the car to see if he could do 'owt 'imself for Tony or any passengers he might've 'ad – a big Police van 'ad roared up on the scene! An' then four uniforms jumped out an' two of 'em ran to him shoutin' at him to stop an' stay where he was. He said they sounded, *'reight nasty an' aggressive they were an'all– like drill-sergeants yellin' at recruits...'*

"The pair of 'em got up to 'im an' actually grabbed 'old of 'im an' still shoutin' they asked 'im if he'd seen what 'ad 'appened an' he told 'em, *'no – I only 'eard it and then rang you - the Police...'* So then they roughly told 'im he'd 'ave to wait back at the farm – he'd told 'em who he was an' where he'd come from - to mek a statement to an officer who would come to him shortly.

"So he were quickly moved away before he could get any closer to the crash an' one of 'em escorted 'im back to his farmhouse. The other one legged it back to the crash, an' Gerry 'eard 'im shoutin' to the others there that, *'it were ok – says he 'adn't seen 'owt...'*

"The one with 'im told him that, *'there weren't any passengers – it were just Tony on 'is own...but...from what they'd seen he was...well...he quite obviously 'adn't survived the crash...but there might be a risk of fire or an explosion as they could smell petrol leakin' so they were waitin' for the Traffic boys an' Fire Brigade to make sure it were safe before they let the ambulance in...'*

"But as Gerry asked me Dad – *''ow come they knew 'is name?!'* An' he 'ad looked back once an' he saw another two men in dark suits, who he said just didn't look or act like plain clothes CID Police – an' why would they be there anyway? - *an' so quick...?!*

"They'd opened the front doors an' started to lean into Tony's car...an' they definitely weren't medics! The ambulance 'adn't even 'ad time to get there! An' he said that the rest o' the Police were sorta hangin' back from them an' bunchin' up an' mekin' a closed up sorta semi-circle round the car, blockin' 'is view - *so then he couldn't see what the two men in dark suits were doin'...!*

"'Anyway...Gerry told us he couldn't've gotten away any earlier than he 'ad done - as the Police 'ad that whole section o't'road blocked an' cordoned off for hours. *So no one apart from them – an' the two dark suits wi' 'em...or the ambulance an' the Fire Brigade coulda got in or out.*

"He were obviously still dead upset an' still in a bit o' shock were poor ol'Gerry, but he started really shakin' like a leaf, an' were spillin' 'is mug o' tea down 'im that me Mum'd made for 'im so bad he 'ad to put it down on't table, when he then said this to me Dad, it were, I remember it more or less word fer word..."

Jake's voice then morphed into the broad accent of the aged and frightened old farmer's: *'Ah reckon' if ah'd abin a minute o' two later cumin' dahn mi ladders off t'roof – an' ah'd seened what'd really 'appened – an' told 'em that I 'ad - well...ah def'ntly reckon ah'd'abin found later at bottom o' me ladders wi' mah neck broke an'all…!*

''Cos them two Police ah saw an' were yellin' at me at first, an' then spoke wi' me weren't like any Police – or even like any other blokes ah'd ever cum across afore – an' ah'm reight glad ah never 'ave! – they were more like...more like thugs dressed up as Police! Ah sensed summat def'ntly, ah say def'ntly...not reight abaht 'em - an' I knew straight off that there were summat reight dangerous abaht 'em – like y'sense wi'an angry bull sometimes when y'just know it's sizin' y'up to charge an' gore y'w'i its 'orns...so y'd best get ah't it's way sharpish...Aye ah did! An' ah reckon ah came dead close to getting' on wrong end o' their 'orns this mornin' an' all…!'"

Jake then turned his head sideways, lowering it whilst raising his brow to stare into Dave's face as he nodded rapidly, to emphasise his re-telling of Gerry's account.

Dave stared back at him wide eyed and visibly shocked. They broke off their eye contact to slump together back against the cliff, Dave drawing his knees up and tightly wrapping his arms around them. Neither of them spoke for a minute or two, playing the scenes and farmer Gerry's last words – and what they implied, through again and again in their minds.

Jake eventually broke the silence, quietly continuing with his narrative, "an' so...puttin' two an' two together...joining the dots - *Taxi Tony were obviously 'taken out' on orders from 'them' that didn't want 'im or the Spotters Club goin' public wi' photo proof o' what 'e saw that mornin'...An' those blokes Gerry saw and spoke wi' – he never saw 'em again – they weren't at the inquest - were obviously just the follow-up-team after the shock troops who actually did it 'ad gone...!*

"What me Dad reckoned actually 'appened - 'ow they worked it - is that one o't'black land-rovers must've chased 'im causin' 'im to speed up – Tony woulda realised straight off who they were - an' what they were after - an't'other woulda been in place to run 'im off the road when he got to that bend. *That shouldn't've killed 'im though!*...He were in a big Volvo estate, front bonnet were as long as a swimmin' pool! - an' they used to build 'em like a tank anyway! - part o'reasons he 'ad one! - but those bastads in dark suits leanin' into the car must've broke 'is neck just to mek sure...and to mek it look like it 'ad been done in't crash...

"He reckoned them that were drivin' the black land rovers wouldn'ta wanted to 'ang about, as there are several cottages dotted round the farm area, all set well back from t'road like, but still wi' some views of it, so they wouldn't want to chance any witnesses seeing a black land rover stop and someone get out, go to the car...finish Tony off...an' rummage around for 'is camera an' photo ticket...then just drive off. So they were just used to set up the crash, an' drove off quick after, an' the - *supposedly* - Police van were ready an' waitin' nearby to go straight in an' finish...finish the job off...by gettin' what they were after, before handin' over to the local traffic Police, an' anyone watching from a cottage across the fields wouldn't've been suspicious of a Police van and uniforms being at the site o' the crashed car.

"Anyways, that's 'ow me Dad reckoned they'd set it all up...'specially when it turned out later that the reason Tony were on that stretch o' road in't first place were because the Taxi firm 'ad 'ad a call from a couple in one o'them cottages askin' fer Tony to come in 'is big Volvo estate to tek 'em to train station wi' a load o'their luggage – an' that road's the only way into that neck o'the woods from Scarborough...An' guess what?! – When the local Police enquiries later turns out nob'dy 'ad rung! At least not from that cottage or any other round there!   None o't folks livin' in any o't cottages knew owt about any 'phone call to book Tony's taxi to go the train station!"

"*Oh My God!   That's what they did!* - But surely the Police...wouldn't...do...or allow that…?!   And they couldn't have just ignored that farmer Gerry's witnessing the black land-rovers either – or the fact of the hoax call for him to go there?!"

"*Huh*...the 'Police', *if that's who they actually, really were - from what Gerry suspected about 'em* - from the van that he saw that day weren't local, who knows who they were…?!

"When the local, 'normal' Police got there soon after they just left Gerry gave 'is statement to one o'them.   Some very 'igh rankin' uniform at the inquest – which were set up dead quick a few days later, just said, *'they were close by in the area only by sheer coincidence and that they were a visiting 'specialist unit', from an outside Force who correctly secured the incident site and then waited to hand the scene of the incident over to the local traffic Police when they arrived'*.   All very plausible, an' it were left at that...no further questions about 'em were asked by the Coroner...

"An' as far as the black land-rovers were concerned he dismissed them, he said, *'land-rovers were obviously a common sight in farmland and rural areas, and it was just a coincidence, and hadn't been worth following up...especially as no drivers of any vehicles matching those descriptions 'ad come forward anyway...an' the hoax call were just an unfortunate coincidence…as well!'*

"Everythin' were: *'an unfortunate series of coincidences'* accordin' to the 'igh rankin' uniform, an' the Coroner believed 'im, swallowed it all 'ook line an' sinker wi'out a qualm...an' then did what he'd most likely been told to do...as they'll all be top Masons won't they...which was to give a verdict of accidental death - due to Tony fallin' asleep at the wheel...no other parties involved...so case closed...!

"I remember exactly what he an' everybody else involved said, as I've got a good memory – me drama teacher at school always said I'd be a good actor! – if I could apply meself to more than just doin' funny mimickin' voices an' messin about! -

"Anyway me Dad told me later that evenin' all that were said when he got back 'ome, I didn't go – I 'ad to be at school! Now the thing is, *yes* - all them farmers round there 'ad land-rovers, 'course they did, but none of 'em 'ad new-ish *black* land rovers – they weren't fashionable then! The ones they 'ad were beat up ol' rust buckets!

"The only places around 'ere that you'd tend to see 'em in them days were at the MoD – Ministry of Defence - Listening Stations dotted all over the area – that one at Staxton is the first and the oldest still operating in the country, if not the World – it were set up in't fifties - an' definitely at that big RAF Early Warning Radar Station over the moors a few miles away at Fylingdales...It's one o' biggest in the Whole World! Which, we know now, might be called an 'RAF Base' but it actually is an American Security Agency that takes over it when they spot an' track a UFO...or UAP. - *'Unknown Aerial Phenomena'*, as they call 'em nowadays.

"I think they started callin' 'em that ever since the RAF Brentwaters case, down South, back in 'eighty one – which turned out to be an American Nuclear Bomber Station - on English soil! Not an RAF base! It had UFOs – UAPs - penetrate the woods surroundin' it for several nights, an' loads o' credible servicemen were witnesses who saw 'em...an' most of them 'ave died mysteriously since...Anyway, that's what the authorities call 'em these days, I suppose it's so they can legitimately claim they've officially closed down all *'UFO'* sightings an' research an' all that years ago...!"

"Ahhh! So as Ander's would say – *'step back, join the dots...see the bigger picture...'*"

"Aye...that's right, for 'them' it were a good result – stage 'an accident' to get rid o' Taxi Tony who'da *never o' stopped showin' 'is photos to The World!* – he woulda made it 'is life's work after that...! Our club an' 'im woulda been famous! So they grab all his photos' an'all 'is camera gear, an' it also sent a big warnin' to the growin' numbers of anyone else round 'ere who might 'ave, well, thought about goin' public with any real proof they 'ad - or might get in't future.

"An' it worked, 'cause the club went underground as I said, an' most of the regulars left, just gave it up, scared like...an' y'really couldn't blame 'em! *Huh*...I remember me Dad sayin', *"Ministry of Defence' were the wrong name, it should be the 'Ministry of Attack'...!'"*

Dave grunted an approval of the black humour of that, and said, "yes, that's actually a much more appropriate name – did you know that from 'forty five – the end of the second World War - to the early eighties they'd started or been involved in over fifty or so 'wars' all over the planet, so God knows how many it's been upto now...?!

"A neighbour's son of my parents joined the Royal Marines in the early-eighties, just before the Falklands war, and he went and fought there, I remember talking to him a few years ago, he'd long left the Marines by then of course, but he was still suffering badly from post traumatic stress. He told me a few things about what he'd seen and experienced...it was horrifying, and he told me that fact about the number of wars was in the Army recruitment brochures they'd given him, back when he was thinking of joining the Services, as if they were proud of it..."

"Blimey – No I didn't know that about all the wars Britain's been in! I do know this though – me Dad told me – that the American military has – since America were founded around seventeen seventy six – it's bin involved in over two 'undred an' forty wars! So basically they've 'ardly 'ad a year when they've bin at peace!

"*Huh!* An' most folk'll think we've all bin 'at peace' since 'forty-five! An' there's only bin World Wars one and two! - well plus the 'small one' as well in the Falklands! - An' there were a lot more 'appenin' down there that was well hidden from the public - about the *real reasons* behind that Falkland's war. Simmo told me about some of it, as he obviously talked shop with mates of his in the various special forces he worked with in later years.

"Apparently it was more about access to a smaller island further South that 'ad some alien technology discovered on it...summat to do with a sentient 'black goo'...they called it...an' some very strange an' disturbin' things 'appened down there – an' it's still goin' on - that's all bin well hushed up...But there's a fair bit of info' about it on-line now though from some brave whistle blowers...

"Anyway...gettin' back to what I were sayin' - me Dad were clever – soon after all that 'appened wi' Taxi Tony he spent a lot o'time teachin' me 'ow engines work, an' he got me into strippin' and fixin' all sorts of 'em, from startin' wi' little ones in remote radio controlled model aircraft we made and flew together, then onto to car engines an' then onto renovatin' ol' motorbikes - which I were really more interested in than cars!

"We'd go to auctions and he'd buy two or three ol' wrecks at a time for me to do up. He'd taught me 'ow to ride a bike on that big car park near the industrial estate – like I told you all when Magda asked me about it last week. Once I'd got the 'ang of it I'd then razz round all the fields an' the woods at the back of our house on scramblers I did up until I were old enough to get a licence to go on't road wi' 'em. In fact I did one up fer Simmo – he's still got it! - for 'is twenty first birthday as a present from us, an' when he came up on leave we'd go off scramblin' all over moors together. Passed me test first time an'all! Then I was on't road wi' bigger machines!

"We built two more big sheds in't back garden just for me to store an' work on 'em, an' me Dad encouraged me to start sellin' a few I'd done up as a sort o' payin' hobby – lot better than a paper-round or stackin' shelves in't supermarkets like some o' me school mates were doin'! Anyway all that sort o' diverted me away from gettin' more involved with the UFO club…

"I suppose, an' I realise it now, lookin' back, that he was protectin' me o'course, 'cause he knew, an' were afraid, that I woulda carried on where Taxi Tony left off – 'cause when I start on summat I find interestin', that's it! - I suppose I get a bit obsessed like, huh! – y'could say I've got 'attention *surplus* disorder' as I always see *whatever* it is I've started on - right through 'til it's finished…*It's just the way I am!*

"...So, anyway, me Dad, obviously knowin' that, channelled me time an' energies into mechanics an' engineerin' an' then usin' them skills to doin' bikes up an' mekin' a few bob instead. - Plus it weren't likely I'd ever get any sort o' 'decent job' round 'ere after leavin' school – *reckon I'd've 'ad more chance o' marryin' into Royalty!* - Not that I'd want to like! So I'm very grateful to 'im for all that, 'cause I luv doin' it' an' it's got me to where I am now like, doin' it as a proper business.

"I started off in the 'world o' work' when I left school, well, just before really! with a sort o' apprenticeship with Ol'Billy, at the garage in town...an' I still enjoy doin' a bit o' mechanicing work for Ol'Billy, coverin' for when 'is lads are on 'oliday or when I've got nowt on..."

Both men then went companionably silent for a good while, just sitting back against the cliff together and staring out to sea. Each deep in their own thoughts.

Dave was feeling quite privileged because of the way Jake had expansively opened up to him about his life, and told him, in considerable detail, everything he had, pleased that their new – not yet a week old! - friendship had just gone up a few levels…

"Anyway mate...that's a good rest from all our chin waggin' together eh?! Let's get on with our walk shall we?" Jake suggested eventually with a big sigh, getting to his feet.

They made their way carefully down to the bottom of the long and steep cliff path onto the rocky promontory, Dave leading the way, his thoughts still mulling over everything Jake had just told him. Once down on the rocks just above sea level, he paused to catch his breath and turned to look back up at the cliff they'd just descended.

"It's not so bad coming down, but it's a right pull going back up! Second time Mel and I came down here we went back along the beach, paddled along the waters edge and then went up that far path over there, *'it's a lot easier on the legs'* Mel said, and she was dead right! We're both looking forward to doing lots more walks around here – away from the city streets, it's great to be out in the fresh sea air and getting some exercise - *we'll soon be as fit as 'butchers' dogs'!*"

Jake laughed and said, *"That sayin' always makes me laugh!"* 'Cause y'don't want to end up lookin' like the only 'butcher's dog' I've ever known – an' that's Big Sammy's boxer – fattest dog I've ever seen, calls it 'Bluto - The Bloated'! *It's true in their case what they say about dogs and their owners endin' up lookin' just like each other!"* He laughed.

"I haven't met him – or his dog!" Dave chuckled.

"Oh y're in for a right treat then mate! Tell y'what - you an' me could go up on't bike t'get the meats for the barbecue off 'im. We'll sort out a day an' time for later in the week, if I ring 'im with our order first he'll 'ave it in fridge in 'is van all ready for us.

"In fact I was thinkin' this mornin' when I was up there 'avin' me breakfast, that you'd do a great paintin' o' the views from the lay-by where he parks 'is ol' van up – missin' out the ol' van tho'! - It saw better days around the time the country came off food rationin' in the mid fifties!" He laughed.

"Yeah – cheers! Great idea!" Dave said, amused at Jake's descriptions of the dog, man and van – and secretly looking forward to going on his motorbike – as it'd be his first time on one!

"...But...y'know...in my mind's eye I can see the van, the man and his dog as being actually central to the whole picture! Set in the landscape – bit like the paintings of people in everyday but lonely environments an artist called Edward Hopper did – I think his work is brilliant. I'd do it in a similar style to the way he painted - one of my favourites of his is just called 'Gas' – as in a 'Gas – or Petrol as we call it– Station'; it shows the edge of a forest – the natural environment – and then there's the man made unnatural monstrosity, all lit up, that's the gas – the petrol - station, and the tarmac road in front of it and everything they represent, that's invaded and occupied it..."

Jake laughed even louder at this, saying - *" 'Unnatural Monstrosity'* – that's Big Sammy in' is ol' van alright! – Best not describe y'paintin' idea like that to 'im tho' – he might decide to sit on y' !"

"Oh crikey no I'd never! I wouldn't dream of it! I'll talk instead about the, about the...*juxtaposition of the old vintage catering van - a relic of man made artifice – set transiently in the eternal natural landscape – which could be seen to cater – good pun! - as an atavistic symbol representing the demise of the proclivity of the hunter gatherer instinct, and which has now become a modern iconic focal point of the nomadic tribal social dynamics of the camp-fire gathering at meal times hosted by the big chief displaying his largesse...!* - People's eyes usually glaze over after a few seconds when I start to waffle on like that!" He said grinning.

"*Hah ha ha! Fantastic! - No idea what it meant though!* But I do know I think you could definitely '*waffle on*' for England mate! Reckon Big Sammy'll be dead impressed! Just 'ope he don't decide to '*display his largesse*'! - That'd well put us off the barbecue!!" He laughed even more, Dave joining in with him.

They carried on walking carefully over the seaweed covered rocks until they finally got to the very end of the promontory. Even though the tide was out the rocks here were far enough out to sea to be surrounded on three sides by the powerful waves that crashed into them. Standing and leaning slightly into a fairly strong wind, on a higher slab of rock right at the very end of the long rocky finger pushing out into the sea, the two men stood side by side in awe and companionable silence for a while again amongst the powerful elements surrounding them.

"So mate...what do you think I, what we, should do?" Dave quietly asked, staring out to sea. Jake's eyes were focused on the distant horizon where the sea seemed to fade into the blue sky, and after a while he replied, "I think the time's come for all of us to refuse to be afraid anymore. 'Cause that's exactly what they want us to be. Ander's made that very clear to us didn't he? 'Cause when we're all afraid they can control us much easier, like all them sheep Magda talked about as well. So when we're afraid they can get us to do what they want us to do, and we now know that that's in no way anythin' like good for us...fact is - it's the exact opposite, and just meks things worse fer us all..."

Dave turned his head to look sideways into Jake's face. He had to look up slightly, Jake being much taller than he was. His face was in profile to him. For a moment Dave saw him as a vision of a mystical Celtic warrior of old - bare muscular arms folded over his chest, long straw coloured hair blown about by the sea breeze, and his grey eyes now flint hard as they stared out to the far horizon. He looked like a bold sentinel visually searching and waiting for the stealthy approach of raiding enemies, but exuding the confidence that they would be confronted, and dealt with...

Jake then said, "so...*I think* we should first tell the girls all about this, an' then try an' arrange a meet up with Magda, 'opefully we'll see 'er then at the Fair tonight when we go, an' y'can tell 'er everythin' y'told me, an' I'll tell 'er everythin' I told you, an' then we can listen to what she has to say about it...then ask questions...

"Because I think we've moved on now from just showin' photo's an' that to the world, as y'said before: 'there's plenty o' folk doin' that now', I think the next step is to, *to...try an' make proper contact with whatever they are, in whatever it was you saw...that's what I think.* An' I think that if anyone'll know 'ow to Magda will, an' she'd advise an' 'elp us do that if we asked her...What d'you think?"

"*Yes!*...I think you're right. I must admit I've had similar thoughts myself. I'll tell Mel all about it now when we get back to the caravan, I didn't tell her yesterday morning, because by the time I'd got back she'd only just woken up, and she thought I'd only just got up as well to make a cuppa for us, which I had actually...and when I took them into the bedroom and saw how she was all so excited about getting started again straight away with sorting everything out...well, it just didn't seem the right time to...Seeing her all happy and keen to get on, I didn't want to spoil it, well, not spoil it, but y'know what I mean?!"

"Aye, I do mate. It's always best to pick the right time to info' drop these sorts o' things on someone, an' I reckon this afternoon'd be a good time – for both Mel and Sophie to listen to your story and to mine."

"Yes, an' by the time we get back they'll probably be ready to have a sit down and a break from sorting out all the unpacking and all that!

"Also I don't want Mel to think I'm being secretive and keeping things from her – about me now owning the caravan that's fair enough, I think, because it's going to be a really nice, big surprise when I do

41

tell her, but then keeping quiet about seeing UF - USO's on our doorstep, might, well, I wouldn't like it if she kept things from me, and she wouldn't anyway, and I just prefer to be open and honest about things...so, well...*that's just the way I am…!*"

Jake slapped his hand down onto Dave's shoulder and said, "Y're a good man Dave, an' I'm glad y're me mate, I mean that. *An' between us, between all of us, we'll do it...it's what we 'ave to do...*"

"Cheers mate! – Likewise! - *And that sounds like a good enough plan to me...!*"

Chapter 3: A Meeting is Arranged

They stayed at the end of Filey Brigg for quite a while longer, talking, taking in the view and soaking in the atmosphere of the place – both of them literally soaking it in when they got too close to the rocky edge and a rather large wave suddenly flew up and with what seemed like gleeful intent it threw itself heavily over them. Realising that the tide was now starting to come in fast they headed back towards the beach and the other longer, but easier path back up to the cliff top and the caravan.

Well before they got to the cliff top their clothes had dried out in the warm sunshine and sea breeze, but salty white streaks had been left on them. The longer but much less steeply inclined path up the cliff lead them to approach the caravan from its rear side. They walked around to the front's timber decked patio area - and came across Mel and Sophie lying on sun loungers sipping cold beers from frosty glasses!

"Oh Aye!" Jake said, looking at Dave in mock exasperation, his hands on his hips. "D'y'know! Typical innit?! - Y'turn y'back f'less than five minutes Dave, an' the workers 'ave their feet up suppin' all the cold beers! I dunno! - *Can't get the staff these days mate…!"*

"Cheek! - Er - do you know these two salty, sweaty and bedraggled men Mel?!" Sophie asked her, her nose in the air as she pointed a finger at them with pantomimed disdain.

Mel giggled and said, "Maybe if we give them a cold beer they'll introduce themselves!"

Jake dropped to his knees and crawled over to the girls, panting loudly, croaking like a man emerging from the desert after days without water, "Me...Jake! Need...cold...beer!" And collapsed onto his back gasping. Dave staggered and swayed on his feet before he too collapsed onto his back gasping for cold beer…

"What do you think Mel? Could we spare *a bottle* for them *to share* between them…?!"

"EH?! *Share a bottle be'twin us!"* Jake popped his head up and exclaimed loudly, "More like we'll *share a crate be'twin us!* Eh Dave?! Me mouth's as dry as the bottom of an empty parrot's cage!"

"Share *a* crate?! - More like *one each* mate…!" Dave replied, suddenly recovered, and up on his feet going into the caravan and coming back out with a cold bottle for Jake and one for himself.

"Crikey me! You two *have* been busy!" You've done it all!" He said to the two girls. *"But where is everything?!"*

"Oh we girls don't mess about! – Said we'd get loads done without you two under our feet didn't I!" Sophie laughed. "We put all the charity stuff in black bin bags under the caravan – in fact we found an old tatty leather bike jacket under there, so it got put in with the charity stuff as well…."

"EH!? *Y'Can't Be Serious!!"* Jake wailed pounding the deck and sounding just like John McEnroe, the seventies tennis player famous for his tantrums when disputing umpires' decisions. Both girls laughed at his antics. Their two bottles of cold beers then went straight down the hatches hardly touching the sides, and Dave went to fetch two more.

"Cheers Dave, last one for me though", Jake said reaching up for it, half lying down on the decking and leaning his back against Sophie's sun lounger, "Otherwise we'll be walkin' back to Scarborough – an' I'm knackered as it is from walkin' back up that cliff! I never do 'ave more than a couple o' beers when I'm ridin'."

"I'll put the kettle on now then, takes a while to boil, does anyone else want coffee – or are you sticking with the beers?"

"I will, please Dave", Sophie said, I don't want to meet Jake's Mum later for the first time reeking of beer!"

Jake said, deadpan, "Oh don't worry about that Soph - *she'll understand!* – I told 'er that Sat'day teatime is the best time for y'to come round for one of 'er teas - *as that's about the only time durin' the week there's any chance of y'bein' sober…!"* He then had to duck down quickly onto the deck to avoid a playful swipe that Sophie aimed at him.

Mel then told Dave all about her and Sophie's efforts, what was going to the charity shop, what they were keeping, and what ideas they'd had between them about decorating and redesigning the interior layout of the caravan, as Sophie's suggestions from her experience of interior design layouts from working at the Estate Agents had given her some great ideas.

"I just hope your Mum and Dad wouldn't mind us making any changes to it though? Should we ask them first?" She asked Dave.

Dave caught Jake's eye before replying, "Oh I don't think they'll mind at all luv, they'd want us to make it just like we want it…!"

Just then they heard the kettle whistle and Dave went off to make the coffees. He came out with them and then went back inside to bring out the second chocolate fudge cream cake.

Jake said, *"By 'eck - it's a good day today!"* – I 'ad chocolate cake wi' me breakfast, now two lots 'ere, an' me Mum's made some for us tea an'all!"

Sophie said, "Didn't I say to you Mel when we first met in 'The Trocadero' that he eats more chocolate cake in a day - *than I do in a month!"* She laughed.

"Well I'm a growin' lad!" He laughed along with her.

The conversation then went onto food and how they'd all started to make major changes to what they ate, and had sourced non fluoridated bottled water to drink now. Jake told Mel and Dave, as Sophie already knew, that he'd fitted water purifiers in his Mum's and Sophie's kitchen that he'd ordered online, to avoid them drinking the flouride and other toxics deliberately put into the tap water.

Their dietary changes were all as a result of the revelations about modern food, which had been part of Magda's informative talk to them last Monday evening. It had really encouraged them to do their own research to avoid all the toxic chemicals in so much of the packaged food on supermarket shelves.

Sophie and Mel shared and compared some of their findings from the research they'd both done – mostly by Sophie as Mel had been so busy with the move to here. Sophie told everyone that she had come across, just yesterday, some very disturbing facts about how harmful to bodily functions modern factory processed, genetically modified wheat flour and grains were.

She said, *"...the modern wheat flour stuff is so completely different to what our Grandmothers baked with – it's now just basically 'industrial filler', mainly to give foods a longer shelf life, for bigger profits, and it's stripped of essential, natural nutrients, but other nasty stuff is added to it - and it's in just about everything when you look at the ingredient labels! Most of the packaged food we eat is riddled with it!"* She shuddered slightly recalling some of her findings.

"So - as from yesterday I've stopped eating bread, which is going to be a challenge - as I've made lunch sandwiches from it for years! But now I've started to realise just how *unhealthy* it is, and how we're conned when we read *'healthy whole grain'* – which isn't, it's anything but! - I won't be any more! I'll send you all some links all about it – really opened my eyes!"

Dave told Mel and Sophie about the proposed barbecue idea for later in the week. *"But it looks like it'll be without white flour bread buns with the burgers then!"* he said.

He then changed the subject, saying that he had something else to say, to tell the girls about, and he'd been waiting for the best time to say it, but he'd told Jake about it when they'd been down on the Brigg...and Jake had got something to say about it as well. The girls were immediately intrigued, and settled back to listen.

Dave then recounted to them everything that had happened and what he had seen early yesterday morning. As he finished he reached for Mel's hand and said, "So I hope you don't mind me not saying anything until now – but I hope I've explained well enough why I didn't..."

"Aaah bless you, of course I understand! But it would've been okay, please always tell me anything anytime, *if it's important to you it's important to me too!"* Dave sat up from the deck at her side, got onto his knees and kissed her.

Jake whispered loudly to Sophie, *"D'y'think we should go off an' give 'em a minute or three?!"*

Sophie giggled, "Not now no! - I'm too fascinated! And Dave said that you have something to tell us about it all as well!"

"Aye! I 'ave...an'...like Anders'd say – *'I'm gonna tell y'...a story.'"* And so that's what he did.

After Jake had repeated everything he'd told Dave earlier when they were sat on the cliff top, and then standing at the end of the Brigg, the girls were very quiet and very still.   They all were, it was an intense motionless silence, the sort that occurs when people realise they now have to commit themselves to making a crucial decision, the outcome of which could have - will have - very significant consequences for each of them...Sophie broke it by saying quite emphatically,

"So...we need to contact Magda *now,* to meet her *later...*if everyone agrees...?"

She looked around at their faces, seeing that they all agreed. "Magda told us that: 'all you have to do is *reach out to me with your thoughts,* as you are all *connected* to me now', didn't she...?! So...shall we try that, *do* that, altogether now...?"

Jake interrupted her to say, "Aye! But before we do I think we should first summon our 'diamonds', them 'psychic shields' like she showed us 'ow to, 'cause, well I dunno, but we might be like a beacon when we all send 'er all our thoughts at once...and it could attract...*them others*...?"

Mel said, "Yes, you're both right, Let's Do It! We've been practising the diamonds haven't we Dave?"

"Yes - and practising trying to see each other's auras, like she showed us how to as well!"

Sophie and Jake said that they also had been practising these skills, and Sophie then suggested, "I think it might be best if we stand up, make a circle, boy girl, boy girl, make our diamonds, then hold hands and focus on contacting Magda, to see her later – but we don't want her to think we're, well, in a panic or in any danger – do we? We just want to ask her if we can meet her later at the Fair - *about something important."*

They all got to their feet, Jake stood with Sophie on his right, Mel on his left, Dave in front of him. "Ready?" Sophie quietly asked. "Perhaps when we think we've made our diamonds, if we say 'okay', then when we're all 'okay', we hold hands to link us all up, and then try to send out our thoughts...to meet her later…?"

They all nodded to her, then closed their eyes. Less than a minute later Mel quietly said "okay", then Sophie did, then Dave, then Jake. Reaching out to hold hands they then sent their thoughts to Magda. Jake imagined he could see her in front of him and his thoughts were as if he was just talking to her normally - *'Hi Magda, can we all meet you at the Fair later? There's no problem, we just need your advice about somethin'...'*

He repeated his thoughts to her again, and incredibly...*thoughts that weren't his own entered his mind, replying to him,* saying, *'Hello Jake, yes of course, I look forward to seeing you all again…'.* Then his mind went quiet. Amazed and not sure what to do now he opened his eyes to look around at everyone else – one by one they too opened their eyes, the same expressions of amazement on their faces. Sophie looked into his eyes with tears in hers blurring his face.

"*Oh my God!* Oh my...it worked! *I heard her!*...She, she...spoke...*she thought spoke to me…!"*

"*Me too!"* He said, just as astonished, "it were like she'd just popped 'er head round the door into a room I was in an' she quickly spoke to me - then she went…!"

Sophie rushed into his arms, completely overcome. "*I, I know I sounded 'all matter of fact' about it before we did it.."* She sniffled – "But, *but when it happened…! And I think I saw her there, by the caravan door, just looking at us – just for a second…!"*

Mel had her hands over her mouth and her eyes were wide open.."I think *I saw her* as well! As if she was just here with us - but only for a moment – but I thought I must've been imagining it! *Oh Wowww!"* She gasped. Dave's arms were round her, his mouth wide open but he managed to say, "I, I need to sit down! *That was...incredible...!* We just did, we just communicated...*telepathically*...and it was easy...! *Oh Woww!*"

They all quickly sat down again and Jake said, "I feel like somethin' inside me 'as just gone up a gear...! I didn't, I never *doubted* what Magda said to us about doin' that, but, until just now, it weren't, sort o' *real* to me, I mean *'real'* like – *'Oh I can do that! I know how to do it...!'* D'y'know what I mean...?!"

"Yes! That's *exactly* what I feel too." Sophie agreed with him, and Mel and Dave both echoed her words.

Dave said, "So now *we know* we can do that...just...imagine...what else, now, and, in time, we could, can do...?! Perhaps what *everyone* can do?! I mean...if someone said – even only thirty or forty years ago, that, *'soon everyone will carry little plastic boxes in their pockets, called 'mobiles', so that you can talk to anyone in the world - who's got one as well'* - you would've thought they'd been reading too many sci-fi mags wouldn't you...?!"

Their positively animated conversation flowed on about what they had just achieved and experienced and its possible implications. Jake then said, "So...*firstly*, we know what we're goin' *to tell* Magda all about, and *secondly*, we now know we're goin' to be meetin' 'er, to do that, so...okaaay...fine...but – *thirdly* - do we know exactly - *what we're goin' to ask 'er...?*

"I mean...it's like we've got all the parts, all the components – *or 'ave we?* What more parts are missin' – that we don't know about, an' we need? An' what are we gonna try an' make with 'em all as an' when we've got 'em? An' to be practical about it - what's *'it'* gonna do? What do *we want* it to do? Where could *'it'* take us...An' what do we 'ave to do on the way - and then when we get there...? - *Er, does all that make any sense...?!*"

"Yes it does mate. It makes a lot of sense." Dave replied. "You're thinking strategically, creatively and very practically, and you've answered your own questions brilliantly as you were doing it! All those are exactly the questions we need to be asking Magda later!"

"Oh...*Blimey O'Reilly! Did I do all o' that!* I'll 'ave to try an' remember 'em all now then!" Jake said in his usual self deprecating manner.

Sophie took hold of his hand resting on her knee in both of hers, and leaned towards him saying, "Yes! *You did do all of that*! – Do you remember when we first met Magda that she looked at you, and she said, *'You have far more power than you now know you have...'*"

"Aye..I do, an' she did...an' 'appen we'll all need all the power we've all got, now we're goin' to try an' do this..."

"Not Just *Try*! - We W*ill* Do This! *We Will!*" Mel exclaimed, "We might think it's just us four, right here, right now, but there must be thousands - millions of people in the world, who are ready, willing and able...to do it as well. So we won't be alone! We'll all join together As One – *because we are All One All Connected Together…!*"

The steely determination in Mel's unexpected outburst surprised them all – not least herself! She blushed and her hands flew up again over her mouth for a moment, then she spread her arms wide open, her fingers spread apart, *"Oh! I don't know where that came from!"* She said in amazement.

Jake, Sophie and Dave spontaneously clapped, whoop whoop shouted, whistled, and air punched to cries of *'Well Said Mel!' 'Go Geddit Mel!'* which caused her to flap her hands and shush them as she said they were making her embarrassed!

Dave went to get some more cold beers for himself and Mel, and make coffees again for Jake and Sophie. When they all had their drinks, Dave, now sharing Mel's sun lounger with her, raised his bottle and said with a pantomimed slurring of his speech as if he had actually drunk a whole crate of beer, "Well! –*'hic'*- here's to the Four Musketeers! All in it all for all and one and all – and all at four to one...*er, no, hang on - that's sshnot right, is it*...now, er, *how does it go…?!*"

They all laughed, their emotions high and excited, Jake said, "Nice one! - *D'Artagnan Dave!* It's summat like that...I think!"

The rest of the afternoon quickly passed as they discussed again the experiences that Dave and Jake had recounted, and what they thought Magda – Gypsy Magda Leah Rose - might tell them about it. *And who she* – and her six sisters, and Anders, Maria, Alfie at the Trocadero Cafe - *and had they really somehow gone through some sort of portal that took them back in time to the nineteen sixties when they'd been in his Cafe…?!*

And the two teenage teddy-boy twins - Eddie and Bert - who were Alfie's friends and worked on the merry-go-round at the Fair - and then that huge stately room! – *had they really gone through another sort of portal to get in there as well?!* - into that huge room where they had sat in an alcove off it with Magda and she had spoken about and demonstrated so many eye-opening, mind-boggling incredible and amazing things to them – and all after Ander's had done similar in the Cafe – *and where exactly was that room?*

…And who exactly all those incredible and so very, very un-usual and amazing people…or what…?!…they really were…?!

They had talked about it all before just as intensely last Monday night when they had had fish and chips at Sophie's house after finally leaving Magda and the Fairground, and after what had seemed like *hours* in the Cafe with Anders and then with Magda in the stately room – when they were finally back at the Fairground – *how come no time had actually passed at all…!?*

The two young couples had first met in the Trocadero Cafe last Monday evening – less than a week ago, and then they had gone together into that stately room, taken in there by Anders, where Magda and all her sisters had been waiting for them…and the others who had been in the Cafe to listen to Anders talk. But later at Sophie's, by then, they had experienced so much that night that they had all been mentally exhausted by it all, so now, after several days of their own thoughts going over and over it all again, the opportunity to share them afresh with the others and delve further into their speculations was most enjoyable.

Eventually Jake suggested that they'd better be making tracks to go back to Scarborough, to Jake's house where his Mum was doing tea for them. Sophie was looking forward to meeting his Mum, and seeing where he lived, so, after arranging a time to meet Mel and Dave at the Fair that evening the two of them rode out of the caravan site back into Scarborough.

Chapter 4: Tea At Jake's

"*That was great Mum!* I'm Full! Thank you!" Jake said sitting back with a contented sigh.

"Mmmm, yes it was, and I am too! *It was all lovely - thank you very much!*" Sophie said.

"Well just as long as you're both sure you've had enough," Jake's Mum replied, she then leant towards Sophie, saying, "You're obviously *a very good influence* on him Sophie! – I usually have to be quick and just grab what I can - *because normally he doesn't stop until he's finished everything off* – all the pork pie, the salad, the chocolate cake – *Pufff! - Gone in an instant! - and I'm lucky to get a mouthful!*"

Sophie chuckled again at his Mum's humour.

"Huh! *More exaggeration!* - What with you Mum, an' Simmo an' Big Sammy – *it's all Pots Callin' Kettles* I say! - Anyway I thought I'd save some for 'Ron' – y'know – *'Later Ron'*...before we go off to the Fair…!"

They were sitting altogether at one end of the large pine table in the big farmhouse style kitchen at Jake's and his Mum's house. The few remnants from the tea-time meal of a huge pork pie, salad, cheeses, fruit and a chocolate cake that his Mum had prepared and baked specially for this tea lay in front of them.

"Well I'll put the kettle on then, clear all these plates away and make us all a nice cuppa..."

"Oh let me help you..." Sophie said, moving to get out of her chair.

"Aye, an' I'll give y' hand an'all! - *I usually get us tea ready every day Soph'*, I set the table, clear up after, do the washin' up an' puttin' away like...*so I'm quite used to it...*" He said deadpan.

Jake's Mum gave Sophie one of those knowing, tolerant looks that only Mum's can give, then turned to Jake and said, "*Well that'd be a first!* But thank you both I'll do it while you show Sophie round the garden – I thought we could sit out there with our teas, as it's such a lovely evening".

"Oh *okaaay* Mum - I'll let you do it – *if you insist!*" Jake got to his feet and reached over to politely pull Sophie's chair back for her as she stood up. Sophie was still smiling from the humorous repartee between Mother and Son, and as she stood up she saw his Mum giving him a long loving look as he fumbled around with her chair.

"Y'know something Sophie - you're the first young lady our Jake's ever brought round for tea and to meet his Mum!...I was beginning to worry he'd never get off his bloomin' motorbikes long enough to meet someone really nice like you are and settle down..."

"*MUM!*" Jake exclaimed in the way that only sons can when they are embarrassed by their Mums' saying something like that, and he quickly ushered Sophie out into the garden.

"So...you thought I was worth the time to get off your bikes for then did you…?!" Sophie teased him.

Oh! *Er, Well, I, er*...Aye! Yes I did...first time I saw you...thought y'were worth all the time, 'All The Time In The World'…as the song goes." He said, his face flushing redly. She hugged him tightly and stood on her tip toes to kiss him on the lips.

"And I'm so, so glad you did!" She said. "C'mon! Show me round your garden...*it's massive!*....And...*errr...how many sheds?!* – *Five...?!*"

"Aye, five! Mum put 'er foot down then! She said, *'it were gettin' like lookin' out onto an industrial estate from the kitchen window!'* Though for t'past few years me Dad didn't call 'em 'is sheds – he called 'em 'is 'Bletchley Huts'. - Hah! That big colour photo' of 'im on the kitchen wall by the back door me Mum put up as a joke - she said to 'im that, *'it were to remind 'er of what he looked like in case it were some other strange bloke in overalls tryin' to come in't back door one day!'* - 'Cause he spent most of 'is time in 'em, an' she said she, *'only saw 'im now an' again these days– 'an' not even that often! - What is it with men and sheds?!'* She used to say!"

"*Oh dear!*" Sophie giggled. "So they are where he invented and made all sorts of things in them, and you did...do...as well, with your bikes...?"

"Aye! It's where I do me bikes - *but I've never invented 'owt tho'!* He were good at it, the best, 'is first big invention were when he came up wi' some electrical systems and the mechanics for 'em that improved power stations' mainframe distribution, he patented it and made enough money from it to give up 'is teachin' job at the Tech' College to research an' do other stuff like it full time. That weren't 'ere tho', it were in their first 'ouse, he bought this big place with some o' the money he made from it, but that was all before I were born."

"Wow...what a clever man...! But why did he call the sheds 'Bletchley Huts'? What's that mean?"

Sophie knew all about his Dad having Alzheimers. When Jake had first told her he had, understandably, got very upset about it, he still was of course, so she was trying to gently steer the conversation away a little from upsetting him too much again, plus she was genuinely curious as to the unusual name for the sheds – huts.

"Well...he told me he'd read all the books he could get 'old of about 'ow the Government, in the second world war, set up a top secret group o' boffins in a big stately 'ome down South, near to London, but far enough out to avoid the bombin' raids, to crack the Germans' military signals and secret radio codes. An' as more an' more really clever an' genius folk got involved they 'ad to build loads o' huts, they called 'em, all over the grounds for 'em all to work an' for some to live in, to invent an' make their machines to crack the codes.

"An' they did eventually crack 'em! - A genius bloke called Alan Turing were at the forefront o' the breakthrough to achievin' that. But then they realised that they 'ad to keep the fact that they'd cracked 'em a secret o' course, which apparently, me Dad said, from what he'd read, turned out to be just as big a challenge as crackin' 'em was in the first place! Because from then on they might know well in advance what the Germans were plannin' to do - but they couldn't just take counter action everytime to stop what the Germans' were gettin' up to - 'cause that'd just be a dead give-away that they 'ad bust their

55

codes...and so then they'd change 'em!"

He shook his head, and sighed, "Apparently they, the Allies – on Churchill's decisions, still 'ad to let a lot o' ships still get sunk by the German U Boats, and worst of all was lettin' Coventry get bombed one night which flattened the city an' tens o' thousands o' civilians were killed.

"Churchill made them 'orrible decisions to keep the fact they'd cracked the codes a secret...'Cause it weren't long after that we invaded Europe, so without knowin' where all the German forces were from intercepting their codes they were still usin' when we did invade - an' they knew we were comin' - we might not 'ave won the war...

"For crackin' the codes, the machines they made were basically the first mechanical type o' computers. An' the stately 'ome where all o' that 'appened were called: 'Bletchley Park'."

"Oh woww...that's incredible, *and so, so horrible too*...All those poor, innocent and unsuspecting men, women and children killed...and all the sailors on the ships...that the elites knew in advance would be...But they obviously thought that their deaths were *'justified'* – just like Ander's said about that horrible female American Secretary of State who commented that she thought the killing of at least half a million children in Iraq was *'justified'*...

"I didn't know *anything* about all that, the history lessons we had at school never mentioned it of course! But I see now why he called them his 'Bletchley Huts'!" She then quickly looked around her and furtively whispered with clandestine mock seriousness, "do you think he was doing something *really secret here too* - in - *his 'Bletchley Huts'?!*"

Jake chuckled, and said, "Well...to be 'onest, *I dunno really!* He never said to me, *'Jake - what I'm doin' now is: Really Secret!'* But he did 'ave...still 'as...one main thing on the go for years - along with loads of other things he did o' 'cause - an' he kept leavin' it when he got all frustrated with it, then a few days later he'd be goin' back to it. I remember 'im sayin' to me, *'You 'ave to think about these kinds o' things very differently an' approach 'em positively an' trustin' your intuition Jake – an' it's not so much askin' 'How?' - it works – it's askin' 'Why? It took Edison a thousand or more attempts to make a light-bulb work, but he didn't call those attempts failures – he called 'em – 'discoverin' a thousand ways 'Why' it won't work'!'*

"...Anyway it were summat to do with a device that made or got its own energy, or amplified a little energy into a lot, somehow, summat like that, that's all I know, that's all he ever told me, never went into any detail about it – which, lookin' back, were strange I suppose, as everythin' else he did he always talked about an' explained to me, an' he always got me involved with 'em all, even from me bein' just a little lad – apart from that one thing...

"He said he'd crack it – just like they did at Bletchley – one day, then I'd be the first to know all about it, but unlike what they did at Bletchley it wouldn't be kept a secret, an' then he said, all excited: *'But We'd Still Win The War! - an' help to change the Whole World between us with it!'* Then he'd quickly change subject and get stuck into 'elpin' me strip an' ol' bike down or summat else like that in *my* two huts – he built them last two – with me 'elpin' - 'specially for me – shortly after what 'appened to Taxi Tony - like I were tellin' y'all about at Dave an' Mel's."

"*Wow...! -* Why don't you see if you can, well, find out exactly what and how he was trying to make then, and like 'picking up the baton' - *carry on with it and you crack it...?*"

"*Hummm, I dunno -* he 'ad a brain the size o' two planets - an' were strugglin'! – *Compared to 'im I'm just a grease monkey wi' a spanner!*"

"*No You're Not, You Silly!*" She rebuked him, "You are *just as clever and just as skilful, you could do anything you set your mind to - I Know You Could!*"

Jake put his arms around her shoulders holding her tightly and said, "I think me Mum were right! You are a good influence on me! – An' with you Soph' I reckon' I could! *Ahem! Anyway - C'mon -* an' I'll show you my two huts, there's two ex-army despatch bikes in one I'm goin' to be doin' up – ex-army as in nineteen forties ex-army! My huts are the ones at the end – we built 'em there 'cause it's closer to the big rear gates - so it'd be easier to load bikes in an' out from a van in the back lane."

Through the kitchen window Jake's Mum watched the young couple, with their arms around each other stroll down the flagstone path to the bottom of the long garden, and go in one of the huts at the end and she smiled, wiping away a happy tear. She then slid the kettle off the Aga cooker, thinking she'd wait until they came back out before boiling it and calling for Jake to come and carry the tea things out into the garden for her.

Jake's huts were each slightly bigger than Dave and Mel's static caravan. One was fully fitted out as a well organised, professional mechanic's workshop, and the other was a spare parts store, with wide shelves all around piled up with bits and pieces from dozens of assorted bikes. Laid out haphazardly all over the floor were larger engine parts, and general biking paraphernalia. Two old, dusty, rusty and matt army green coloured motorbikes were on raised stands next to each other at the far end of the workshop hut all ready to be worked on.

He told Sophie the brief story of how he'd come to own them – a couple of weeks back one of his mates from Ol'Billy's garage had gone down to a farm near Bridlington to do some welding on a tractor plough, and in conversation the farmer had told him about them – they'd been in one of the barns since the war, obviously been left there and forgotten about, probably by the Home Guard, but there'd been loads of other army units all over the area as well in those days. Then they'd been sort of forgotten about again, by him, since he was a kid and used to play on them in the barn with his brothers.

"'They'd just been left, shoved in a corner collectin' dust ever since', he'd said to me mate – an' he were goin' to be 'avin' a big clear out soon, and demolish that ol' barn to build some holiday cottages in the field behind it, as he needed the space it were on for part of the car park for 'em, 'cause the farm itself was struggling as a business.

"So he were goin' to put an advert in the paper to try and sell 'em - and loads of other stuff that were just piled up in there. Anyway me mate then rung me straight-away and told me all about 'em. I dropped mi tools an' nipped straight down there an' then on me bike – an' after a bit o' hagglin' we did a deal fer cash, put 'em in a double 'orse trailer an' the farmer drove 'em up 'ere for me - an' so here they are, but as yet I 'aven't 'ad the chance like to mek a start on 'em.

"An' the next job now tho', after Wednesday, when the 'Easy Rider Chopper' is finished an' collected, is gonna be the Norton Commando Cafe Racer that Reg wants me to do for 'im - so all in all, I've got quite a bit to be getting' on with! - *An' ah'm lookin' forward to it!*" He said enthusiastically.

His lips then pressed together in a grim smile as he said,

"an' it's all down to me Dad tekin' the time to teach an' show me 'ow to do all o' this, so it means I can always mek some money doin' what I love doin', I'll always be grateful to 'im fer that..."

His sad smile then quickly turned into one of humour as he said,

"...s'pose I'll soon 'ave to put a photo' o' me up as well by the back door so me Mum don't forget *what I look like!*" He chuckled.

"Anyway – let's go back an' 'ave a cuppa - talkin' about me Mum she'll be wonderin' what we're upto!"

"*Oh I think she probably knows!*" Sophie said with a big smile and reached upto kiss him again.

" - But you're right, we'd better go back and join her, it's not polite to be ages! I think your Mum's great, and I think she likes me too!"

"Oh aye she does! I can tell! - *Much more than the last dozen or so floozies I brought round for tea!*"

"Oh...and here's me thinking I was the first...!" She said rolling her eyes at him and then laughing.

" - *'Course you are!* Only jokin'! You're The First...The Last...You're my…...."

"I'm your what…?" She whispered coyly.

"...I should've 'ad the CD player set up to play the Barry White track right now...'cause the next word is...*Everything...*" He whispered back.

Which then lead to much longer kisses and hugs…

Jake's Mum saw them eventually come out of the far hut and she slid the kettle back onto the Aga's hot plate. She then took a large plate laden with buttered shortbread biscuits she'd made that morning as well, as a surprise, outside to the garden table and chairs which were sheltered from the sun under a large cream coloured canvas parasol. All the while with a happy smile on her face.

"Jake - would you be a luv and carry the tea tray out for me please? The kettle's nearly boiled."

"*Aye! Will Do!* Oh magic Mum! *Butter Shortbreads!* - Me second favourites after y'chocolate cake! But, er, isn't anyone else 'avin' any? *There's only my plate there…*" He said with mock surprise. His Mum gave Sophie another one of those looks.

The kettle whistled loudly. "Kettle's boiling!" His Mum said.

"Right! *I'm there!*" He said moving rapidly off into the kitchen – but not before swiping a biscuit off the plate, just managing to avoid a wrist slap from his Mum.

"Well Mrs. J. …" Sophie started to say a while later, after the tea and biscuits had all gone, "Oh please Sophie! - It's Helen! - Only the Butler calls me 'Mrs. J.', and it's his day off!" She said with a grin.

"*Huh…!*" Jake said, joining in, "*That bloomin' Butler has more time off than I do…!*" Sophie laughed once again at their easy, relaxed and funny patter that had come to the fore whilst sitting out here in the sunny garden, leisurely drinking their teas, and she realised that Jake's dry humour came in no small part from his Mum. *The funny Mummy and the genius Dad, traits that are so evident in Jake's character,* she thought.

"Well – Helen – thank you again! - It's been really great to meet you and come to your lovely home, I've really, really enjoyed it! I hope you won't mind though if I say I must go home soon and get changed before we go to the Fair – I've still got my work clothes on!"

"Of course I don't! And very smart and attractive you look in them too, *you never know…your smart and stylish dress sense might rub off*

60

onto some others round here we know..." She said looking pointedly at Jake in his salt and sweat stained black cut off frayed T shirt which now also had shortbread biscuit crumbs and buttery smears stuck all the way down the front of it.

Jake looked over his shoulder as if to see whom it was she was talking about before turning back and pointing at himself in surprise. "*Who...Me?*"

"*Yes You Dear!* You're surely not going to escort a lovely smart young lady on an evening out in *those clothes* are you...?!*" Sophie had to put her hand over her mouth to hide her grinning.

"Huh! *I was* just about to get changed an'all! I just 'ope that Butler pressed an' laid out mi evenin' wear before he swanned off for the day..."

He then stood up saying, "I won't be long Soph - a quick shower – er, it is Sat'day innit? - Aye it is! – So it's shower day, *and* change clothes day – I do it every Sat'day - *even if I don't need to...!*"

As he started to walk away he pulled his T shirt off over his head, scattering crumbs everywhere, and revealing his muscular torso.

"Oh Please Jake Jackson! *Go inside – you'll frighten the horses!*" His Mum shouted over to him, waving her hands towards the house.

Sophie and Jake waved goodbye to his Mum who was waving back by the front door as they rode away down the long drive, then he accelerated out onto the road, skilfully weaving his way through the traffic to go to her house.

Chapter 5: To Scarborough Fair

"I think she might be on her last legs." Dave said sadly to Jake and Sophie, after apologising for arriving late to meet them in the car park field next to the Fair.

"She's not running anything like she used to, been like that for a few weeks now, hope I'm not going to lose her – we've been together for years...She did her best and finally managed to start *just before* the battery went flat."

He looked disconsolately at his car. It was an old Citroen 2CV, it's paint work a dull battleship grey, the body work scarred and dented in places, but still something of a classic in its own right.

"Nah, won't come to that, from what y'sayin' *it'll be summat or nowt mate.*" Jake said to him reassuringly. "Beauty o' these is that y'can take a spanner to 'em, parts are cheap enough, an' there's no computers in 'em that cost a fortune to reset – even if y'can, so y'can take parts out an' fix 'em or put new ones in wi' no hassle. Drop it off round at the garage sometime next week, Ol'Billy'll sort it, he 'ad one o' these years ago – he'll still 'ave loads o' spares – as he never throws owt away!

"Y've gotta keep these ol' cars goin' mate! – They've got character! Not like all these modern ones 'ere, most of 'em all look the same to me!" He said gesturing disparagingly around him at the rows of cars in the almost full car park.

"An' *none o' these* are made to last 'alf as long as this ol' girl *already has!* - I reckon she's good for years yet!"

"Oh I hope so!" Mel said. "I think she just needs a bit of TLC and I'm sure she'll be as right as rain again!"

"Aye! That's it! *Amazin'* what a bit o' *'Tender Lovin' Care'* can do it innit?!" Jake chuckled, catching Sophie's eye with a knowing look...

"*Mmmm - There's Nothing Like It!*" Sophie replied with the same knowing look and a slightly blushing smile at him, as she linked her arm under his, "so...shall we...? Oh! Look! *There's Ruth!*"

Ruth was one of Gypsy Magda Leah Rose's six younger sisters, and she was waiting for them near the entrance to the Fair. Ruth had waved them off when they all left the Fair last Monday night, and she was now waving again, welcoming them back. They all hurried over to her. After hugs and kisses of greeting Ruth said, "Magda asked me to come and wait for you all, so now you're all here - let's go in and you can see her!"

They walked into the busy Fair all together, just another group amongst many other groups of people doing the same thing, and the three girls talked non stop to each other. When they were still a little distance away from Magda's old fashioned, classically styled Romany caravan Ruth stopped to say quietly to them all,

"...if you and David, Melanie, go in first, then give it a few minutes or so before you and Jake go in Sophie, that way it will be less obvious to everyone around us, especially if you can make it look as if you weren't intending to go straight in - but had just decided to on the spur of the moment - is that okay?"

Mel said, "Yes of course – come on Dave I can't wait! See you later Ruth!"

They separated from the others and then walked off seemingly aimlessly, but towards the Romany caravan. As they ambled closer to it they paused to read the large, antique looking, ornate and gaily hand-painted standing sign in front of it. It detailed the scope of all the revelations about your future - that would be revealed to you once you went inside! Then, smiling widely and nodding at each other, as if coming to a sudden agreement to go in, hand in hand they walked up the steps and went inside. Their actions went completely unnoticed by the crowds milling past them.

"Wow!" Sophie said, "They did that well! You'd never've known that they *actually intended* to go in to it all along! - It was like watching a clip from a spy film!"

Ruth laughed. *"Yes, it was! I'm very impressed!"* What they did is actually called *'Trade-craft'*. A big part of it is the art of doing everyday seemingly normal things, so that you just pass by unnoticed...

"The trick is: *to live your cover and be completely natural with whatever environment you're in,* so you blend in without creating any give-away signs to anyone who might be watching – *because those using tradecraft have a secret purpose that is camouflaged by the normal things they are doing!* It looks as if Melanie and David are naturals at it! *I'm sure you two are as well!* Okay then - it's your turn now!"

Jake was enjoying himself as they slowly wandered off amongst all the people moving around them, apparently just another couple meandering along.

As they got closer and closer to the caravan though he deliberately slowed right down and lowered his noticeable height by bending slightly, acting his part well by pretending to be doing something with the leather and canvas bag he was carrying with their helmets in.

Whilst he was doing this Sophie read the large sign, she then pointed to it, shaking his arm, looking questioningly at him copying the way Mel had nodded to Dave, and then she lead him up the steps.

Ruth smiled wistfully to herself as she watched them appraisingly, recalling how many, oh so many years ago on this planet, she and her sisters had all had to learn how to perform such seemingly innocuous actions themselves, but in those faraway days it had been in a different country and amongst a suspicious, hostile and very dangerous, armed occupying force...She moved slowly away and blended in with everyone around her, and if anyone had been watching her - she seemed to then...just disappear…

Once inside the dimly lit caravan Jake and Sophie saw Mel and Dave sitting at a round table. They were talking with another of Magda's sisters whom they'd seen last Monday. She was sat opposite them and had her long pale fingers wrapped around a large glowing crystal sphere on the purple velvet covered table top.

"Hi again!" Mel tittered. *"This is Lucia!* She's been telling us about doing crystal ball readings!"

"Hello and Welcome Again Sophie and Jake! We didn't have the opportunity to talk last Monday - and I don't think we will have tonight either! *But another time we will!* - Magda asked me to let you all go straight through – I'll just suspend the ward of protection on the entrance portal for you..." She went quiet for a moment, her eyes closed, as she concentrated...

"There! *All Done!* - You know the way now!"

Lucia said with a smile, turning slightly in her chair to flutter her hand airily at the floor to ceiling length, exquisitely woven heavy tapestry in the back corner, which depicted a scene of snow covered, high mountain peaks under a full moon.

The last time they had seen it both Sophie and Mel had commented to Magda on how beautiful and realistic looking they thought it was, and she had further amazed them all by saying it had taken over six months to hand weave in silk, wool and silver thread no thicker than a human hair, in a master's workshop in Belgium...*in fifteen thirty two...!* - And it was just one of the many superb Flemish tapestries she had commissioned from those weavers...

Behind it they knew there was what looked like a narrow doorway, perhaps leading into a small bathroom, to all outward appearances, but they now knew it was also a portal, a portal that lead into and out of the wondrous stately room they had been in for the first time last Monday night.

"Oh – er, shall we just go through then Lucia...? It seems a bit rude of us if we just say *'Hello And Goodbye'* straight away to you!" Sophie said.

"Oh Bless you! *Not at all! Please do! Go through!"* Her voice warm and friendly.

"I'd love to listen to you talk some more about your crystals sometime when it's convenient for you Lucia..." Mel said as she stood up. "I design and make jewellery and things, and, well, when I can find or afford really nice samples I use them in my designs too, if you wouldn't mind I'd really appreciate it – you know so much about them...even in a few minutes you've said things about them that I never knew...!"

65

Lucia smiled at her and said, "Of course Melanie I'd love to! I'll bring some interesting ones with me to show you when I come – I have some special ones from Russia, given to me by...by someone who, who was a friend and he lived there once...*and I'd love to see your jewellery as well!* Just contact me when it is a good time for you – you know how to now! and I'll come! You can show me round *your* caravan as well then...!"

"Oh thank you Lucia! *Wow, that'd be great!* – I'm looking forward to it already...! Er – but - *how did you know about our caravan...?!*"

Lucia smiled at her again, "Magda will tell you! But please hurry, all of you, or the warding will fade and automatically reset."

Jake went through first, carefully holding the very old and surprisingly heavy tapestry aside and opening the dark polished wooden door for the others to pass through. They all felt again the slight tingly feeling all over their bodies as they stepped through a portal once again, then they walked a short distance in single file to another door, opened it, and went into the immense stately room beyond...

Chapter 6: The Stately Room, again.

Magda was standing just inside it and waiting for them, a happy smile of welcome for them all on her face. "Hello Sophie, Jake, Melanie and David! How *lovely it is* to see you all here again!"

She then seemed to glide over to them – *how does she do that?!* - Sophie thought to herself again - then she was hugging her in greeting. After they had all hugged and said a few words with Magda, Sophie stepped back a little, looked up and down at her and said, "*Wow Magda!* You look *absolutely fabulous! That dress is incredible!* It, it, you, you look like – *if* you don't mind me saying – you look – well - *just like - a Fairy Queen!*"

Magda was wearing a full length formal evening dress of a shimmering silvery satin like material, the long sleeves belled out from her elbows and were deeply edged with swirling patterns of tiny glittering silvery crystal gem stones, surely they couldn't all be diamonds – could they? Her long reddish auburn hair had a broad silver tiara covered in – diamonds? holding the front of it up and the rest floated around her shoulders and all the way down her back.

A large multi facet cut and polished pale green and silver streaked milky quartz like crystal shone with a subtle inner luminescence of its own, hanging from a delicate silver chain around her neck, and it complimented the intense emerald green of her eyes. The silver rings on each of her fingers had a smaller stone of the same mounted in complex and differently filigreed designs.

"Well *Thank You* My Dear! It is *very kind* of you to say so! Such generously flattering comments I do not mind at all! - *But please - not so loud!* I am not of the Fae Folk, the Daoine Sidhe, and if Her Majesty, Medb, their Queen, heard you say that about me she would be *very* jealous – and that would *really not* do at all!" She laughed, but had quickly widened her eyes to emphasise her last words...

"I like to wear this dress when it is going to be a full moon here, the material responds to and glows so delightfully in the moonlight! Anders is escorting me to our soiree here later, to thank all our helpers for everything they have done this past week, as this is our last night here, for a while. In fact you will see him shortly before he has to go and give his last talk.

"We managed to securely ward the entire area of the Fair with a lasting glamour of protection in the early hours of the day after you all left, so the marquee was reinstated for him.

"The Watchers' and particularly 'The Wreckers' malevolently used abilities are neutered under such a powerful warding glamour, so perhaps, with hindsight, we should have done that at first. But we decided not to initially because sometimes it is advantageous for us to allow them to reveal themselves, so we can monitor and gauge changes in their dark arts and tactics...drawing them in...like a multi-dimensional game of chess...

"The parasites controlling their servile elites and *their* servile minions may be highly skilled in the Dark Arts, but so are we...but in the countering Arts of Light. So are all of those whom are *allied with us from their own choice and free-will...*

"Just as we have the parasites also have their forms of *exotic technologies* as well of course - that they are having constantly weaponised by...misguided human scientist minions who are shown how to by them.

"But for all their Dark Arts and Dark Technologies they will ultimately never supersede all our far older...*natural, positive, love and light based, free-willed living abilities*...from which stem all the associated glamours and wardings that we can call upon..."

"Wowww...!" Mel said quietly. "Listening to all the things you say Magda, I think, well, you not only look like a Queen - *you are a Queen*! And you certainly look very *glamorous*! Your jewellery is exquisite!"

"*Thank You Too My Dear!* Some of this jewellery was made by early Russian lapidarists, they were gifts to me from...a friend...when we stayed there once with his family...but some are...much, much

68

older...

"'Glamour' is such a lovely word I think, its true original meaning is quite different to the way it is used in these times of course, although the modern sense of the more superficial changing of physical appearance is similar I suppose...but shall we go and sit down? – because it is *all of you* who have somethings to *tell and ask me about* from what I understand!?"

She lead them towards the same alcove with the reddish brown silky fabric covered chesterfield styled sofas and matching high backed chairs, where last Monday night she had talked about and introduced them all to such amazing and life changing wisdoms. All of those coming more or less immediately after Ander's incredibly insightful lecture in 'The Trocadero Cafe', which had had a profound affect upon them by opening their eyes and expanding their perceptions of themselves and of what was really happening in the world around them all as well.

As they walked across the warm, creamy coloured marble floor – Sophie noticing that Magda was walking now, not gliding, Mel asked her, "Magda? - Lucia said you'd tell us how you knew that Dave and I - *are now living in a caravan...as well!*" Magda smiled back at her.

"Yes of course I will my dear – but let us sit down first."

When they were all settled, sitting in the same familiar places as they had done last time, Magda started to explain.

"When I received your 'psycomms'...your psychic communications...this afternoon – and I must say that it was *very thoughtful* of you all to say to me first that you were all fine – that you just wanted to meet me to tell me about something important and ask me some questions about it!

"I say so because for a split second when you all first came through to me so strongly at once I was very concerned that...well...that there might have been...a problem. It *seemed* that there was not, but, nevertheless, as: *'Assumption is the Mother of all 'f...' ups'*, to quote Dwight - the late American President Eisenhower - he always had such a pithy and direct way of talking in private...! - Actually he had

69

that particular statement engraved into a plaque to stand on his desk!

"Anyway...I decided to remote view you all just to make sure...as one never knows...I would not normally of course, dream of intruding on your privacy by doing that...but I just wanted to, to make *no assumptions* and so reassure myself, that all was well, so thank you all for doing that.

"Melanie and David y*our new home looks lovely! – and I saw you have a 'Home Sweet Home' tapestry inside it above the door just like mine!* Your caravan is in such a pleasant location so close to the sea! I'm sure you will be very happy in it! And I think you, Sophie and Melanie – *you were both actually aware of me and saw me there?*"

Mel's and Sophie's hands quickly went upto their cheeks in astonishment on hearing this. "Yes! *Yes I did!*" They said together.

"But we thought, we just thought after, that we'd imagined it - seeing you! So we really did then? *We really saw you?!*" Mel asked her.

"*Yes, you both did!* I thought you had! Your natural psychic abilities - especially your 'clairvoyance' – from the Old French word for 'clear-sightedness', is obviously more than *just starting to re-emerge...!* So well done! You were both aware of my consciousness being present and your minds' eyes decoded that into a fleeting image of me.

"You must have been practising all the things I showed you when we last met, and that has started to...*resurrect*...your other senses, abilities and talents as well! I also saw all your protective diamonds quite clearly – so *I do know* you have all been practising! – *So Well Done Everyone!*"

Sophie quickly recalled how she'd felt last Monday lunchtime when she had been sat on one of her favourite benches in the sunshine at Scarborough's harbour, just before Jake had come to say 'hello' to her.

She clearly remembered thinking and realising then that she was becoming more and more aware of: *'lots of other senses as well, that were still in the background a bit – but I know they are coming closer towards me'*, so this 'glimpse of clairvoyance' must be one of those...!

70

Mel interrupted her recall as she enthusiastically exclaimed,

"Yes! Yes we both have haven't we Dave?! And you've been explaining and showing me how to meditate as well haven't you?"

"Yes I have! - Not that it took much showing you! - You took to it like a duck to water!" He laughed.

"In fact I think it was from me meditating early yesterday morning that started this whole: *'wanting to meet you tonight thing off'* in the first place Magda! - Err...not that I need to meditate first - *before wanting to see you Magda* - of course!" He quickly added with bashful humour.

"Well thank you David! - *That's always nice to know!*" Magda replied teasing him with a smile as the others laughed.

Jake asked her, "This *'remote viewing'* Magda, Anders mentioned it last Monday an' me Dad did once to me, but that was all, he didn't say owt else about it. So what is it exactly?"

"Well Jake, it is a big subject to go into in depth and *fully* explain – so I think doing that will have to be for another day, but for now let me just answer you by saying that it is the ability for your consciousness to go out of your physical body at will, and then it projects to view and see things at a distance – any distance – from one room to the one next to it or out to other galaxies far away from your physical self, *in time and space*, in effect it is similar to astral travelling that I mentioned last time.

"'Remote Viewers', as people who have developed their abilities to do this are called, have been secretly used, unbeknown of course to the public masses, and by the people or installations targeted, by the Intelligence gathering agencies of many countries for decades.

"A male remote viewer called Ingo Swann, an American, used by that country's Intelligence Agencies recently 'spilled the beans', as they say, on much of these types of covert psychic activities. He managed to do so before he unfortunately...passed away...

"It is something that you are all capable of doing quite naturally...though there is nano-technology which is now being developed further by the military industrial corporations of the elites which enhances the ability to do it. And predictably - weaponise it...which is a grave concern and will be a subject for another day as well.

"To do it naturally, at first, it is essential that you have some instruction and guidance, and then you practice and practice it...just like you do when learning anything new. But look at how well you all performed your telepathy! - or 'psycomms' - as we call it, to me for the first time you practised it!

"And there are...many other things you can do as well, as you become more aware of the nature of your true reality and abilities...

"In fact, just as an aside, if mobile telephone electronic communications had not been so deliberately and rapidly deployed across the entire planet over the past very few years most people would by now have naturally developed a basic ability to psycomm with each other...so there are dots there that you can join to make a picture...however, I say again - another subject for another day...

"...Actually I will ask Lucia to do so with you, as she has an extra-ordinary ability with remote viewing and its associated skills – such as psychometry – which is similar to reading auras, but is the ability to hold an object – particularly jewellery which is Lucia's speciality, to discover its history and that of the person, or persons, whom wore it...!"

The two young couples let all this incredible information soak in, amazed yet again, at the things Magda revealed to them so matter-of-factly. Mel thinking as well that what Magda had just said about Lucia would be another incredible facet – ha! good pun! - to the experience of meeting together to talk about crystals and jewellery - *as soon as possible now!*

After a few moments Sophie asked Magda, "talking about travelling and viewing - if you're all going away from here after tonight though Magda, how will we be able to, to come and see you again?" A tinge of concern and sadness in her voice.

"Oh do not worry about that my dear! To meet me here again you

just psycomm your thoughts to me and I will tell you then where my little caravan will be, because when you have thought to me I will know where you are – like your mobile telephones do – but the difference is *they* do that all of the time...another reason they are promoted so cleverly...and then my caravan and I will go somewhere nearby to you.   My unicorn, Beau, is very adept at earthly navigation...!"

"*Your...Unicorn...?!*" Sophie gasped.

"Yes, although I say *'my'* he's not really *'mine'* at all, he's a helper too, along with the others, partnered to us all to navigate our little caravans and their portals to wherever we need them to go. Outwardly, to just about all humans, and...those whom are not...he, and the others like him, looks like any other normal working horse! But that is just a powerful glamour specifically designed by them to be seen in that form *on* the Earth plane...In fact Sophie - you've already met Beau...!"

"W,wwhaaat!?...I...but I haven't seen any hors..*unicorns*...Oh!...*The merry-go-round!* But they, they were just nearly life-sized models...! *Weren't they...?!*"

Magda laughed. "Oh yes – of course - in the differently glamoured forms you perceived them all then they were, and it was Beau you rode on then, he told me. They all *do so enjoy* the times we have when we come to the Fair, as they get to play on the twins' merry-go-round giving rides...mainly to children and young people like yourselves.

"Unicorns have a great affinity to the young, in fact very, very young children, particularly girls, can naturally see their true forms of course, but that is only in the few short years before society at large, starting with the restrictive compliance programming of their own social milieu which they grow up in, repeatedly tells them in their all-too-soon later years: *'no you can't see them! Don't be silly! They don't exist...!'*

"So, sadly, and all too quickly, they, and their perceptions, become ever more limited to conform and comply with only the socially engineered and acceptable, group or 'milieu mindset', and they believe just that...so then, they can't see them, or everything else they could before, anymore of course..."

"Oh wowwww!" Was just about all that Sophie could manage to respond to Magda with, as she flopped back into the sofa, her lips silently trying to form words that just wouldn't come out of her mouth.

"Blimey...!" Jake muttered. Then he grinned mischievously as he looked first at Sophie, dumbstruck on the sofa, and then at Mel and Dave, who both were similarly gob-smacked, saying, "Well I know now that if I want some peace an' quiet from Soph' – I'll just mention...*Unicorns...!*"

Which resulted in Sophie playfully pummelling at his arm in mock high dudgeon as they all laughed.

"Well it is wonder-full when conversation wanders as it does all on its own with such enlightened young people like you all are, but you want to tell *me* about something...and David you said, *'that it started from when you were meditating...'*?"

"Yes, that's right...well, just before that really, when it woke me up yesterday morning I suppose. I, I've tried to remember everything exactly as I saw it, and what happened yesterday morning for you, well, *I hope I have anyway!...*

"I told Jake all about it this afternoon, and then he told me all about, about somethings he'd experienced that were related to it - but all of that wasn't yesterday - it was a long time ago, wasn't it mate?"

"Aye, it were, it's a bit of a long story an'all, but it's all related like Dave says, in fact Magda, it's really just Dave and me that *'have a story to tell you'*, as we told the girls about it all this afternoon. And when we've both told you, if Dave goes first, I, we, well we all 'ave some questions – I've tried to remember all of 'em! They're really about what you would advise us to do - *about what we've all decided we want to, try to do...!*"

"Excellent! I am most intrigued! In that case then...until Anders joins us in a few minutes time - *he's just told me he's been slightly delayed* - I told him earlier that you were all coming this evening; if

you do not mind, I would first like to just briefly pause from going ahead with that, only until he arrives, and take this opportunity we have together now to give you some relevant, general, background context first though – about talking and communicating generally, before you tell me all about this important issue.

"It may seem that I am going 'way off topic' a little at first, but I am sure you will all soon 'join the dots'! I will try not to be very long, and then I will have a suggestion, for you both, which, hopefully you will agree to...is that acceptable to you all?"

They all keenly nodded their agreements, and Jake said, "Aye, o' course it is Magda – *it's great Anders'll be 'ere in a bit an'all as well!* Anythin' you've got to say that fills in some o' the blank squares for us, so to speak - is more than welcome!"

"Thank you Jake. I do not want to seem as if I am deflecting away the impetus and obvious importance of what you wish to tell and ask me - us, but, as I said, until Anders gets here this is a good opportunity before you do, to give you a relevant 'info drop'."

Magda then steepled her long slim hands under her chin, displaying the exquisitely crafted rings she wore on each of her fingers, as looked at them all.

"Talking, communicating, debating and discussing things, sharing one's own thoughts, ideas or memories about them 'face to face' with others, using all the arts of good conversation are *natural*, wonder-full human experiences as I have said.

"But, as I mentioned a few minutes ago, sadly there is so much *unnatural* but highly addictive communications technology now seeping into and contaminating your societies, and it is doing so because it is strongly coupled with insidious social programming agendas - which are major parts of its latent 'psyops' - 'psychological operations' - agenda, which is designed to deliberately diminish these human conversational arts, abilities and experiences...

"Why? And How? Well, let us start with just a couple of the aspects of the social programming behind it all: - *everything you communicate with electronic technology is constantly being monitored.* Why? - Well, because surveillance is an essential expedient of population control...

"...and in particular, persistently using communications technology detrimentally targets the inner, deeper thought processes of the human mind that fuel a truly natural, insightful exchange of ideas and thoughts during a meaningful conversation...or a critical thinking debate.

"It reduces it instead into merely superficial, short and limited 'messaging' or 'sound bytes', rather than meaningful, insightful and extended verbal communications.

"I said it was 'seeping' into your society, well really it has achieved much more than that – *it has saturated it.* Research into this has shown that most people now consume some form of mainstream media for *at least* a third of their waking hours...

"However...moving on...try doing this the next time you talk to someone in a social setting – and I mean actually talking to communicate with serious insight about something – not just a quick verbal exercise in repartee and swapping shallow and brief sentences riddled with the flippant, and current 'buzz words'.

"It could be about something important to you, and to them. Try to do a mental count of how many seconds pass until you realise that their attention is wandering. You will find that as you talk, after about seven seconds, *at the most,* with the majority of people, you will have lost their full attention, even all of it, and with a lot of people it will be much less than seven seconds.

"Yes, of course, brevity and the ability to be succinct, yet still communicate the essence of what you want to impart to others is a desirable skill. In it's place. But it so often just degenerates into unfeeling terse and blunt *'corporate email speak',* that could almost have come from a programmed machine...

"Also, try this as well - watch a modern film or some current 'programme' on television – particularly the adverts. Do a mental count of how many seconds pass before each scene or camera angle changes.

76

"You will find that on average it will be between three to seven seconds – and much less in the adverts - which exist to subliminally train you to be a good and compliant consumer – which is extremely effective whilst you are in a hypnotically induced alpha brain wave trance state - as a result of watching the television screen, which achieves that by flickering a certain amount of times a second - which is the same as the brain's alpha wave frequency, *so the brain entrains with it,* and therefore becomes totally receptive and open to suggestion...

"*The Alpha Trance State then 'lets everything in', as it disables all your critical filters...*

"*Realise as well that* what *you watch between the adverts are called 'programmes' for a reason...*television is a hypnotic propaganda machine that easily feeds tremendous amounts of false information to the masses, because it teaches people *What To Think – not How To Think!*

"I would be guilty of going a little bit too far off topic if I were now to go *too much* into the details of the deliberate truncating of speech patterns – and the diminishing amount, variety and quality of the words used, for example, by the very carefully selected actors in the popular – particularly the very popular plethora of 'soaps' - programmes people are exposed to, and often, all too quickly become addicted to them.

"To say nothing of the, shall we say – *less than ideal* or beneficial - moral, behavioural and attitudinal roles those types of *'programmes'* and many others, if not all, portray – so I will only just mention all of that in passing...! *Oh – last comment on those types of 'soaps-programmes'!* – Watch some and you will notice the camera angle very rarely – *if ever* – includes the sky or horizon shots.

"This is deliberately done because the overall impression you are then hypnotically receptive to is that of confinement, limitation, and totally absorbing the negativity of close up exposure to traumatic and stressful life-styles, these 'programmes' are inflicting on you, mainly in interior environments, as if the people are helplessly trapped in them. Which the viewers' brains' hypnotically entrain with...and so their perceptions identify with them as being just the normal state of human affairs..

"All that rapid scene-view-changing is done because those whom create what you are watching are well aware that the current human verbal and visual attention spans have been reduced to, on average, between three to seven seconds – and after that you have, more or less, lost them…

"And by designing media technology like that they are also subliminally, constantly reinforcing that short time – and deliberately, gradually, succeeding in shortening the human attention span even further.

"Incidentally, that flicker rate, or the flashes on a screen to give the illusion of smooth and continuous movement, is between twenty five to thirty five a second, which, as I have just said, just happens to be the optimum amount to induce a highly receptive, alpha brain wave trance like state in someone sat, transfixed and hypnotised, as they stare at it…for hours and hours, everyday...

"The next thing to try is, when you get the chance to, as an interesting comparison, is to watch some films made in the early seventies, or earlier. Do the same 'scene-change and camera-angle seconds count', it will average out to around seventeen seconds! On average that is about three times longer!

"Having done all that, you will have witnessed an ongoing psyops mainstream media programming exercise. To use a 'buzz-phrase' – it is an intentional *'dumbing down'*.

"I am not not saying that true conversation and debate are soon to be extinct arts – certainly not! Much diminished though – yes! Because at this time of your race's global awakening, those...entities...who are desperately trying to prevent that awakening...are rapidly stepping up the Technocratic aspects of their agenda against you...

"You will, perhaps remember what Anders first quoted to you all from Zbigniew Brzezinski's writings backing the concept and desires for the 'Technotronic, or Technocratic Era' last Monday evening…? It is all part-and-parcel of the same latent agenda…"

"Aye I do Magda!" Jake said, "an' it wound me up! Not for *just* what he said, I mean that did an'all o'course - *but really, well, because y'can see an' hear it cumin' true an' 'appenin' all round y'wi' so many folk!* It were this he said weren't it?" Then in a snidey, contempt filled, American accent he said:

'...the public will shortly be unable to think or reason for themselves, they'll only be able to parrot the information they've been given on the previous night's television news...They will come to expect the media to all their thinking for them...The Technotronic Era is the gradual appearance of a more controlled society, dominated by an elite free from traditional values, and they will influence and control the people...'"

Magda clapped him loudly – the others quickly joining in!

"That was remarkable Jake! *It could have been the despicable man himself sat there talking!* And *Very Well Remembered!* You obviously have some excellent and very special gifts - an eidetic auditory memory, coupled with an extra-ordinary gift of mimicry! An eidetic memory is very, very rare, in fact almost non-existent amongst adults in Western societies now, often it is found in just a few young children, before it is lost…" She smiled widely at him, her eyes intense and fascinated as she stared at him with great affection.

Sophie beamed an admiring and loving look at him and then cheekily said, *"so don't you dare stop being like a big kid most of the time – or you might not be able to do it any more…!"* and then, giggling, she put her arms around him to give him a quick, big squeezy hug.

"Well...thank y'all good buddies!" This time in an upbeat, friendly, American accent. He then reverted to his normal Yorkshire accent, "Aye, it's just that I came across him talking in some research I was doin' online last week, so I put his voice onto what Anders'd said. I'm not tryin' to show off! - it's just that I think I've still got *verbal-itis* from talkin' so much about things that different people said this

79

afternoon!"

Dave was nodding and said, "I was amazed this afternoon mate, when we were sat on the cliff top, at how you could just remember everything people had said, *and how they said it*, from years ago, when you were telling me about all those things that happened... they're fantastic gifts y've got mate!"

"Oh blimey! Cheers! Never really thought that much about it meself! Just always been summat I could do! Got me into no end o' trouble at school tho' when I used to tek off the teachers an' mek everyone laugh! S'pose it might've cum from bein' when I were a little kid an' I listened so much to what me Dad were sayin' as he explained 'ow to do, use, an' mek things in't sheds wi' 'im...? I dunno...!" he shrugged his shoulders.

"That will certainly have helped you Jake, but it perhaps just helped you to maintain the gifts you were born with..." Magda commented.

"Well, going back to what I was saying about true conversation and debate...I must quickly add that it is with delight I can see, and hear - with all of you, that all those deleterious effects I mentioned are not evident, but, disturbingly, they are – as you just said Jake, with so, so many...especially, but not confined to, the younger generations.

"If you addict a four year old – or even younger child - to the entrancing programmes of dumbed-down media content on a hand held screen they consume in isolation – or absorb whilst in a trance from watching dumbed-down television programmes – often eye catchingly colourful cartoons - specifically designed to target them - what do you expect...? Well, computer programmers would reply: 'GIGO', which is an acronym for: *'Garbage In – Garbage Out'*...!

"Also, constant close range exposure to the very powerful microwave frequencies all these devices – particularly the hand held screens and mobile phones - receiving and transmitting, has been proven to cause cancerous tumours and other grave long term illnesses and other problems due to them interfering with and damaging the human body's natural electro-magnetic cellular functioning and harmony in a disturbingly high percentage of people.

80

"There is much, much research and evidence of this just in the recent years of their proliferation, and in the longer term the harmful effects *can only increase as the radiations become even more powerful,* so please do research it for yourselves – it is of course, all dismissed and attempted to be buried away by the manufacturers and promoters of these devices, ostensibly to protect their profits, but in doing so it also continues the parasites latent agenda.

"The mainstream media, as you would expect, flood the airwaves with false news and disinformation about it all, generally ridiculing all the concerned voices, and learned research papers - when they even bother to approach the subject, so the average citizen 'in the street' is quite easily persuaded that there is nothing sinister at all going on.

"Incidentally, I recently learned during my researches – initially through remote viewing – then by accessing documented evidence in the public domain, that inside the Head-Quarter's building of the elites' so called 'World Health Organisation', these electro-magnetic-frequency millimetre-wave frequency radiations – called MMW - are absolutely minuscule compared to those in the outside environment, due to effective shielding from them being in place – so why would they go to all that trouble and expense of shielding in there if they are harmless? - well, because they know the truth about the dangers of exposure to them of course - so they have protected those *who work for them* in that environment from them...

"In the same vein, another relevant fact to think about is that many years ago Lead was removed from the petrol fuel for your cars' engines - because the microscopic particulates of it were proven to be having harmful effects on you when they were discharged through an engine's exhaust pipe and out into the atmosphere you breathe in. And the public were too well informed and aware of that particular danger – and demanded changes! They are not so well informed now though! *That was a lesson the elites quickly learned!*

"The public are now, of course, deliberately ill-informed and un-aware, about more and more. But the harmfulness to you of the EMF micro-wave MMW emissions from so many devices are now many hundreds of thousands of times a greater danger to them than the Lead emissions ever were – but nothing is being done now about them – in fact their usage is being accelerated at an alarming speed…

"Talking about breathing in harmful metallic particulates – all across the planet humans are breathing in vaporised metallic particulates of aluminium, barium, strontium and many other metals, from the chem-trails, which lodge in various parts of the body, particularly in the brain, and unless you regularly follow certain straightforward procedures to de-toxify yourself from them, by flushing them out of your system, they build up and aggregate.

"Now just as a simple example - if you've ever - by mistake - put something in a micro-wave cooker which had even tiny traces of aluminium or another metal left on its packaging and switched it on – you might have seen what immediately happens when it reacts - by exploding, burning and crackling violently! So imagine what happens at a microscopic level in the human brain and other areas of the body – particularly the skin and eyes, but there is a long list of adverse biological effects – when targeted micro-wave radiation reacts with those absorbed metallic particulates…and the more there are of the particles the greater the destructive reaction of course…

"The elites' agenda is to soon cover the entire planet with even more powerful, military grade, so-called 'Fifth Generation', or 'Five G', EMF MMW discharge emissions, *and over twenty thousand* orbiting satellites to blanket humanity with a lethal, irradiated, MMW toxic electrosmog are already in place to do so…

"Along with millions of small cell tower transmission masts, every five hundred feet or so, mounted on electric utility poles. This means that they will be able to send, at the speed of light, tightly focused beams of intense, extremely short wave, phased array, microwave radiation, like a bullet, at each specific 5G device – *and not just at devices.* Specific people – due to facial recognition cameras, and crowds generally, can be irradiated. Crowds because it will prevent them from massing in protests, or if they already have, it can be used to quickly disperse them. This targeting is a policy called: 'Active

Denial'.

"The feeling targeted people experience when the power and intensity of the MMW is deliberately 'turned up' is like having their skin burn from the inside...*which is exactly what happens* because the sweat ducts on the skin act like mini-amplifying- antennas – and gradually boil...prolonged exposure leads to a human body shutting down...*and dying*...due to massive shock...if he or she cannot get away from the irradiated area...

"When all those satellites and all the Earth bound transmitters send the MMW to each device, it will send a beam of radiation back to the satellite or transmitter, that radiation will pass through human bodies and through the whole bio-sphere, drastically disrupting and damaging natural electro-magnetic cellular harmony...and has been proven to cause single and double breaks in living, sentient creatures' DNA, *the very 'building block' or 'blue print' of creation...*

"The transmitters are being put on public buildings and schools, on bus shelters, in public parks and along every city's and town's streets.

"The reason so many city streets are having all their lovely trees cut down is to give the radiation – *and all the cameras* - a clear and unobstructed pathways, or lines of sight. I was in the lovely city of Sheffield recently, visiting a group there. It is a city which has had many of its streets which were lined with fully mature and magnificent trees, cut down – on the orders from the local, parasite and elite infected city council. It is heart rending to see, but there is a resistance movement within the city's populace, so let us hope they can eventually stop the psychopathic policy there.

"Some people will be rubbing their hands together with glee because they are making huge profits of course from all the harmful technology products, which are mostly manufactured in China...

"Wi-Fi devices for the Five G grid are also being put into every home – the 'internet of things', they are called 'Smart Meters' and will be connected to all your household appliances...well, you can now join the dots...dots that at the very least, reveal a macabre picture showing they are all part of the engineered dumbing down, distraction, control and surveillance of the population, and ultimately...a crucial element in the elites' de-population agenda...

"...de-population because exposure to the 'military-weapons'-grade-strength' of Five G MMW radiation destroys around seventy percent of the testosterone in developing boys, kills fifty percent of the active sperm, and in pregnant women it kills the six to eight weeks old female embryo's mitochondrial DNA in the ovaries which develop around that time, which, over five to seven generations, will extinct that family...*if they have not all perished from the toxic carcinogenic radiations well before then...*

"The Big Pharma Industry and the Medical Institutions are already making billions in profits from selling their 'fertility treatment' products to couples struggling to conceive, and that is from the lesser damage done by the existing two, three and four G radiations - plus of course the food, water and vaccines' toxic additives...

"*Anyway – Look! There I go! I am now starting to go well off topic and wander talk again!*

"But I did think this was a good opportunity to just 'lift the lid' a little, so you could all peer in and have some...*alternative but truthful* insights to this area of the vast subject of 'Communicating'. So I thought it would be relevant and interesting for you to know - *as well as giving you some pointers for more of your own research!*

"...And I hope as well that I have 'filled in some blank squares' as you put it Jake?!".

"Aye – you've certainly done that! Thanks Magda. More than a fair bit o' food for thought there...! Everythin' – apart from the testosterone, sperm an' ovary damage, y've just said about the Five G radiation me Dad told an' warned me about, but he didn't know about that, a few months back.

"He were really angry, an' desperately concerned about it – *as everyone should be*...but most folks 'aven't got a clue what it's gonna do to 'em 'ave they...? *An' p'robly don't care as long as they can download a film wi' it in seconds...*

"Anyway...Hah! Funny you mentioned puttin' summat metal that

84

y'shouldn't in a micro-wave cooker – made me remember when me Mum played pop with me years ago when I were just a lad an' I put a Chinese take-away in a tin foil tray in it to warm it up. She'd only recently bought that latest, big an' fancy, micro-wave cooker, well, I switched it on at full power and it went *Bang!* Wi' a big bright Flash! An' 'alf filled the kitchen wi' smoke an' fireworks and blew all the electrics! Gave me a right shock an'all! I don't think I've ever really trusted 'em since to be 'onest! - *micro-waves that is...not...Chinese takeaways...!*"

Which caused chuckles and groaning laughter from everyone.

"But seriously, just goin' back to what y'were sayin' about the TV, that were fascinatin'! *Didn't know owt about any o' that!* I personally don't watch that much of it - usually too busy! But I think - Soph - we'll 'ave to watch some o' them ol' black n' white British comedy films you've got that you like, an' I do an'all! - one evenin' wi' a takeaway - an' we'll 'ave a go at that scene-camera-seconds-count you were talkin' about Magda. Sounds interesting that! *An' I promise not to go near y' microwave Soph'...if the takeaway needs warmin' up!*"

"Excellent!" Magda replied still smiling at his humour - "*and you can both have a good laugh as well whilst you do! There are some films from that era that both Anders and I find particularly amusing and certainly make us laugh!*" Magda chuckled back at him.

Sophie said that was a date to Jake, but then quickly added, grinning, that she'd: "*make sure the micro-wave was unplugged - just in case...!*"

She then wondered to herself if...was it possible...remotely possible...that Anders outwardly presented himself with having a sort of amalgamation of all the genial character traits that were so similar to those played by one of the prominent actors in those old comedies – the actor Alistair Simm? Is that what he's done?...not just mimicking the voice – like Jake can do – but basing *his whole persona,* his 'outward character', *on those characters*...using them to interact easily with people?!

Magda had paused for a few moments, silently gathering her

thoughts before continuing. "I obviously sense, very strongly, that whatever it is you wish *to communicate to me* is obviously very important to you all, it is clearly not *'a-run-of-the-mill'* occurrence you want to inform me about.

"So...*before I went off 'wander-talking'! -* I said I wanted to suggest something to you - David and Jake, and it is this...instead of you having to consciously recall and then adequately verbalise everything – all over again! - to communicate to me about...the occurrence, we could do it with a *'mind fuse'* together instead.

"Please understand that I am *certainly not implying* that you could not do so adequately *by verbally communicating to me!* But a mind-fuse means that all your memories, conscious *and sub-conscious,* of whatever it is - are *all revealed* to me, because so often merely relying on the conscious recollections of an event then putting them into words can miss out somethings that are very subtle and very important, but the subconscious mind sees and remembers – *everything.* Which is the basis of all hypnotic therapy treatments of course.

"So...David and Jake, for example...if you were to cast your conscious minds back to whatever it was you were doing *prior to whatever it was that occurred,* that would be where we would start, and we would finish, and defuse, when it ended. To do that though I need your permissions, as fusing with someone's mind must always be done with their agreement...So, would you both agree to me, to us, doing that…?"

"Er, y, yes, *I agree* Magda. As long as you don't mind all the rest of the clutter I've got in here!" Dave said with a slightly nervous chuckle, tapping his head.

"Aye! Me too, *I agree as well Magda!* But like Dave says – *'y'll 'ave to excuse all the clutter' - in me attic!"* Jake said smiling and pointing to his head.

"Thank you both! Thank you for your trust in me. But please be assured, None Of That Clutter as you call it will be within the scope of our fusing. This will just be what is called 'a partial'. It will only be over a period of time that you set, and is relevant only to the memory of the occurrence, whatever it is. It will only be from whatever you were doing just before, to when you think it ended. It is an often used technique we all do when we need to *really impart everything about an important occurrence and do so in a short period of time...*

"Also, as we normally do, I will put in place, in my mind, a 'psychic diode', a diode is, in the physical plane, an electronic component that allows electricity to flow through it in one direction only, so a psychic diode only allows the passage of memories one way – in this case from yours to mine - *which means you will not be burdened with all 'The Clutter' I've got up here as well!"* She said with a smile tapping her own head.

Chapter 7: A Mind Fuse.

Dave drew in a deep breath and asked Magda, "Okaaay then...if I'm going first, how - *what do I have to do exactly Magda?*" She immediately sensed the trepidation which had now crept into his voice.

"Oh please do not be concerned – all that you both have to do in a partial mind fuse is easy and straightforward. What we will do is in three simple stages: first, we will sit closely together, you will close your eyes and breathe slowly and deeply to relax, to quieten and focus your mind, readying it to go back to the time of the occurrence. Then, and only when you are ready to start - you just open your eyes and nod to me and I will place my fingertips lightly on your temples and I will look into your eyes and you will look into mine.

"Then secondly, you start to remember what you were doing just before the occurrence and play it all back from there in your mind's eye as if you are watching a film, and include everything you remember about it.

"Finally, thirdly, when you have done all that and come to the end of the occurrence, simply lean back, so I am not touching you, look away from my eyes, and the connection between us will be immediately stopped. I will need a moment or two after that to...to process...what you revealed to me, but your part in the fusing will be over David. Then you and I, Jake, we will do it as well. Is all of that acceptable, and clear, to you both?"

They both said it was. "Excellent! Then I will need to disturb you Melanie if you do not mind, as I need to be sat next to David, perhaps we could change places?"

Melanie got up from the sofa to sit in the chair Magda vacated for her, Dave shuffling sideways as she sat closely next to him. They both sat very still, breathing in deeply through their noses and out of their mouths and after less than a minute Dave opened his eyes and nodded to her. Magda raised her hands very slowly to lightly touch the tips of her fore-fingers to his temples. Her emerald green eyes then looked deeply into his and the nervous trepidation that he'd been feeling dissolved immediately and he fully relaxed, still breathing deeply. Then very quietly she said to him, "when you are ready David...just start to recall..."

Magda's eyes seemed to expand, filling his vision, and his inner, mind's eye also seemed to expand with them and move forwards to meet and merge into them. The feeling was like slowly wading out into the still, deep waters of a warm lake of emerald green, and when the water was at his chest height he let himself go, surging forwards to swim effortlessly into it.

His body seemed to be held weightlessly afloat for him as he moved ever forwards, further into it, and then his memories started to flow from him into the warm emerald lake which absorbed them all.

He'd started them when he was laying in bed, very early yesterday morning, in the hypnopompic state just before he was fully awake, and feeling the urge to go to the cliff top.

Fascinatingly though, deeper, subconscious memories containing images, sounds, scents and feelings flowed out as well that he had consciously forgotten. He felt exactly as if he had somehow gone back in time and was actually reliving everything he'd experienced, all over again...

But contained in these deeper sub-conscious memories now he heard a faraway echoing female voice calling to him just before he had fully woken up, calling for him to come to them, and where they were. He then fast forwarded to when he was sitting on the cliff top as the sun was starting to come up, and when his mind had slipped into a calm meditative state.

He heard the same voice again, but it was much clearer now, it was greeting him, and he saw the immense craft out to sea materialise, seeing it in much finer detail now. He knew somehow that the friendly voice was coming from it, but it seemed to be as if whomever was speaking was just in front of him.

The voice was friendly and congratulatory, it told him they just wanted him to hear her voice and see their vessel for now, and next time she and the others would reveal themselves to him and show him more of their vessel, and they would be able to communicate about many things for much longer.

Then the voice receded and their vessel suddenly flew away into the sun's rays over the sea and disappeared below the surface.

Then he was walking quickly back to the caravan, barely feeling his trainers get all wet from the heavy dew on the long grass, which he had forgotten about as well, his astonished thoughts going over what he had just experienced. But he realised now that at the time, for some reason, he hadn't consciously remembered the female voice he'd heard...then he was making tea for himself and Mel, and going back into their bedroom…

He moved his head back, away from Magda's fingertips, and looked away from her for a moment. As he did this he felt as if he was in a fast action rewind of all the sensations of entering, floating and swimming in the warm emerald green lake waters...until he was back again, sat on the sofa.

The others had been silent, still and utterly enthralled as they had watched them both intently. He quickly inhaled a really deep and loud breath, as if coming up for air, at the same time looking wide eyed at Magda.

Then he slowly turned his head to look at the others and let it all out loudly in a rush, exclaiming,

"Wwwwwow! That...Was...Something.….Else…!

"And The Voice…! I hadn't consciously remembered the – *Her* - voice at all! - *Her Voice…!* My God! Magda! *You were so right! - Of course you were…! But Why? - Why didn't I remember her voice…?!"*

Magda smiled at him, "Well done David. You see now how the conscious mind can so easily filter things out, but your sub-conscious mind *remembers everything*...It is not uncommon for the conscious mind to, to mis-remember some things as it immediately relegates them into the subconscious – the process is rather like quickly storing

90

a, a container of something, something that makes you uneasy – or even fearful of it, so you hide it away and store it in the vast warehouse of your subconscious memory because you don't want to face it, open it up and look into it right then, but will, perhaps at a later day.

"Your conscious mind sometimes does all that to protect itself from things it is suddenly exposed to that are way beyond its current frames of reference. The being who spoke to you obviously realised all of that, which is why she had only the briefest of communication with you, because next time your conscious mind will be more, more...able...to, to cope and accept it, and not immediately box it up and push it away into a corner of the warehouse...

"Just let your conscious mind be aware now that the female being was absolutely in no way a threat to you, but quite the opposite, she was displaying a great care, gentleness and compassion for you, from an obviously deep understanding of your human psyche...So next time your conscious mind will be more accepting and *it will allow...*

"Let me now just process and go over it all again slowly in my mind, I will not be long..."

She leaned back into the sofa and closed her eyes. Dave glanced at her and lowered his excited voice to just above a whisper, and leaned forwards on the edge of the sofa towards Mel, Jake and Sophie. He described in detail to them everything he'd just felt, and recalled to them what the voice, he only now consciously remembered, had said to him.

Magda opened her eyes. She smiled at him, nodding almost imperceptibly. They all looked at her expectantly, sensing a subtle change in her demeanour. It seemed to them as if she was forcing herself to contain an exhilaration and the happiness from it radiated out from her.

"My my, David...This is marvellous..." She said quietly. "Quite marvellous...Thank you for sharing it with me...Before I explain more of why I say that, to you all, I think I must first share your recollections Jake, as you have both said they are related. Could we all play at musical chairs again and I will come and sit next to you?!"

A minute or so later when Jake had relaxed himself by taking slow, deep breaths he opened his eyes and nodded to Magda, she then touched his temples and looked into his eyes. Jake felt the same sensation of floating into warm, emerald green, lake waters just as Dave had described.

Then he was suddenly a young boy, laying all curled up, comfortable and sleepy in his warm bed. He had just been woken up by a loud banging and shouting coming from downstairs at the front door...

Then his memories flowed on, and so did many, many details in them that he had long forgotten...He replayed them all, right upto when his Dad was showing him how to strip down his first motorbike engine in the new shed they'd just built together.

Jake had to break off then, the clear focus of all the forgotten details had become too much for him emotionally...This wasn't like the scratchy cine film recollection of just the main events he had had that morning at the garage, or this afternoon when he'd verbally replayed it as he told Dave, and then the girls.

This had been like a lucid dream, when you are awake but know you are dreaming, and in it he had actually been reliving, in his mind, everything that had happened, it was, as Dave had said, as if he had time travelled back into his past. All his senses had been remembered as well, particularly the sounds and smells of everything - particularly of the Old Spice aftershave his Dad had always used...And he slumped back into the sofa he put his hands over his face, his shoulders quivering with emotion.

Magda looked with great concern at him and then to Sophie who immediately moved over and threw her arms around him, cradling his head, hers pressed to his, cooing softly to him.

After a few anxious minutes for them all, he started to recover, but when he took his hands away from his face it was pale and his eyes were red and watery.

"I am so, so very sorry Jake, if I had known all about your Father I

would not have suggested we did it like this...because *all those deeper memories were evoked and came through to me as well...*" Magda said to him, barely above a whisper, immense compassion and concern for him in her voice.

"*No...no that's alright Magda*, don't think that, glad we did in a way - fact is you've 'elped me 'ave some better, even clearer memories of 'im that's all..." He then sigh chuckled, "Huh! If he could see me right now he'd be sayin', '*C'mon then me lad! – It'll all be alright! –* C'mon let's be getting on wi' summat together, it'll take y' mind off it - *y'big lummock!*'"

Just then they all saw Anders Starrman hesitantly stop walking towards them whilst he was still some distance away. He raised a hand in greeting to them, "Oh I'm *very sorry* – I didn't mean to intrude on you all." He said quietly, stepping backwards gingerly to retrace his steps. He had instantly recognised the four young people sat with Magda. He remembered them from 'The Trocadero Cafe' last Monday evening, and they had been the first of everyone else from there that he had escorted through the Café's portal into this room afterwards.

Clearly now though the big chap in the leather motorcycle jacket – Jake was his name he recalled, sat between Magda and his girlfriend was upset about something. *I'll sit over here for a moment*, he thought, *might not be appropriate to just butt in on them all...right now.*

"Nah...no..y're not Anders – *good to see y' mate!*" Jake called out to him, sitting up and shaking his head. Magda asked Jake, great concern for him still in her voice, "*Are you sure* you are feeling even slightly better now Jake?"

"Aye! *I'm fine*, thanks Magda, and don't you worry! *'S not your fault or owt like that! Prob'ly done me good to be 'onest!* Better than bottlin' it all up - or just shovin' it away to fester in't warehouse like y'said! Best to face things like, get 'em out into the open *an' get on with 'em!*"

"Thank you Jake, you are a remarkable human being, I said as much to you when we first met. You have such great depths of compassion and empathy...and...your tremendous gift of humour always makes me *laugh so much – and my sisters too when I tell them of all the funny things you have said and done...!*"

"*Oh!* Er, Well Thank You Magda! *But 'ere - steady on!* - 'Else with that on top of everythin' else nice y've said about me tonight – 'appen I might not be able to get me head back through that narrow portal-door later...!" He chuckled. Magda smiled lovingly at him, and reached out to squeeze his large hands in hers.

"Perhaps if I go and have a...a word or two...with Anders, and leave you all here for a moment, it will give you chance to have a...recuperative break. Jake – David – would you agree to me sharing with Anders what you have both revealed to me? As they are *your memories to share – not mine.* It is very fortunate though that Anders *has arrived right now,* he will want to talk to you about all of this, and help you with the answers to the questions you want to ask...and perhaps...I more than suspect, he will have some answers to those you have *not yet thought to ask...?*"

Jake and Dave agreed immediately, and they all said it would be great if Anders would come and join them. With a final quick squeeze of Jake's hands, Magda stood up and walked out of the alcove and over to Anders. Then, side by side, they started to slowly walk in a large circle, as Magda talked rapidly to him. The two young couples heard some initial snatches of what she was saying, just before they went out of earshot – but whatever she was saying – it was in a language they did not understand...

"*Are you really okay?*" Sophie asked him, still holding him.

"Aye, *I'm okay now*...thank you Soph'." He replied giving her a long loving hug. Over her shoulder he saw that Magda and Anders had stopped walking and she was now facing him, her fore fingers touching the sides of his head as they looked silently and intensely into each others eyes.

"'*Ey Up!* Looks like Anders is gettin' the memory treatment as well!" He chuckled.

The others looked over to them, and Mel said, "I suppose, for them, it must be *quite normal* to do it. I mean, it's quicker, and, and obviously everything gets passed on...but for you two, especially for you Jake, it, it's obviously, well, it can be very unsettling - *are you sure you're ok Jake?*"

"Aye, I am now thanks Mel. As I say, I think it's prob'ly done me good. An' like I said to you Dave when we stood together at the end o' Filey Brigg..."

Jake paused, and looked at them all, his grey eyes now clear, hard as flint, and said: "'The Time's Come - for us to not be...afraid any more'..."

He blew out a big sigh, "...An' I'll admit, o' course part o' me was afraid – like me Dad an' all the rest were, an' it sort o' rubbed off 'em on to me.

"Fear's a very contagious thing innit, 'specially with all the implications of what 'appened to Taxi Tony...*BUT I'M NOT NOW!* An' I'm not about what we've all decided *To Do*. Well, yes, a bit I s'pose, but that's only natural, an' healthy innit? - Keeps y'on y'toes! When I said all that to you Dave, yes, I meant it about all o' that *in the past*, but I really meant it more now - *for in the future* – d'y'all know what I mean?" They all nodded slowly in understanding as he paused, then continued,

"...An' for *me, more personally*, I 'ave to admit, I've been *just as afraid as well, but in a different way*...sort o'...well, afraid of all the sadness that just does me in when I think about me Dad...*like it were takin' over at times an' depressin' and controllin' me, but I've just called it out* – draggin' it from that warehouse – opened it up, confronted it and faced it all down now, an' it's backed off an' gone – just like a school-yard bully would - *an' the bein' afraid of it's gone...*

"...an' now, well yes, o'course I'm still sad about him, but now it's *a positive* sort o' sad, not an afraid an' fearful *negative* sad, because instead *I choose to remember now* all the really great an' positive things about him, as he was before...An' they're better, brighter, bigger an' much more powerful than, than what I did feel like - *because they are positive*. An' I know that's what *he'd want me to feel like...*

"Hah! What was it Magda said about 'hypnotic therapy'!? - Feels like I've 'ad more than a bit o' that! - *Look-Into-My-Eyes...!*" He chuckled.

"...An' thinkin' about it, an' knowin' now what Anders said to us all about there bein' '*no such thing as coincidences*...but they are all events and experiences, '*that we deliberately create*'...well, I must've, deep down, *obviously wanted and needed what just 'appened now to 'appen!* - So I could sort o' confront it, an' well, get rid of all that bein' afraid an' negative stuff that were festerin' away inside me...

"So it feels now like I've been mentally flushed out or 'de-seized-up', like brakes on a bike can seize-up sometimes, an' slow y'down. So now I can move on freely, properly...*an' be stronger for it!*

" - An' it's a bit like one o' them sheep as well that Magda talked about last Monday - puttin' two fingers up at the dogs an' shepherd it were afraid of!

"So...anyway...I 'ope all o' that makes some sort o' sense to yous! Y'know me! - I'm better wi' me tools than me words! – Struggle wi' 'em a bit I s'pose when it comes to talk about me emotions an' all that!" He grinned and then said, "So...if you did understand any or all o' that – *could y'explain it to me...?!*"

He then clumsily – deliberately so, but very gently, with robotic movements, clamped his large hands around Sophie's head, mussing up her long glossy black hair, pushed his face into hers until their noses were touching, opened his eyes wide, made them go cross eyed and stared into hers, and said slowly in a very deep baritone voice, "*Look-into-my-eyes-there's-something-I want-to-know...!*"

Sophie, greatly relieved at how quickly he'd bounced back and with his humour in high gear again, promptly joined in with his horse-playing, stuck her tongue out and blew him a raspberry! Then she laughed with him, her tears gone, his humour eradicating all the remaining traces of distress and trauma.

Dave, taking his cue from Jake's sudden, back-to-normal clowning around, slowly reached out with his hands, moving them robotically as well, the fingers spread wide, towards Mel, whilst saying in a low and droning voice, *"Come-Here-You-There's-Something-I-Want-To-Do-To-You...!"*

Mel squeaked, pressing herself away from him into the corner of the sofa, her right wrist dramatically pressed over her forehead and partly over her eyes, the palm facing him, her other hand trying to fend him off, as she rapidly gasped, "Not *Here* Dave! Not *Now!* - *Later! - At home* - YES!" Which caused them all to laugh together.

"Well, Well, Well! – Proof again *that it is quite amazing* - what Love and Laughter can do!" Magda said to them, laughter evident in her voice.

They all rapidly looked up, smiling at Magda and Anders, and quickly shuffled themselves back to sitting normally in the sofas, amused as well at feeling a little bit like naughty school children caught messing about in class by the sudden appearance of their teachers.

"Well Hello To You All! - Sophie, Jake, Melanie and David! I *must* say I really am s*o very pleased* to see you all again! This is a *most pleasant surprise* for me, indeed it is." Anders said to them in his cultured voice full of old school, olde worlde charm.

"And *thank you all* for inviting me to join you! - Magda's told me that you've all very kindly agreed to put up with me for a short while!" His eyes twinkled with good humour. "Unfortunately it will only be for a short while now though, due to the unavoidable delay that cropped up earlier, so I'm sorry to say I'll have to be away quite soon as I'll be due again for my last presentation in the marquee."

Magda had been pushing another chair over for him whilst he greeted them, and placing it next to hers they both sat down. Anders was dressed the same as he had been last Monday evening – wearing the dark greeny brown tartan tweed three piece suit, collar and tie, and shiny brown leather brogue shoes.

Sophie just couldn't help thinking again that he reminded her so much of all those endearing characters the vintage actor Alistair Simm used to play. She now felt it was more than likely, based on what Magda had said earlier about them both enjoying those old comedies, *that he must've based his outward appearance and character on the roles he'd played.*

Because *outwardly* Anders presented all their stereotypical mannerisms of a polite, bumbling, elderly, humble eccentric. But she, and all of them, now knew from their experiences of listening to his presentations and being in his company last Monday evening, that they were all just parts of a disarming façade he deliberately used to interact and communicate with effortless charm, as it immediately put people at ease and in a friendly, receptive state of mind.

But behind that façade, yes, the charm was still there, but there was also a powerful radiance of brilliant intelligence, full of ancient wisdom, and phenomenal insights of the modern world. His mind was, in short - as sharp as a razor...

What they didn't know though was who he *really* was, where he came from - or just how old *he actually was* - because during his talk, lecture, presentation – whatever you'd call it, last Monday evening, he had sometimes inadvertently or perhaps he had done it deliberately, said some things that indicated he was far, far older than a normal human life span could possibly be.

They all had the same wonder-ings as well about Magda, who had done exactly the same when they'd been with her afterwards. And her sisters, and Maria and Alfie in the Cafe and the twin teddy boy brothers on the merry-go-round – they were all...as well...what...? Who were all these amazing people? *Were they even 'human people'?!* But they all felt, as they had discussed all of this again at length amongst themselves that afternoon, that Anders and all these very 'extra-ordinary' individuals would reveal those answers to them in their own time...perhaps when they considered that the four of them *were ready to know...?*

Right now though, looking at him sitting there, once again they all sensed the charismatic and immense force of goodness that radiated tangibly from him as he rubbed his hands together, then lowered his head to rest his chin on his knuckles for a moment in concentration, before slapping his palms down decisively onto his knees and started to speak to them in quiet, intimate and congratulatory tones.

"Well done...*Very* well done - *All of you.* And my thanks to you two splendid chaps for agreeing to share all of your deep memories of this *with me* as well."

He then paused, crossed his legs, sat back and said, "I'm going to sit back with Magda, *and we're going to listen to you talk now,* as you all take the floor, so to speak, to tell us about the decisions you've made based upon these experiences so far, and ask the questions you obviously have.

"Magda has suggested that I - because I have to be away to the marquee soon - that I attempt to answer your questions first and explain things. You see, by doing that, by listening to them it will give us, in addition to your shared memories, an excellent insight to the level of knowledge and understanding, that *you all* have of these, these types of events...of their background and context...and what you think they could lead to, and the level of commitment you intend to, well, to embark upon with...So, please...the floor is all yours!"

Dave looked at Jake and said, "Well mate, I think it's over to you then! This afternoon you pretty much summed up what we all wanted to ask Magda - about what we want to do, and what advice she – and now Anders, could give us...to do it..."

"*Ah!* Ok then! Right! *Oh 'eck! - I'll do me best to remember!* But jump in anyone if y'think I forget owt!" He leaned forwards and taking a deep breath started to speak to Anders and Magda.

"Well, the best way *I* can put it is like this: so far then, I think it's like we've just found and opened up 'a container' – like you said Magda – but for me it's more like a big old, heavy box, an' we've emptied it out and now we've got a lot o' parts, components for summat like, all spread out on a work bench in front of us, and now we wanna put 'em all together an' make summat useful wi' 'em - but there's no instructions how to in the box...!

"...So right now we *think we know* what it is we could make with 'em, but we're not really sure about *what it is exactly* – an' we don't even know if all the parts are there - there might well be some missin'!" He paused momentarily to further assemble his thoughts.

"But we do know, we do understand, that it's somethin' very important we could make or do with 'em, even though, an' this might sound a bit daft – even though we don't really know what the end result of *'it'* is, an' what'll 'appen - what *'it'* *'ll do exactly* - if we manage to put everythin' we've got – includin' any missin' parts – an' by 'parts' I mean missin' knowledge o'course - all together - an' make whatever *'it'* is - *an' we...switch it on an' fire it up!*

"But we do know that we are all an 'undred percent committed to doin' it...'cause it just feels like the right thing to do. *I'm – we -* are – trusting our intuition about this – like you both 'ave said we always should...!

"So, as best as I can remember, what we thought this afternoon, was once you knew everythin' that'd 'appened so far, all that's what we wanted to ask you Magda! - An' o'course you now as well Anders. P'raps y' might know what them missin' parts, missin' knowledge, an' end result, or results, are, or might be - an' what the missin' instructions were to achieve it...?! I 'ope all that makes some sort o' sense to yous! 'Ave I left owt out anyone?"

He looked to Sophie, Dave and Mel, who shook their heads. They all thought it had been clever of Jake to describe it in the way he had, using the workshop imagery, processes and context that he was familiar with. He had clearly inventoried and pictured what they had right now, what they needed, and what they wanted to do with it all. Mel then had a sudden feeling though that it just needed something adding, something more specific...

"That was great Jake, but can I just add something, do you mind? - Magda, Anders, I've just got the feeling that we need *to specifically, to definitely ask you for your advice and help.* I remember you saying last Monday evening in the Trocadero Cafe Anders, *'that we can't be like the Cavalry coming charging over the hill to rescue you – only you can do that for yourselves...!' And We Will!* - But our 'Charging Over The Hill' would have more chance of success if you two could, well, just advise, guide and help us to *understand more* and *prepare* for it better, before *we did...Our Charging...!"*

Jake, Sophie and Dave all smiled at her, nodding in agreement, recalling the outburst of passion with which she had spoken about this earlier in the afternoon.

"Well...my goodness...! *I think this is just what we've been hoping and waiting for,* on this part of the world, for quite a long time, don't you Magda...?" Anders said, looking at her excitedly and nodding his head slightly, a knowing smile on his lips.

"Yes, it is...*at last...*it is wonderful! I am so pleased. All that time and energy invested in the communications and diplomatic efforts have, once again, proven to be so worthwhile, so fruitful..." She then turned to look at Mel.

"So Yes, Melanie, and Yes to all of you, of course *we can,* and of course *we will* help you now - because you have asked us directly from your own free will - we can. We could not just impose that help upon you otherwise...your feeling about that was quite right Melanie, it is just how – just how these things have to work, *our help can now be permitted"* She replied quietly, her eyes sparkling.

"Yes, and of course I quite agree with you Magda, *well put!"* Anders said, "and...perhaps...but only if you think it appropriate and agree to it of course - before I get into starting to answer those questions first, and all their implications, should I - or would *you* prefer to outline, or go a little deeper, into some of those *'communications and diplomatic efforts'?*

"Because it was you, a long time ago now, who initiated them, and you've been so heavily involved in them ever since, in the background to all of this...do you think it would be appropriate? It might just help to give our young friends here some concept of their broader implications, relevance and context to them?"

This was interesting, because the two young couples sensed something more now than just a polite deference in Ander's demeanour towards Magda.

They had, upto now, just assumed that he was 'higher up' in whatever organisation they were part of. Mainly because he seemed to be more prominent, and whether they were aware of it or not, their social conditioning was conducive to expecting an elder or senior *male* to 'be in charge', as that was still, by and large, a lingering 'tradition', and so more familiar to them.

Also in their society, it was more familiar to them for organisations to have, as well, archaic, vertical, power hierarchy structures, always with a boss or manager above you telling you what to do and supervising everything you did.

But Sophie had noticed a few times before today, well, she'd just vaguely sensed them really, that the occasional behaviours and subtle attitudes from Anders towards Magda implied the opposite - it was Magda who was really, well, 'higher up', and 'in charge'...or was she? Did they actually have 'one person in charge'?

She made a mental note to ask Magda at some point this evening, or at another time, just how they all worked together, how they structured their organisation. She was genuinely interested in how people worked together and interacted in organisations.

When she'd left school after getting four 'A Levels' with high grades, she had decided not to go to University to study Business Administration, because she couldn't see the sense in starting her working life off afterwards with well over thirty thousand pounds of debt hanging round her neck, and with no guarantee at all of getting a decent job at the end of it.

So she had decided instead to take the trainee's job, which had good prospects, at the Estate and Letting Agents that she'd successfully applied for, do further relevant studies in her own time, and make her own way from there in the world.

Which had been a good move, as she now, in her early twenties, had a little terrace house on a mortgage, no other debt, and a reasonable income.

Everything she'd achieved so far compared favourably to most of her friends who had graduated from the Universities a few years ago. She really felt for them because so many were still having to live with their parents, back at home, or in rented flats, in a lot of debt, and were either 'signing on for State benefits', or were doing boring, dead-end jobs just managing to survive on the minimum wage they earned.

So she was really interested, because whatever organisational structure these amazing people had created, it seemed to function so positively, efficiently, and, well, so *harmoniously!* And she remembered Anders saying last Monday evening, in The Trocadero Cafe - about some quick and vital responses that he and Maria, and others had implemented, when a threat from the parasites' underlings had been realised by them, he'd said: *'the beauty of good teamwork eh?'*

Those quick responses had obviously been seamlessly implemented because the people in their organisation, the people whom she'd met so far anyway, were clearly devoted to doing whatever individual, and inter-linking-with-each-other tasks they did, and in complete accord with helping each other to achieve them whilst they were working on them.

The way they were all working together was very different – compared to some of *her* 'working-together' experiences in an office which was now a branch of a large national company.

The previously local family who had originally started up and run the business, and had done so for three generations, had sold out to the much bigger company a couple of years ago. It had been expanded considerably since then with the taking on of more staff, and moving to larger premises.

Anyway, her working experience was very different...because she had to, frustratingly, spend a lot of time being 'diplomatic' herself - to try and avoid getting sucked into all the distracting, petty office-politics, personality clashes and power struggles designed to *hamper others* whom they were supposed to be working *with* - but were more often than not were just regarded *as rivals!*

Rivals for praise, accolades and 'pats on the back' from those 'higher up' yes - but usually the rivalry was just to achieve promotion, which really just meant more money for them. Admittedly it was only some of the people she worked with, who often seemed more inclined

103

to spend a lot of their time and energies *negatively* engaged in doing all that conflict stuff, rather than *positively cooperating* and getting on with each other, and getting on with all the – ever increasing - workload they were supposed to be doing in the first place!

But even just a tiny few 'awkward malcontents' still managed to disproportionally corrode a positive and productive working atmosphere for everyone else!

*Anyway...*she sighed mentally, eagerly focusing her attention quickly back to Magda as she had started to speak again.

"Yes, you are right, I think *'an outline'* and some *deeper filling in* is necessary first. I will do that, but leave the bulk of the 'filling in' and question answering to you Anders." He bowed his head almost imperceptibly to her.

She looked up at the high ceiling for a few seconds, organising her thoughts. "Anders said, just a few moments ago: '*I think this is just what we have been hoping and waiting for - on this part of the world - for quite a long time...*' He was quite right, we have.

"The development into a 'Unity Consciousness', which is where everyone – the entire human race - realises they are: 'All One Together' - rather than being in a 'Dualistic Consciousness', which means, basically: 'I Win - So You Lose!', by the humans *on* Earth, has been, *for a very, very long time,* of considerable interest, not only to us, but also to many races of non-terrestrial, and higher inter-dimensional beings...

"...Especially so in the more recent decades because of the increased potential for great changes that are happening *on* Earth *now.* Some of *us* have been - and I was, and still am, in an instigatory, coordinating and liaison role for the group *of us who chose to work to promote that Unity.* Quite recently I was, well, *elsewhere,* involved in a fresh round of re-establishing contacts, diplomatic negotiations and communication protocols with...others...*not of this Earth...*

"With the communal consent of all who were involved, we agreed it would be more effective to establish a working strategy for all our purposes, with just one of the benevolent extra-terrestrial races, *to start with*, and keeping all the others informed of our progress.

"You, David, have been the first amongst you here to experience the initial processes of how we all agreed they would make contact...."

Dave couldn't help himself from interrupting her, "Oh Wow...! *This is completely amazing...Again!* But do you mean - 'the first amongst you here' - as between *us four here now*, or 'you' as, well, as other humans – *world-wide generally...?*"

Magda smiled at him, "*Amongst you four sat here now* – yes, but not amongst 'you' as humans generally. On a few other areas of this country, and '*world-wide generally*', lots of others, both individually and in small groups like yours, have had the initial – and further - in many cases, contact experiences."

She then looked at Jake and said, "when you shared your memories with me Jake I became aware of course that several years ago, your Father and his friends had set up a group, from their own volition, to observe some of these visitors. Well, to observe their crafts at any rate, when they deliberately revealed them – their intention was that they would be seen, by such groups, on and around these parts of this country. And also by many other similar groups on and around the whole World.

"Each of the many extra-terrestrial races had been acting independently of each other for thousands of years until, finally, we all agreed to operate along the lines I have mentioned. At times, I have to say, achieving that was similar to overcoming what I imagine the difficulties and intricacies would be if you were to play hundreds of games at once of four dimensional chess...for well over half a century...!

"Of course, I am now also aware of what happened, tragically, to one of your friends, in your Father's Club, as a consequence of him being determined to put his photographic evidence out to the World. The decision to take that callous, prompt action against him would have been made - as you, your Father and other friends rightly surmised – would have been made in the highest levels of the so called 'Security Agencies'. Because the psychopathic elites occupying the very highest levels in those organisations have almost constant contact with, and close supervision and instructions from, their parasite overlords of course.

"That tragic incident was not, *by any means*, the first they have been responsible for in recent decades.

"All over the World similar incidents have occurred, time and time again, with different methods and procedures - but they all had the same tragic results. The predictable ferocity of the parasites'-elites' direct action response has always been of grave concern to us, and to the off-planet visitors...and was a major factor we had to consider in our early planning stages.

"We initially devised a series of flexible processes to make contact *far more safely* – for both parties. Even so..." She sighed heavily, "...many of their crafts were still shot down, and those they had contacted were killed - or silenced by other means. Some of the shot down crafts were totally destroyed by the hidden, advanced technology, directed energy weapons used against them, some were not completely destroyed and were retrieved, and the occupants were then either killed or captured..." Magda took a deep breath and sighed heavily again, pausing for a few moments.

"...So, with us all working together we have now finally established procedures and protocols for far more safer, and more frequent contact - particularly with more and more of those humans whom *we* have, as one of our roles in this process, profiled for *them* as being more receptive...

"But not just receptive to seeing them - and then, quite understandably, rushing out to immediately tell everyone they know – and don't know! of what they have seen – because that can have, as you all know now, at its worse...some very dire consequences. No, what I am saying, what I mean, is receptive people who are more able...able to cope more calmly with their first exposures to paradigm shattering realities, and then go further as an 'experiencer'...

"Part of the reasons for initiating Ander's, and all the others' presentations all across the World, was to attempt to enhance the collective perceptual awareness, hand in hand with the rising of the collective, connecting consciousness…

"You have all calmly taken the first crucial steps and have been exposed now to a broader and deeper education from us, of the many, many things not touched upon by your mainstream education – for all the reasons Anders and I explained to you last Monday evening.

"When Anders talks in his presentations, the script is always flexible, according to the audience. But what is constant is the very wide-ranging 'connecting of dots', of events, because doing so dismantles the handicapping scourge of 'compartmentalisation'. What do I mean by that? Well, the 'compartmentalisation' of information occurs to such a degree in your societies that people inadvertently create their own prisons, it is a 'gate keeping' effect. A way of narrowly defining, monitoring and controlling the breadth and depth of something – so the whole Truth is never revealed, never seen…it is a very effective method of censorship and control.

"Now *we* face the opposite challenge of not revealing *too much too soon!* – which can sometimes lead to 'knee-jerk' reactions that are over-simplistic, black-and-white, 'accept-or-reject' thinking, which all facilitate 'gate-keeping', and other methods of deliberate distraction."

"Sort o' like what 'appened with the Enigma code-crackin' breakthrough at Bletchley…!" Jake suddenly blurted out.

"Sorry for buttin' in Magda – I'm followin' everythin' y're sayin' – which amazes me I can! - but what I mean is…" He then quickly covered the subject of what the code breakers of Bletchley Park had to do about carefully rationing the dissemination of what they knew, as he had explained it to Sophie earlier that afternoon.

"Yes Jake, thank you, that was an excellent example of this process." Magda then smiled mysteriously below her raised eyebrows as she looked at Jake.

"You must talk with my sister Angela one day…she was very familiar with the work Alan and the others were doing in hut eight at Bletchley Park…in the guise she was then under…in fact some of her many, carefully crafted, instructive throw-away comments to them, for example, along the lines of: *'instead of asking 'How' it works, perhaps we should be asking 'Why' it works – once we know, of course, on what dimension it operates...'*, were all the sorts of ongoing cues and insights she subtly gave them towards them achieving *their own* eventual success...because it would have been – inappropriate – *for her to have simply told them...!"*

Just like Sophie had responded to hearing about the unicorns - this time it was Jake's turn to flop back into the sofa utterly gobsmacked...his lips silently trying to form words in reply!

"However, moving on...have any of you heard of something called 'Milab'?" She looked around at them seeing shaking heads and confused expressions.

"Milab is short for 'Military Abductions'. Often in the past, and it still goes on today of course, selected experiencers whom reported their...initial contact experiences to the authorities...would then soon after be abducted by the military using secret, very high-tech' means, and false, or, what are called: 'screen memories' implanted in them, of which the norm is for them to falsely relive and only recount afterwards a very unpleasant, stressful and even painful experience, when that experiencer had been previously – they would now believe - *'forcibly'* - taken aboard – and *'abducted'* – against their will, on an 'alien' craft.

"One of the reasons for doing this means the experiencer will then unwittingly add many fearful and highly negative elements into the communal punchbowl that so many are keen to drink from to slake their thirst for knowledge of this crucially important subject...Or to continue with the imbibing analogy – it is like poisoning the well...

"So...instead it is of course highly preferable and much safer for all concerned for contact to be made to 'profiled' individuals; to initiate a covert interaction with them and then establish ongoing relations with them...to achieve mutually beneficial ends...These are the early days, or years, of this process we are involved in, but so far, it all looks very promising.

"There is another factor at work as well for going about the whole process like this. And that is similar to something Ander's talked about to you last Monday evening in The Trocadero Cafe, it was, is, called: *'The Hundredth Monkey Syndrome'* – I'm sure you will all recall what he described: how *one* monkey on an island was shown and learned how to do something, then, after a hundred or so on the island learned how to do it, eventually – and it was not too long afterwards - *all the monkeys of that species - all over the world - knew how to do it!*

"That knowledge had become a part of their collective, 'Unity Consciousness', and they immediately shared it – sub-consciously - so it could be tapped into and used to benefit any or all of them when any or all of them needed to use it. So that knowledge was downloaded and installed as a default skill set across the entire species.

"Quite unlike a 'Dualistic Consciousness' where just the individual, who had learned how to do the task, and then, perhaps, just a few he selected to 'let in on the secret', and so get the reward, kept it all to themselves – *so then of course all the others of the species whom had deliberately been kept in ignorance of it...'lost out'...from the reward!"*

They nodded their heads eagerly, telling her they did remember Ander's description of this phenomena, and they understood what Magda was saying about it, in more depth now, within the context she was telling them about.

"So just try and imagine the implications, over time, of that same process applying now to humans in relation to experiencing 'visitor' contact, with their true memories of it...the ongoing relationships with them and the inevitable revelations and *understanding* that would come from 'working' with them! – But obviously it all has to be done very covertly at first.

"Coupled with the raising of consciousness...well, eventually *everything* will change from being covert to overt – it will all be 'out in the open'. It will all be out in the open for *everyone* to see, realise, know and *understand* exactly what has been really going on for so long.

"The majority of the seven billion or so of then-aware-human-beings will not be vulnerable to the threats from a few thousand parasite aligned elites...Indeed, way before then the parasites would have either abandoned the planet as their sustenance rapidly diminished, or they would have been destroyed...

"Either way - *they would no longer be here...*

"As for their elite minions...and from them, right down every level of those whom willingly collaborated with them - the legions of those whom were instrumental in implementing their atrocious policies, to those whom knowingly and deliberately spread all their lies and disinformation to back the process up – the 'talking heads' on television, the 'writing hands' of the print media, and all the others who played their supporting roles in the wickedly deceitful agenda, well, what happens to them as they are gradually and irrevocably exposed and brought to account will be upto humanity then to decide...

"We will promote 'Truth and Reconciliation' to play the dominating roles then, as there will be many who genuinely regret and will atone for their actions.

"But there will be many whom will just have to be permanently isolated from the rest of humanity, for as long as they remain alive, because they, to all intents and purposes...no longer have any vestigial traces remaining of what it means to truly be a human being...and there are some of those - who are irredeemably just far too evilly corrupted and ultimately despicable, even for a lifetime of secure confinement, so as they are rooted out - they *will be* no longer...

"Remember – what I'm telling you all, for now, *is just an outline and brief filling in of just some of the bare facts!* – In recent years, as part of our role with the visitors, we have stepped up our efforts and strategies against the parasites, their elite minions and those in supporting roles; and just *one way* we have been doing that has been by Anders and many others like him giving enlightening talks to transfer knowledge and promote *understanding*, to people who are awakening - and to try to awaken other people to all of this, who, as yet, are not, all over the World."

Sophie was nodding her head again. Her now much more rapid and insightful thought processes enabling her to quickly 'join all the dots' of the outline Magda had revealed, and visualise the images they formed within...showing the great potential there was now for all these re-constructive events that would take place in a positive, soon to come, future time line...

'There's no fate – but what we make...' She thought, remembering again the inspirational words of Sarah Connor in 'The Terminator' films.

It also revealed most of the answer to her earlier, unspoken question - of how they all worked, operated, and achieved so much, so well, together...She did voice one further, related question to Anders though.

"So all that's part of and just *one reason* why you, Anders, gave that quote by Einstein, when we were in The Trocadero, the one when he, Einstein, said: *'Peace can only be attained through 'understanding'...'*?"

Anders nodded and smiled his confirmation to her. Magda smiled as well, saying, "well remembered Sophie. Yes, the word: *'Understanding'* really is The Key - and not just to unlock and open the door to Peace. Because Peace is the fundamental basis, or foundation, for the fantastic edifices of positive change that can be built upon it on a Peace-full Earth, that you will be able to *'stand-under'* – and so – *'under-stand'*...

"Actually, I think I will diverge from my intended outline now a little bit, although I have really sketched out, more or less, what I wanted to let you know.

"I will give you a further 'ledge' to help your awarenesses to climb up from, let us call it: another 'know-*ledge*! I will explain some more about what I meant by saying all that about knowledge and understanding, it is highly relevant to what I and Anders will continue with afterwards anyway, as you will see, *and under-stand...*!

"...It is a difficult, and very challenging mission, which Anders and all the others are engaged upon, in many ways, and he has detailed some of them to you already. Not the least being, is succeeding in putting those whom come to listen to him, and to the others, in a position where they are – to use a motorbiking analogy...” she smiled at Jake - who had now seemed to have recovered from his earlier shock about what she had said about her sister Angela and Bletchley Park...

"...'kick-started' - and so they then, hopefully, become 'intrinsically' motivated, which is the desire and the motivation from within, to do it for its own sake – to do something positive to explore and strive to actualize their potential - by investing their own time and energies to open-mindedly research and enjoy learning far more about 'it all' on their own, and in groups like yourselves.

"The opposite of intrinsic motivation is extrinsic motivation – which is the behaviour, often of: 'having to do something', and it is driven purely by the expectation of gain, of an external reward – a paycheck, money, fame, praise et cetera...Most of the activities that need extrinsic motivation are, by their very natures, repetitive, boring, and full of drudgery...I am sure you can all think of many examples...!

"So...how often does a teacher say after a lesson: 'Oh if only we had more time! This is just a drop in the bucket!' Hence, of course, why Anders suggested throughout his presentation, and I have as well, so many starting points for you to do your own 'homework-research' from, on a variety of topics, to understand them a lot more – and be intrinsically motivated to do so!

"Because 'Understanding' demands a much closer examination of any prior 'Knowledge' and all the assumptions by which we claim something to be that 'Knowledge'. That is the meaning of the word when Einstein, as a scientist, used it.

"The philosopher Socrates gave us the best 'model' or 'way' to do this – it is actually named after him, and called: 'The Socratic Principle.' It is when you repeatedly question the claims of 'Established Knowledge' in order to Understand and thus learn far more. Because when we are helped to ask certain questions, such as: Why is that so? Why do we think that? What justifies such perceptions? What is the evidence? What is the argument? What is being assumed? What are the consequences? When we do all, or even some of that, we go through a powerful transfer: *the ability to grasp, to realise what, or who, actually makes or made that previous 'Knowledge'.*

"So you can then start to rapidly climb up the 'ledges' and discover a more refined, truer, factual *'Know-ledge'*, rather than *'Mere Belief'* - which so often simply comes from the compliant, 'plugged-in' and programmed mentality that just accepts – *'well that's just the way it is!'* Which is all just dogma, diktat, and propaganda from those whom want you to *perceive* and so then *believe* things only in a certain way - *that suits them...and their agenda,* etcetera.

"Hence doing all that puts you in a far better position to increase your *True Knowledge*...and then of course that leads you to a...*Real And Solid Foundation of Under-standing.*

"Basically the difference between Knowledge and Understanding is that Knowledge just gives us the – *apparent* - facts, whilst Understanding - gives us *The True Meaning* of those facts..."

Jake jumped in. "Yeah, yeah I actually do understand – ha! - *that's not a pun!* I mean I do really get all what you're sayin' Magda, good job I've found some higher gears in 'ere to shift me thinkin' up into than what I 'ad before!" He said, tapping his forehead.

Mel then said enthusiastically, "Yeah! *I really get all what you're saying as well!* I really do, but a week or so back – no way I think I would've! – it'd just've been a load of convoluted words! I really do get it, as well, I think, because that first Sunday night Dave and I listened to you speak at the Fair, when you were in the marquee, towards the end you were so right when you said Anders: *'as your consciousness expands, your whole way of thinking will change...'*

"That was so true, and it's not just me, it's all of us, we all feel like that. So what you are doing and sharing Anders - and you Magda, has certainly worked - and had great rewards and fantastic benefits for us so far!"

"Thank you Jake and Melanie - thank you all, from both of us, and *from all of us,* that is so..." her head lowered for a moment, as she breathed deeply, "...is so reassuring for us, and so kind of you, of you all, to give us that. Thank you..."

She turned her head to look intensely at Anders for a few moments, as if transmitting her thoughts to him. Then she turned back to address them - verbally though, again.

"So...to summarise, and I admit to the brevity of this outline...for various reasons we have agreed a series of protocols – which are 'agreed terms' – with another very advanced race. One of those protocols is that they will initially appear, at an appropriate moment, and place, just very briefly at first, to those whom we have recommended to them as being ready to...*understand.* Clearly an appropriate opportunity for them to do that safely, first occurred early yesterday morning, with you David."

It was now Dave's turn to slump back into the sofa! But after a second or two he managed to reply, albeit rather quietly, *"so...they've been, like, watching me, us, and just waiting for an opportunity to show up...?!"*

Magda nodded, "yes, but they were not following you all around all of the time watching everything you do, just waiting for an appropriate opportunity, whilst remaining invisible to you, although they can quite easily do that...

"To put it as simply as I can...they remotely monitored the auric fields of your individual consciousnesses, to alert them when it was in a favourable phase – just prior to waking up or going to sleep are two of the ideal phases. They are called the hypnopompic and the hypnogogic phases or states of consciousness, and they are two phases when you would be most receptive to communicate with, well, certainly for the first time.

"For you Melanie, Sophie and Jake, it is very likely they would have attempted to make an initial communication – very delicately at first, as they did with David, but if your conscious minds were...engaged...on other thoughts preoccupying, or dominating your minds they would not have attempted to get through.

"They could have 'forced their way in', but one of the protocols we agreed was that they would not do that, not initially anyway. Think of it as being similar to telephoning someone you want to talk to - but they are talking to someone else, so you get the engaged tone!

"I'm aware that you have all had a very busy week with lots of preoccupations, so all that would contribute to make you 'engaged'. But perhaps David, due to you being alone on the cliff top, and to your calm meditative state, which quietens and clears the mind whilst you are fully awake, that is why you first heard their call…"

Jake jumped in again saying, "So it's like you gave 'em our mobile numbers to ring us - but we were always busy talkin' to someone else when they rang…?!"

"Yes Jake, in its essence that is exactly the process, initially. Let's say that if someone unknown to you rang you, you would perhaps listen to them introduce themselves, and then if what they had to say you found interesting and relevant, then, depending on the circumstances, and the nature of the call of course, perhaps you might agree to a face-to-face meeting with the caller at a mutually agreeable time…for whatever purposes."

"Aye, I understand! - Oh – I'd better be a bit more careful 'ow I use that word from now on as well!" He chuckled, "I can't 'elp but say though that I often, an' so does everybody else I suppose, when an unknown caller rings it just gets ignored – 'cos usually they're just tryin' to sell y'summat!"

Magda laughed, "yes you are quite right Jake, my mobile telephone call analogy only goes so far! In the case of the initial 'call' from these beings though, I assure you that they would not be trying to part you from your money – *and sell you anything!*

"In fact it is only on Earth that the false concept of 'money' exists in the multiverse…particularly as it is used as a form of manipulative control over you by the banking families of the elites who control it – and they can do that partly because they also 'own' and use most, if not all of it!

"The creation and emergence of 'money' on Earth, goes back to

115

Babylonian times. Money had, and has, an energy attached to it that influences and motivates people almost as if they were spell-bound by it. Which, indeed, most people are...and which is why it was designed and created of course."

Magda looked at Anders and said, "I am aware of the time passing for you, and you soon have a final presentation, so perhaps if I stop now it will allow you to add to the answers to those questions Jake voiced earlier from everyone, Anders."

Chapter 8: Anders talks.

"Yes, indeed, tempus fugit! - *Time flies!* Thank you Magda."

He then looked at Jake, "I think the way you used analogies to help you sum up and explain what you have now, and what you want to do with it was well done Jake. As you all well know by now I too find analogies extremely helpful to get messages and information across that are...complex.

"So if you don't mind - I'll start to reply by using one now, well, in a minute or so, and forgive me – all of you - if on hearing it, and then what I'll say after it, if you all think I am being...shall we say...more than a little dramatic...and exaggerating things...

"But it is important, very important, that firstly you are all fully aware of, or as much as possible, so you *understand* - all of the future implications, consequences, and the ultimate goal or achievement of the course of action that you all clearly now intend to, to embark upon.

"Plus, you need to know of course, more of the past history and background, the 'Lie of the Land' – Oh! I'm sure there's another pun there! - that you are going to journey and 'charge over' so to speak...and as the military men – *particularly those in the Cavalry!* - always say: *'time spent in reconnaissance is never wasted...!'*"

He uncrossed his legs and leaned forwards, his elbows on the chair arms, and interlaced his fingers.

"The analogy and imagery of the big, old, heavy box you used Jake, was most, most apt, and I think it's quite accurate of me to say that that big, old, heavy box you've found has a name, and it is: 'Pandora's Box' - although what Pandora was given was actually a 'jar', not a 'box', that was a mistranslation of the ancient Greek into Latin back in the fifteen eighties – but we'll go along with 'box', as it is, as I've said, most apt here.

"It is, because if, and when, you eventually and successfully release what you can assemble and make from all of its contents, having found any missing ones first of course, and it is what Magda and I think it might be - 'once it is fully assembled', as you put it, and openly revealed to the World, it will cause turmoil in the short term, but in the mid to long term, *immense changes* to *your World* that will be irrevocable...

"It will be 'A New Reformation', literally a '*Re – Formation*' *of your entire World.* But unlike the disclosures that Martin...Martin Luther proclaimed - which slowly started what historians now call 'The Reformation' - mainly on his own, *but with a little help*...that happened *mainly in Europe* during the fifteen hundreds – *these* revolutionary, re-formatory disclosures - once they are all present and assembled – and openly displayed, they would be, *in these times*...driven rapidly...once they are out there, by the mass of humanity *and across the entire World...!*

"*Why? - How come?! -* What Revolutionary Disclosures To Change The World?! - *Surely I'm exaggerating!* Well, I assure you - *I'm not...*

"Like many others have already done, you have made contact – or rather – they have made contact directly with you – with your group. Contact from highly advanced beings that are not from this world, but from...somewhere else in the Multiverse.

"Somewhere that is hundreds of thousands of light years 'away', and they are from a much higher dimension than this one...Just so you are aware, there is a difference between 'extra-terrestrial' and higher 'inter-dimensional' beings.

"The extra-terrestrials have physical bodies, and are fifth, sixth and lower seventh dimensional, generally. The inter-dimensional beings are seventh and higher dimensional beings, and generally do not have physical bodies, but appear as 'light bodies', energy fields, and they do not need 'physical' craft to appear, as they use an entirely different methodology.

"Oh – also - just so you all know, a 'light year' is the *distance* that light travels – at one hundred and eighty six thousand miles per second, in every one of the thirty one million, five hundred and thirty six thousand seconds in 'a year'...it's a hard sum to work out the distance in total! and that's just for one light year! – *but it's quite a long way nevertheless, as time and distance are currently measured - I think you'll all agree...*

"So it's quite obvious that the extra-terrestrials' means of transportation is definitely from a very highly advanced technology! They are certainly not shovelling in, or pouring in, and then burning, in some huge combustion engine vast stores of fossil fuels they have dug out of the ground and are carrying around in a huge tank for their energy supply!

"No, of course they're not! Instead they are using energy systems and inter-dimensional time and space vacuum singularity technologies, that are coupled with and interface with their consciousness.

*"Imagine it! - their conscious thought interfaces with and controls that technology...*Because if they had to physically move to press a button, or move a steering wheel to adjust their flight path for example, even travelling *at only the speed of light,* just three seconds to decide and then do that button press or wheel turn would mean they'd've moved well over half a million miles! – *Not really very practical for accurate navigation and arriving at exactly where they want to get to!*

"With all of these beings their civilizations' spiritual and technological advancements are millennias, and even more, ahead of those of the current human civilization *that is on* the Earth. Although the majority of the human race would be, *will be,* shocked, as and when *the coming, undeniable disclosures and revelations* make them fully aware of just how advanced human technology discoveries, *in these areas, especially energy, really is.*

"But...it has all been kept secret and suppressed from general release, so that it only 'benefits' a select few and their agenda. – And so we're back to that 'Duality Consciousness' at work again - and the inversion, or opposite, of 'the hundredth monkey syndrome'...!

"It is advanced technology which would, of course, have been of great benefit to humanity. *But it is only used by,* by small, so called 'elite' factions of humans, as I've said, for their own dark agenda...and in the forefront of that agenda of course is their determination to maintain their hold and control of power, and their hegemony over humanity *on this planet...*

"Just *one* example of the sort of hidden technology I'm talking about is the so called 'Anti-Gravity Flying Machine'. Although *'Anti-Gravity'* is not really a very accurate description of what actually happens, that is more of a 'comic-culture' definition. The truer description is 'Electro-Magnetic-Gravitics', or EMG.

"Well, the fact is, these types of craft utilising this EMG technology have been successfully manufactured in America since the early nineteen fifties. The final breakthrough to fully achieve that was in October 'fifty-three if I remember correctly...

"That success followed on from the pioneering works done before in Nazi Germany since the mid 'thirties...mainly by the same scientists and researchers...as they were, the majority of them, secretly re-located to the Americas, just prior to and after the end of the so called 'Second World War'. A war that Germany lost, but the Nazis didn't, they just relocated, reformed and recommenced...but that's by-the-by...

"That re-locating programme was called 'Operation Paper Clip' - by all the allies' secret security agencies involved in doing it. It was called 'Operation Paper Clip' because at the Nuremberg trials of the Nazi war criminals, any of them whose file had a paper-clip on it were destined for relocation and to continue their work...having avoided prosecution...

"Works that were not just confined to rocketry technology either...pioneering works of a very dark nature into mass and individual mind control techniques by their scientists all came under the protection of Operation Paper Clip. The reason the American mind control programme was, is, called M.K. Ultra, of which M.K. which stands for Mind Kontrol is a nod to its Germanic originators.

"At those trials in Nuremberg after the war, less than two dozen war criminals were actually convicted – out of tens of thousands whom really should've been. The whole trials were really just staged public relations exercises, but that's a 'by-the-by' as well for today, another time I'll explain more..." He grinned at them saying, "...and you can also research it all for yourselves of course!"

"The EMG advanced technology has been used by many flying crafts in the Earth's skies over the past few decades since then. Those crafts have often been seen and thought to be 'UFO's from other worlds' by those whom saw them. But they were – and I don't mean *all of the unidentified flying crafts of course* – but these were, and still are, in fact, a result of human, terrestrial manufacture...!

"Let's now think about *just some* of the implications of that technology for a moment...this energy and propulsion technology.

"Well, for one thing, it clearly eliminates entirely the need to carry and burn fossil fuels – particularly oil...and all its derivatives, so if it *had been openly disclosed* to humanity the world's current macro economic geopolitic system which is based on fossil fuels and the global economic money dominance of the 'petro-dollar' - would not have been spawned...or at least it may have been, for a while, but it would by now all have been obsolete for a very long time.

"So the *very - money profitable,* constant wars to secure those resources – quite unnecessary; pollution creating, but *money profitable,* transportation industries – quite unnecessary; to say nothing of there being no need to – *money profitably* - tarmac millions of miles of roads all over the planet's surface...! And so on, and so on...and Magda has already explained to you that money equals, or means...control...*by those whom have the most, if not all, of it...*

"What I've just very briefly described, merely - pun intended! - only 'skips over the surface' of how different your world would have been over the past *SEVENTY* or so years...It would have been – *it should have been - an entirely different technologically and socially structured civilization...on the surface of this planet!*

"Actually - one more example! – A crucial part of all this is the so called *'Free Energy'.* Well, the technology to harness and supply, at hardly any cost at all, safely and far, far more efficiently than burning fossil fuels, or using dangerous, and potentially catastrophically so, nuclear fission energy using radioactive uranium, as evidenced by the recent disasters at Chernobyl and Fukushima - the latter of which was *certainly* no 'accident', and the former we are highly suspicious *wasn't either*!

"Instead of harnessing and supplying the *clean, safe and naturally abundant energy already present on and all around the planet*, and I say again - *non-polluting* energy - *For Everyone* - *in every city, town and village on this planet*, that technology was just about perfected *again* in the modern era by Nikolai – Nikolai Tesla, *and by others* working in that field, in the first decade of the nineteen hundreds...*Over a hundred years ago...!*

"Just as a quick aside, whilst we're touching on this subject – many, many tens of thousands of years ago other advanced civilizations *on* the Earth's surface understood and utilised *similar* technologies, particularly so in Africa - as evidenced by the thousands of stone structures there being discovered now in very recent years that some brilliant, open minded researchers are realising were designed for utilising and amplifying the energies of planetary acoustic harmonics, which are 'just' another form of the abundant energies all around us...

"Those stone structures were not confined to that continent alone of course, they were, are, all linked with others across the planet, hence the many similarities in design from one continent to another. But modern mainstream historians bleat on about the stone circles in Africa being: *'just for primitive peoples corralling their livestock'* – despite them originally not having any entrances to get them in there!? *- And the pyramids were built by the Egyptians as tombs for deceased Pharaohs* - despite no dead Pharaohs or funereal items *ever being found in them...!*" He shook his head despairingly.

"Anyway – back to Nikolai's work...*tragically for humanity it was all very quickly suppressed!* The instigator of that suppression was the moneyed coterie of the global elite families, whose banking businesses financed, and so ultimately controlled, the conglomerate of industrial cartels; the moneyed coterie of bankers was headed at that time by a man called John Pierpont Morgan, J.P. Morgan.

"It was he who instantly realised, after watching a demonstration of the energy technology given by Nikolai, who had approached him, naively, for funding to set it up on a national scale, that the way the usable energy was transmitted, was such that the industrial cartels the coterie owned wouldn't be able to put coin meters on it to make any profits from it. And if he couldn't do that, he obviously couldn't charge money to use it – money from just about every single member of the population - for using that type of energy.

"He also realised that it would also cancel out the need for countless thousands, millions, of miles of copper wire, copper, and many, many other metals and associated materials of course - which all came from the mines that he and his cartel of industrial associates owned and made huge financial profits from...

"It would also have decimated, possibly even eliminated, all the financial profits from all of the other associated production industries they owned, that went hand-in-hand with using fossil fuels as the primary energy source...

"And it wasn't just the 'money profits' that were at risk. The elites also profited and benefited in many other ways, all in accord with the darker, parasitic agenda – because by controlling the world's energy and power sources and charging populations for its supply they had, and still have to this day, their hegemony of power and the contrived dependency of humanity on all the social engineering programmes, and the manipulative geo-political-economic system allied to them. Which is just what...'they'...wanted to continue then – and want, even more desperately to hang onto now...

"In fact right up to the present day many independent scientists, researchers, and inventors, after years of research and work to successfully re-produce 'free energy technology', with the motivation to re-introduce it to the world to benefit humanity have been constantly suppressed, by subtle and by brutal means – but nevertheless the technology *Does Exist!* If it didn't – why would they go to so much effort to suppress it?!

"Sadly, many – most – *all - in some cases* - of those brave and pioneering people, who had a benevolent Unity Consciousness, and so they were motivated to try to independently bring it out into the world for everyone's benefit - no longer *do exist* though...They have either mysteriously disappeared, or died in unusual circumstances and their work somehow couldn't be found afterwards...all of Nikolai's original research papers and working models just disappeared – quickly taken away by the American FBI and other Deep State Agencies.

"Oh – just as an aside - a curious fact about that FBI removal operation, and the analysis of it all afterwards, is that one of the people involved in it – brought in from academia as a consultant, and who was very involved in its planning, execution and later analysis, was called Professor John G. Trump – and he was the uncle of the current American President...!

"One modern day example of an *un-usual death* was that of the American inventor Stanley Allen Meyer, on March the twentieth, 'ninety eight. Seconds before he died, after taking a sip of cranberry juice he gasped: *'They poisoned me..!'*

"Indeed 'they' did...because he had invented a small device that extracted the energy from hydrogen and oxygen – in water, and he successfully used that 'free' energy to run his car – and the device could've been easily adapted and used to fuel and run all the existing cars being driven around the planet – *on water!*

"*So it would have eliminated the need for expensive petrol or diesel to be used in them!*...and he was on the verge of releasing that technology to the world...but after his unexpected, sudden death...he was in good health prior to it - *the crucial parts of his research papers and work could not be found...*

"Some inventors succumbed to death *threats* to them and their families, and other intolerable pressures to cease their work.

"Some actually sold their research for vast amounts of money to the huge multi-national corporations whose immense profits and power would have been threatened by it. Then those corporations, once they'd got their hands on it just 'boxed it all up' and shelved it, hiding it away of course. There are few better, more classic examples of the

Dualistic Consciousness in operation:- *'We've just Won! – So you lot have just Lost...!*

"However! - Right about now you're all possibly thinking something along the lines of: *'what on earth has all of this got to do with me, us, sitting on a cliff top and seeing and hearing extra-terrestrial entities...?!'*"

He paused, giving them some moments to absorb and digest what he had said so far, watching their outward reactions closely, which, predictably, went from initial astonishment as he had started to speak, to the dawning realisation of the implications of the picture he had briefly sketched out for them as they inwardly 'stepped back' and then 'joined all the dots' of the facts he'd just presented...

Dave cleared his throat and said very quietly, "So if all that's true – and I don't mean *'if'* - I mean, obviously I believe you, I believe it is, *of course*, it, it – starts to show a picture of a world that could be *utterly, totally different* - to the world we know and experience now...in fact I can't, or I'm struggling to, to even try to partly imagine what it would all *really be like...!*"

" - *Aye me too an'all mate!* - But it sounds like we'd 'ave 'ad *flyin' motorbikes - wi' no petrol tanks or fiddly electrics* - for one thing! - For the last *sixty odd years...!*" Jake commented with his irrepressible humour.

"*Sorry!* – Sounds like I'm bein' a bit flippant but I'm not really! It's just that I'm a bit, well, *more than a bit bowled over as well like*...But as you've just said, *asked*, Anders,' *'ow do we go from us all sittin' on a cliff top seein' an' hearin' extra-terrestrial entities'* - an' all that – just 'ow do we go from there?

"An' 'ow does our part, the part we can play - *whatever that is*, actually fit in exactly, with, with everythin' else, with all these other parts, you've just told us about...?'"

"*How Indeed?!*" Anders replied in a grandiloquent genial manner, then he turned his head towards Magda

"Well - that is something I will have to ask you, Magda, if I may, to continue with, as I really must go now to the marquee, I am due to start there in a few minutes...do forgive me for having to leave you right at this juncture! – But I hope I have managed to fill in some of the 'background blank squares' for you all – so you start to...*understand*.

"We must all get together again very soon, perhaps if I could further prevail upon you Magda to arrange that as well?"

"Of course Anders, when I see you later I will let you know.   You and I can 'get our heads together' before we all meet together again to decide upon the best way to go about moving forwards and supplying those 'missing instructions', components and 'parts' that can be played - *as Jake was so eloquent in putting it*."

She rose up with Anders, and as Jake, Sophie, Dave and Mel were starting to get to their feet as well Anders said, "Oh please don't get up! *Thank you all so much again!* - I look forward to our next meeting and continuing with you on our - *your...quest...!*"

" - *The Pandora Quest!*"   Mel burst in loudly.   "I think that's a *Good Name* for what we are going to do Anders!"   Anders paused in mid step and cocked his head to one side, saying, "Yes, *yes it is rather!* It's a *jolly good name*! - I shall tell her! - *She'll be most pleased...!*"   And with an endearing wink and a wave to them all he walked away with Magda at his side.

" - I will not be long, I am just going with Anders to the portal doorway for the marquee and then I will be back with you."   She called over to them.

Jake was scratching his chin and slowly shaking his head.

"You still okay Jake?"   Sophie asked looking at him, and with a slight concern creeping into her voice.

"Yeah, I'm fine, yeah thanks Soph' – but...well, no...*I dunno about it...*"

"About what? All of it? Any of it? - The *name*? – '*The Pandora Quest*'?" She asked him.

"No! *No – It's a great idea! - Great name for it Mel!* No, it's just that I've been called a lot o' things in me time...But I've never been

126

called that before…!"

"*Called what?* Who called you what? *When?!*"

"*Magda did just now!* She said I was: eluquen – eloquon – *good at clever talkin'*…!"

Sophie one handedly slap pushed at his shoulder and he fell sideways onto the sofa laughing silently.

Sophie rolled her eyes at Mel and said to her, "*I don't know Mel!– Just can't get the staff can we!*"

Mel grinned back at her, and Dave said, "Well, to that, as 'D'Artagnan Dave', I say – *'touché'*!"

Chapter 9: The Missing Parts...

Magda was soon back, and she asked them if tomorrow, Sunday, would be a good time for them all to meet again with herself and Anders, as they had just decided that it really would be preferable to meet again as soon as that.

Mel and Dave explained that they were hoping to arrange with Jake's mate Reg, whom they'd be seeing, hopefully, at the Fair sometime later this evening, to help them in moving the remaining stuff from their old flat in his big van, and then going to Sophie's friend's charity shop with loads of their stuff after, so really the early evening would be best for them.

Jake said that he had booked a midday coaching session for himself at the Archery Club that he must go to as he had been told a few days ago that he had been picked for the Archery Club's team in the County Long Bow Championships, and he needed to get some practice in after it with his new bow, and test the arrows he'd made for it, but he too was good to go from the late afternoon onwards.

Sophie said she would be free from the mid afternoon onwards, as she had some computer work to do at home for the Estate Agents, so the four of them then agreed to Magda's suggestion that tomorrow evening at seven o'clock would seem to be ideal, as she and Anders would by then have had a meeting to: 'put their heads together'.

Sophie then said, "I know this *might sound* a bit silly Magda, but here we are trying to fit in an important meeting, and all of us are saying what we're doing, and where we're going first – when, compared to, to *'the magnitude'* – is that the best word for it? - *'Importance'* definitely is! - Of what both you and Anders have been saying, part of me sort of thinks we should, well, be putting that first, making it our priority, but, life just gets in the way!

"What was it that John Lennon said? - Something like: *'Life's what gets in the way of all the plans you make...!'* But it doesn't mean we're not all totally committed! *D'y'know what I mean?!*"

"Of course I do my dear, and please do not doubt yourselves. Tomorrow is a very busy day for us too as it is 'a Moving Day' as the Faerie folk call it when they relocate, and we all have various commitments because of it during the day as well.

"You all have lives that right now have other important commitments and priorities too that you must maintain of course. It is going to be a case of just being flexible, and planning ahead when you know and understand more, and the more you know and understand the better the plans you can make will be of course.

"At the moment you are obviously not fully aware of what and how: *'sitting on a cliff top and starting to communicate with extra-terrestrial entities',* could, and hopefully will, proceed from there.

"Or how it is going to impact on your lives...so let me put it all into context for you...and at the same time give you some more...*'knowing'* so you can start *to understand* more of all the background to it - *it may take a little while!* – One of those few seconds only 'sound bytes' will not cover it! Oh – and as you said you are meeting your friends at the Fair this evening as well, please do not worry about being late for them – remember that when you leave here it will be the same time 'back there' - as when you left...

"So...where would it be best for me to begin – from where Anders left off...?" She quietly asked herself, looking up and tapping her fingers on her knees. The answer obviously come to her in seconds as she quickly lowered her head to look at them.

"It is not just the Human Consciousness that is re-awakening now - so is the Earth's. They are both starting to re-awaken, rise up and get onto their feet, so to speak, this time in close conjunction with each other. The previous *six occasions* when these events occurred they were not quite so much in synchrony as they are this time. Which is the main reason why humanity did not achieve their throwing off of the shackles that the parasites had harnessed them with. So coupled with that and the parasites efforts to hinder, handicap and prevent the full re-awakening. on those previous occasions they managed to stop it.

129

"But each time they did it, it became more and more difficult for them to achieve that prevention. This time the odds are really against them from achieving it. Which is why Anders and I have said to you before that that is why they are now: *'throwing everything they can at you to prevent it'*. And they have had many, many centuries to prepare...but then again – *so have we...*

"...Everything in the multiverse tends to move in cycles. One of those cycles is called the 'Precession Of The Equinoxes', and its implications were known about to civilizations here on the Earth many, many thousands of years ago. They left monuments and artifacts in connecting patterns all around the planet, designed to serve as reminders of this that would survive the passage of time.

"The Precession is a twenty five thousand eight hundred years, approximately, cycle of the synchronised elliptical energetic movements of many planetary systems, including the Earth. At this time one major cycle, or Yuga, of it is ending and another is starting.

"As I have explained previously, *everything is energy*, and the energies now coming to Earth, as part of this new cycle, *are aiding this awakening and rising of the consciousness of the Earth and humanity.*

"To give you some basic ideas of how these things work - imagine two or more – *or even a room full!* - of violins, or guitars, positioned in close proximity to each other. By repeatedly playing the same musical note – which is a transmitted energy frequency - on one of them, the other, or others, *will tune and harmonise themselves to that one dominant harmonic energy frequency they are being exposed to.* This is a natural phenomena and it is called 'entrainment'.

"People, as I explained to you last time, tend to react in the same way to the dominant emotions they are constantly exposed to, as emotions are the transmitted energy frequencies of another person...which are visible in their auras, as we talked about last Monday evening.

"So...in a similar way, *both the Earth and the humans on it* are re-tuning, re-harmonising and so *entraining*. Most humans are doing so

130

mostly subconsciously, but many awakened humans, since the end of the year of twenty twelve, which was the end of the Mayan calendar, the end of a cycle, and the ushering in of a new one, are becoming fully conscious of the entrainment changes...to the synchronising, surrounding flow of these higher vibrational positive energies, in both the humans' electromagnetic fields and those of the Earth's.

"The *basic* 'elements or parts' of this energetic phenomena can be measured, partially, even by mainstream empirical scientists, who call it, that part they can measure, the 'Schumann Resonance', after Winfried, the physicist who discovered it as a mathematical concept in nineteen fifty two, *and it is rising significantly...*

"And just for your interest; the emotional frequency of pure love is transmitted on the five hundred and thirty four Hertz wavelength, and some aspects of the Schumann Resonance frequency are steadily approaching *well over* half way to that...

"Another example like the entraining tuning of those violins, guitars – and people! - *is what whales do!* Those wonderful, huge, gentle creatures periodically – but more often so now in these current times, dive into the great oceans' depths, sometimes having travelled thousands of miles to do so, to nodal points on the Earth's natural energy grid.

"Once there they position themselves vertically, and then in concert and perfect synchrony with many hundreds of others of their kind, over vast distances, *they all 'sing' together...*they all emit sound frequencies that they know will re-harmonise, re-pair and re-entrain the imbalances they have sensed in the Earth's energetic frequency grid.

"These sounds, these 'songs', have been recorded, and the 'songs' of whales are quite delightful. But mostly they are not understood, or, more accurately, the *significance* of the whales' songs have always been understood by some, an elite few, but never, ever, openly revealed to the masses what they are *actually, really doing* of course.

"What their singing achieves is the real reason why they have been, and still are, hunted and killed so mercilessly. The financial profits

131

from the industrial scale of killing them for their oils and other body parts being just 'an added bonus' – *the manifest agenda.*

"Not that in the old days of individual hunters in rowing boats, poised and ready to hand throw their harpoons - to the captains and crews of the modern, state-of-the-art weaponised, huge sea going abattoirs are, or have been, ever aware of *the latent agenda* that they are fulfilling...

"Like so many examples of human affairs, those in the lower levels of the pyramidal, vertical hierarchies of power, have no notion at all of the true reason, or reasons, of what, why, and for whom exactly...they are really doing what they do. Only the elite few at the very top, and the parasites beyond it, in the dark shadows do, and they control it...

"Going back to the positive light energies being transmitted from Galactic centre, and now coming to, and starting to reach the Earth – and the associated changes in the frequencies of radiations from the Sun, they are some of the reasons why the agents of the parasites - those elites at the top of the pyramid, have organised, for the past fifty or more years, the flooding of your skies with 'chemical trails' – so called 'chem' trails'.

"It is quite possible that in the early days the pilots flying those aircraft had no notion at all of the true contents and real reasons for all the spraying. However, these days with the helpful and informative publicity this spraying has received – such publicity never, of course, coming from the mainstream corporate media – who have denied they even exist...! but has stemmed from very concerned citizenry all over the world, whom have provided so much evidence of the damage being done to the Earth and to peoples' health, by this spraying.

"So it has to be more than likely that the pilots and all the support staff, these days, must know what deliberate damage they are doing, *yet they continue to do so...*

"Most of the spraying is done using a poisonous three part cocktail mixture containing in one part, genetically modified bacteria, fungus, and viruses, in the second the metals, microscopic metallic particulates of vaporized aluminium, barium, strontium and others, and thirdly, the nano-technology.

"The contents of the sprays impact devastatingly on many aspects of human behaviour, and physical and mental health.

"Explaining how all these effect, and harm a human body is obviously a big subject and would take quite a while for me to explain, so we will just continue touching upon some of the main points today, and come back to it again in much more in depth another day.

"I will mention now though that the nano-technology is highly vulnerable to pulsed negative magnetism because the electrically based metabolism of these dangerous, artificial-life programmed organisms is fatally disrupted by it and they 'die'. Which is very effective in treating Morgellons disease– but – more specifically on that, and other de-toxing procedures you can do as well, will have to be in more detail another day!

"The metallic compounds in the sprays, are, in part, an attempt as well to reflect some of these Cosmic energies away. They do have some limited effect in achieving that, but it is not considerable. But the parasites know this, it is just a desperate, delaying tactic.

"The main function of most of the microscopic nano-technology is designed to be responsive to the radiated transmission frequencies in WiFi and other communication devices' transmissions, and then perform certain tasks in a human body, which, like all the spray contents, they are ultimately designed to adversely effect, and take over the natural, proper and healthy functioning of the human bio-electro-neural systems.

"We talked earlier of what happens with a domestic microwave when metallic particles are – *inadvertently as you experienced Jake!* - put in it and it is switched on..! Hence the metallics in the sprays are one reason for the increase in recent years of so many dis-functions and dis-eases of the human body – particularly the brain - causing unnatural behaviours of those heavily exposed to it.

"The metal Barium, for example, is a toxic heavy metal, and when it is ingested and stored up in the body, it acts like an aerial and a sponge enabling the body to attract and absorb very high doses of harmful radiation...so when the latest Five G radiation transmissions start to flood the airwaves *in and around everyone*, well, it will just amplify the damage it will do to a human body, not least to the reproductive system – as I touched upon earlier, so all the harmful effects of it are obviously of grave concern to us...*as a mass grave is where it is all intended to lead to...*

" - You may have seen, or heard of, an interview with the famous singer called 'Prince', on an American television show, when he openly talked about witnessing at first hand how these sprays, soon after an area had been covered by them, adversely affected the behaviour of the inhabitants of some inner city ghettoes. He also had many first hand accounts from those unfortunate people trapped in the lowest socio-economic groups that populate the ghetto areas, of an increase in lethal drug overdoses, suicides, homicides, violence, general aggression and extreme anti-social, unnatural behaviour..

"He was passionate about revealing detailed information of the connection between what was being sprayed over them and their radically altered behaviours, and he would have, with no doubt, soon have reached a global audience with what he was saying, hugely reducing the numbers of those unaware of any of this, which, indeed, was his stated intention in that television interview.

"He really would have quickly achieved that due to the platform his fame and celebrity status gave him - had he not been very rapidly silenced, killed, so soon after that, and the other, initial broadcasts, to inform people all over the world...

"It is highly likely that Prince had observed, and understood, that what he had observed were the ongoing field trials and experimental works of this wickedly used technology. It was, and is, mainly developed by DARPA, the American Government's: 'Defence Advanced Research Projects Agency', one of the most sinister and secret organisations on the planet...and when I say that, just think of all the global competition they have for that negative accolade...!

"It was DARPA who instigated the global spread of the World Wide

134

Web Internet...*which is now enmeshing most of humanity into that net, and the artificial-intelligence – or more accurately, the artificial-life that dwells there...and was their latent agenda for it to do so all along...*

"But great damage is being done as well by all these poisonous toxics, not just to humans, but to the whole biodiversity of the planet. *Over sixty percent of animal species have been made extinct over the past fifty years...*and the planetary surface is being gradually devastated. *It is ecocide...and 'terra-forming'. Which is exactly what the parasites require...*

"Another musician, John Lennon, who also had world-wide fame and celebrity status, tragically fell prey to the same dark forces at work behind all this – and more - as well, in nineteen eighty, when he was shot and killed by Chapman, who was, without doubt, an MK Ultra programmed assassin.

"What most people do not know is that John was about three weeks away from embarking on a long, nation wide speaking tour, when he intended to visit every, or as many as possible, of the University campuses in America, to promote Peace, and an end to War.

"It is quite possible that he too would have had tremendous successes in his positive endeavours to wake people up - particularly the younger generations – which was something that the Deep State's Military Industrial Complex could certainly not allow – or even consider tolerating the risk of him going ahead with any part of his tour...

"...especially as back then they didn't have quite the control and monopoly of the mainstream media corporations that they have today, so the publicity of his tour, actions and messages would have been very significant...

"However, moving on...using the same broad brush to fill in just some areas of very relevant background...

"...the deliberately started, catastrophic and raging fires in California, Colorado and Oregon recently, which are still destroying huge tracts of forested and inhabited land, and have already killed many thousands of people, and made many more homeless as they have lost everything to the conflagrations, have been in areas where prior heavy spraying was commonplace.

"The initial fires were deliberately started with phased array particle beam, micro-wave energy weapons, which are very much a reality despite mainstream media denials...evidence of their usage is indisputable – I will mention some in a minute, and the fires spread so rapidly partly due to the abundant presence of particulate aluminium, which has been proven by samples of it from the spraying that were managed to be taken before the conflagrations. It is also an active ingredient in many types of high explosives...but with the fires it acted as an accelerant and intensifier of the flames.

"When aluminium is absorbed by a tree's or a plant's roots it also prevents the further absorption of water and nutrients by that organism - *humans too are similarly affected* - so the tree or plant, or human...gradually 'dries out' and dies – *dry wood and dry plants of course burn a lot easier...*

"The mainstream media, *quite predictably of course,* just ascribe the cause of the fires to accidents, *probably by errant campers...!* But groups of boy scouts and hikers having a small camp-fire get out of control do not cause people to be reduced to charred skeletons inside cars that literally melted instantly around them before they could get away...houses to be reduced to ash - yet some trees nearby be untouched...that sort of accurate targeting and end result can only come from a deliberately aimed, battle-field weapon system...

"The weapon system works by transmitting multiple, short wave length, pulsed micro-waves, as phased array radiation from ground antennas spread over a wide area, which are then bounced off the – *now metallic particulate saturated ionosphere due to the chem trails –* which enables them to be then all focused back down to the planet's surface – and below its surface as well - onto very specific targeted areas.

"So if cars are driven through those specifically targeted areas - where all the pulsed radiations converge - the people inside the cars are immediately incinerated, *and all the metal will melt under the extremely high temperatures.* Which is also what happens to houses and other buildings – because every metal wire, appliance or metallic item in them will immediately superheat, ignite and melt...*It is a devastating, hidden technology, battle-field weapon...!*

"Many photographs of cars and other vehicles – barely recognisable as they are just molten lumps, are out there on alternative news sites, but they never appear in the mainstream sites...as you would expect. *An out of control camp fire being the cause of such destruction, as they claim - is obviously and completely, sinisterly ludicrous...!*

"A very simple, basic way of imagining it is what happens when you focus the sun's rays through a magnifying glass, down to a small dot – if you do it onto paper or wood it will burn it. It is not quite the same process of course, and I am perhaps really over-simplifying it, but that sort of comparison gives you an idea of it.

"Several researchers and observers have noticed that another curious and callous feature of the Californian fires is that some of them follow and cover most of a route that had been proposed for a new, major high-speed rail-road train transportation system...a bid for those works has been accepted from a consortium headed by Richard Blum, who is the husband of a local elite, and extremely wealthy, high ranking politician, she is actually a senior Senator for California, called Diane Feinstein...

"...and now that most of all the forests and the people living there, which and whom would have been in the way of it, have been destroyed by the fires; or they died in them, incinerated in their cars, as they tried to flee - which was deliberately done to them so they would not be able to return and re-build...*no doubt now the land value along that proposed route will have been considerably reduced...*it will probably be available soon for just a few cents on the dollar of its previous value. Curiously...the Consortium that Blum is involved with – their bid was the lowest of five others that had been received for the high-speed rail link – almost as if they had had prior knowledge that the land costs and legal hassles from – now non-existent - residents would diminish considerably...

"As I say, that reduced land value also comes with the added attraction of its population having been heavily denuded - so mitigating all the predicted lengthy delays due to legal proceedings stemming from their objections - if they had still being living along the route of it...

"...it is another callous example of the elite psychopaths' mantra of: *'The End Justifies The Means...'*

"Most normal, good, but unaware people will say, *'oh they wouldn't do that...!'* Well, yes *they* would, they do such things all the time.

"*Three thousand plus dead on 'nine-eleven', and all the destruction, just to achieve their ends? – so what? - not a problem..!*

"In some parts of the world huge swathes of forests are dying because of the poisonous spraying. *Without the addition of fires.* And the devastation goes right down to the infesting of the plankton in the seas, the insects on the land – and bees particularly – because they pollinate about one third of all the food sources grown for human consumption.

"They are all being culled by the 'chem' trails'...so destroying the natural food chain. All of which is part of the parasites' human *de-population* agenda...and the *land clearance* agenda, which will force people to move into surveillance riddled, and highly regulated 'Smart Mega-City' micro-apartment ghettoes, all heavily irradiated by Five G...They are already well underway in their construction, all across America, under the specious 'Sustainable Development' programme, of what the diabolical elite politicos, social planning architects and psychopathic manipulators call: 'Agenda Twenty One'.

"All of this is also relentlessly moving towards the terra-forming of vast areas of the planet to make it much more conducive for the parasites to eventually attempt to manifest in as their domain...where there is a vastly reduced human population who are only allowed to reside in certain, highly controlled, permitted zones...like a farmer would corall his livestock...

"Oh - just a little more about the microscopic nano-technology in

138

the chem trails and the focused radiations – *and that will be enough about them for today...!*

"It can be breathed in and absorbed through the skin of humans, in a similar way that chemical weapons are. This so called 'Smart Dust', is also activated by microwave transmissions from the several huge, secret microwave transmitting stations sited around the planet.

"The transmissions have other purposes as well as 'simply' causing massive fires and melting cars with families in them - not the least of their other applications is the weaponising of weather systems and generating and amplifying Earth movements underground such as earthquakes and volcanic eruptions – which are rapidly increasing across the planet.

"It is the weaponising of weather systems *to create extremes 'on demand'*, usually as a tool of macro-political blackmail, which is what has happened to Japan, with several devastating events that have occurred there in recent years, for example...

"These transmissions are from H.A.A.R.P. - the 'High Altitude Aerial Acoustic Resonance Project', the first one is a huge complex and was built by the Americans in Alaska in nineteen ninety three.

"Also...the saturating presence in the atmosphere of the nano-technology and the microscopic metallic particles helps the detection, by advanced technology radar stations – and one of the world's largest and most powerful is near to Scarborough, at Fylingdales, as you know - of the materialising into this dimension of the extra-terrestrials' crafts, rather like a spiders web transmits tiny vibrations to the spider in the centre of it.

"Hence a lot of craft, like the one you saw David, are materialising here now in the oceans, they are literally coming in 'under the radar' as the expression goes, and hence the billions invested in so called 'nuclear deterrent' super submarines, to detect, attack, and destroy them...and the schools of hundreds of whales when they come across them in the oceans' depths of course.

"The ET craft need to come into the third dimension 'cloaked' and 'under the radar' to avoid the militaries' new generation of three dimensional 'battlefield imaging' technology - because many of them have been shot down and destroyed by advanced weapon systems, using some of that hidden technology Anders has talked about.

"So, understandably, when they make an initial direct contact with humans it tends to be very brief at first, until certain protocols can be arranged between you to help avoid detection – of both parties - a sort of intergalactic trade craft! - And Ruth told me just how good you all were in your first attempts at basic tradecraft earlier - when you approached my caravan…!"

Mel had become, quite understandingly so, increasingly more and more agitated on hearing all about this.

"Oh my God!" She burst out, almost in tears.

"I knew about this! Well, not *everything of course* you've just said about it Magda! - but my friend at work – you remember I said last Monday evening that she had told me about the dangers of the flouride poison in our water supply? - Well…she told me at work the other day that she had emailed her local politician about her concerns over these 'chem' trails' – and she got a polite but snotty and condescending reply saying, *'…they didn't exist, they were just 'con' trails' – natural 'condensation trails', and that so called 'chem' trails' were just an internet hoax…!'*

"Then - *later the same day* - her nearly brand new computer – she'd recently upgraded to the latest model – and had had it for less than a month – she'd used it to email him with – *it just crashed!* So she rang the helpline technicians from the internet service provider, and then the manufacturers - and none of them could understand it!

"There was no obvious fault they could find or explanation for it! – So it's going to be nearly two weeks apparently before she gets it back from PC World who said they'd send it off to be stripped down, check it all out and eventually get it up and running again – or give her a new one if they couldn't for any reason, but they said a preliminary assessment had showed lots of data had somehow gone missing from her hard drive!

"She's also had to get a new router, as the old one just won't work, and she's had to open a new account. All that carry on is really pissing her off and she's probably lost loads of stuff for the print company as well that she'd been working on and hadn't got round to backing it all up!

"So she reckoned that it was obvious that when someone emails the local politicians, they've all been told to forward the email on to their central office, who then send it somewhere else – probably that GCHQ spying base down South, or some other devil knows who 'Security Agency' who locate and then somehow frazzle the sender's computer – as a warning...so she said: *'that there's no point contacting the local politicos about all this...As they're part of the problem...and whether they know it or not they set off this process of sabotage..!'"*

"Oh dear Melanie, it sounds to me that your friend might have already been 'flagged' as a *'Person Of Interest'*, as they are called, by the so called 'Security Services' – which is a definite oxymoron – what *'Security'* and what *'Service' - for whom exactly?!* – Well...we all know who *really benefits from them - and it is certainly not 'the man, woman or child 'on the street'!*

"She will have been flagged because if she had previously been raising concerns to local politicians about the dangers of flouride as well, and now about the chem' trails, what you have just described was obviously a deliberate, subtle attack to discourage and inconvenience her.

"*But*...I have to say...I have had similar reports from many others who have emailed local politicians *for the very first time* about chem' trails, people whom have never raised any concerns or contacted them *about anything before*, and then they too had sudden and inexplicable computer crashes..."

Sophie joined in and said, "*Mmmm*, I'm really glad you've both told us about that! I *had been* thinking about doing the same - with a colleague *of mine* in the tech' department at work who told me that he had downloaded a programme, for just a small monthly subscription, that's like a radar flight control monitor...!

"It tells you all the details of the planes that are flying around, and a

141

lot of them, when you see them spraying the chem' trails, are either military - or have no details at all given about them – or they just don't show up! – *Even when he can see them spraying from high up in the sky above his neighbourhood!*

"He'd got concerned about how often and just how many planes there are, and they're just openly doing it, making 'criss-cross patterns' in the sky, because he reckons now, with hindsight, the toxics in the chem trails were responsible, six months or so ago, for killing all the special Rex rabbits that his girlfriend breeds locally. They all died quickly within twenty four hours.

"At the time he didn't know anything about any of all these dangers, he wishes now though, now that he does know, that he'd had one or more properly autopsied to find out exactly what chemicals did it to them.

"The vet said is was just some sort of contagious virus that lots of small animals and birds seem to be suffering from at the moment! *Not surprising if they're outside all day being sprayed with poisons!* They were both really upset about it as you can imagine.

"Anyway, since then he's done some research into the chem' trails…but from the bits he's told me he didn't know anything about them that's anything like – well - on the same level that you've just told us all about Magda!

"In fact he reckoned the paintwork on one of his neighbour's new car was damaged by it – in quite a few spots – but the dealership collected it more or less straight away, and left him a courtesy car, and are now completely repainting it!

"He'd wanted to get a small sample of the damaged paint before it went, but they came so quick and during the day when he was at work that he didn't get the chance to! Anyway, so I, we, thought – and all this was only just a couple of days ago, about spreading the word to friends as well to research it for themselves – and sort of, pool all the info we found out - and then we'd all contact the local politicians with what we all knew.

"But now, if we do, I'll set up, and advise them all as well, to use a different anonymous email from an internet cafe though!

"- A crash on my system and on his so we'd lose all the work files and stuff that's on them – plus everything else! - would be a disaster!

"I meant to tell everyone about all of that this afternoon, but what with everything else that we were doing and what happened when Jake and Dave came back – I forgot! *Sorrrreey!*"

Magda said, "Thank you for telling us all that Sophie. Yes, doing it that way would be good advice from you. I would advise as well, without wanting to sound overly dramatic or paranoid, that if you do start to use internet cafés for email communications – *just for these sorts of things,* do not go to the same one too regularly, and walk there along different routes each time.

"On your way there wear a baseball, or similar type of cap, and not the same one each time! Start a collection! Pull it down low, and hide away your lovely long hair! They are just to counter the facial recognition cameras on your route in – which is called your 'in-filtrate' route.

"In fact spend some time doing 'a recce' – a reconnaissance – of routes with no or only minimal camera coverage first...

"Also – *and now you might think I am really being over-dramatic and paranoid!* - but I have often taped a small stone in a different part of either shoe each time to change my walk, causing just a slight change in the way I balance when I am walking – because a lot of cameras now have 'gait recognition' capability as well as facial recognition...

"Change your outer appearance for every visit by wearing different coloured but not too noticeable clothing each time, Go at different times on different days, preferably when it is busy, do not stay too long in there, always have the right coins to pay with, and try to just blend in unnoticed.

"When you leave, or 'ex-filtrate' the area, have places you previously noted where you can quickly, unobserved, remove your outer garment, a jacket say, and roll it up to carry it unnoticed and remove the stone from your footwear – but do not do that in the toilets of a department store – those places are riddled with cameras! *Well, maybe not the actual toilets, but you know what I mean!* Doing all of that is just sensible and necessary 'trade-craft', it will soon become a habit, and is well worth doing...*for obvious reasons...!*"

"Oh my gosh, I wouldn't've thought of any of that! But you're right! - *I'll feel like I'm in an episode of 'Mission Impossible'!*

Magda laughed. "Or even better – 'Mission *Possible*', Sophie!"

Jake, full of his usual humour, despite the seriousness of the topics, said, "Aye! *But I can see me 'avin problems blendin' in though!* – I'll 'ave to wear dark glasses, a big rubber nose, false beard an' 'ave a limp like Inspector Clueless – Clouseau, did in one o' the Pink Panther films!"

Everyone laughed this time, even more so when Sophie said ingenuously, "Oh? - The rest of it yes, but...*Why would you need - a big - rubber nose...?!*" He studiously ignored that as she giggled silently behind her hands.

Magda then resumed, still chuckling, "May Your Humours Never Desert You! Well, I need to back-track a little to – 'Back-Ups!' - Even back-ups of your computer files would be compromised under such an attack as Melanie described, especially the so called 'Cloud Back-ups' – they just corral and make everything accessible to them 'in one place' – in one go! Which is why they are promoted so much of course.

"The tech' departments' 'super computers' and the new generation of 'quantum computers' of the American N.S.A. - the National Security Agency - *can locate, get through passwords, monitor, access and retrieve any electronic data from anywhere on the planet.* So I would suggest you purchase large memory external hard-drives for back-ups, and only connect them to your computer when you want to use them, and keep them locked away somewhere safe when not in use.

"Advise people where possible by word of mouth, *or even write 'good old fashioned letters'* to them, possibly addressed to P.O. boxes you can rent for anonymity, changing them frequently, *and to definitely not*, initially, use social media – because that is also totally

144

open to constant, discrete monitoring, to find things out about people, which was the major part of the latent agenda of its design and formation of course. It is all done initially by their algorithms that detect certain key words, then once triggered, they focus in on you...and go through everything about you. So, we are back to 'old school trade craft' again - *as all electronic communications are 'unsafe' and are monitored all of the time!*

"Having said all of that though and decried using electronic communications because of their vulnerability to being hacked, I will, however, now give you all a procedure, that 'sort of' uses email, that we often use when we need to securely and rapidly communicate data and information to our human groups we cannot psycomm to...and they do not have access to the 'Dark Web', which requires a greater level of expertise to navigate safely through...This whole procedure is not one hundred percent secure, but used correctly it is not too far off...

"It is this: set up an email service account under a false name, with different user name email addresses, using an internet café's computer, *not your own computer!* - and change the service regularly.

"Write the email with whatever it is you wish to communicate. Ideally not 'in clear', which is normal language, but preferably in a 'book code'. This uses only a book both you and the recipient knows about and has a copy of. The lines of numbers you then write in your email identify the page and letter numbers that make up your message...it takes a little while – obviously you do all that before you write all the numbers down quickly into your email! It is an extremely secure method of encrypting a message.

"In fact without knowing which book has been used, and without knowing how to navigate through it using the numbers you write – you may have to read them backwards and mentally double each number and then subtract the number of the day of the week it was written on for example - from each written number that is read – it is unbreakable.

"Save it in the 'Drafts Folder' – *do not actually send it!* Then telephone – *not from your mobile phone!* - the intended recipient – when they answer, alter your voice and ask something like: *'...is Alfie there?'* This is a one time use only of one of the pre-arranged verbal 'trigger' signals you will have already established between you and the recipient. They then reply with, *'No – you've got the wrong number!'*

"If a pre-arranged reply omits any word or words, for example. *'No – wrong number!',* they are secretly telling you that they have been compromised. In that case access the email and delete it and change to a new provider immediately. Inform all the others in your group, and try and find out what has happened to the recipient...without revealing yourselves.

"A trigger might even be a conversation you have with a trigger word embedded in it towards the end, for example you've had a general chat and towards the end you casually mention that, *'oh, I saw Josephine the other day - et cetera et cetera blah blah...',* 'Josephine' was the trigger word, the signal, for her or him to then go to the email service as soon as possible, access the draft email, read it, and then delete it.

"But perhaps I am getting a little too advanced for you, for now – but do you understand the principles...?"

"Blimey, yeah I do thanks Magda!" Jake replied, "it all gets a bit serious dunnit when you talk about secure communicatin'?! You okay with it all an'all Soph?"

"Mmm, yes, yes I am thanks. I'm just thinking that we'll have to decide on what book we all use now won't we?!"

Mel said, "well, my friend at work has just loaned me a book to read called: 'It Awaits Us' by Ian McHale, she said it was brilliant and well worth reading – how about we use that?

Magda looked up at her quickly and smiled, "yes Melanie, she was quite right! Ian's book is well worth reading, and that book would be a very, very good choice...As it happens I am seeing him, *here,* again next week – *so I will tell him...!"*

"Oh Good! And if you recommend it, well - it must be really good Magda! I've been so busy this week I haven't had chance to start reading it, but I'll start on it as soon as I can now! *Actually, Soph and Jake!* – I'll order some copies from Amazon tomorrow as a *'thank you'* to you both for everything you've both helped me and Dave with this week to move into our caravan, I've been wondering what to try and get for you both, so I think it'd be ideal!"

They expressed their gratitude to Melanie, saying they looked forward to having a good read, and sorting out how to use it as their book code...! Jake, deadpan as usual, muttered something about, *'opin' there wouldn't be too many 'ard sums to work out in his head!'*

Dave asked Magda about the 'Dark Web' she'd mentioned, saying he'd heard about it, but it was all a mystery to him, the others agreed, asking her to please tell them some more about it, and so Magda explained something of its origins and usage, and why it existed.

"Actually, whilst we are on this particular subject, and this is very relevant to everything I've just said, various so called 'terrorist groups' are currently achieving many successes in their orchestrated atrocities – partly because it is *intended* that they do so - and partly because the 'Security Services' say that these terrorists – who are often *their 'proxy agents'* – several steps removed from them so there is no comeback of course - are totally refraining from using electronic email communications.

"So the Security Services then have a plausible deniability claim in the face of *'public outcry'* – which is always whipped up hysterically by their allies in the corporate mainstream media - as they can then claim that they had no prior knowledge of an attack from monitoring the 'Persons Of Interest' emails or mobile telephones!

"And as I've just explained they use the Dark Web anyway and not the 'standard internet' for emailing! *And systems like the book code!*

"This admission, by the Security Agencies, is designed of course, to cause more fear, anxiety and uncertainty for people holidaying on beaches, shopping in malls, or just walking along the city streets.

"Because if the Security Services say they are struggling to electronically or cyber detect the planning of attacks in these normal everyday places that people and their families naturally go to, then the 'problem-reaction-solution' paradigm smoothly kicks in – the imposition and willing acceptance of more overt surveillance, more intrusions into privacy, more suspicion, more division, more social engineering - to accept being willingly compliant to the 'authorities'' demands – *'because it is only for your safety'…*

"That 'public outcry', I mentioned, is part of the classic stratagem called the 'Hegelian Dialect', or more commonly known as: 'problem – reaction – solution', which means: cause the problem - the masses then 'cry out' for something to be done – which is the 'reaction' – then offer the pre-planned all along - 'solution', which invariably then justifies more surveillance, more State powers, and less freedoms for the populace, all being predictable steps on the road to the Totalitarian Fascist State of The New World Order the elites' desire and are relentlessly working towards.

"And of course the outpouring of all the deliberately created negative emotional energies of fear, anxiety, insecurity and suspicion create a veritable banquet for...those...that feed off it…

"Some people shout against those pointing out these increased State powers saying: *'Well if you've nothing to hide – you've nothing to worry about!' - Look at all the terrible things that happen if we don't let them protect us…!'* That argument of: *'well if you've nothing to hide – you've nothing to worry about!'* was created and first used so very effectively by Joseph Goebbels, Hitler's Chief Propagandist...who also stated: *'if you are going to tell a lie, make sure it is a big one! – and keep on telling it – the people will soon believe it...'*

"But when those people who fall for, or are taken in by, this false belief, and they vociferously claim: *'so what's the problem with it? - I've nothing to hide…'*, what they do not ever seem to realise is that they are just as vulnerable – *and perhaps even more so* - to the intended final outcome - *because a well planned offence will just about always defeat an unplanned defence…*

"It is like them standing on a raised patch of sand – an illusory 'moral high ground' patch of sand – and saying: *'We'll be alright, and*

148

quite safe now, because we've obeyed and complied with all of the authorities' instructions - like we were told to, so the dangerous tide won't reach us here, we're safely above it...'

"But that black insidious tide will soon, just as surely, surround and engulf them, and when they finally realise that everything has changed, and they no longer recognise the world around them...it will be far, far too late..

"As the masses are encouraged to become more and more addicted to using their cell phones and emails and all their other addictive devices, it makes the 'SIGINT' – the military and Security Services' term for 'Signals Intelligence' - electronic eavesdropping and surveillance, that much easier of course...

"Just to finish off, and depart for now, this 'train' of conversation – but which has all been very relevant to have a ride together in and visit a few stations that were admittedly *slightly off the route* from what I was originally on and talking about!

"I quite understand your friend, Melanie, being exasperated and saying: *'there is no point contacting the local politicians...'* but imagine if five thousand, ten, twenty thousand or more did, over a few days – imagine that! There is security in numbers! As individually you can be just 'focused on' or 'zeroed in on' and 'picked off' too easily...

"Remember that the hidden and permanent Deep State is the Master of these 'bought and paid for' politicians, who are 'only here today and gone tomorrow', and they do not want their dark secrets brought out into the light of mass awareness...and of mass action, because then they would not be able to so easily contain it...!

"That concept of 'security in numbers', is one of the reasons for the protocols of initial contact with our visitors that I helped to design, and was outlining for you earlier.

"Soooo...moving on...or moving back!...*With my broad brush!* Anders and I talked to you the last time we met, about 'The Manipulative Institutions', particularly the corporate controlled mainstream media. Well, we did not tell you then that during the nineteen fifties to the early seventies, in just North America alone, there were well over eighty separate, independently owned media corporations and organisations – from television stations and radio stations to publishers of thousands of newspapers, to highway billboard sign printers et cetera, et cetera...

"Other countries all had hundreds more of their own independent media organisations as well of course. So globally there were many thousands of different ones! Each one putting out its own independently investigated information to its consumers.

"But...but, but! - For a long time now, over twenty years, most, *over ninety percent - of all the mainstream media in the entire World* has been bought up and is owned by...just...*Six Global Corporations!*

"This all came about under the Presidency of Bill Clinton when he signed the Telecommunications Act of nineteen ninety six, which allowed the giant corporations to monopolise and buy up thousands of media outlets, to increase their control on the flow and content of 'information' – *propaganda* - all around the world...The Act has resulted in having tragic and destructive consequences for all of humanity...for democracy, which was, of course, its intention...

"*' never have so many been held incommunicado by so few'*, said Eduardo Galeano, the Uruguayan journalist, who wrote extensively about freedom, democracy, slavery and dictatorships, in response to this act...

"The six, monopolistic Media Giants now are: Time Warner, Walt Disney, Viacom, Newscorp, CBS, and NBC Universal - and most likely, *actually without any doubt at all,* those six are all owned and controlled by just one board of directors, about twenty or so elite, super-wealthy individuals, controlling and ruling over all of them – and behind that board, controlling and ruling over those Directors – are the parasites...

"So what the monopolistic corporate mainstream media now offers *their Global Consumers* is well orchestrated, tightly controlled and often pre-scripted. The same 'News' messages, or other content, can now be instantly published or broadcast in dozens of countries at the same time, for instant absorption by those populaces. Which dovetails in nicely to the modus operandi I've already mentioned of Josef Goebbels, who said, and I'll say it again: *'If you are going to tell a lie, make it a big one – and keep telling it! – the people will soon believe it...!'*

"Jake – you kindly gave us an excellent rendition earlier of a related quote from someone from the same, 'mould', as Goebbels, but that was from Brzezinski, President Carter's National Security Advisor, and was part of his, and still is, his fellow elites' vision of the 'Technotronic Age', or Future...

"I agree with you as well when you said what you said about *'it now being all too evident'*...because sometimes when I go out and 'mingle and mix' amongst the un-awakened masses, I too don't have to look or listen too hard or go very far, to find proof of it seeming to be coming to pass, as it is, all too often, sadly, all too evident...anyway...one day...soon...that will not be the case...*we hope*...and continue to work to achieve...!

"In the mainstream media the days of the truly independent, free thinking, investigative journalist able to have their work - exposing all the Chains of Illusion, printed or broadcasted – without censorship from an elites' puppet editor - are over.

"Now, they are all - or ninety-nine percent of them - just 'eye candy', and programmed repeaters of the 'information' – the propaganda – and all the frequent lies – and biased, false news it is always riddled with, that the 'News' agencies receive multiple times during the working day – which is twenty four hours - from a centralised source for them to read out, parrot fashion, on the 'News', or print in their papers...And they are very well paid for doing so...

"If they object to just doing that, well, they will soon find themselves out of a job. Or worse...much, much worse – as, for example the killing of the nationally loved, B.B.C. television presenter, Jill Dando, who was days away from revealing to millions, the truth and proof on a mainstream television show about so many of that country's elites' involvement in the evil networks of paedophilia...

"This is the globally homogeneous – which means it consists of parts or elements all of the same kind - mainstream media that most of the masses now watch, hear, read and generally consume. It is where they get their 'information' from – the selective and deliberately packaged biased 'false news' from, so the modern mainstream media has *tremendous control* over what the masses think, perceive and so...what they believe, basically they become 'like putty in their hands'...to fairly easily mould them into whatever 'shape' they want!

"Everything the mainstream consumer sees and hears in that media concerning extra-terrestrial existence and UFO sightings is in tune with an orchestrated narrative developed decades ago for them to be just so programmed and indoctrinated with – *a sceptical narrative of ridicule, disdain, and disbelief.*

"The Hollywood Mind Control Capital and all it's 'propaganda and predictive programming' films are in the forefront of this. Actually, 'holly wood' as a material, is what the most powerful of magicians' wands, particularly those of the Druids, are made from - curious do you not think, that the name is the same...? It certainly waves its powerful magic wand to en-spell and en-trance...millions...In fact Walt Disney, a name synonymous with Hollywood from its earliest days, was making blatant propaganda films before and during the Second World War for the American government.

"Most curiously his house is exactly the same as the 'Kehisteinhaus' or 'Eagle's Nest', a building on one of the peaks of the Hoher Goll, a mountain range that overlooks the nearby town of Berchtesgarden, in the Bavarian Alps. It was used by the elite of the Nazi party, and as Hitler's retreat as well as one of the Fuhrer HQ's.

"There are researchers who claim that some of the filmed footage of the Nazis' leadership there was cleverly fabricated using Disney's own home – which was, is, identical in its construction... Himself and many actors who appeared in those propaganda films achieved much fame and fortune in later years as a reward for their services...

"Actually, again according to researchers, the forty ninth greatest villain in the past one hundred years of films, was called 'Auric

152

Goldfinger', in the nineteen sixty-four James Bond movie 'Goldfinger'. That villain was played by the German actor, Gert Frobe, *who had actually been a member of the Nazi Party.* Some of the footage shown for propaganda purposes ostensibly taken from the 'Eagle's Nest', shows a remarkable likeness of him to Hermann Goering...

"I'm digressing slightly I know, but Disney's propaganda films were found to be so effective he continued to advise and make them for the government after that war, manipulating the perceptions of the general population...Particularly targeting the minds of children – the adults of tomorrow - with the story-lines and visual, subliminal content of cartoons.

"Here in England one of the early Director Generals of your BBC was Sir Hugh Green, previously in the Second World War he had been an army officer extensively involved in 'Psyops' – 'Psychological Operations' - in the Far East.

"'Psyops' is defined in the American Army's Field manual as: *'Any form of communication in support of objectives, designed to influence the opinions, emotions, attitudes, or behaviour of any group in order to benefit the sponsor, either directly or indirectly'.*

"So...manipulating the perceptions of a target population with a controlled media is a vital, well used and extremely effective tool...to use in achieving what their 'sponsors' desire..."

Mel sat forwards, indicating that she wanted to say something again and Magda smiled and nodded at her to do so,

"I know what you mean about the media's attitude – all of us here do now. And what's interesting as well is that, again at work, in the design department at the printers where I am, we've noticed, well, a bit of a change in it about UFO's and all that...

"I wouldn't normally read mainstream papers and magazines - but because the company prints loads of different things – from calendars to magazines, we get lots of the current, popular and relevant publications, and loads of general other mainstream media on subscription, it's just so our design department can be upto speed on trends and changes in popular, current design layouts, fashionable colour scheme co-ordinations *and so on etcetera etcetera!*

"So it's not so much for the content, but y'can't help read some of it as you study layouts and all that. And I've noticed a lot of publications are changing their attitude and doing what seem to be quite sensible articles about extra-terrestrials for their readers – especially some of the on-line newspapers, but not yet so much in their print versions - so that can only be a good thing - can't it…?"

Magda nodded slowly before replying, "Yyyes, and well spotted Melanie, it can be, *it should be* - but I, we, have noticed this too, and we are concerned that it is motivated by something else, that is far removed from being a good thing...Let me explain why...Let's keep looking at films first.

"'All of a sudden', after decades of media ridicule, and of them portraying 'aliens' in films as fictional but *almost always as a dangerous fantasy enemy and threat* – from 'The War Of The Worlds' to 'Alien' to the 'Independence Day' films from Hollywood – and interestingly, or rather, I should say disturbingly, the recent Independence Day film had a lot of subliminal military recruitment propaganda embedded in it.

"Disturbing because prior to, and during the First World War, young men lined up in just about every village, town and city to 'sign up' with the military, most went away with them...and never came back. Most of those who did come back had had their minds shattered by what they had seen...and done...

"That 'mass-lining-up-for-signing-up' would not happen these days, because the structures and mindsets of societies have changed considerably since then. But instead, by using the appeal and influence of exciting films, and evermore 'realistic' video war and combative games, often based on those films, and all targeted at the younger generations of heavily programmed consumers, *they* have been proven to be very effective in increasing military recruitment.

"Very effective as well in many other areas of the consumers' behaviour, not the least being the psychological numbing of compassion and care for others, from a young age, due to intense exposure to the atrociously graphic violence in so many of the video games that 'a young gamer' can 'inflict' on others...

"However...Now other *'backing up the message'* media is showing obvious signs, as you have noticed Melanie, of changing their attitude to sow slightly different seeds in the masses' perception: *that the possibility of aliens existing is actually now a very sensible one!*

"The mainstream corporate media has so much experience and expertise they know that they can absolutely manipulate and programme the mass of the people to perceive and believe whatever their agenda requires them to think and believe.

"So if they manipulate and change the masses' perception to be more likely to accept believing in the *sensible possibility* of them, and then...the next step...of *the reality* of advanced extra terrestrial beings, the masses would then be well and truly primed to believe in a *'false flag alien invasion.'*

"Because then they can be portrayed *as a really existing, very dangerous enemy, posing a very great threat to you!* – Just like the predictive films I have already mentioned – and there are many, many more of that ilk - portray them to be...and all this has already been planted into the fertile, unsuspecting ground of the masses' subconscious...it is called, as I have said, 'Predictive Programming'.

"And after all, the continuance of the existing elites' power structure necessitates the masses believing that they have lots of...*Enemies!*...'to be protected' from!...*And an Alien enemy would be the 'Grand Daddy' of all Enemies!*

"The German scientist Wernher Von Braun, was an ex-Major in the Nazi's Shutzstaffel, the 'S.S.', their foremost agency of security, surveillance and terror. Photographs exist of him wearing that distinctive black uniform in the company of Himmler, Hitler's deputy.

"Von Braun was a leading figure in the development of rocket technology, and of the V One and V Two rockets to deliver high explosives as a long distance weapon for the Nazis, and they devastated parts of London, killing tens of thousands of civilian men, women and children.

"Then, after that war, which Germany lost, but the Nazi's didn't...he worked for the Americans, who welcomed him with open arms, as part of 'Operation Paper Clip', and was, in his later years in the top echelons of NASA, the initials said by some to mean: *'Never A Straight Answer...!'* but is actually their space agency. He also worked in other *unacknowledged* agencies, *and he actually warned of exactly this false flag 'Alien Threat' on his death bed.*

"The American President called Reagan claimed - in a speech he gave to the United Nations: - *'...nothing would unite The World more than a threat of an alien invasion from beyond this planet...!'*

"The craft and the weaponry that would be used in a 'false flag alien invasion' are already being used as Anders has said. False flag 'terrorist' operations have long been 'the stock-in-trade' of the covert 'black ops' – black operations - departments of all Governments' Security and Intelligence, and of corporate businesses' agencies.

"Justification for massively escalating the Vietnam War was started on just such an operation, by falsely claiming attacks on American naval vessels in the Gulf Of Tonkin...to the recent false flag claims of chemical weapons being used by the Syrian government - to justify another invasion and more warfare...plus of course..."

Dave had been nodding at this, and said, "Yes, *sorry – I'm interrupting* - but I think, well, I hope, that anyone with even a slightly open mind is now starting to question the official, mainstream version of events like all of those – the classic of course was the false flag, 'inside job' demolition but so called 'terrorist attack' on the twin towers - and the other buildings - that they used to justify all their sweeping 'security' measures, and then invading so many countries afterwards in their 'War on Terror' – *that they'd planned for all along!*

"In fact I'd call it their *'War on Peace'!* It's just like you said Jake – when you talked about the 'evidence' given by the authorities for Taxi Tony – *'none of it stacks up'!* "

"Absolutely right David." Magda replied. "Using the 'Socratic Principle' I mentioned earlier, another question you could ask, and particularly in relation to the horror of the twin towers event, where

156

they killed over three thousand people, is: 'Qui Bono?' or 'Who Benefits...?'

"So...*why exactly* would they...want to 'stage-craft' a false flag alien invasion? Well, we know that the masses have been, and are continuing to be, drip fed and programmed by the mainstream media to eventually believe in its genuine possibility, so if and when it *apparently* happens it will most certainly not be questioned or doubted by that media.

"The few questioning voices from the masses and the alternative, true and independent media – or at least those parts of it that haven't been heavily infiltrated, will quickly be drowned out by the tidal wave of accepting it to be true from the majority of the programmed masses and the corporate mainstream media. As they will have by then, very effectively created what is called *'manufactured consent'* by the globalist marketing companies.

"And that is assuming, of course, that the independent, questioning voices can still be heard by then, broadcasting on the internet, or by any other means, as the plan also includes the total governmental control and regulation of the internet to prohibit any dissenting voices from being heard.

"Here in England that is already being openly proposed, whilst being secretly, gradually implemented, by your major political party in its manifesto, they are claiming: *'it is merely to protect you by preventing 'hate speech' or 'radicalisation' from spreading'*, the implication is that they are simply concerned about *your feelings* and they want to protect *you*!

"The evil mendacities and hypocrisies from the 'bought and paid for' politicians are always quite breathtaking...!

"...Eventually, if it is allowed to go to the extremes that the elites really want it to, this plan of theirs would make it illegal not to believe, or to *even question* what their mainstream media 'Orwellian News Speak' tells you is true. Those who still persist to disbelieve and question it would be classed as 'mentally unstable' - they must obviously have severe psychological problems.

157

"To add credibility to this *totally specious argument*, in the eyes and ears, hearts and minds, of the masses, as per classic psyops tactics, certain University Social Science departments, specifically selected to back this claim up, have already started to state exactly that in many mainstream publications. *It is pure Sophistry!* – Which is The Dark Art of False and Misleading Argument. And they were selected and attractively commissioned of course to say exactly what was required of them..

"This *'Demonising of Dissent'* tactic has already been proven to be very successful. It resulted in countless numbers of 'dissenters' being locked away in state mental hospitals, or sentenced to years of cruel slave labour in atrociously inhumane camps in the Gulags of Siberia - or they were just simply killed.

"All that happened in communist Soviet Russia, *and not so many decades ago either...*I say *'countless numbers'*, well, that's not quite true now...some of the survivors and researchers of it have since meticulously investigated it and concluded that *sixty million* went in to those horrific places – and when it was all over, *twenty million* did not come out alive...

"It is an all too true warning, what George Santayana, the great philosopher, essayist, poet and novelist said:

'...those who cannot learn from their history are doomed to repeat it...'

"And we can very appropriately follow that by another quote from a great mind, this time from Confucius, who said:

'Study the past – if you would divine the future...'

"So...The corporate media repeaters and talking heads will all continually broadcast and keep repeating their given scripts of exactly what they have all been told to say...as per Goebbel's dictum - the major part of their hyped up reactions to this so called 'alien enemy invasion threat' will jingoistically be the demand, based on the *'obvious necessity'*, for a globally united, centrally controlled, super powerful military force to counter this new, potent enemy from another world.

158

"This united military force will be a 'One World Army' to be coordinated by a 'One World Government' - to be the only effective responses to *fight back...! - Just as President Reagan said decades earlier in his speech to the United Nations.*

"The multi-national corporate military industrial complex will then have a new potent enemy to fight, justifying their future rapid expansion, with the programmed masses cheering them on.

"*'Look! Told you! We were right all along! Aren't you glad you didn't listen to all those disbelieving, dissenting, obviously psychologically deranged voices!'* they would claim.

"They would also make billions upon billions in profits of course, and once most of the staged conflicts were over, the remaining humans on the planet would end up, from then on, being ruled over by a One World Order Of Corporate, Militaristic, Fascist And Totalitarian Government Of Elites, in a world divided up into, as far as we know at present, ten administrative regions – as named countries as a concept would no longer exist in their *'New World Order'*...

"The planning and predictive programming of this aspect of their latent agenda is already well underway – here in Europe you are no longer a citizen of England or Italy or France – but a citizen of the 'European Economic Community', and those with eyes to see who can join the dots, can see the bigger picture and understand why the peoples' concept of National Identity in all these countries, and in many other countries around the world, that are all being grouped into 'Economic Communities', is being constantly undermined...

"I said *'the remaining humans'*, because this false flag alien invasion is the parasites' - *who are directing these events from the deep shadows beyond the pinnacle of the elites' control pyramid -* opportunity to gorge on and store up all the terrible energies released from the killing of billions of people, in a relatively short space of time.

"Most of the now awakening humanity, would be gone...along with those whom were yet to awaken but whom soon would have done...Their intention is to reduce the global population to a much

159

more controllable and manageable - *for them and for their ruling elite puppets* - four to five hundred million, or even less, from around eight billion! – From Eight Million Million!

"Population reduction on this scale has always been one of the vital, major components of their New World Order Totalitarian Agenda...*in fact it is literally 'written in stone'* – in eight modern languages and four ancient languages – including a form of ancient Sanskrit - on the huge granite 'Georgia Guide Stones' which were unveiled on land near Elberton, Georgia, a town in the South East of America, in nineteen eighty...and recently it was revealed that the site is constantly maintained and secured by a department of the American government...or more accurately, of the Deep State.

"Which is absolutely, breathtakingly incredible when you think that on any of the social media platforms if you now post anything the elites' artificial intelligence operated algorithms construe as being *hurtful, disrespectful, racist, sexist, promoting hate et cetera et cetera* – those posts will be quickly removed! - Yet here is a huge, stone monument put up, secured and maintained by the Deep State Elites openly stating the *desirability of killing over seven million-million men, women and children*...and then *maintaining* a global population of no more than five hundred million! *It is utterly, utterly sickening...!*"

Dave sighed, slumping back into the sofa, then saying, *"it's all just so way beyond what most people could get their heads round isn't it?* I had actually heard about them, but only recently, and 'by accident', and it certainly wasn't from any mainstream source.

But...*what or who is this 'Deep State' exactly Magda?* Is it just a group of some of the long serving, career and top ranking politicians?" Dave asked her.

"Good question David, I should really have explained exactly what it is for you all before. Yes, it certainly does include some of those lifelong career politicos, but it's ranks are comprised of much, much more than just them.

"In fact in the true balances of the real powers at work in the world they are pretty much insignificant. Basically, *they* just say, do and act out the wishes of whichever hidden hand is pulling their strings at the time wants them to...and they comply from either their own already corrupted volition for reward, or they are eventually forced or blackmailed into doing so, after having been set up in some scandalous manner. The Intelligence and Security Agencies are past masters at arranging such incidents...

"Many of them do really embark, at least initially, upon a political career to change 'the system' – unfortunately the system usually ends up changing them – or destroying them...

"The reason they and the whole pantomime they play in are stage managed to be so prominent in the public's perception of their performing, is that they give the public the feeling that they have some say, by 'voting', in what is 'going on'. Nothing could be further from the truth of course, it is all: 'Just An Illusion', to quote that song by a group called 'Imagination' that I rather liked in the nineteen eighties...! So it keeps them relatively docile...compared to an outright, anarchic, and mass rebellion from them..

"Those elected politicians from their political parties the public sees are really just the *'here-today-and-gone-tomorrow'* 'bought-and-paid-for' transitory figureheads, then another lot rise up, *and basically continue the same agenda as before...*

"...But...the 'Deep State' conglomerate is always the real and *permanent power-base...*

"...and anyway, ultimately it is the elites' Deep State that selects, nurtures, orchestrates and dictates who gets to high public and political office, and once there, tells them what policies they must pursue. The Kennedy brothers are a classic example of what happens...if they do not...

"For example, in America you would think that the President is the most powerful political individual and office in the country, not so - *there are thirty five levels of security clearances above the President!* culminating in 'Cosmic Top Secret', which only the crème de la crème of the hidden elites have clearance for...

161

"Curiously they call it 'Cosmic', indicating something 'out-of-this-world'...why not 'Tree Top' or 'Mountain Top' Secret? Which would imply something more terrestrially bound...is it because those elites who really know, know that their ultimate 'Top Secret' is something beyond the confines of this Earth...?!

"*Oh dear!* You may all think I have rather a skewed opinion about politicians - and 'their' political system! Well...after centuries of being involved with them, and the systems they operate in, I regret to say that in all of that time, for ninety-plus-percent of them, what I said was, and will be, sadly, an appropriate epitaph...

"So...having dealt with the politicos – *in a nice, calm and objective manner...as you all will have noted...*", she said with her tongue literally in her cheek and a wry smile, which made everybody laugh, Magda composed herself to explain and fully answer David's question.

"The Deep State is really made up of those elites at 'the very tops of the poles' - and also in high positions up them - in the permanent manipulative institutions of Banking and Finance, the Crown in England and other countries with a Monarchy, the Legal and Judiciary Systems, the State Bureaucracies, the 'Education' Systems, the Health Systems, the Militaries, all the alphabet soup Security and Intelligence organisations, the predominant Religious groups, the Mainstream Media, Industry and the multi-national Big Business Global Corporations.

"But at the *very, very tops* of all 'the poles', where all the joint geo-politic and socio-economic policy decisions are made, having been first instigated by, or approved by, the parasites - and are then quickly disseminated through the ranks of the secret societies – and then into all the relevant, controlling bureaucracies, *are the ultra secretive and the ultimate elite*: 'The Illuminati', 'the enlightened ones'...but 'enlightened' by Lucifer, their deity.

"The world's power elite of the elites, The Illuminati, who are at the *very, very tops of all those poles of the Deep State institutions;* usually around eighty of the most powerful individuals in them, have been

162

meeting *all together*, once a year, for over half a century. They are summoned to the very private meetings to attend by invite only. No agenda or any topics discussed are ever made public by them, and certainly no journalists are allowed! – *they own the global media anyway!*

"Collectively they are called: *'The Bilderberg Group.'* Which is now, effectively, a Shadow World Government. Their Grand Design is to soon come out of the shadows and implement an overt, 'One World Government, run by a One World Company'.

"They want it to have a single global marketplace, policed by a one world army, a cashless, one electronic currency society financially regulated by a One World Mega Bank.

"The One World Mega Bank is coming ever closer, because there are now only three countries left without a Rothschild's controlled central bank – apart from Russia, where President Putin threw them out.....Those countries are Iran, North Korea and Cuba. *Libya is now off the list*...does it all start to make sense now...?

"The remaining populations will all be micro-chipped, and live in huge, heavily monitored, 'Smart Cities', saturated in the Five G radiation.

"Just to point out for you all some of the stepping stones this particular group of the top elites have worked on ceaselessly for decades to put in place, *and continue to do so* – although their actual agenda goes back centuries...to achieve this Grand Design of theirs, are:

"...the centralized control of the world's populations by 'mind control' – in other words, by controlling public opinion. Oh - you remember I told you that nearly ninety percent of media organisations are now owned by just six global companies? - well, *one hundred percent* of any print or electronic media product in the English speaking world is now owned by a Bilderberger...

"They organise all the crises and perpetual wars. They are achieving the absolute control of education, purely - although there is nothing 'pure' about it - to program the public's minds, with only the *'officially accepted'* perceptions and therefore only the *'officially acceptable' beliefs.*

"They want no 'middle class' – just their elites and then the serfs or slaves; with a global welfare system where the obedient slaves will only be pitifully 'rewarded' and the non-conformists, and *'the useless eaters'* to quote the husband of the current Queen of England, will be targeted for extermination. Which would be easily done - when everyone is micro-chipped...

"You will have heard of The 'Universal Credit' system of welfare benefits in England, which is being implemented by a vast bureaucracy there first. It is part of this agenda.

"A callous spin-off, a 'two-fold benefit' of this Universal Credit system - *for the elites* - who control the various regional councils in England where it has been implemented – is, the 'first fold': the rapid escalation of the already thousands of suicides as a result of the destitution, despair and homelessness this Universal Credit bureaucratic system is inflicting on the most vulnerable people in the lower levels of society.

"Many of those people have *severe* physical and mental health problems, *all legitimately proven by their own Doctors,* and previously they automatically received welfare payments and were excused from looking for work. But now they are having their health capability for work 're-assessed' - by the Universal Credit system's own contracted underlings, who are not Doctors – or have anything like approaching their qualifications or expertise – and then, after such an *'assessment' - surprise, surprise!* - they are now 're-classified' as: *being fit for work!*

"So then, if those claimants with degraded health issues – *or indeed any other claimant* - in those levels of society, *cannot prove and show evidence* – that they are actively looking for work – in jobs that are basically non-existent, and upto fifty miles away from where they live...mainly by daily filling in an on-line 'Journal', and doing so upto thirty-five hours a week, they are 'Sanctioned'.

"They can also be Sanctioned for any number of other petty, minor misdemeanour's, including having *'the wrong attitude...'* To be 'Sanctioned' means that their money – much reduced anyway from the previous benefit system's payment scales, and which is now paid electronically, and monthly, not weekly or fortnightly, which many find difficult to manage, *is stopped...*for upto, potentially, *three years...! So how do they then pay their rent, or buy food for themselves and their families...?*

"The 'second-fold' benefit *for the elites* is that they are now setting up their own, local, Funeral Director Services to profit from the increasing suicides and all the related deaths - *which will only increase* when the whole country is under the Universal Credit system...*and that is just sheer, unadulterated, sickening psychopathy."*

"Aye...y'dead right Magda" Jake sighed heavily, *"...more than a few mates o'mine are really sufferin' from now bein' on that Universal Credit system.*

"One of 'em was tellin' me all about some o' the tedious an' petty controls they enforce an' put on y', just the other day. *Huh!* He told me he'd 'ad to 'old 'imself back from goin' over an' slappin' this middle aged bloke in a shirt an' tie behind a desk – despite there bein' all the uniformed security guards that were all 'overin' all over the place...!

"This official bloke were on the phone to someone 'avin' to set up an' to register on it, in their offices in Scarborough, when me mate were waitin' for his weekly grillin' - *appointment* – it's more like an interrogation session tho' he said. He'd bin there just before he'd cum round to mine to have a brew wi' me after it - *an' unwind a bit!*

"He told me this 'robot-like-official-bloke' in't Job Centre office on the phone, were goin' on about: *'the great thing about Universal Credit is...'* and: *'it's really much better than the old benefits because it's to help you...'* He were goin' on an' on, an' on...like that.

"Me mate said it were just unreal as he listened an' looked at this bloke, a grown man, *bein' all obviously - to anyone with eyes to see – obviously so falsely enthusiastic* an' spoutin' out all the long, pre-programmed an' well scripted bollox – oh – *'scuse me!* - to some poor sod on't phone, *an' he just couldn't believe what he were 'earin'!*

165

"*Huh!* me mate said: *'blokes - people – men an' women - like that one – an' place were full of 'em, all sat be'ind desks, grillin' an' interrogatin' claimants, like he'd bin summoned to be – an' if he 'adn't gone he'd abin 'Sanctioned' – they'd've stopped what little money he eventually gets – so how do you buy food to eat then?! Or they were just starin' into computer screens checkin' up on claimants.*

"He said that all of 'em were: *'...just the types that'd be just as easily be programmed one day to be sayin', with a big enthusiastic smile, 'well, the great thing about the new gas chambers is...an' they're really the best for you because...!'*" He then shook his head angrily.

"Yes Jake...sadly...that is all too true, *they would most likely be...*And sadly, well, some people *are* so easily, even willingly, programmed to behave like that…" Magda's sigh then echoed Jake's earlier one.

"*But when they are confronted about it though...*they invariably, and immediately use what is called the: *'Nuremberg Defence'*, which came to be called that after the trials at the end of the second world war, when so many concentration camp guards and callous bureaucratic officials said; *'...it's not my fault! Don't blame me! I was just doing what I was told to do! I was just following my orders – just doing my job...'*, in relation to the gas chambers, and all the other, obscene and inhuman atrocities they facilitated..."

Sophie jumped in then, saying, "I went to a conference of Letting Agents and Landlords at the Spa in Scarborough last year, for the first time, I hadn't been to it before. I was representing the Company I work for, because the boss was on holiday.

"A senior politician and her crew of assistants from Westminster were there on stage to explain about Universal Credit to us. She was doing a tour round the North East regions where Universal Credit had been inflicted – but she called it: *'being rolled out'*, a few months previously.

"Towards the end of the morning I was getting so wound up – and you could tell just about everybody else there was as well! at what she was – like your mate said that official bloke in the Job Centre was Jake – *what she was so falsely and enthusiastically* spouting on and on about, that I stood up and informed her that between the Estate Agent and Letting Company I work for, and another two in town, over forty families had been evicted so far since Universal Credit had been recently imposed - due to their rent payments being delayed for months!

"*We'd never known anything like it!* And most of those evicted ex-tenants had ended up being homeless on the streets! And nearly three quarters of that number again were over two months in arrears, and after three months of rent arrears eviction proceedings are started!

"*And we knew all that because we had got together and compared notes earlier in the coffee break!* - they were all in arrears because of months and months of delays in payments under this new, 'all on-line Universal Credit system' - and the payments - *when they eventually got them! - were not enough to cover the rents anyway!*

"Then a large group of private landlords sitting near to me joined in, all saying more or less the same thing – that they'd had to evict dozens of tenants between them as well, for the same reasons – *and in future they would all be refusing tenancies to 'Universal Credit' applicants!*

"But the politician, *she just literally shrugged her shoulders at all those true facts and responses from everyone!* She obviously didn't give a toss! Just muttered something like, '*it was very unusual!*'

"Then a chap in the front row of the audience piped up loudly and asked her - *I can't remember every word of what he said but it was along the lines of*: 'if what she'd just heard then from this group of professionals here today, '*was very unusual*'; so obviously she must be confident in saying that - because she, and, or, her Department, must've compared Scarborough to other towns and cities – and so, therefore, for her to say that, her department must have detailed statistics – now that everything was 'on-line' - of the numbers of people being made homeless throughout the country where Universal Credit had been implemented because of her departments policies...?!

"But she got all shifty and really defensive then at that, and she basically waffled and skilfully ignored it, and just carried on to talking about some other, irrelevant bureaucratic stuff about, *'key roles in community partnership initiatives'* instead...! - Which can all be best described by the *'B...'* word you used Jake!

"What's wrong with these people...?!" She flapped her hands in the air in frustration, *"oh – that's a rhetorical question everyone! We all know what! You've explained it all - and all about politicians very well already Magda...!"*

"Well, thank you for saying I have Sophie. I am sorrowed though to have heard about your and Jake's experiences - *and all those poor people about whom they were really about.* It is important though to talk about such 'real life examples' of 'the system' as you have experienced them in your local lives and keep on informing others about them. They are easier for people to relate to as they are local and even personally relevant.

"It helps to make other people aware, and hopefully encourages other people then to constantly ask questions, and not just blindly, meekly, comply. Which is what the bureaucratic apparatchiks want them to do of course. It is a crucial part of everything you can all do to oppose: *'the system'...!*

"There was an excellent film made by Ken Loach, in twenty sixteen, called 'I, Daniel Blake', which really shows the distress and hardship inflicted on one person – but also by implication, on many hundreds of thousands of others as well, by this uncaring bureaucratic system.

"This particular system, and the many others, is part of the 'Iron Cage Of Bureaucracy' that Max Weber, the philosopher, and one of the three founders of Sociology, mid-way in the nineteenth century warned about.

"He described it as being a trend in society to move towards a form of bureaucratic, 'official' control. Weber wrote that the 'Iron Cage' traps individuals in a totally unfeeling system based on *'rational'* calculation - *and we all know what lies at the end of the road of*

'Rationality'...it is the silence of the mass grave...

"...and where large amounts of power is managed by just a small number of people. Those who control these bureaucratic organizations control the quality of peoples lives. Their desire is ever towards a technically ordered, highly controlled, rationally rigid, *and dehumanized society.*

"All the Iron Cages' Of Bureaucracy thus trap individuals in systems based purely on efficiency, rational calculation, the individual's productive and consumptive capacities, and they have overwhelming control of those whom they are administering.

"Weber also described all of this as:

'...the polar night of icy darkness'.

"Because the 'iron cage' of bureaucracy is *the one set of rules and laws that all are subjected to and all must adhere to*, which keeps you locked in that iron cage, *and so it drastically limits individual human freedom and potential.*

"It is the modus operandi, the way of the manipulative institution, *where you do not have any choices anymore.*

"It is like some huge, uncaring, psychopathic machine you seem to be being powerlessly pulled into - without any alternative options...

"...a huge, uncaring machine that its basic concept, design and creation were all done by...psychopaths...and it, *all of them*, are willingly operated by well-programmed, mind-controlled, compliant worker-drones...

"All the psychopathic elites' bureaucracies - all their uncaring machines - will become more and more dominating over time - *unless – unless* - they are resisted - and stopped...then finally switched off, *dismantled, and permanently disposed of...!*

"Well...! *That is what you are all a part of doing now!"*

Loud whoop-whoop agreements, air punching and clapping from Jake, Sophie, Mel and Dave followed that statement for a minute!

"Talking about the elites' bureaucracies we are back to the Bilderbergers...! And thank you both again for sharing your

169

experiences....

"I could go on and list seven or eight more stepping stones of their Machiavellian Totalitarian designs, but I think you are all getting the picture by now!

"One final comment about the Bilderbergers for now though that is particularly relevant to everything we have been talking about – particularly yesterday, is what Henry Kissinger, a Bilderberger, and an American diplomat, but who is really one of those manipulative architects of geopolitics from the same mould as Brzezinski, whom both Anders and I have told you about - and Jake quoted for us so eloquently!

"He said at the nineteen ninety two meeting, and it was very similar to what President Reagan said to the United Nations, five years earlier, about an 'Alien Threat' from beyond this world...Kissinger said:

'Today, Americans would be outraged if UN troops entered Los Angeles to restore order; tomorrow, they will be grateful. This is especially true if they were told there was an outside threat from beyond, whether real or promulgated, that threatened our very existence. It is then that all people of the world will plead with world leaders to deliver them from this evil....individual rights will be willingly relinquished for the guarantee of their well-being granted to them by their world government.'

"He could not have made their plans any clearer I think...

"I briefly mentioned the 'secret societies' just before – well various inter-connecting orders of secret societies have seeped into those top and higher levels, of the Deep State manipulative institutions, and they are riddled with them; and not just at the top levels, because from around the lower management levels upwards, any future significant promotion usually depends upon being accepted into their ranks, so they start to permeate from there, because *just one of their main functions* is to be a rapid communications network amongst the members, whose primary loyalty is to the 'secret society' they are indoctrinated into.

"To eventually succeed in climbing up those greasy poles to the

170

very tops of those manipulative institutions; as well as being a member of one of the secret societies – often the Freemasons, *you must also have psychopathy as your dominant, default, mindset,* it is an essential, mandatory requirement, because without it, you may be promoted some way up them, *but you will never get to, and be accepted by those...at the very top.....*

"...To get to the very top you have to be obsessed with, and proven your skills at, manipulating others purely to achieve your own, or your coterie's, self-serving ends, and *whatever means* you used to do that, you must always have considered them to have been totally justified in achieving those ends.

"You will have no conscience, care, compassion or concern, no empathy, for any others, however injuriously they are affected by the deployment of those means you used...they are the hallmarks of the true born psychopath destined for a top elite role - *and they are*...abominations and an aberrant, utterly vile, sub-human species...

"Anders and I have talked at length about all the 'Manipulative Institutions' before, well, think of them as the individual branches, and the 'Deep State' as the huge, overall, deeply rooted tree all those branches connect into...

"Oh dear me! *I must apologise at once to all the trees for using them in such a horrible comparison! - My Druidic friends would be horrified!*

"In summation then, the Deep State, 'shadow government' - and the one word of *government* comes from the two Greek words meaning: *'to rule',* and *'the mind'* - is a nebulous, but very real structure of all the permanently powerful vested interest groups that wish to maintain the status quo, or slant it purely for their own benefits and agendas. It is the base distillate of the Luciferian Dualistic Consciousness manifested...which is: *I, We...Win – so You Lose...!*

"Does all that help to explain something of what the Deep State is David – everyone...?"

"Wowww! Crikey! Yes, yes it certainly does! And some...! Thank you Magda."

171

The others all vigorously inputted their own, some lengthy, comments and agreements with Dave's.

"So...going back to what I was saying earlier...about population reduction...as a key element of the New World Order. All of that has to be done 'relatively quickly', because the parasites are running out of time as the galactic energies now flowing in and helping humanity's global awakening are gaining in strength, and causing an acceleration in the rise of human consciousness.

"It is the raising of consciousness, and therefore of awareness and perception, and then *the understanding of it all* – which *are the only things that can prevent this nightmare scenario from happening. And of course - to finally rid humanity, and this planet Earth, of the parasites...and all their minions!*

"The parasites have not been 'taken by surprise' at all by these positive events. They knew they were coming, and they already had their long planned responses in operation - created for them by, and activated through, their elite, psychopathic, human minions. Oh, and by 'long planned', *I mean as in many, many decades – running into centuries long* - to counter these positive events for humanity.

"They are going to be deploying the Five G radiation as well of course to support their agenda, but its effects are more medium to longer term. Although *'longer term'* with that means just a few decades...two to four generations...

"In fact it is likely they were, arrogantly, not *too desperately* concerned – after all they have successfully countered them before many times, and have been secure in their position here for thousands of years. So it was initially more of an 'amber alert' rather than a 'red alert' - as there have actually been *six other occasions* in the long past when this cycle and event potential occurred, but humanity and the Resistance was 'beaten back' every time by them during each of those occasions.

"We all do think though, that now, in this seventh cycle of events, that *the speed, power and intensity* of the rising up of human consciousness, awareness and understanding, coupled this time with

172

the Earth's synchrony to it, *has been a surprise to them,* because it has definitely caused their plans for a New World Order to be thwarted so far.

"They had planned for, and really did expect it to be already well established by now. To 'blow our trumpets' - we have had many successful involvements, *and many are ongoing,* to prevent those plans from coming to fruition. So everything I'm telling you is certainly not all: 'doom and gloom'! Not by any means!

"Their New World Order should have been in place for a long time, *many years,* by now...Hence the increasingly drastic events unfolding now, and in recent years, and decades, to counter the Resistance.

"All the poisoning of water, food, the environment, all the manufactured diseases, all the warfare, the global corporatising of the mainstream media and the other Manipulative Institutions, and all the rest of the malevolent methods they have been using, that we have both talked to you about previously, are constantly pushing their agenda along of course, *but not quickly enough for them now...*Because the Human Resistance is gaining ground...

"Many of the super-wealthy elites who are 'fully in the know' about the parasites' agenda – *because they have been at the forefront of implementing it* - already have fully operational, secure, well stocked, underground - some are partially above ground – but those are mainly in New Zealand, very comfortable accommodations, 'in-out-of-the-way' places, all over the world to escape to.

"Just like some secret elements of the world's militaries have with their 'D.U.M.B.s' – 'deep underground military bases', and some of those are the size of cities. Nearly twenty five years ago now, there were one hundred and thirty one active ones in America, and fourteen hundred and seventy seven world wide. With the technology they have now they are able to construct two in just over a year...the tunnelling rate is now around seven miles a day.

"They are well away from the denser population centres, to avoid the surface conflagrations for a few months, or even years, and on average are one to three miles underground.

173

"A significant amount of the 'missing two point three trillions of dollars' - that Donald Rumsfeld, the Secretary of Defence under President George Bush mentioned just before the Twin Towers attack, which they both played their parts in planning, and then as the reason and justification to implement all their pre-planned actions afterwards - had mostly been used to finance all these 'black budget project' underground installations and the projects they ran in them...

"Interestingly, if that is the right word, in twenty thirteen, just twelve years later, Elizabeth Coleman, an Inspector of The Federal Reserve, admitted that there was then *nine trillion dollars unaccounted for...*!

"In fact many elites have already moved to them, or at least to the immediate areas where they are sited, for rapid access into them. Or they are now predominantly in locations where they can quickly access them using the thousands of miles of secret tunnel systems they have created under and across the planet.

"Some of them have been too late to do so – and are currently residing in Guantanamo Bay and other prison camps, as the covert, surface world's Alliance forces have acted swiftly as the sealed indictments against them have been opened and acted upon.

"Some did not have that option of enforced confinement, and were quietly executed, having been found guilty of heinous and treasonous crimes by the Alliance's official military tribunals, including, recently, a prominent ex-senator - and an ex-President...

"The tunnels vary between forty to sixty feet wide, and were made using nuclear tunnel-boring technology which burrows through deep rock heating it to a magma - a molten state, so there is no 'spoil' or excavated waste to dispose of. The result is a tube with a smooth, vitrified, glazed lining. These NTBM's or Nuclear Tunnel Boring Machines, have been in use since the nineteen fifties, and we think it was the Rand Corporation that first constructed them, they certainly had photographs of them back in 'fifty nine. Patents, hidden up until now, were registered for them around that time.

The tunnels are linked to vast subterranean areas with the super high speed, single rail, advanced 'Magnito Leviton' - magnetic levitation - technology driven trains, with speeds of upto Mach 2, which is just over fifteen hundred miles an hour..."

"*Oh My God....!*" This time Sophie gasped, her face pale, stunned by all this, her comment echoed and added to in just as shocked and stunned voices from each of the others.

Jake was dismayed, stunned and just as shocked at this deluge of information Magda was giving them. He, just as they all did now, realised exactly why Anders had said earlier, '*we might seem to be being over dramatic*', before he had started to explain things further.

Jake, before today, much more than most, had realised, ever since what had happened on that tragic day to Taxi Tony, and all the sighting experiences prior to that, with the Spotters' Club, just how serious, and just how real all these things were.

But now he was realising, and starting *to understand* as well just *how colossally huge and inter-connected* all of this was.

A big part of his dismay stemmed from the fact that it had been going on for such a long time, all around them - *but incredibly*, the sheer scale of it all was unknown about to most folk.

Because it had all been so well hidden, and was all just too big, too gargantuan, too outlandish for them to get their heads around – perhaps even if – *when* – it was all eventually revealed to them - especially if the next episode of their favourite TV Gameshow, football team or Soap programme was due on to entertain and distract them...

The wicked endgame planning of it all was just something everyday-folk were totally ignorant of. In fact, he thought, it's like a dark, hidden, parallel world that would not just drag them all down if the worst came to pass, but it'd take over, and literally eradicate the one they lived on now – and most of the folk on it!

Huh! They'd all certainly had a full delivery – *and then some* - of all those 'major missing parts' – and 'what they'd do when assembled and switched on', since he'd asked Magda and Anders...!

175

"Sooo then...Fu...ooops! - Er - Crikey Me! - Sorry! - Ladies Present! – I nearly came out then wi' a bit o' choice Anglo-Saxon instead!

"So...you've been 'diplomatically dealin'' with all these extra-terrestrials Magda...an' the fact that Dave, an' others all over the world, have had actual contact with 'em, as a result o' that, means, obviously means, that *they* are aware of all you've just said, and what Ander's said, an' prob'ly a lot, lot more, an' in more detail an' all... An' they said they want to have more contact, so some'ow, mebbe, with more contact, an' even proof of it...if they'd let us, to make folk aware an' *understand,* 'owever we could do that, an' then get it further out into the World, is that what we could do? - Before those ways we could do that all get shut down, so I say again – *"owever we could do that'* – to help make people understand.

"I think it's 'avin' to somehow convince more an' more folk that, yes, they should be taken serious – because look - 'ere's the undeniable proof that we've got! An' then further down the line it'd help folk to understand the mainstream media's plan to reveal that they do exist...an' why - for all the reasons you've explained.

"I'm just thinkin' off the top o' me head Magda, that's all - just wanting to do summat!" He flapped his hands up and slapped them down onto his knees, shrugging his shoulders, in obvious frustration. Everyone thought he had finished talking but he then leaned forward and continued.

"We'd be in a position to then say: *'Yeah They Do Exist! – But they're Not Hostile To Us! Well, at least not the ones you've bin workin' with Magda* - an' they've already proved it! An' even if they were – Crikey Me! - Just Think About It! – With the technology they've obviously got if they were hostile to us we'd've all been 'wiped out' a long time ago! - They'd've just come in an' 'Boom - Flash!' Game over!

"...especially as 'we've' been provokin' 'em by shootin' 'em down for decades…! So obviously conflict and warfare - industrial scale killin' - what some humans seem to be easily made to do - just ain't part o'

their make up, *because they've developed way, way beyond all o' that...?'"* He raised his hands in a questioning and frustrated gesture again.

*"Ohhh I dunno, I s'pose I might be soundin' a bit naive like. After all, they – the Deep State elites, killed a friend o' mine who tried to do just a bit o' that as y'know...*I'm just thinkin' out loud, y'know, tryin' to, to think how to put things together an' throw a spanner – or summat much bigger! In their works!"

"Of course you want to do something Jake, and all of what you have just said was a commendable response, that emanated from your positive thinking. So well done, and well said. You are already thinking of countermeasures and strategies you could attempt to create.

"However...I have to say and try to assure you...*and this is some more of The Good News!* - that all those lines of strategies you just mentioned are well underway *now*, by many, many others, all across the Earth, who have had contact – and *much more* as well – and they have access now to extensive resources and methods to implement and achieve them.

"Soon an unstoppable avalanche of undeniable, and unredactable – it cannot be stopped, blocked or erased - media in all forms of data will go viral globally...so watch this space...! But in the meantime - I am not saying do not participate in helping others *to understand*, I am not saying that at all. Please do so, whenever you can. At a 'grass roots level' every person you help to become aware and who starts to share in this understanding is a great achievement."

Magda then steepled her hands under her chin, and looked up for a few moments, almost appearing to be in the classic pose of prayer, before dropping them back into her lap. She smiled at Jake and said,

"There is however, *something that you can do*, and be part of Jake which will be more than akin to opening and releasing the contents of 'Pandora's Box' as Ander's described it earlier.

"It is something *all of you* can participate in, but I would prefer to go into what that is at our next meeting tomorrow.

177

"For now, all I will say is that it is going to be the major component of the second wave of the globally viral data to be unleashed. I want to give you some further background information and context to it, today, which will be essential for you to have, and to understand, before we talk about it in much more depth tomorrow."

He nodded, "Okaaay, thanks Magda. I'm relieved and glad to 'ear that *summat like* I was sayin' is underway…!" He then grinned at her sheepishly, and self-deprecatingly, *"o'course y're all bound to be streets ahead o'whatever I could cum up thinkin' of!* – an' it's on a mega-scale an'all from what you've just said! An' it's good to know there's summat important that I, we – all of us can do an'all. *'Else I don't suppose we'd all be sat 'ere right now…!"* He said with another grin.

Magda grinned back at him, then at all of them, and said, very quietly, and very intensely, "Oh Yes...*there most certainly is..."* She then sat back, looking much more relaxed.

"Yes Jake, you were quite right when you said before, *'they must've developed way beyond all of that'...*'That' being the 'Industrial Scale killing' you referred to, but there is much, much more they have: *'developed way beyond'.*

"So...various scientists over the years have worked on categorising planetary civilizations. For example a planet inhabited by what is called a 'Level One' Civilisation knows how to use the naturally occurring energy of the planet for the benefit of all of its inhabitants. It has no warfare or murderous conflicts, and the level of consciousness of each of its inhabitants is much higher than humans is at present – but human consciousness is currently going through the 're-birth' pangs to evolve up to that.

"There are many other Levels, some extra-terrestrial and inter-dimensional civilizations will be at Levels Thirty or more! But do not worry - I will not be going into a lengthy explanation of them all now! Other than to say that here *on* the Earth, the Level is...Zero...

"Part of the ranking system of planetary civilizations is based upon the energy systems used by those civilizations. When the inhabitants *on* Earth move to and globally embrace the usage of free energy systems for and by everyone, which can only come about by a rise in consciousness, awareness and understanding, to annul the negativity dominance of the parasites, will those birth pangs be over and Earth's surface bound humanity be re-born, into a Level One civilization, and ascend onto an Earthly existence in the fifth dimension.

"It is the most potentially dangerous transition period for a planet to go through though, from Zero to One, as those negative elites controlled by the parasites will desperately want to hold onto their power structures – all those Deep State vested interests...And they have the capability and sheer evilness to cause horrific destruction first, before this Renaissance happens...It has happened here before, and it has happened on many other planets as well...

"There are, you will all be relieved to know, like you said Melanie, *many millions of others* like you all over the planet now, connecting consciousnesses and their numbers are growing daily.

"*People* whose consciousness, awareness, perception and understanding, are all rapidly rising...

"*People* who are transforming mere left brain intellectual and limited academic *'so called knowledge'* into clearer realisations *of much deeper, profound understandings and wisdom...*

"*People* who are attaining the higher states of enlightened *fully functioning, unshackled minds* to dispel the corrosive, destructive, deliberately manipulated and programmed virus like habits of greed, ignorance and hatred which create all the negative energies for the parasites...

"*People* who have great compassion and empathy for all living, sentient beings...

"*People* who are throwing off all the chains of illusion and limitation put upon them by the parasites and their minions...

"*People* who are re-becoming what you, even as a young species, all once were...

"*...People who radiate positivity and fully consciously exist within*

179

the reality of those infinitely more powerful positive energies of Light and of Love..."

Magda then had to pause, the emotion and the energy she had put into her latterly spoken words had made her voice strain, and her eyes to fill with unshed tears. She put her head back, blinking rapidly. There were no unshed tears though from Sophie and Mel, their eyes were streaming.

Their men, just as emotionally impacted held them close. Jake looked over to Dave, who was looking just as pale and wide eyed as he was, but also looking just as determined...

"I'm sorry everyone..." Magda said quietly, *"sorry - not for expressing my emotions,* but for having had to put all of this in front of you, *all at once.* I, we, do not do 'fear-mongering', or 'doom and gloom' promotions. But you asked...and you needed to know the context, the broader, panoramic background, to all this, and the future probabilities, consequences and possible outcomes of it. *To Understand.* But Always, Always Remember, Always Know:

'The Future is Not Written, it is Yours To Make...' "

Wiping tears off her cheeks, Mel jumped in again with a bursting intensity of emotion, *"Yes! Yes it is!* That's so like, well, it means the same anyway, as what John Connor's warrior Mum, Sarah, said in the film: 'Terminator Two', she said: *'The Future's not set – there's no fate but what we make...'*

"And please don't be sorry Magda, *we asked - we needed to have the knowledge! – and we needed to really understand it all!*

"Speaking for myself I'm very glad you did, it just makes me all the more determined to do whatever I, we, all of us, can do to oppose, and to stop what *they* want to happen, what *they* are bottle feeding the masses to create for them...

"And yes, we did ask you for your advice and what 'missing parts' there were we didn't know about...and you and Anders have done all that brilliantly...*so thank you...thank you both"* Her voice wavered, her tears flowing again, Dave put his arm around her, holding her.

"Aye! Y're totally right Mel! I agree with you an' 'undred an' ten percent! An' thank you Magda, and please say thanks to Anders for fillin' us in on what's really goin' on wi' all o' this. *It's all a lot more involved than anythin' we thought...* 'Ow's you feel 'bout it all Soph'?"

Sophie nodded her head emphatically, her glossy long black hair falling partly over her face, she then straightened up, pushed her hair back with her fingers, her elbows high, her chin raised, her pale blue eyes looking upto the high ceiling, and in a quiet and steely determined voice that Jake hadn't heard from her before, said,

"we know now what they want – but they're not going to have it! I'll do everything I can, and then some, in being part of something to make sure they don't...!"

Jake looked at her in awe and great love for a long moment, he was thinking that right then she looked exactly like a picture he'd seen a long time ago in a textbook he remembered from his school history classes, a picture of Boudicca, the warrior Queen of the Celtic Iceni resistance fighters. She had been holding the reins of her chariot in one hand, and brandishing a long shining sword in her other as she lead a ferocious charge against the massed legions of Roman invaders...

"So Will I!" Dave exclaimed loudly. "And I know something else now as well - *that this is what I came here, to this Earth to, to take part in, and to do everything I can, with the skills and gifts I have, to be part of helping humanity at this time..."*

Magda looked at them all, her eyes still moist, her red lips smiling, and then she seemed to withdraw slightly, nodding to herself as if she had finally come to a decision.

"Thank you, all of you...

"I believe that you are four of the very many, and very special young people whose souls chose, volunteered, to be incarnated here, *on* Earth, at this time now.

"I believe you are all of the third generation of Indigo, Star, and Crystal Children...another time I will explain more of what that means - but you could also of course do some research into it before then for yourselves as well.

"We will come to a close for this evening but before we do I want to say to you that you are all now sufficiently aware of, have a good basic knowledge of, and understand the, the opposition, and the scenario, the outcome, the parasites and their human elite agents desire - but you are not yet *fully aware of exactly who and what - 'is on your side', and what is being done and is being planned to do, to help create a different scenario, a different outcome, a different fate...*

"So tomorrow when we meet again at seven o'clock that is what I, and Anders, will tell you all about...*but more than that – we will show you*...and I have just decided on this, because the time has come now - *for you all to know much more about us, who we are, and where we come from...*"

After a moment or two Magda then said with a smile, "well my dears, perhaps we sisters ought to retire to the Ladies' Room for a minute or two - *because what will all your friends and mine think* - if they see us looking so bleary eyed and tearful?!"

She rose to her feet and Sophie and Mel did the same, moving quickly into her open arms and they all hugged each other close. The three of them then walked slowly away together leaving Jake and Dave talking quietly and intently between themselves.

Chapter 10: A Respite With Friends

J ake, Sophie, Dave and Mel were all back in the crowds, noise and lights of the Fair again now, after taking their leave from Magda, who remained in the huge stately room, to finish the preparations for their soiree later that evening.

They had had brief goodbye chats with Lucia on their way out, and Mel had arranged with her to meet at the caravan site's cafe at ten o'clock, and then go to their caravan on Wednesday morning. They had departed from the old Romany caravan in the same way they had first entered it, in pairs, a few minutes apart.

Magda had psycommed with Lucia before they left the stately room, just to make sure that she had no clients with her having a crystal ball reading. Magda had chuckled when she'd said, 'I think you will all agree with me that it would be preferable if no one was with Lucia - *when four people suddenly emerge from what looks like a tiny bathroom!'*

Jake was sniffing the air, the aroma of fried onions was enticing him, and he said loudly, "Well I dunno about anyone else! But *I could eat a scabby donkey!* - But I'll settle for a *hot dog or three!*"

A suggestion unanimously agreed to just as loudly by the others. So the four of them made their way over to the nearby Hot Dog Van.

"Mmmm, *weird innit?!*...When me head gets filled up wi' so much like it just 'as been wi' all Magda an' Anders were sayin', it's like me stomach feels left out an' wants fillin' up an'all!" he commented, before taking a huge bite out of his first giant sized hot dog.

In his other hand he was holding two more under it on paper napkins. They were all piled up in the same way with extra onions and fully doused in mustard and ketchup.

"*Oh Bugga!*" he exclaimed through a mouthful of sausage and onion, as nearly all the mustard and ketchup on it had drizzled out in great globs down the front of his black leather jacket. Sophie had to turn away to avoid choking as she tried to stop a fit of the giggles whilst chewing on a mouthful of a more moderately sized hot dog.

"Yeah, I know what you mean, it's draining a bit, well, a lot – just like your hot dog is...!" Dave replied, trying desperately not to smile as he tried to studiously ignore the splattered condiments all running down Jake's jacket front. But then he couldn't help himself as he glanced at Jake's attempts to wipe it all up with a soggy napkin, but instead he just made a smeary mess of all the red ketchup and yellow mustard on the front of his jacket. His high top black leather biker boots hadn't escaped from a liberal splattering either...

"I should leave it as it is to dry now mate, the colours make a nice pattern and they sort of match the colours on your back patch…!" he commented, and on hearing that Mel had to join Sophie in quickly turning away to avoid a fit of intense giggle choking as well.

Just then a loud stentorian parade ground like voice from behind and off to one side of them bellowed out above all the ambient Fairground noise, *"What did ah say t'y'all 'bout 'ow to find Jake in 'ere? - 'Follow y'noses t'nearest 'N.A.A.F.I. Wagon' ah said!' - Didn't ah say that?! – An' was ah right - or what eh?!"*

Immediately recognising that unmistakeable, booming, drill-sergeant-like-voice Jake turned to see Simmo emerge from the surrounding crowds. Then eleven others, eight men and three women, all similarly clad in black leather jackets adorned with the biker club's back patch appeared with him. The crowds around them promptly detoured and thinned away slightly to avoid getting too close to the sudden appearance of this large gang of bikers.

"Bloody 'ell Jake! Y're supposed to eat 'em not rub 'em all over y'! An' anyways - *ah keep tellin' yer* that it's *Leather Polish* y'put on y'jacket an' boots - *not Mustard an' Ketchup!"*

He guffawed loudly, hands on his hips, his long beard jiggling up and down at this irresistible opportunity for shadenfreude mirth. Jake grinned back at him, shaking his head.

"Fine! Fine - carry on! I can tek it! An' I won't even say a word, not one, abaht that time in Spain when y'fell back'ards off y'chair after abaht sixteen jugs o' sangria in that cafe an' spillin' 'alf a gallon o'

184

garlic olive oil an' mushrooms all over y'! - Or even a word about that pan o' boilin' 'ot tomato soup the time we were livin' in't caravan an' y' spilt - but no – *no - I won't even mention it…!*"

Simmo laughed even louder, all the other bikers joining in. Meanwhile Sophie had asked the man in the hot dog van for a large damp cloth and she handed it to Jake who finished cleaning himself up with it.

As he was doing so he introduced Sophie, Mel and Dave to them all whilst they were moving up to the van to order hot dogs for themselves. The twelve bikers were from about their ages and upwards, the eldest were a couple who looked to be in their late fifties or early sixties, they all seemed very pleasant and genuinely pleased to meet Jake's friends and his girlfriend Sophie.

Leaving Sophie and Mel chatting with the three female bikers, as all the men jostled boisterously with each other in the queue for hot dogs, Jake, with Dave, went over to Reg and he explained to him about Dave and Mel needing his help to load up his van with furniture and stuff from their flat and caravan, and then to drop it all off at a charity shop, ideally in the morning if it'd be possible.

Reg agreed straight away, saying to Dave, "as long as it in't *too* early a start mate - after a days ride an' all that walkin' about at the classic bike show, an' now some more in 'ere - I'll need a bit of a lie in!"

As Jake was about to leave the two of them together and go back over to Sophie, whilst they sorted out the details between them, Reg said, "*Oh aye Jake! – Na then!* - Them two old ex-army BSA despatch bikes y've got to do up…there were four of 'em at the show today that 'ad bin all done up!

"Think they were the same, or more or less like, as yours, from what y'were sayin' anyway about 'em this mornin' at Big Sammy's. *Well they looked brilliant!* Total renovations on 'em, proper job done like you do, *an' y'd best grab onto summat now as y'll fall o'er when I tell y'price tags that were on em!*"

"*Go on then!*" Jake grinned at him.

185

"Between...*Four To Six Grand Apiece* mate!"

"*Bloody 'Ell...!*"

"*Aye! They were!* The bloke who 'ad 'em just specialises in vintage ex-army bikes, I've got 'is number in me phone now, I'll text it t'you later, told 'im about yours an' he asked me to ask you if you'd consider givin' 'im first refusal on 'em when they're all done up like, if y'were thinkin' o' sellin' 'em then - *an' he said it'd be a cash deal an'all!*"

"*Oh ho ho - nice one!* Cheers Reg! - y're a star! But I'll get y' Cafe Racer done first then do 'em, *oh brilliant!* - Thought it were worth forkin' out a good few 'undred to ged 'em when I first saw 'em in that ol' barn! - But I've been that busy wi' getting' the chopper finished an' one thing an' another I just 'aven't 'ad chance to get round to doin' any work on 'em yet!"

"Er, well, I'll tell y'what mate, as it looks like I'm comin' down an' drivin' round Scarborough an' Filey now tomorrow - I could put the Commando an'all the bits fer it in't van in't mornin', an' drop everythin' off at yours first – I'll come round to back lane an' we can get it all in y'shed if that's ok wi' you, then I'll go on an' meet you Dave at y'caravan, load up there an' then we'll go on to y'flat an' get done all what needs doin!"

So, arrangements made, and mounds of hot dogs eaten with much friendly bantering between them all, the large group then moved off all together to continue wandering round the Fair. They all rode on the merry-go-round and Eddie and his twin brother Bert had greeted Jake, Sophie, Mel and Dave like old friends.

As they got off their rides and had started to walk away Sophie turned round and waved back to the unicorns, and said quietly, "*Thank you Beau! – See you again soon I hope!*"

Hearing her say that Jake had grinned and given her a big one armed hug, and he repeated the same words towards the unicorns now spinning round again amongst the flashing lights and the loud music, now playing, appropriately, The Three Degrees: *'When Will I See You Again?'*

The gang of bikers then came across the archery stand where the

186

last time he'd been there, the previous Monday evening, Jake had won a carnival glass vase and given it to Sophie – and first thing the following morning he'd arranged for the delivery of a huge bunch of flowers to her at the Estate Agent's office during the afternoon, for her to put in it - just as he'd promised her he would! The unannounced arrival of them had caused many amused comments and questions from her colleagues in the office at the time!

With much excited shouting and argy-bargy all the men formed in to two teams to compete fiercely against each other. The ladies wisely declined from getting involved and decided to move away to just spectate instead, as they suspected that it was going to get more than a little boisterous.

They were right, and laughed long and loud as they thoroughly enjoyed watching all the juvenile but very funny antics of these supposedly grown men...

This time Jake personally won no prizes, because the opposing team, well aware of his skill with a bow, had managed to keep hampering his aim by 'accidentally' pushing into him and blatantly distracting him, causing his arrows to fly anywhere but the target – completely unsportsmanlike actions which were vigorously reciprocated back to them when it was their turns to shoot, much to the consternation of the young lad running the stand – but he was too intimidated by this loud rowdy gang of 'mature' bikers to do anything but stand well out of the way and just let them get on with it!

When this raucous and vehemently disputed competition was all over, Simmo, as the self appointed captain of the eventual winning team - that he had first selected Jake to be in – like schoolboys do when they select sides for a game of football at break time in the playground, leaned over the counter and tipped the lad a fiver saying to him, *"Sorry abaht all these noisy cheatin' 'ooligans messin' abaht lad! Can't tek em' anywhere!"*

The lad had grinned back at him obviously made up with his tip, saying, *"Cor Thanks Mister! Nay worries! - Good laugh that were!"*

Much later, on their way out to the car park, Sophie, her arm linked

187

under Jakes, said to him, "y'know...meeting all your friends and just having a nice and normal-everyday-fun-time with everyone was just what I needed after everything with Magda and Anders..."

"Aye! Me too an'all Soph' - sort o' helps y'to switch off fer a bit and keep y'feet on't ground dunnit?!"

"Yes, it does, but it's also a bit strange knowing all what we do now, *especially what we learned tonight*, and then meeting, talking and mixing with nice, normal people who have no idea about it at all...and are just...unknowingly...getting on with their lives, doing everyday normal things...unaware of what's...do you know what I mean...?"

"Yeah, yeah I do - an' even ol'Simmo can be *nice an' nearly normal* - sometimes! Seriously tho', yeah, yeah I do. I've got thoughts goin' round in me head – I 'aven't put 'em all together yet tho' – that I want to...some'ow...*let 'em all know as well...*

"...Dave said to me this afternoon when we were at the end o' Filey Brigg, that he, 'didn't like keepin' secrets from Mel, an' I feel like I am, well, sort o' keepin' secrets from people who are important to me in me life as well. The Whitby crew would be open to it all, an' so would them still left in the UFO Spotter's club, but until we know even more – an' after tomorrow night's meeting with Magda and Anders, we will...

"...So, well, I think I, we, should keep it all to ourselves for the time bein', *but only for the time bein'*, a bit later I think we might need to get everyone together an', well, *after we've worked out 'ow to*...to present it all to 'em...*or even better!* – if we mebbe ask Magda an' Anders to...as they'd do it a lot better...!?"

He grinned down at Sophie, then chuckled, "What you chuckling at?" She grinned up at him.

"Ha! I was just imaginin' the look on Simmo's – and all the others' faces – if they walked into 'The Trocadero Cafe' with us - an' Anders an' Magda explained everythin' to 'em! Well, who knows, maybe we will, a bit further down the line...?!"

"Yes, I hope so! I'd love to go to the Cafe and see Alfie again! And Anders did say we would didn't he?!"

188

"Aye he did! - *An' I could 'ave some more o' that brilliant chocolate cake Alfie's missus makes!*"

Sophie hip bumped him, shaking her head, "*The Future of the World is at stake and he's on about chocolate cake!*" She said in mock and humorous admonishment.

" *- Nowt wrong wi' a good steak either...!*" He quipped back, jogging forwards, both of them full of childlike fun as she chased him out to Dave's car.

Nearby the Whitby M.C. bikers were all revving their bikes loudly and getting ready to ride out. Jake stopped jogging to turn and say to Sophie, "'ang on a minute Soph', I'll just go an' 'ave a word wi' 'em – I was goin' to ride us back wi' 'em as far as Scarborough – but I think we'd be best followin' Dave and Mel – looks like they're 'avin' trouble wi' startin' the car again, if it packs up on their way 'ome, I'll 'ave to ferry 'em back! Only be a sec - would y'tell Dave an' Mel what I'm gonna do?!"

He returned a minute later on the back of Simmo's bike with Reg following them.

"Simmo an' Reg 'ave kindly offered to follow yous back an'all Dave - in case it packs in f'good, 'cos if it does y'll 'ave to leave it to get towed back wi' Reg's van in't mornin'. But fer tonight they could give you an' Mel a lift back, Simmo's brought a coupla o'spare 'elmets over, if it does come to doin' that."

A while later, just the four of them were sat in Dave's and Mel's – now much tidier and less cluttered caravan - thanks to the efforts of the two girls that afternoon, chatting and having a coffee before Jake and Sophie went on to Scarborough.

The old Citroen had finally managed to start and leave the Fair, but had stalled about half way back to Filey, and wouldn't start again, fortunately it had stopped on a flat stretch of road. But on Jake's suggestion of just having a go at bump starting it with himself, Simmo and Reg all pushing together it had bump started again easily enough.

Soon after that Simmo and Reg had roared off waving but without stopping, when, hopping and stuttering, the old car finally entered the

189

sanctuary of the caravan site's car park – and finally packed in just as they were pulling into a vacant slot, so at least they'd arrived home safely!

Jake had pulled in behind them, and he'd easily pushed it in the final few feet himself. He'd left his bike parked there as well, chained to the car's rear bumper, to avoid disturbing the other caravans' residents by riding it through the site, as it was by now quite late, and the four of them had walked together to the caravan.

Now sat around the dining table, chatting about all the evening's events the three of them admitted to Jake that they had been slightly overawed - *'and a bit unnerved at first!',* Mel admitted, by the sudden, imposing presence of the twelve black leather clad bikers - and then the loud banter from the stocky, powerful body-builder figure of the long bearded, but bald headed and heavily tattooed Simmo, the obvious leader of the biker gang.

"- But, he was really funny and nice, a real gentleman! - and how good of him was it to follow us back and then have to push the car! – And Reg too – and for Reg to give up his Sunday morning to help us out as well! *Just shows - you should never judge any book by it's cover!"* she said.

"Aye it were." Jake said, "But that's 'ow the biker fraternity is, they just 'elp each other out, sort o' like a tribe does like."

Dave said, "Yes, Mel's dead right - an' I'd like to do a large charcoal portrait sketch of Simmo sometime, try an' capture his character with it, charcoal'd be ideal, and I'd give it to him. An' that's interesting what you've just said Jake – ties in with what I read in a book a few months ago.

"It was about different tribes, all over the world, some that are well known about, and some that've only just been discovered...and the amazing similarities of how they all organise themselves.

"It said, in the book, that the early native American indigenous tribes had what the author claimed to be, perhaps, the best societal systems. Because apart from them not having money - and therefore no tiny elite of bankers having power over them and controlling

190

them!...everyone in a tribe was important. They all had an important role, shared their necessities, and they all made important decisions that affected the whole tribe, together.

"They all knew all about what was happening in their world, because secrets weren't kept from them about it by those at the top of the totem pole!...and they respected, looked after, and cared for each other...

"I realise now that everything Ander's was saying earlier about 'Unity Consciousness', *was obviously how they were...*

"But all that was, of course, before the 'white European man' invaded their lands and...more or less wiped them all out...it must've been unbelievably horrific...devastating...for them, the book went into some details of the obscene violence the Americans' forces inflicted on them – their women and children as well, I won't go into the details...And done mainly for the reasons he'd told us about last Monday...plus sheer greed, and....and..."

He shook his head, exhaling heavily, and got up to make some more coffees. When he was sitting back down again with them Jake explained that he'd known Simmo for years, and he was like an older brother to him. He'd first met him at the UFO Spotters' club when Jake had been just a young lad and Simmo had been in his late teens.

Then Simmo had gone off and joined the 'Paras' – the Parachute Regiment, for fifteen years or so, and gone all over the world with them. But he'd always kept in touch, and several times a year when he had some leave he used to ride up from Aldershot where he was based - when he wasn't away for months on end at some faraway trouble spot and in the thick of it - and he'd stayed for a few days with Jake and his Mum and Dad.

His parents had sold up in Whitby and moved to Tenerife to live out there in a sort of early retirement, a few years after he'd been in the Paras. They'd had Simmo, their only child, late on in life.

In the Paras he'd got to the rank of Staff Sergeant, and was in line to be a Company Sergeant-Major - but he would have been more or less desk bound in an office back at base on light admin' type and recruit training duties, as he'd been badly wounded in his left leg, which was why he had a slight limp, which ruled him out of future active service. It had happened when a patrol he was leading had been ambushed one night by the Taliban in some remote mountain village in the wilds of Afghanistan.

Two of his close mates had been killed immediately in that ambush and a lot of the other soldiers wounded. But because of his leadership in immediately counter attacking, despite being repeatedly wounded himself, he had more than likely saved the lives of all the remaining soldiers in his patrol; plus they'd eventually achieved the elimination of an entire large unit of a very dangerous enemy, many of them single-handedly by Simmo...despite his injuries…

A while afterwards he was awarded the Military Medal, with a silver bar, for his actions in that contact. It was one of the highest awards for NCO's in the British Army, and just below a Victoria Cross for bravery in the face of the enemy, particularly whilst wounded himself. So he'd certainly seen and done more than his bit during his time with the Paras, plenty more, as Jake had seen all of his other medals and framed citations as well, and spent many hours with him over the years listening enthralled to some of his hair raising stories of service in 'The Maroon Machine' – the nickname of the Paras because of the colour of their berets.

Simmo was now in business running his own gymn' he'd set up in Whitby, where a lot of local ex-army blokes were members and he spent most of the rest of his time involved with the Whitby Motorcycle Club as its 'President'.

"He's 'elluva bloke! - a bit like the 'Big Chief' I suppose - from what you were sayin' about them Indian tribes Dave!"

Jake then told them that just before Simmo had finally got back to civvy street, their mutual mate, a farmer, who had, and still has, a lot of land about halfway between Scarborough and Whitby, had back then been having some bad problems with a criminal gang from further up North who had started to use some of his land for illegal hare coursing betting, having threatened him to turn a blind eye and

192

say nothing...or else...

"But between us all in't bike club - an' then Simmo suddenly in the line up o' the team – or 'the tribe' - we, well, we sorted that gang – the bad tribe! – *Sorted 'em well an' truly out!* An' they didn't bother our mate, or us, again...So it was a good result all round - an' we all 'ad a good crack doin' it!

"Ha! – *Literally more than a few good cracks for all o' them nasty sods from up North! In fact we had 'arder time from stoppin' ol'Simmo from properly finishin' em' all off like he'd done after that ambush in Afghanistan...!*" Was all Jake said to them about that episode, apart from finishing off by saying:

"It also gave Simmo the chance whilst he was sharin' a caravan wi' me durin' that time at the farm, to look round for somewhere permanent to live an' find some suitable premises in Whitby for the gymn' business, which he soon 'ad done.

"Both his parents sadly passed away a few years ago, leavin' him a bit of an inheritance and their villa in Tenerife, which he still has, but is now a holiday rental. I've been out to it with him, Reg, and two others, on the bikes, like I was tellin' y'about Dave about earlier this afternoon. We went over to sort it out an' giv' 'im hand getting' it cleared an' done up for a local 'oliday rental company to manage it an' let it out.

"He'd also saved up a fair bit o' cash over the years, plus he'd had a payout for his injury, an' he got a loan as well to buy a big ol' derelict warehouse near the 'arbour entrance and made the gymn on the first floor, with a massive garage for parkin' an' storage an' all that on't ground floor, an' he 'ad a big flat made for im' to live in up in what were the roof space.

"He did a lot o' the buildin' work to do it all up 'imself, an' with 'elp from some o' the lads in the bike club – tribe! I did a fair bit o'labourin' work on the site when all the work started - knockin' walls down, shiftin' materials around an' all that! - Good, honest, but back breakin' graft it were an'all!

"He's got some mega views over the harbour an' the sea from up in't

193

flat, it's got a sort o' balcony there an'all, an' he still does a bit o' sky watching with a massive telescope he's got up there – bloomin' thing's linked upto a laptop, it's an amazin' bit o' kit!"

Having finished his tale, and after chatting some more he and Sophie then drank up, said their good-nights to Dave and Mel, and rode back to Scarborough.

Chapter 11: Sunday Afternoon

Sophie's mobile rang mid afternoon the next day just as she'd nearly finished doing some work related spreadsheets at home. Looking at the caller ID she saw it was Mel.

"Hi Mel! - Hey - *how's it all going?*"

"Hi Soph', you ok? - *We're all done at last! - And I'm worn out!* Even with Dave and Reg doing all the heavy lifting!"

"Heyyy! Oh that's great! - *I mean it's great you're all done! –* Not worn out!"

"Yeah! Ha! - Dave's now ipso collapso here on the sun lounger! He says he aches in places he didn't know he had! Reg did a great job, he's just had a mug o'tea and gone, he even brought us back here after taking everything to the charity shop! Oh yeah – your friend Michelle at the shop – she's really nice isn't she – she was made up with all the furniture and stuff!

"They don't normally open on a Sunday but she went down to open up specially just for us to unload it all – they're going to sort it all out tomorrow – and she asked me to say *'Hi'* to you! So we just wanted to call and say thanks to Jake and you for setting it all up! – I tried Jake's mobile but it went straight to his answer-phone."

"*Oh that's great! I'm made up that you're all sorted now! I bet you are as well! Must be a big relief!* I knew Michelle'd be really pleased with everything you've donated! I told her you had good quality stuff, so it was really generous of you both, and it'll be a big help for the charity!

"Jake must still be at the archery club, he said he'd ring or text me when he's finished and he's bringing pizzas for us before we go to see Magda and Anders again. *But I might not be speaking to him when he does get here...!*"

"*Oh Dear!*" Mel giggled, sensing the humorous undertone in Sophie's voice, "*Why's that...what's he done?!*"

*"Wellll...*he rang me this morning - to see if I fancied a pizza later – *'yes, great idea',* I said, and then he said that now he's got a proper English longbow, and he's just finished making his own wooden arrows for it, he wanted to look the part and do the whole *'Robin Hood thing'*...and he was going to ask me if he could borrow a pair of my green tights!...But then he said, the cheeky man, *'but I won't bother asking you as I've just realised they'd be far too big for me!' - Cheek of it!"*

She heard Mel laugh loudly at the other end. *"Oh that's a good one!* Dave'll crack up when I tell him that!" And she laughed again.

"I wanted to suggest something for later as well – with our little car being so poorly we thought that it'd be best – well, we've no choice really! - if we got a taxi there and back to the Fair tonight, so do you want to come here and we all go together in it, or, do you and Jake prefer to go straight there on his bike?"

"Oh we'll come to you then we can all go together! Might be best to ring now and book it though, as there'll be four of us so they'll need to send their little minibus. What d'you think – book it for half past six?"

"Oh right, good, yeah I'll do that! Okay then, we'll see you both later! And thanks again! - *Oh! - Soph' – I can't wait to hear what Magda says about who she and they all really are...and where they come from...I think we're in for another mind blowing session don't you?!"*

"Yes I do! And I've wondered if we've been anything like – 'on target' as Jake'd say - about all that when we've talked about it...?!"

"Well...knowing Magda – *the truth will be stranger than fiction!"*

The two girls chatted for a few minutes more before hanging up. Sophie then put the finishing touches to all her spreadsheets, feeling really pleased with herself for finally achieving what had taken her several long sessions at work and at home to do, and backed everything up on an external hard drive she'd just got a few hours ago from her tech' friend at work.

It was the same chap who had the radar system download on his

196

computer to try and identify the chem' trail aeroplanes. She'd told him over the 'phone – apologising profusely for calling him on a Sunday morning - that she was worried about losing all this work stuff on her computer, that she'd just finished doing, due to something crashing it – which she'd explain about tomorrow at work – so he'd kindly dropped it off for her on his way out with his girlfriend for a drive over to Malton for Sunday Lunch at a popular Pub's carvery there.

She unplugged the hard drive – which was about half the size of a paperback book - and put it back in the shoebox sized little safe he'd brought for her as well, and she was going to ask Jake to bolt it to the floor for her, hidden away under the desk.

Then she printed off everything that she needed to show her boss tomorrow afternoon when he was back in the Scarborough office after a meeting at another branch, and put it all in her large shoulder bag ready to take with her to the office.

Just as she did so her mobile pinged with an incoming text, it was from Jake, opening it up she read: *'Robin to Maid Marian – wot pizza u want? - Friar Tuck's Sherwood Forest Special'?*

She grinned lasciviously and replied: 'Triar who...?'

His reply came back immediately: *'Robin on his way right now!! – Pizza can wait!!'*

Chapter 12: Moving Day and Artists

"Taxi's coming!" Mel shouted, leaning over the railing to look around the end of the caravan's patio. The four of them quickly walked out onto the roadway as it drove up. They all got into it feeling the same excited anticipation as if they were embarking on a 'big night out on the town' that they'd been looking forward to.

Jake sat up front as he and the driver had recognised each other. The taxi was from the same firm that Taxi Tony had worked for all those years ago, and the elderly driver remembered Tony well, so as they made their way to the Fair he and Jake reminisced and chatted about those days and events.

When they pulled into the Fair's car parking field it looked very different to how it had been last night – because all the rows of parked cars had gone, and instead there was a constant toing and froing of towed caravans, large wagons, and long flat-back lorries with dismantled fair ground attractions stacked on them.

What looked like a small army of people were still dismantling the remaining structures of the three Fairs that had all been together there for the past week. Now though it all seemed like organised chaos to them as the Fairground people – of all ages - from older children to their grandparents and great-grandparents from the look of some of them, were gradually clearing the entire site and getting ready to move off in convoys to their next venues.

"*Oh Bugga!*" Jake said, grinning, as he turned around in his seat to the others – "Looks like I got the day wrong folks! *They're shut!*"

Dave, joining in with him, replied with dead-panned disappointment, "*Aaaah No!* I was so looking forward to going on the rides as well! Ah well, I've got *'The Sound Of Music' DVD we can all watch instead back at home!* So Neverrr Minnnd!"

The elderly taxi driver looked slightly confused on hearing all this, so Jake, still grinning, said to him, "*Nah! - It's alright mate, only messin'!* - We're just seein' some friends off from 'ere tonight! We'll giv' y'a ring later to go back, cheers mate!"

"Oh right! – Ah thought when y'booked it that it were strange – *as last night were it's last night!* They're all splittin' up again now an' goin' off to Lincoln, Leeds an' Durham overnight for next week - which's y'friends goin' to?"

"Errr...down to Lincoln...!" Jake replied, quickly ad- libbing, "right then, well it's bin good t'see y'again - an' thanks a lot f't'lift mate! – We'll see y'later to go back - cheers!"

Standing in the field they looked in amazement at all the activity and the transformation of the view in front of them. Jake then grinned again, and looking sideways at Dave he said to him, "Err -y've got: *'The Sound Of Music' DVD?!*"

"Yeah! *Great film man!* - and Mel's right when she said in the taxi that she thought Magda looks a lot like Julie Andrews who plays Maria in it!" Then he put an arm around Mel and broke out singing loudly and definitely way off tune:

"I'll do anything for you Dear! – Anything - For Youuuu...!"

Mel giggled and said, "Er – No! - That's from ' *'Oliver'* - *The Musical'* Dave...!"

"Ah! *Is it? Ohhh...!*"

They all laughed, in high spirits, and then Sophie said, slightly bewildered as she looked around at everything going on, "*wellll*...somewhere in all that lot is Magda's caravan! Looks like it's been moved from where it was. I think we'd best go the long way round tho' and look for it away from all these lorries going in and out - *before we get run over!*"

"Aye! An' we'd best be quick about it an'all! Here's another one cumin' out!" Jake said quickly striding away from the front entrance, his arm around Sophie safely propelling her along with him. They all stopped a safe distance away to watch a huge, fully laden, articulated flat back lorry rumble noisily past them.

Mel was quite fascinated at everything that was going on. Her eyes then narrowed slightly in deep thought about it. After a moment or

199

two she said, having to raise her voice over the noise of yet another lorry piled high with various large fairground structures, that was now crawling along close by to them in low gear, "I was just thinking...when we've been here before, when it was all set up and running, with the crowds, the noise, the lights, the smells and – *the sound of music!*"

She paused, grinning at Dave, "...and everything else! It all seemed so, well, *real and permanent*, and we didn't even really think about it or question it! Because - *we were just in it, and, like, mesmerised by all of that...*and just, well, *accepted it,* too busy just *accepting and being distracted by it, and being in it,* I suppose...

"But now it's all being dismantled in front of us, and it's all going away. So now we can really see how it was all just façades, deliberately put together - like a big film set is to create an illusion for us...

"*But it's all going now...and what'll be left is what was there all along, before the illusions came, but we didn't really see it then - the real Land, the real Earth...*so it makes me think you could compare all this that's happening to what we're part of now...'*The Pandora Quest'!*

"...Because from everything Magda and Anders have told us about, once all the façades and all the distracting illusions have been started to be dismantled, we'll all start to see the true reality, bit by bit, and it'll be unstoppable by then – just like what's happening here now! – As here they're not going to suddenly stop are they - *and put it all back!?*"

She scrunched her shoulders and raised her hands up, her fingers spread wide, "Ooops! - That's a bit heavy isn't it?! I know it's got a few holes in it – because it's just going somewhere else - *But can you see what I mean...?!*"

"Yes...yes I *certainly can* my Dear, and that's *a very astute* observation and comparison you have just made...!"

They all spun round to see Magda smiling at them.

"*Welcome to you all again my Dears!* I thought I had better come here to meet you as we have had to move the caravan over to the far corner so it was not in anyone's way. It is only a few minutes walk. And please excuse my appearance! - I don't normally greet friends who come to visit me when I am still dressed in my 'moving-day-working-clothes'! – But we've all been having and enjoying *such a very busy day!* - I do intend though to change out of them when we go in!"

She was wearing a pair of vintage looking fawny coloured baggy dungarees, the knees of which were stained with mud and grass. Around her middle a wide brown leather belt with a big old fashioned square brass buckle gathered it all in, a very faded blue denim shirt with the sleeves rolled up, and muddy hiking boots on her feet. A brightly patterned headscarf was tightly knotted over her coiled up reddish auburn hair.

They all walked together over the large field, with Sophie and Jake on her left, and they had to occasionally step over some fairly deep muddy ruts in the earth made by the heavy vehicles that had previously passed over it. Magda stopped for a moment or two every now and then to point out some of the dismantling endeavours that were going on, and she called out friendly words to those who were doing them as they passed by. After she had done this a few times she said,

"Now...as far as everyone who has seen us is concerned, you are just a group of my friends who have come to say goodbye to me and I am showing you around, so it is unlikely now that they will give your presence here a second thought, especially as they are all so busy doing everything they have to do as well. - It's just that old 'trade-craft' again, and acting quite naturally just about makes you invisible...! I must admit that it has become something of a habit with me, with all of us, over the years! - *A habit that has stemmed from absolute necessity though - on many occasions...*

"Only Lucia and Ruth are still here this evening, my other sisters have already gone...as they were expected in...*other places*...but they all asked me to say 'Hello' to you.

"Oh – before she left Angela asked me to say to you Jake that she would be happy to talk about her experiences at Bletchley Park with you sometime, as I had told her about your and your Father's interest in what happened there...

"Lucia and Ruth have been helping today by entertaining the Fair ground folks' very young children, safely away from all these works going on, so all the rest of their families can work together doing them.

"My sisters' magic acts, games, rides, picnics and funny dramas are always enjoyed so much by the little ones!

"Anders is all ready and waiting – and...here we are!"

She pointed over to her Romany caravan which they could see was now safely tucked away in a corner of the field in some long grass, it was alongside a tall and bushy hedgerow and small copse of trees that lead into the big, sprawling forest behind them.

Munching contentedly on the grass in front of her caravan was a pale haired horse...Sophie gasped and pointing to him she asked Magda, "*Oh! Is, is that...Beau* – Magda?!"

"Yes it is! *I told him you were here!* - and he said he wanted to come over and say 'Hello' to you all! Then he will go back to Lucia and Ruth to carry on giving the little children rides around the other fields, and come back through the forest - after they have all finished the picnic teas Ruth and Lucia made for them earlier and they are all tucking into now - and then had some time to let their tummies settle!

"He can give five or six of the little ones a ride at once with them all holding on tightly to each other, whilst my two sisters walk along both sides of them all - to steady anyone who might be about to wobble off! The other children walk with them as well, all happily singing along, and they keep changing places to rest and ride on Beau's back!

"It really is such a lovely sight to see! All the little children love him so much, and he does them. We do find it very amusing when some of the little girls - *who can see him as he really is of course* - and who are always *so excited* to tell their parents, when they come to collect them that:"

She switched her voice to a high falsetto little girl's voice:

"...'Mummy! – Daddy! - We've been for rides on a unicorn!'

"And then the little boys say..." She changed her voice to that of an indignant little boy's: "'No - it wasnnn't! Don't be silly! – It was just Beau! - Magda's horse!'"

The two young couples laughed loudly along with her, as they imagined the scenes Magda had described. Sophie was laughing and smiling widely with absolute delight as she pictured the idyllic and oh-so-endearing sight of the horse-unicorn walking slowly around the fields, and through the forest, carrying a group of excited, laughing little children all clinging together on his back as he slowly walked for them with Magda's sisters, and the other little children all walking and singing alongside. Still smiling with delight at the lovely image, she walked slowly up to Beau saying very quietly,

"Hello Beau! Thank you for coming and waiting to see us! I'm so pleased to see you! - We all are!

The...horse...raised his head and whinnied softly to her in reply, and shook his long, silvery haired mane. Then he became very still as he looked down, and deeply, into Sophie's eyes.

She saw and sensed in his a great intelligence, an otherworldly, incredibly benign intelligence radiating from them, and she reached up slowly to gently stroke his velvety muzzle, lost for words at the sudden intensity of his aura and overwhelming presence so close to her. Then, incredibly - just for a few milliseconds, just for the briefest flashes of thoughts - she saw him reveal his true and magnificent form to her! It was much larger, more muscular, with a brilliant pure white-and-silvery gleaming coat, and a long barley twisted shining horn sprouting proudly from his forehead...

"OHHHHHH!" She gasped, staring with totally delighted awe at him, and then she flung her arms around the broad base of his long neck, her eyes instantly watering, then the tears of an overwhelming joy freely flowed as she pressed her cheek to him, hugging him tightly.

"You're so beautiful! - I saw you! I saw you! Ohh Thank You!

Thank you so much - Beautiful Beau!" Her voice watery with the tears of an intense, ecstatic joy flooding through her...

Magda smiled with delight as well at Sophie, saying quietly,

"Yes...yes he most certainly is...and if I am right - *I think your pure, inner child, just saw him* – am *I right my dear...?"*

Sophie could only turn her head to look at Magda as she hugged Beau, and softly bite at her bottom lip as she nodded a 'yes' to her, as her tears of happiness ran freely down her cheeks.

Dave quietly said, "I've just seen, in my mind, a painting I want to do, of the scene you described Magda, of Beau and all the little children sat on his back – lead by your sisters, and they are all laughing and singing their songs together - journeying over the Elysian fields..."

"Oh that would be wonderful David! Yes!...*Elysium!* – It is such a wonderful place...*and State of Happiness...!"* She replied wistfully, her glittering emerald eyes moving over the fields in front of them to the far horizon. She then promptly turned back to face him and said,

"David! - *You have just reminded me! - And I must apologise to you!* - Because I did not say to you yesterday evening that I had been to see your painting - and all the others you have on display in that lovely little gallery, on the steep cobbled street, your friend has in the Old Town in Scarborough!

"But to be really honest it was not that I forgot to tell you – I had intended to - but with everything you and Jake...'told'...me, and then Anders, yesterday, and then everything we spoke about afterwards, I thought at the time, that well, perhaps right then was not really the right time to...and partly as well because I also wanted more time to talk about Art and Artists and all your lovely paintings with you.

"Ruth and Lucia were with me – we all went together yesterday afternoon – *we were actually on our way there just as you all psycommed to me*!

"I have to say *we were all very, very impressed with your work!* You obviously have an extra-ordinary talent. The depiction of the

204

scene on the long dark road where the young couple have broken free from the long lines of people just drudging along it, and who are running away together towards the sunlit mountains, discarding all their baggage is really quite superb!

"We thought that the mountain could perfectly represent the Yang in the Eastern philosophy of the Yin and Yang, where the Yang is often described as *'the side of the mountain with the sun on it'*...

"We could also see in it touches of the natural skill and ability that dear Gustave, Gustave Courbet had in depicting an ethereal illumination over a landscape, and the figures in it have so much of what Vincent could do when he captured peoples' postures, movements and expressions, which are the crucial elements that he so effectively used to illustrate human character, perception and experience. *Particularly in his earlier, more draughtsman like works -* of which we actually have quite a collection of on display in our galleries - that he so kindly gave to us...

"But you are clearly developing your own style and techniques, which naturally amalgamate all of theirs...and all the others... *So we are all definitely looking forward to seeing much more of your work in the future!"*

Jake, sensing that Magda and Dave were going to carry on talking about his Art together, thoughtfully said, "...Er, 'scuse me fer a bit you two – I'm goin' over to say 'Ello to Beau as well!"

He then went over to join Sophie and Mel who were both now hugging and stroking Beau and talking excitedly together.

Dave said, "Well...Gosh! Wow! *Thank you very much Magda!* Good of you all to go and see them, and to say what you've just said about them...*Nicest things anyone's ever said about my paintings!*

"But?...*But do you mean - Vincent?*...'Vincent' as in - *'Van Gogh'*...? And He...*He - Gave - You...?!"* He was quite stunned, and barely managed to get his last words out.

"Oh - oh yes...*yes I do! And yes he did Bless him!...He was always so generous!* We got to know him quite well - and his younger brother Theodorus, we called him Theo', who helped him such a lot as well with financial and emotional support which helped to keep Vincent painting. We got to know lots of other wonderful artists when we went to Paris of course, and we helped a lot of them as well with...various things.

"Vincent insisted, on that last evening with us, before we left, on giving us such a lot of his early and quite exquisite figurative drawings and paintings that we had all admired...We all, my sisters and I...*Ohhh My Goodness!* - *We all so enjoyed our times with all the artists when we were in Paris!* All those wonderful painters! - And the wonderful writers! – especially dear Emile – Emile Zola, all their ideas and perceptions were all *so radical* for the time and went on to have such *a lasting and profound effect on society's ideas and perceptions* about Art and Literature...

"In the century or so before, we had seen Paris become the centre of powerful political and social movements that really did have lasting and hugely transformative effects for all of Europe. So many of the old and established traditions had been challenged - and firmly shaken to change society – *and they still were being!*

"The painters and the writers who then emerged in those later years – *they all helped* to bring in new ways of *seeing and creating* with Art and Literature, and of perceiving other realities in the world around them; overall, *realities*, that were more relevant to, and often reflected the everyday lives of, the general public, *and so they helped so much* to change the perceptions through Art and Literature in the minds of the public masses.

"*They were all ridiculed, criticized or laughed at, at first of course!* – The ruling elite's Establishment Salons and their State Galleries scornfully refused to display their works!

"But...we, and others...let's just say...we became involved...and through many independent exhibitions, promotions, and displays of their works - *especially in places more accessible to the masses*, those artists, their ideas and works of Art, gradually came to prominence. Especially when a few forward looking dealers...whom we initially met with and introduced to the artists...found other markets overseas

206

for their works as well...

"After those far sighted dealers put on exhibitions in London and New York - those painters became, and still are - *internationally famous!* And most of them have been household names over the decades ever since! - Vincent, Berthe, Gustave, Edgar, Paul, Claude - *and all the others...!*

"*Ooooh David - how we so enjoyed our meetings, talks - and just the times we spent generally with all of those so enlightened, bohemian crowds! You would have loved it! -* But who knows...?"

She then looked deeply, soul searchingly, into his eyes for a few long moments, her emerald eyes twinkling, before very quietly whispering: "*...Perhaps You Did...?!*

"I say that...partly because...well, as I have said, I also recognised in your works - especially for one so young - *just so many natural similarities to theirs!* - Particularly to dear Gustave's techniques and the ways Honore Daumier and so many of the others depicted such intense and questioning social realism in their drawings and paintings!...

"*Ohhh!...And the auras and energy atmospheres they all created when they got together in all those wonderful Cafés! - So positive and so lively!* – Our favourites to go to were the 'Cafe Guerbois' and the 'Cafe La Nouvelle Athenes', they were *such fun* and *so conducive* to free and creative thinking, and it was all spoken about and discussed quite openly - *so many wonderful ideas and dreams were shared by all those creative bohemian crowds of wonderfully gifted artists and writers!*"

She dug both of her hands deeply into the single, baggy, front pouch-like pocket on her dungarees, hunching her shoulders, and looked down at her muddy boots, clearly enjoying a few moments of her own private reminiscences of all she had just spoken about.

David was totally, utterly, enthralled – his mind was spinning – dizzying him once again! – at everything Magda had just said. He was bursting with so many questions, but all he could come out with was:

"Magda...that's...*so fantastic! I mean fantastic! - As in fantastic and wonderful to hear! - I can just imagine it!* And *it does just seem so, so...somehow...incredibly familiar!* And – and you were, *you and your sisters were all actually there...!?* I'm, *I'm, I dunno! - I'm just too knocked over by it!* Oh wow! *Oh Wowww! HaHa Haaaaa!*"

He tilted his head right back, laughing loudly and uncontrollably in sheer pleasure as he looked up into the evening sky, his eyes wide, breathing deeply between exhilarated bursts of joyous laughter.

"*Wowww!* - Oh I'm sorry Magda! - *I'm not usually lost for words!* – Jake said yesterday - *'that I could Waffle For England!'*"

Magda slowly raised her head, her glittering eyes seemed to be dancing as she smiled, all the while looking at him with great affection.

"I thought you would like to hear a little something of all those times. Another time – when you come to see all the Art we have collected in our galleries, I will have more time to talk to you – to all of you - about those days – and others – from earlier times a little more..."

"Oh Yes! *Yes Please!* That'd be fantastic Magda! *Next week! As soon as possible! We must arrange a date! Mel will be absolutely entranced by it all as well! - I can't wait to tell her!* - Oh good! Look! - *Here she comes!*"

Mel was wandering back over to them, leaving Sophie and Jake with Beau, she was grinning broadly at Dave, having first heard his exclamations, then his laughter and seen the expressions of delight which were still on his face. She skipped the final few steps upto him and hugging and hanging onto his arm she looked up at him saying, "*Wow! You look happy about something!*"

"I am! *I am! - Even more now!*" He said laughing as he hugged her tightly and kissed her.

"I'll tell you everything Magda's just said later - *about Paris and all the artists – she, she and Ruth and Lucia and all her other sisters were there! – And they all actually knew them...! - But it'd be best if you were sat down first before I do, I nearly fell over, I might still do!*"

208

He laughed again, then looking back to Magda he said,

"I, I wanted to see if you liked my painting of all the people on the dark road, and the couple running towards the sunny mountain, first, then, if you did, I was...well, *I was going to give it to you!* But, from what you say about all the Great Art you have in your galleries, well, *I think mine might look a bit like 'the poor relation'...compared alongside to all of them...It...I thi..."*

Magda's eyes brimmed with tears as she reached out to gently touch his shoulder and quieten him, her face too was a picture of delight, radiating a warm maternalistic love towards him.

"And that giving would have been *so typically generous of you too..David!* - But you cannot *give* it - or any of them to me, to us...now...because I saw little yellow round stickers next to them – which I believe, from what your friend, Shirley, at the gallery told me:, *'means that they have all now been sold!'"*

"*Wwhhaat?!"* OH NO! I mean...*OH YES! I mean That's Fantastic! That's great, oh wowww that's amazing!* I mean...I mean - I should've given it to you before! - But I, I didn't - because I didn't want to *just presume* you'd like it...*but now it's too late...!* Oh no! But...*Oh yes!* But - but Shirley – it's her gallery – she hasn't called me to tell me they'd all been sold! - *She'd've been onto me straight away if they had!?"*

"Yes, I am quite certain that she would have done so normally – but I asked her to please not contact you – until you contacted her - because I told her we were meeting you that evening – just a few hours later - and I wanted it to be a nice surprise for you then – *so with one thing and another I am really sorry you have had to wait until now to find out!* I also said to her that we thought the prices were too modest, *so we paid thrice the prices being asked for them...!"*

"*Whaaaat?! Y'YOU DID?! – YOU B'BOUGHT THEM?!...ALL?! - All of my paintings...! Y'you really liked them all - that much...!?!"* He stared at her in absolute shock.

"*And F, For Th' Three Times!...THREEE TIMES the prices on*

209

them...! Oh My God Magda! Oh Thank You! Thank You so very, very, mmmuch...!"

His shocked voice finally broke down and he sobbed quietly, his chest heaving, tears running down his cheeks.

Magda quickly stepped in and spread her arms around both of them, holding them both tightly to her for a few moments as she remembered so many similar occasions she had done exactly this, when, long ago, her young artist friends then had responded in just the same way...

She knew that sometimes that was all it took – an input, a burst, of positive fertilising energy to them at this stage – simply done just by giving encouragement and showing a true and genuinely knowledgeable appreciation of their talents to help them towards overcoming all the early self-doubts that could so plague and sometimes even stall a young, artistic, creative mind.

With such a burst of positive energy given to them their belief and confidence in themselves would then have a greater chance to carry on growing, and to flower fully, and then seed and create more and more, free from some of the choking weeds that can stifle it so much. And in such a fertile and nurtured ground, their talent and output had a greater chance to keep on growing and blossoming, and so produce an ongoing harvest of more and more wonderful works...She stepped back from them both and said,

"I also asked your friend, Shirley, if they could remain on display there for a while, so other people can go in and see and enjoy them, and she agreed – she also said that she wanted to talk with you as soon as possible about having the local press come and do an article about you and your quickly sold out exhibition!

"Over the next few days we will contact as well some of the prominent people whom we know in 'The World Of The Arts' – because I know they will be very interested in your work...so...*I don't need Lucia's crystal ball* to foresee for you many more exhibitions in many other places - *and much publicity for your work in the future!* Because what you are capable of, *and what you are doing right now*

David – will – and indeed it already is - adding enormously to the positive energies now starting to flourish again here on the surface of this Earth!

"...Wellllll...Beau is telling me that it will soon be time for him to take the children around the fields, as they have finished their picnic teas, and Sophie and Jake must be wondering what on Earth has been going on between us three! – So you had better tell them! Then we can all go in and join Anders!"

Sophie and Jake were absolutely thrilled to hear Dave's good news, Jake slapping him on the back as Sophie hugged him. They had both gone together to see his exhibition one lunchtime earlier in the week, and been amazed at the range and quality of his works, and sent him lengthy texts to say so. Jake, laughing, said to him, between manly back slaps,

"*...By 'Eck Mate! – Y'll soon be that rich an' famous we'll 'ave to make appointments wi' y'Personal Assistant to cum an' visit y'!*"

Dave replied with mock pomposity, his deadpan humour so similar now to Jake's,

"Well...she might be too busy to – *mightn't you Mel...!?* - So...possibly an option to resolve that potential time conflict issue could be that we'd just have to organise and construct my ongoing schedule of specific commitments and just diarise instead certain set days with mutually convenient windows of opportunity for times to accommodate visitors within it...!"

Jake laughed uproariously at that. "*Ah said y'could 'Waffle Fer England!' Did'n I mate!?*"

Mel was giggling as she said, "And...if I'm going to be a top flight PA to a famous artist I'm going to need a new wardrobe for it...and..."

"*Eh!?*" Dave expostulated, and still being humorously obtuse, he said, "But there's a perfectly good wardrobe in the caravan! *And there isn't room in it for another one...!*"

Jake quickly followed up on Dave's humour, by saying, with apparent seriousness, "*Quite Right Mel!* – But don't you worry! - I bet

211

Reg'll 'ave an ol' spare one in 'is store – y'could get Dave to paint it up an' put it *outside the caravan on't patio*, an' put some plastic sheetin' - or mebbe sellotape some bin bags together or summat like that to put o'er it to keep the rain off – *that'd do – wunnit?!*"

Mel, with pantomimed dismay, turned away from the two men to look at Sophie and Magda, her hands on her hips, rolling her eyes and shaking her head as she sighed loudly, and said with mock dismay,

"*Men! - They just don't understand do they?! And you just can't seem to get a sensible conversation from them for very long at all these days can you...?!*"

They all laughed uproariously together, Magda delighting in the excitement, fun and humour of her four young friends, even Beau whinnied loudly, pawing his front hoofs at the ground.

"Aye! *Y're prob'ly right Mel! -* At least not from us two! *But there's another man waitin' for us now who I reckon'll more than mek up for it...!*" Jake said to her.

"Yes – and we'd better not keep him waiting any longer!" she replied. Then looking over to Beau she said, "so...we have to say *'bye bye'* for now Beau! And See You Soon!"

She skipped back over to him and hugged him, then moved aside as Sophie did the same. The two men went and patted his neck, saying a few words to him, and then Beau whinnied loudly again, turned around and took himself off to rejoin the children, Ruth and Lucia. They all watched him trot away through the trees, then they went in to join Anders...

Chapter 13: Magda Starts The Revelations

They were sitting once again on the comfy sofas in the same large, but intimate, cloister like alcove they'd been in before that lead off from the immense stately room. After a few moments of general, settling in and welcoming chat with Anders, Magda told him that Dave now knew all about his paintings, and that she had also said to him they were going to contact and ask some of their friends whom were now prominent 'movers and shakers' in the Worlds' of Art and of its Marketing, to start to further promote his work - as they had discussed together at the soiree last night.

She then stood up and asked them all to excuse her whilst she went to quickly bathe and change out of her working clothes. Anders replied, politely standing as well for her, saying,

"Splendid! Quite right too! *Oh My!* - I certainly didn't mean you *needing to bathe and change your attire Magda!...Ha ha!*

"I'm going tomorrow morning to see your exhibition myself David, I would have gone before then but I must admit that this past week has been an unexpectedly busy one for me, and I just haven't been able to, so I am looking forward to it!"

Sitting back down he looked up at Magda who was just about to walk away and said, "I knew you had much to occupy you today Magda so I thought I'd leave it until now to let you know that I spoke with Jurgens in Germany late this morning, and based upon the glowing and enthusing recommendations from you, Ruth, and Lucia, *he is very keen to see David's work – with a view to hosting an exhibition of it!*"

Magda smiled in pleasure at this, and excusing herself again went away to change.

"So David..." Anders said, "... ideally, and as soon as possible really, what you'll need to do is perhaps organise a photo session of all of your paintings and then email them to Jurgens – and please do copy me in as well", he took out a silver business card holder from a waistcoat pocket, clicked it open and handed one of the ornately embossed cards over to Dave, "...all the relevant address details you'll need are on there for you ol'chap. When I get them I will forward them onto several of our other friends and associates whom are also very active in the world he operates in, and they will be more than interested to see them as well!"

"*Oh yes definitely! Wow! Thank you so much Anders!* I'll have to do it at the gallery though – *perhaps I could meet with you there tomorrow and photo' them then...?*"

Sophie quickly interrupted to say, "*- call in at the office first Dave -* and you can borrow one of the new professional digital SLR cameras the company's just bought – they cost a fortune! But the quality of the images is absolutely incredible, and as there's only me and two others in the office on Monday mornings – the boss will be at the Pickering branch until the mid afternoon, you could use one and when you bring it back I'll download the photos and email them to you, you can then sort them all how you want them and send them on!"

"Oh Fantastic! *Thanks Sophie! Awesome!* I will! Thank you! My digital camera is just an old average quality cheap one so Thank You! - I'll go from your office to that new internet Cafe near the harbour to access my emails as we won't have our internet at the caravan for about another week, so I can then email them all straight away Anders!"

"Well that's all excellent! *Nothing like teamwork and having good friends is there?!*" He chuckled.

"I think meeting you at the gallery is an excellent idea as well David, it'll give me the opportunity to listen to you talk about your works, I can also give you a hand if you need to move the paintings around for photographing as well.

"Our friend Jurgens is in Berlin at his main gallery in the city centre at the moment, he told me he's currently hosting a Rauchenberg retrospective exhibition, and then several exhibitions of more contemporary prominent artists for a few months, but he always keeps gallery space open for newly discovered artists to exhibit..*so...I must say - everything's looking extremely promising!"*

Conversation then flowed around other things involving them all for a few minutes – in fact it was less than five minutes before Magda returned to them, completely transformed wearing a canary yellow, flowing sari style dress of chiffon with delicate embroideries on its sleeves, the vibrant colour matched her freshly painted finger nails and the toenails of her bare feet, her freshly washed – but somehow almost totally dry – very long auburn red hair hung in an elegant but stylish loose coiffure down her back.

Jake looked at Dave, his mouth and eyes wide open in pantomimed amazement, then in a loud cheeky whisper he said,

"*Crikey me Dave!* If Soph' said she was goin' to bathe an' do 'er hair an' get changed I could put a DVD on an' watch most of it before she got back...!"

Sophie firmly pushed at his shoulder muttering mock embarrassed admonishments about him being so rude!

"Yes, I know what you mean mate..." Dave responded, with a tolerant sigh,"I usually go and walk to the end of Filey Brigg, do a bit of fishing, go back – *and still have to wait for ages then...!*"

Mel responded to him in exactly the same way Sophie had to Jake.

But at the same time both girls did wonder to themselves *Just How On Earth* had Magda reappeared so quickly looking as immaculate as she did...!

Sophie thought that her doing so was just like one of those impossible-to-explain scenes from 'Mary Poppins'!

Magda's shoulders shook in silent laughter at them. As they quickly settled down again to listen to what was going to be revealed to them now, she could only hope that she was doing the right thing...but in her heart she knew that the four young people were now ready to progress again, and take the next momentous step to proceed further along on their path of knowledge...and to know...

Anders slapped his palms down onto his knees and said, "*Righty Ho then!* To start things rolling, as they say, I'll quote you from last night David when you said to Jake, *'well it's over to you then...'*, by saying now: *Well, it's over to you then Magda!* - I defer to you to explain further...and tell our story..."

"Thank you Anders...You are all very aware now, from previous talks given by Anders and myself of the background to the current state of human affairs *on* the planet generally...and when I briefly summed up at the end of our get together yesterday evening, I said that you are now fully aware of what the parasites and their human agents are planning to take place *on* the Earth with regards to their black, negative agenda of most likely staging a devastating false flag alien invasion, the planned depopulation and the ultimate goal of a centralised, globally controlling, fascistic corporate bureaucracy to finally usher in their desired 'New World Order'...

"I also said that: *'it is time for you to know who and what is on your side...and who we are, and where we are from...'*

"So...that is what I am going to do...But firstly, before I jump right into all of that, I want to add to your background knowledge and understanding, by talking about some of the history of planet Earth, which will include some of those, whom...within...its orbit, are allied to your ideals – and are *'on your side'* - who have been, and will continue to, work tirelessly to do all they can to prevent that dark agenda's ultimate goal from happening. And if it does become...unavoidable...to attempt to minimise its impact on humanity on the Earth...and of course for the Earth herself.

"Also this evening, I want to further add to your knowledge and understanding of the non-terrestrial races who are making contact with you...whom also desire, and are determined that the dark agenda will fail, and for your race to ascend and advance, which will only happen once you have overcome and expelled the parasites...

"Sooooo...to begin...

"...The planet Earth has been fairly accurately calculated by mainstream scientists to be four and a half to five *billions* of years old. With that in mind, if we were then to say, 'let us imagine, for the sake of this example, that *all of those years* are represented *as being a*

216

twenty four hour clock'...and then we were to ask: *'At what time did human beings* - as recognised and known about by mainstream science - *appear on that clock?'*

"The answer you would be given is: *'somewhere between sixty to twenty seconds before 'midnight'...or hour twenty four...'*

"Your next question might then be: *'So what was happening on the Earth during the previous twenty three hours, fifty nine minutes...?!'* Mmmm, what indeed?! The detailed answer to that question is something we can approach another day, for now though I think the previous answer gives us a very clear background, or representation, of the comparative historical time scales of humanity appearing on the Earth and the age of the planet, that is more meaningful to place what I am going to talk to you about now, in to.

"So...if we now go way back in time, looking, as we do, at all the *known* evidence of recorded human history, *and then we go even further back*...we will soon find a thread, which, if we then follow it, will lead us into the fabric of traditions woven from a true knowledge communicated by the stories of a truly wondrous place.

"Those stories became the central theme of so many ancient lores, traditions and beliefs across all of the continents which were passed down orally from generation to generation before writing appeared.

"The essence of all those stories was that there really does exist a magical, sacred, holy place, a place where there is an earthly paradise, where the highest ideals, attainments and aspirations of humanity are an everyday reality...

"To put it a little more poetically...you could say that: *this was the place where all the wonderful, aspirant dreams of childhood innocence could be realized...*

"...and there is a hidden, secret path that leads to this place, this blessed domain, to this seemingly invisible world, this esoteric and occulted domain. Seeking and then following this path has been one of the central quests of all the past and present mystery teachings.

"For example, in the mythology of the mystery schools of ancient Greece this heavenly land was called Mount Olympus, and The

Elysian Fields. The symbolism of the mountain is interesting, because the peak of the mountain is in the sky, the middle is on the earth and its base is in...the...intra-terrestrial world...

"...Speaking of the writings from those long ago days of ancient Greece, to Jason and The Argonauts it was accessible through what they then called the Land Of Kolkhis, and they sought it in their quest for the Golden Fleece...

"...The ancient Egyptian Mystery Schools, in their 'Book Of The Dead', called it the Halls Of Amenti...

"...In the very early Judeau-Christian teachings it was called the City Of The Seven Kings Of Edom – or *Eden*...

"...It was called The City Of The Seven Petals Of Vishnu in the Brahmanism tradition and teachings....

"...The ancient Persians - Persia is now known as Iran - called it Alberdi or Aryana, The Land Of Their Ancestors, who arrived from the North, hence the word *Aryan* as a racial description...

"...The Hebrews called it Canaan, the Mexicans Tula or Tolon, the Aztecs Mayapan, and the Spanish invaders – El Dorado...

"...To the Celts it was called 'The Land Of The Mysteries' – or Dananda, from which comes one of the old Gaelic names for their pantheon of Supernatural Folk – *the Tuatha De Danann*...

"...The early Chinese philosophers called it: 'The Land Of Chivin...'

"...In the Middle Ages of England, it was called 'The Land Of Avalon', and legends of that time tell us that this is where the knights of The Round Table went under the leadership of King Arthur and the wise guidance of the white magician – Merlin, on their quest for the Holy Grail, which, to them, was a true symbol of many things – but mainly of Justice and Immortality...

"...It is the Land of Valhalla to the Germanic and Northern European tribes...

"...It is the 'Utopia' written about by Sir Thomas More...

"...The Shangri La of the Tibetans...

"...To the Buddhists it has always been...'Agharti'...The Land Of Immortality...

'Ag' means inner, and 'Hartha' means Earth, which are words derived from the ancient language of the Zhang Zhung culture which Tibetan Buddhism later evolved from. It is the hidden intra-terrestrial world within the hollow planet of Earth that all Buddhists believe in, and is central to their Faith.

"The capital of Aghartha is the city we call Shamballah, which is Sanskrit, another ancient language, for: *a place of peace, tranquillity and happiness'...*"

Magda now paused, not because of any intention to deliberately create a dramatic effect, but simply because what she was going to say next would be a momentous admission for her to make, and one that over the centuries, she had only rarely made, and then only in circumstances that she had considered totally justified it.

Amongst her kind her status and high position permitted her to make this admission, and so she had decided, towards the end of their meeting yesterday evening, to make it again, because these four, brave and shining young people, despite having been made fully aware of all the malefic intentions of the parasites and their human legions' false-flag-invasion agenda, *and everything else connected to it* - they were still resolute in their determination to ally themselves to do whatever they could to prevent this aspect of the negative forces' apocalyptic agenda.

She had informed Anders last night at their soiree that she had decided to tell them – and he had, and not just from his deference to her status, agreed wholeheartedly that the admission was totally justified - saying that he too had been tremendously moved by the fact that the four young people had still been resolute in their determination to proceed with – what Melanie had called – 'The Pandora Quest'. So now, they needed to know...this...

She silently took a deep breath whilst looking into each of their expectant faces, and then very quietly she said to them:

Sophie, Jake, Mel and Dave were immediately stunned and instantly became utterly still and silent, it was as if they had suddenly fallen into a state of catatonic mute immobility. Their shocked and astounded minds claimed every vestige of their physical energies to work frantically as they started to try and process this overwhelming revelation that Magda had lead them to.

Movement returned to them after a few seconds, although it was only to slump, one by one, back into the sofas, but they were still quite mute behind their wide eyed staring at Magda and Anders, their minds spinning in high revs'.

Magda knew that right now each of them was having to deal with the struggle and uproar of their own mind's immediate-response-survival-mechanism of *'cognitive dissonance'* – which comes immediately into play when the mind, and particularly the ego-dominant part of it, is confronted with new facts and therefore new explanations and implications that are so completely different to the established and fixed paradigms of belief it already firmly holds, that those new facts are immediately, reflexively resisted as they are perceived as being a threat to its stability.

She knew, of course, that most humans respond, most of the time, quite negatively during the 'cognitive-dissonance phase' – and sadly most of them never progress through it, but remain trapped in it, due to being quite unable to open their minds to welcome and accept *any other facts which differ from their existing 'understanding', explanation and perception of reality* – because the 'new' facts which verify contradictory knowledge and wisdoms severely threaten the world view that they have so assiduously built up over the years. So it makes that edifice of beliefs suddenly very vulnerable, and their minds respond predictably with vehement denials and refusals of the new factual information that has been revealed. Their minds then, sometimes, 'pull up the drawbridges', locking them in, and keeping the unwelcome invaders out, safe they think, in their own impregnable and familiar castle.

A castle which then, all too often, becomes the refuge of a cynical, fear-full, and sceptical person, who ultimately, if they never leave it, and venture out beyond its confining walls, they will, sadly, accomplish very little more in that self-restricted lifetime...*Because it makes them quite unable and unwilling to welcome and accept the truth of anything that contradicts their own preciously held belief systems, which, as they perceive, are now under siege.*

This is the, all too often, usual reaction in varying degrees...of incredulity, cynicism and even hostility, from the masses of the people in their 'dodgem-car-like' cyclic everyday world of home, workplace, and the popular venues of their social gatherings such as the pubs, clubs, and institutions, all full of people who mostly only get their information about what has happened, and what is currently going on in the world, from mainstream education and corporate mainstream media publications and their constant propaganda barrages of TV 'News' broadcasts...

The cognitive-dissonance *'drawbridges-up'* reaction is even more emphatic and acutely hostile from those men and women who have achieved prominence in the world's of Education, Science, Media, Finance, Politics, Military, Law, Industry and Religion – because those institutional groupings are the bastions of people who only rise to the higher echelons of them if they *'toe the party line'* unquestioningly, with their dogma programmed, and therefore tightly closed, shut off minds.

But at least those brave, shining souls who dare to bring forward alternative *but true facts* opposed to these elitist dogmas and agendas are no longer *publicly* executed by those determined to hold on to their elitist dogmas - by being burned alive in public tied to a wooden stake for example – like Giordano Bruno was by the Catholic Church for first stating, and with proof, that the Earth moved around the Sun...and not the Sun around the Earth...and he was just one of hundreds of thousands – nay - millions - of men women and children that they tortured, burned alive or killed in other obscene and horrific ways for believing and promoting the so called 'heresies' – beliefs and knowledge that didn't concord with all the 'official' dogmas...

All those Institutions were, and still are, all guilty of similar heinous acts to maintain their hegemonic dogmas, and therefore their power, by brutally stamping out any opposing fact-ions. *Nowadays though, using the vast armoury they have built up of their media mind-controlling psychological weapons, and their advanced technology of energy beam physiological weapons, all that tends to be done much more discretely* than in the earlier centuries - sometimes it is called *'death by ridicule'*, as that ostracises and falsely discredits the proponents of truth revelation and alternative explanations, all those deviously subtle methods of manipulation and control can be just as effective as the brutal methods...

However...Magda knew - as all of those thoughts rapidly flew through her mind - *but one could never be a hundred percent sure -* that each of these four young people *still had their own, open minds,* untainted by the hierarchical, dogmatic institutions, and so they still had the moral strength and capability to welcome and embrace revelatory truths. She and Ander's had both witnessed the proof of this from the two young couples' reactions to everything they had told them about so far in their previous meetings together...

So she continued to wait, sitting silently with Anders, for their minds to process in their own time, what she had just revealed to them.

It was Sophie who first managed to pass through the cognitive dissonance phase and regain her voice to say very quietly, her voice and her whole body shaking with emotion:

"I, I knew it would be something like that...but, well, not...not in a million years would I have thought it was that...! I've never even heard anything about it before...about Aghartha, and about the Earth – being hollow! - And, and...all of that...! But now, to me, it, it just means you are all even more wonderful and even more, more...very special, and...and...amazing."

She had to stop talking then as her voice finally cracked and her eyes filled and overflowed with tears. Jake was next, but right then he could only manage to nod vigorously, allying himself to her words as he put his arm round her and she snuggled into him, still looking, as they both were, in great awe at Magda and Anders through tear blurred eyes.

Mel, now looking very pale, then said,

"I, I – We – knew, of course, because we've talked a lot about it, that you, that all of you - were...are...very different – I mean a very special different – very...well...wonder-full, brilliant, magical, and...just...just so wonder-full! – And now...for me too, you, you all still are of course - but even more so as well! Oh My God! It's real! It's all true isn't it?! - It's like I said to Sophie on the 'phone this afternoon: '...knowing you - Magda – the truth will be stranger than fiction!'"

"Thank – You - My - Dears...your kind words touch me, they touch us...deeply...because they come from beyond the mind, they come from the heart, which always knows...And yes, it is all true..."

"Aye! I agree totally wi'y'both, Soph' an' Mel, an'all!" Jake blurted out, having finally found his voice.

"Y've both wrapped up pretty much 'xactly what I feel...o' course I already knew that you Magda, an' your sisters Ruth an' Lucia - that we've talked to so far - an' you Anders, an' everyone else we've met since we first came t'Fair last week– the two lads on the merry-go-round, an' Alfie an' Maria - were, are, just, well - special an' amazin' people...an' I think I am, an' we are, definitely incredibly privileged to know an' be so trusted by y'all...so...well...that's it!...Thank You!"

Dave nodded even more vigorously to Jake's words, and in a hoarse voice he said, "Yeah...that's, that's exactly what I feel too, an' I just want to add too, to say, thank you to you, to you all, for your trust to tell us, and for your help and for all your time with us...I, we, we'll, we'll never let you down..."

"And – I - Thank – You – Jake and David...Please know that Each Of You, that All Of You, are very special and amazing young people To All Of Us As Well..."

Magda tilted her head sideways to look at Anders and said to him,

"I think that now our young friends have managed, *on their own*, to safely pass through the Dark Domain of Dissonance, it is the perfect time *for all of us* to go over to the balcony and into The Light...as I'm sure the view from there will be of interest to them...and we will continue from there…"

"Yes! *Yes I think it will be! - Splendid idea Magda!*" He replied, then he smiled widely to the two young couples, and sprung to his feet with an agility that belied his great age.

Chapter 14: The High Balcony (I)

Anders courteously pulled back Magda's chair for her as she rose too, but rather more elegantly to her feet. He smiled at them saying, "I think you will all *be a tad amazed* at the lovely and *quite breathtaking* view we have from up here - *in case you haven't been amazed or breathless by anything else so far this evening that is!*"

"Thank you Anders. We are only going across the room my dears, just over there, to the crystal doors – they are hidden behind the curtain voiles, then we will walk out on to the balcony." Magda said to them as she watched them all get unsteadily to their feet.

"Oooh! *My legs have gone all wobbly!*" Sophie exclaimed, as she stood up, staggering slightly, as Jake steadied her.

"Er, well – look - *y'can 'ave a piggy back if y'want!* – An' don't worry - Ah've bin doin' a few more workouts at Simmo's gymn – *so ah think ah should be able to cope wi' all extra weight like…!*" Jake said to her with cheeky seriousness.

"No thank you very much! *I'm quite capable thank you!* - Cheeky! Give me your hand! – I'd better hold onto it! - *We don't want naughty little boys wandering off now do we!?*"

She replied to him in a mock strict school ma'm's condescending voice – promptly giving back as good as she got!

Their quiet and spontaneous laughter together at the funny banter between them made everyone else smile and then chuckle along with them as well.

Magda lead them all across the vast stately room, which was nearly as wide as two tennis courts placed end-to-end to each other are long. The two young couples were full of a tingling, excited anticipation, which increased with every step they took.

They walked towards the giant, cinema-screen sized, cream and golden, silky voiles that were draped and swagged in folds from high up in their ornate rococo styled gold gilted pelmeting, and then flowed

225

right down to swathe slightly on the floor, obscuring any details of what lay beyond. A bright, but softly diffused light passed through them.

When they had entered this vast stately room for the first time last Monday evening, Sophie had thought, as she looked around with her 'estate-agent's-eyes', that the subtle but bright illumination coming through the voile curtains was from dimmer switched, multiple and hidden light sources, but was probably using daylight type bulbs, as the quality of the light was so much better, and more natural looking than what you get from normal light-bulbs - especially the drab light from the so-called energy saving ones. She was about to find out that she couldn't have been more wrong…

When Magda was fifteen or twenty feet or so away from the voile curtaining she slowed her walk and gracefully moved her arms as if she were opening them manually, and then swung her hands forward in a door opening gesture. The many layers of silky voiles then started to quickly and silently fold back and smoothly glide to the sides to reveal a pair of huge, arched clear crystalline doors, that then slid soundlessly sideways into the thick walls, creating a huge arched entranceway to a large balcony outside, that ran in parallel to the inner room.

The balcony was paved with large multi hued pastel coloured and highly polished flagstones. A waist high, ornately carved, white marble balustrading ran along the balcony's front edge, which was about half a tennis court's length away from the entrance, but they saw that it swept and curved gracefully outwards, extending much further out from both sides of the immediate entrance area.

As soon as the voiles had rapidly moved aside to reveal the huge, clear crystal, glass-like doors, they had all been able to see through them to what lay beyond...Anders had said the view was 'a tad breathtaking', and he had been absolutely right – apart from his typical understatement of it being a lot more so than just 'a tad'! The two young couples had had to gasp loudly several times to get their breath - at the sight then only partially revealed in front of them.

Once the crystal doors had fully opened and they had walked, very slowly, half a dozen paces onto the balcony together, each couple had then stopped, and clutched at each other, swivelling their heads from side to side in absolute, total amazement.

There was just so much for them to see and take in from the panoramic view they now had. This was unlike anything any of them had ever seen before. The warm and fragrant air welcomed and enveloped them, as the soft but bright light from above and all around them, bathed them all in its ethereal glow.

Magda and Anders had stepped to one side, and slightly behind them so as not to obscure their views, and to observe their reactions with smiles on their faces.

Sophie had a sudden flashback to how she used to feel as a child for the long awaited Christmas morning, having rushed excitedly downstairs with overflowing anticipation, rushed across the hall and pushed open the door to the lounge – and then, wide eyed, delight overwhelming her, she stood as still as a statue as she saw all the colourful and gaily wrapped parcels of presents, all waiting for her to open them, piled up high at the foot of the decorated tree.

Those very same emotions of delighted excitement, pleasure and sheer joy that she had felt as a child had all come suddenly flooding back to her again now, but multiplied a hundred fold, as she exclaimed with unrestrained delight:

"Ohhh! Jussssst Loooook...!"

They were very, very high up, and way, way below, out in front and all around them, going all the way to far off horizons was a city landscape. But it was unlike any other city or landscape any of them had ever seen before. It was futuristic looking, yet at the same time it was somehow, obviously, very ancient. As she gazed at it all she thought that some parts of it did look *slightly* similar though – but on a much vaster scale - to dwellings she had once seen on a holiday, when she had been on a tour to some of the cliffs and caves in Tunisia, which had been made into luxurious homes and a four star hotel.

But here there were myriads of immense, circular, smooth and creamy coloured crystalline stone towers, where she could see scores of tiny windows, doorways and balconies on each of them – but they were only tiny because of the sheer distances away they were. The towers looked as if they might be gargantuan stalagmitic pillars reaching up and disappearing into the glowing light above.

Then, with even more mind numbing astonishment, she – as they all did! - realised they were also actually seeing, ovular and disc shaped objects of various sizes flying around in the air! Some were stationary, just hovering at different heights, but it seemed like there were dozens – scores - of them rapidly flitting everywhere in all directions - and were doing so quite soundlessly. They looked as if they were made of shiny chrome, glinting as they flew, reflecting the light....

Jake, as mesmerised as the others were, pointed with a slightly shaking arm to a large ovular craft that had come rapidly towards them and then stopped to hover nearby but was now passing rapidly and silently away from them in front of the white marble balustrading. His mouth was wide open as he stared at it, a rapturous expression on his face, elation swept out of him in waves and he barely managed to gasp out loudly, *"Wwhat isss thhhat...? Ww, what aaaaare they?!"*

Magda replied, now with a wide grin on her face, "I am sorry to say Jake - that we do not have any motorcycles here! Even flying ones!" She laughed then, quickly adding: *"But there is a very interesting thought, as there is no reason we could not!"* And she looked meaningfully at Anders for several seconds. Turning back to Jake, she said,

"We have, what we call our *'silver-crafts'* instead, when we want transport to go to another place that is too far to walk to...They are all crafts which anyone can summon, anytime they need them. The large one that just passed us thought that we might be in need of it, but passed by when we didn't contact it..."

"Wowww! - Y'mean it - or 'ooever's flyin' it – knew... some'ow...that...?!"

"Yes, that is correct. But no one actually flies them – by having to

228

first sit in a cockpit, and then physically operate its controls - like a pilot in an aeroplane does. Instead, the crafts' have an operating system which is an intelligent, self-programming and interactive technology, which means we can link, attune and interchange our psycomms' transmission wavelengths with them, to summon and direct them.

"I'm sorry to say though that if you were to try and summon one it wouldn't come to you! That is because it, they, have not been calibrated to recognise *your* unique DNA profile, which, when they have been, activates their operating programs to receive and respond to the specific profile of your individual thought transmission wavelengths for instructions...

"Theirs is a form of non-living, artificial, specifically parametered and limited 'cyber-techno-engineered-consciousness' – that is not self-aware, *whereas we, and you, have a living, self-aware, sentient consciousness that is potentially unlimited...*

"If we had been wanting to go somewhere else *right now,* either Anders or I would have simply thought – psycommed - to it, for it to come and hover on the wider part of the balcony, over there, so we could enter it, and having psycommed our destination to it, it would take us there...not at all too dissimilar to the taxi services on your world really...well...similar in purpose – but just different in method!

"*- And of course there are no fares to pay because we do not have or use money here...!* Well - we have access to vast amounts of it, but it only has any practical value to us when we use it on the surface World!" She laughed lightly.

"The crafts' propulsion system is based on electro-magnetic-gravitics, which we have talked about to you before - in relation to the hidden technology used in the more basic types of flying crafts certain elite factions use on the Earth, which were, and are, developed in their secret, unacknowledged projects, in hidden, underground bases.

"And now...*you are all totally aware* - of the existence and reality of *our flying crafts!*" She laughed again, saying - *"in our, secret and hidden - 'underground base'...!"*

229

Magda continued looking at Jake, still mesmerised at the sight of them, his head rapidly swivelling from side to side, and up and down, as he followed their movements. She had intended to say what she was going to say next to him, much later that evening, but right here and now seemed a more appropriate time.

Her lips formed a small smile as she then said to him, "...and it is with you specifically...Jake...that later this evening, Anders wants to arrange a meeting with you, for another day – but soon - when he would like to introduce you to some of our friends from here, who are the...design engineers... for them..."

Jake reacted to that by doing an almost cartoon-like double take as he dragged his eyes away from them to stare at her...

"Whaaat?! I c,could get t,t,to meet the b,blokes who actually made 'em...?!" He gasped.

"Yes, of course Jake...the reason for that meeting – with the *men and women* - which would be the first of many - would be to start discussing them with you in much greater depth...and to instruct and guide you to become fully aware of, of the, of the engineering, the mechanics and all the operational specifics of the propulsion technology – *why and how it works* – *and why and how to make it operate a craft....who knows – maybe a future project might well be a 'flying motorbike'...or perhaps even a whole fleet of them...!"*

A verbal response to that was way beyond Jake right at that moment, he just stood immobile, staring wide eyed at her.

"Because we are hoping you will consider project managing your own – but working with all of those whom he will introduce you to – your own, initially secret, initially *'unacknowledged-hidden-project'*...

"The ultimate goal of doing so, *along with many others doing similar work on the Earth,* is to openly reveal this technology to all the peoples on the Earth *at the same time...!* However, that process of revelation would actually be carefully – *very carefully* - stage managed and synchronised by many others of us. Us, and those beings not of the Earth, with whom we are now in those protocol accords with...

"You would, as well, of course, and very effectively so, be continuing the work - *that your Father had already made great inroads to achieving...* "

By then the means of vocalising any coherent words in reply had definitely failed Jake, due to the compounding of, firstly, the actual reality of the crafts' existence, then the matter-of-fact but completely astonishing revelations of how they operated, then, above either of those - *all the implications of what Magda had just suggested...*

He put his hands on the back of his head, looking down, then up, as he staggered slightly, slowly walking round in a tight circle, blowing out deep breaths. He then stopped his pacing to look intently at Magda, then Anders, then back to Magda, and slowly, in an emotionally filled, quiet and hoarse voice, he managed to ask them,

"Y,yymean...y'think...I...Me!...Could...could...be...would...be able - *to be part of summat momentous like, like that...?! "*

Magda replied just as slowly and just as quietly, nodding her head to emphasise her words.

"Yes, yes...we...really do Jake. *You are more than able to...* "

Sophie, her eyes now brimming again, stepped in front of him and reached up to gently lower his hands, which she then pressed together with hers, looking up into his face, gazing silently into his wide open eyes, full of love for him. Then she said, her voice just as quiet, and just as filled with emotion,

"Y,you remember me saying, in the garden, at your Mum's, just after our tea with her yesterday, and after you'd said that compared to your Dad – that you were: *'just a grease-monkey with a spanner!?'* And I said: *'No You're Not, You Silly!* You are *just as clever, and just as skilful, you could do anything you set your mind to - I Know You Could!'? "*

He nodded slowly to her, Sophie then said, *"well, I meant it all, every word of it!* And in a similar way Magda - and Anders – *are saying exactly the same to you...* "

He blew out a deep, loud breath and disengaging his hands from hers, he gently pulled her close and put his arms around her, stooping slightly, to hug her, his chin resting gently on the crown of her head, his eyes screwed tightly shut. After a moment he opened them, blinking rapidly, and again looked over to Magda and Anders.

Sophie felt his chin move and she realised he was gently nodding. She slowly leaned her upper body backwards to look up into his face, as he then drew in another deep breath, and managing to find his voice again, but which only came out as a whisper, he said:

"...an' then I said: '*I think me Mum were right! You are a good influence on me! – An' with you Soph' I reckon' I could!*' An' I'm sayin' it again now...so Thank You, thank you for that Soph....!"

He smiled widely down into her eyes, pulsing out his love for her. He then looked across to Magda and Anders, and said, "*An' Thank You Both an'all!* If all three of yous think I'm upto it, well...*who am I to argue?!* Reckon y'might be right! So yeah, *I'll give it me best,* an' thank you, *thank you*...we'll 'ave a chat later then Anders - an' start the ball rollin' – *or flyin'*...!

"*Blimey! - It'll put any other project I've ever done right in't shade…!*"

He called out to Mel, "'Ey Mel - when y'called it, 'The Pandora Quest' – *'ow bloomin' right y'were!*" In reply she grinned widely and raised her hand, clenched into a tight fist and shook it in the air to him.

He laughed out loud as he then looked up to watch the flying crafts again, his head back, and his mouth wide open. He was even more enthralled now and utterly transfixed at the reality of what he was seeing - and the reality of what the future was now going to be unfolding for him. He glanced back over to Dave and Mel who were reacting similarly, and shaking their heads from side to side as they hugged each other, and stared up at the flying crafts.

Chatting excitedly together they soon all walked over to the marble balustrading and the two couples just stood there gawping at the surreal views. Mel said, as she leaned forwards and looked over the marble balustrade and down below them,

"Oh My God! *We're so high up! - It's like looking out of an aeroplane window when it goes just below the clouds!"*

She quickly stepped back a few steps, having a sudden shiver of vertigo, disconcerted by the height and sheer scale of their surroundings. She looked back behind them towards the room they had just left, and tilted her head back saying, *"Look! It goes up just as high again!"* They turned and looked up, and up and up, seeing that they were in, or rather, on, one of the huge ivory coloured crystalline stony pillars as well.

Magda and Anders didn't intrude upon them, instead they just let them soak it all in, in their own time, but after a few minutes they pointed out and briefly explained some of the features they could see.

Dave thought back to when they had all first entered the stately room behind them, last Monday evening with Anders, after leaving the Trocadero Cafe, and then, when they had all sat down on the sofas in the alcove with Magda, one of the first questions he had asked her had been: *'where are we Magda?'*

He recalled that she had answered him by saying, *'This room you are in exists...let me just say for now...in a different part or layer of the same third dimension...'* And he realised now of course, and it was so obvious - that had she just blurted out there and then that: *'they were actually way below the surface of the hollow Earth in another world - that would've completely freaked him - all of them! – well and truly – Out!'*

His smile stretched a bit wider as he admired the technical truthfulness of the answer she'd given him then...and also the obvious concern she'd had not to alarm and distress them by revealing too much at once...

Magda saw that he clearly wanted to ask her something, but out of politeness or awe he didn't want to just interrupt her chatting quietly with Anders, so she smiled and nodded to him.

"Oh thanks...er, can I...I wanted to ask you before but...could you, er, *just so I get it totally clear in my head* – once and for all - could you just confirm that I'm right - that we are now, *we're all now actually somewhere deep inside the Earth...*?"

Mel jiggled his hand, smiling at him saying, "c'mon Dave – *catch up!*"

"Of course I will David – *yes* - we are currently over two and a half thousand miles below the surface of the Earth."

"*...Right...oookkk thanks*...I, I, well it might seem as if *I'm being a bit thick*, but...it's just taking me a while to actually get my head round it...*or in it!*"

"Oh please do not berate yourself David, I think you are doing remarkably well so far to take it all in and *'get your head round it – or in it'*, as you say, as quickly as you have – *I think you all are!* Do you agree Anders?"

"*Absolutely! I really am very impressed!* Most of the people from the surface world who've visited here before you, took *considerably longer* to come to terms with it all!

"There have been occasions - I must say though that fortunately there's been *very few* of them, when they just couldn't, as the reality of it all was just too much for their minds to come to terms with, and caused them to panic and become very stressed.

"So...on those rare occasions we promptly returned the visitors back to the surface world - but having first erased their memories of coming here...sometimes it's for the best..."

"*Right, thanks Magda - I've caught up now! - Not usually so slow!*"

Chapter 15: The High Balcony (ii)

Magda suggested they all moved over to the central area of the balcony and sit down for a while on the three sofas arranged there in a triangle around a circular, gold and shiny black lacquered, low, oriental looking table. The sofas were long Chesterfield styled ones like those in the alcove off the stately room, but these outside ones were an apple green coloured silky fabric not reddish brown. Once they were all settled, or as settled as they could be considering the surreal environment they were now in, Magda started talking again, explaining more about where they were.

"As you have all seen...many, many others also have their homes here, and there are lots of other cities, all very similar to this one which is called Shamballah, and is our capital city. Some of the citizens of Aghartha stem from very ancient societies which pre-dated the major civilizations of the Earth's surface humanity - and there were many of those which are as yet completely unknown about to your modern historians, that disappeared from the surface world without trace...mainly due to the sea level rising many hundreds of feet, scores of thousands of years ago...

"Our benevolent monarch resides here, in Shamballah, as well – in the edifice I pointed out to you, his full title is: 'The King Of The World', and he is our supreme representative, but is aided by a Tribal Council, although all Agharthan citizens can participate, should they desire to, in the decisions and the formulating of policies, which would affect everyone. Because everyone here has a voice that is listened to...and everyone is made aware of everything that is happening. For example, your presence here with us now – is already known to all...

"One of the primary responsibilities our Monarch and Tribal Council has is to disseminate - to make information available to everyone - because we have no biased, controlled media – or any 'media' as such! - keeping secrets from the populace, and publishing or broadcasting all their propaganda lies and their 'false news'.

"The parasites cannot survive here even if they did somehow manage to get in, because of the higher fifth to mid sixth dimensional frequencies of our environment, and society. They have not attempted to anyway because they sensed that there is no nourishment here for them from negative energies; and also because they know they would just burn up like a vampire would if he or she walked out of a dark room and went out into the sunlight…

"The Earth above, the surface world, is still in the third dimensional frequency…*for the time being*…which is why they are able to so devastatingly influence it to have all the negative energies created for them to survive and flourish, from the lower levels of the fourth dimension where their colonies exist and operate from.

"So there are none of the myriad…*contaminations*…their elite minions and their tiny ruling cabal of 'money-wealthy elites' willingly create for them. For example, by using a financial and banking system they created as a tool of control, and to make debt slaves of the citizenry, *because we do not use, or have, 'money' here*…instead all the requirements each individual citizen needs to live a long, healthy and happily fulfilled life here are freely available to all, and shared by all willingly.

"We have instead what you would call 'a barter system', where an individual's time and particular abilities can be exchanged with another, or others, for something they particularly desire.

"For example, you David, might teach and help another – or many others - to develop their artistic abilities, and as a willing token of gratitude, in exchange, he, she, or they would, say…arrange to help you further develop *your* abilities in meditating or remote viewing…or whatever area of ability you wished to learn more about, enhance, and become more proficient in – which, in time, you would ultimately share back into the whole society of course, for the benefit of all…that is the essence of a Unity Consciousness...

"My sisters and I have many responsibilities, not the least of which is regularly communicating directly with our Monarch to appraise him and our Tribal Council, of the progress of events we are all communally involved in on the surface world. Many others do so as well of course, but there are...*specific areas of interest...that we are involved in, and have the abilities, resources, experiences and aptitudes to perform*...all of which mean we have spent, and still do spend, significant amounts of time on the surface World, both covertly and overtly.

"When we are 'up there' we use whichever one of the appropriate personal *'legends'* – which is trade craft jargon for a 'false' but credibly back-stopped assumed identity we have painstakingly created and maintained. 'Back-stopped' means that identity is fully verifiable – if it is ever investigated.

"We have to use them because we intermingle in many societies in many countries...and in all levels of them - from 'the bottom' to 'the top'!"

Magda smiled wistfully then, for some reason she had just vividly recalled one of those legends which she and Anders had frequently used a few decades ago, but hadn't been able to quite so much in recent years.

She then thought that a few minutes recounting one particular exploit whilst under the cover of that legend, would be a lighter and amusing tale for her young friends to hear now, as the things she and Anders were telling them were obviously much weightier, and an amusing tale might help to balance them a little bit, so she decided to recount an exploit they had carried out a few decades ago...

"Just one of the legends that Anders and I had were as antique dealers - importing and exporting all sorts of things all over the world. One of our specialities being vintage fairground equipment that we had had renovated for export to clients and collectors with private collections in America and Europe, and quite a lot went to public companies in the African and Asian countries. We mainly sourced the 'antiques' from the many countries in the then Eastern Europe and deeper into Communist Soviet Russia as it was at the time.

"The business is still based in Amsterdam. There are large

showrooms and we have extensive renovation workshops there as well to bring all sorts of things back to their former glory!

"Other helpers have now taken over and run the public face of it for a long time of course – as it would take some explaining if we were still doing so – and were seen not to have aged at all over the past eighty years!

"We set the whole enterprise up several years prior to the 'Cold War' starting as we foresaw that event happening. When it started the legends based on an established business made it much easier for us to carry on making frequent visits to, and travel around, all what became called then the 'Iron Curtain' countries, on our buying trips. Plus the guards at the entry check points we used all knew they would be at least two months wages better off everytime they rubber stamped our entry permits!

"On one such trip; *the real reason for it*, as we were ex-filtrating via Berlin, East Germany, was to smuggle out a Polish bio-chemist late one night, who had all the details of a deadly new biological-weapon the communist elites had ordered him to create, and had forced him to do so by threatening the lives of his family...and he desperately wanted to get himself and his family out and deny them the weapon, so saving thousands – possibly millions of lives…as the communist elites intended to field test it at several camps of the Gulag's 'dissident' prisoners within weeks...

"Others of us were in position all ready to get his entire family out of a village in Poland where they were under constant surveillance by the The Political Police of The Ministry of Internal Affairs called the MSW, at the same time on the same night, in a cloaked flying craft, invisible to radar. That was an option we had, but for various reasons it could have meant us possibly having to abandon the antique business cover afterwards, which would have closed down a very effective and well established pipe-line in and out of the Soviet bloc.

"Our opportunity came when he managed to let us know that he was to be in East Berlin for two days at a scientific conference. So it was our job to just get him out - on our way back from a buying trip

238

we had timed to do just that.."

Anders had realised by now of course which escapade she was referring to, and he had put his hands over his face, shaking his head as he slumped his shoulders. From behind his hands he said, "*Oh my goodness! I'll never forget that night! I still shudder!* It proved that: 'Assumption is the Mother Of All...*'Hick-Ups'...*" Magda smiled widely at his reaction.

"Well, to cut a long story short, we had been to Estonia and Lithuania for several days previously where, amongst many other things, we had bought almost an entire, and very old, fairground's collection of mechanised rides...which included: *a 'human firing cannon...'*

"After a lot of brain-storming, planning and calculations it was that big cannon, mounted on the back of a truck and backed upto 'The Berlin Wall', that Anders decided to use to...*fire the scientist over it with and land him into a large net on the other side, safely in West Germany!...*

"*Which we did!* But it was all very tense as we had to first decoy and disable the two KGB minders the scientist had constantly following him - as they all went back together to the hotel they were staying in, after having had a late dinner at a restaurant and much vodka afterwards...

"Anyway...everything worked out – *or fired out!* As we had planned, and he was then whisked away safely by others waiting on the other side of The Wall, who had also set up and dismantled the big net, and he was soon reunited in the West with his family. But we had removed any memories of that night from him and his family, so they would have no recollections of how they all had got away so quickly and safely...

"We, innocence personified, just travelled as we usually did, through the main checkpoint, after having all our trucks and possessions thoroughly searched, *in case we were smuggling anyone out across the border!* and paying the usual hefty bribes to all the guards of course...

"However...*however*...! It was only later when we were safely driving back towards Amsterdam, and Ruth psycommed me - that we found out the scientist, *unbelievably,* had *actually been carrying a large test tube full of the first – and only - batch of prototype liquid virus – incredibly he had managed to smuggle it out of the laboratory, having replaced it with an identical test tube full of water! What he had in that fragile glass tube was enough to kill just about everyone in Western Europe! – It was actually in his inside suit-jacket's pocket!*

"We had...*'assumed'*...he was just carrying all the original research documents of its formula...which he did have – they were hidden in his jacket's lining – *but not a sample of the real thing as well in just a glass tube!...So if anything had gone wrong with our trajectory and ballistic calculations...and it had been broken...!*

"To be fair to him he had really panicked and probably tried to tell us that he had it on him after we quickly and quietly got him away from his half drunk guards - he was in a similar state himself - we had immediately disabled and left the two of them on the floor of a shop's doorway – after dousing them with vodka so they looked and smelt as if they'd just passed out blind drunk, as they turned round the street corner.

"So we grabbed him and ran him across the street to one of our large trucks waiting there to drive him off – the one with the cannon on it - and he saw the huge cannon mouth sticking out from under a tarpaulin which he obviously thought he was about to be stuffed into – *and then he realised he was not just going to be smuggled out hidden inside it -* because one of our helpers was there with a helmet and a bulky 'flying jacket' ready for him to put on – *so we were obviously intending to fire him out of it!*

"He must have been just starting to warn us that he had the glass test tube full of the deadly virus on him – after he had at first shouted questions about the safety of his family, but he was suddenly making far too much noise in that quiet street so I had immediately put him into a sleeping trance - like I had done to the guards! *So we never knew about it! -* until much later when Ruth had de-tranced him!"

Fascinated, amused, and then shocked enthralment from the two young couples had been their reactions throughout Magda's brief telling of this amazing story. Questions then abounded and she fielded them deftly, wishing to get back onto the main theme that she had been talking about previously.

"Anders is one of our venerable Elders whom have chosen to dedicate part of their time to informing and educating our citizens here – particularly our younger ones." She couldn't help herself then and immediately followed that by saying: *"...when he is not busily engaged on firing scientists carrying deadly viruses out of cannons mounted on large trucks over high walls in the dead of night...of course!"*

More loud laughter erupted again from everyone as she leaned towards him and affectionately squeezed his forearm. *"Never again, never again!"* he was muttering! They all soon settled and Magda continued.

"Although 'younger' and 'age' have different connotations here! And of course, on the surface world he is known as a leading light, with many others, for doing the same and similar presentations you have all been to. My sisters and I have had the pleasure of working with you Anders for many, *oh...so many, many years..."* She reached out to gently squeeze his arm again, smiling affectionately at him.

Anders bowed his head with graceful humility to her, saying,

"Thank you, my dear, but I assure you - *the pleasure has been all mine..."*

"On the surface World our Monarch's covert representative, and primary *human* contact, is the spiritual leader called the Dalai Lama, a name which translated into English means: 'Ocean Of Wisdom'.

"For many centuries the incarnations of the Dalai Lamas used to reside at a monastery in the mountains of Tibet, however, since nineteen fifty nine he has been in exile and living mainly in nearby India, but he travels all over the surface World continuing his life's work to help and aid the spiritual development of humanity there.

"Ander's has had much involvement as well with all the Dalai

Lamas, along the same lines, especially so in their younger, formative years, by guiding and helping them to...to 're-acclimatise' when they go back there once again in the third dimension, from the seventh or eighth - but now in a corporeal form that is fifth or sixth dimensional...*it is quite complicated sometimes...!*"

Anders smiled discretely to himself, nodding at many memories. Then he said, "yes indeed, and that has always been a great pleasure as well, *but I have just been one of many others involved with them of course,* particularly in their early years." He replied self-deprecatingly. Magda smiled at him again, and continued talking,

"The Dalai Lama is based now in India because the Chinese military invaded his country and he wished to stay alive, in that particular physical, corporeal form, to continue helping humanity. The Chinese political and corporate elites, whom are totally controlled by the parasites, desired of course, to negate his and his fellow Tibetan monks' positive influences on the World.

"The Western, corporate mainstream media, paid then, and still pays now, scant attention to the barbaric tortures and ritual mass killings of the Tibetan monks and their fellow compatriots done by the Chinese military – often by vehicular dismemberment – in public squares - but I will refrain from going into further details of all that - and the many other totally inhumane and *un*-human atrocities they are guilty of…

"Communications between the Dalai Lama, the King and The Tribal Council are mostly made by using our psycomm telepathic networks. Physical travel and contact between here and Tibet, and to many other surface locations, used to be only made – and on occasions it still is made, by using the secret tunnels, and passage through them – and all the other tunnels to many different places on the surface world was, and still is, done by using our silver-crafts.

"But many centuries ago we rediscovered and redeveloped the portable 'Stargate' portal technology, so now, for those of us who need to go to the surface world on a regular basis, we usually just go through the mobile portals we have created - like the one you all used to come here..."

Magda paused then for a moment, before she continued talking.

"I realise that you must all still be bursting with lots of questions! But if I carry on by giving you more information – more 'info-drops!' - and more knowledge, first, I can - hopefully - cover and answer most of the ones you must already be thinking of...*But if there is something you really need to ask me – please do!*

"Soooo...Here in Aghartha there are none of the diseases or ailments associated with living on the surface World, and we have naturally...'reprogrammed'...our physical bodies to counter most of the degenerative effects of ageing.

"The current short lifespan of a surface human is not a natural occurrence. Many thousands of years ago your DNA was...*tampered*...with by the parasites; considerably reducing the following generations' life-spans was their primary aim when they did that, their secondary aim was to severely limit your spiritual awarenesses, so most of it was decommissioned – and surface scientists now call that 'junk DNA', it is not 'junk', it just needs...'re-commissioning'..

"As an analogy, imagine it like this: previously you had twelve cylinders in your 'engine' all firing together, then nine or ten of them, having been tampered with, just stop working - they are still there, but now they just do not do anything at all to help your engine's performance. Well, that engine is not going to perform anything like it did before, and those two or three remaining cylinders, now having to do all the 'work' of twelve, will be overloaded, and 'burn out' a lot quicker...

"Now contrast those tampered with and *changed states* to these: imagine, when 'everything' is working properly...if you knew you would, as long, long ago *you did*...that you would live healthily for many hundreds of 'years' – how differently would you live your life...?

"Imagine...or try to, the type of society that would create...what wisdoms, enlightenments, advancements, knowledge and

243

understanding every individual living in such a society would achieve…

"Imagine...when your physical death did *naturally* occur, *from your own choice for that to happen*...your soul, which you knew is immortal, could then choose, with advice and guidance from much, much higher, benign, over-seeing and guardian entities, to go to any of the many, countless, other worlds to experience, develop and learn more, in another physical dimension's life-form...

"Sometimes, depending on the individual's circumstances, and their choices of where to go, they will do so with the full recollections, in their new birth, of previous incarnations…and sometimes not...

"Sometimes, your soul would take on the role of what is called a 'walk-in', which is when, with the agreement of the soul incarnated already into a physical body since its birth, and that body has grown to a certain age and maturity, that soul will then depart it, and yours will enter that body to then continue its work...there can be many reasons for this being performed...

"Overall, please try to realise that *you are not just a 'one time only' temporary physical body - with a soul or 'spark' that 'fires it up'* – which, when it is extinguished from that body, it is judged, and then sent either to a 'Heaven or a Hell' for all eternity! - *simply based on its actions in one short lifetime on Earth when that temporary body dies!*

"No, no, no – what you really are is *an immortal soul that will occupy many hundreds, thousands, of temporary physical bodies*, until 'you' eventually, as a result of all those cumulative experiences, ascend to much higher realms, and go beyond the need to engage in the cycles of physically re-incarnating; beyond what is called 'The Cycle of Karma'.

"Imagine that to be like graduating from an institution of true learning. Once you have successfully passed through all of its classes, you go beyond, using all your accumulated experiences, skills, knowledge and *understanding* - to go on to do even greater things…

"At that time, and often before then, you will have full access to what are called the 'Akashic Records', which are a memory bank *of*

244

everything you have thought said and done, *in all of your many 'life-times'*...

"Everything I have just said are *the greatest, most important Truths,* that have been deliberately kept from you since the parasites invaded...

"One reason for that is because, just imagine, if throughout a physical life *all* individuals knew that Truth...then, after the physical body dies, if a soul was advised and chose to return there again, re-incarnating into another physical, say, human body, once again, to continue and expand upon the works it had been engaged upon previously - after a few short years, once that soul's-memories, knowledge, and understanding were fully 're-realised'...imagine what great works it would achieve in that new, physical life cycle...in service to others within such an enlightened society...Works that it would have re-commenced from, say, before the ages of four or five, or slightly more...

"Ask yourself, for example, how it was possible for a child of of eight or nine to compose a full symphony...like Amadeus did – Amadeus Mozart...and throughout Earth's history there have been many, many others, of course, in many different fields of endeavour, particularly in the creative arts, who had 'unnatural' ability from very, very early ages...

"That type of society would not be one that the parasites, working through their elite minions could easily – or if at all – maintain control over. Because there would eventually *be no* misguided, malign, 'powerful' 'elites' by then to do their bidding anyway.

"Because even if the parasites and their elites did manage to penetrate it, and establish a degree of hegemony of 'power', eventually over time of course, as that society grew ever rapidly in its numbers of enlightened individuals, eventually they would not be able to control or manipulate them at all...so with the increasing diminution of their sustenance which is entirely based on the negative energies they manipulate the masses *to create for them*, they would...have to go...elsewhere...or simply perish...That situation is close to where the surface world is at right now of course...

"Imagine a shepherd and his sheep dogs - an analogy I have used with you before, when we first all met together - they may be able to control fifty or five hundred sheep – but not five thousand or five million, or more...So the parasites, long, long ago, when they covertly invaded, had an immediate priority to change the true and proper longevity functioning of your physical bodies, *and your awareness of your True Reality...*

"They also, at that time, had 'a net', a trap, installed around the planet, so that each human soul, as it left the 'deceased-sooner' physical-body, was caught in it, and that soul's physical lifetime's memories were then erased. That soul was, is, then recycled, without choice, promptly *back onto the Earth*, knowing nothing of its past... like a blank clay tablet they could then impress with whatever they wanted into it...

"We have talked at length with you previously about *'manipulative institutions'* – well, I don't want to go over too much of that again at the moment, but the Hollywood psyops film media industry is one of those institutions in the forefront of maintaining this entrapment and recycling process.

"How many films have you seen where departed souls go to 'The Light'...? *Well, 'That Light' is the illusion – It Is The Trap!...*

"Those films are made to subliminally pre-programme the unconscious mind to do that. Many people are now aware of this and whilst their souls briefly retain those memories of the just passed physical life, they repeatedly demand that they *'be permitted to return to Source'* - and so they are - *because despite the soul trap, you cannot be forced against your free will into being immediately reincarnated here – but You Can Be Deceived Into It – so then it is speciously justified by the parasites as being 'your choice' from your 'Own Free Will' – after all you chose to go to The Light...! which is in accord with Multiversal Law...*But all that is pure sophistry – which is the skill to promote a misleading, false argument, and yet make it entirely plausible...

246

"'Sophistry' abounds in the surface world and the elites there are masters at it...Most of humanity is *totally unaware* of all of this of course - and so they are just continually recycled back onto the surface...remembering and therefore learning, nothing...for them it is just like getting back into yet another 'dodgem car' and going round and round the *same old limited track, over and over again...*"

"So then, of course, that human, from its earliest years was unquestioningly absorbing, and being imprinted with, sometimes irrevocably so, in that lifetime, the prevailing, and ever increasing, false programming of the societal milieu it was now living in... Becoming just another victim of the parasites' and the elites' many weapons of *'Mass Distraction'...*

"And as the years passed, and that human grew and interacted in all the desired ways with its society's programming, exactly as the parasites wanted it to - using all of their ever expanding 'manipulative institutions' and the malevolent machinations of their elite minions, that we have talked to you all about before at length - *it could then be 're-harvested' of all the negative energies it would unknowingly be manipulated to create, purely for the parasites' sustenance...*

"*But all those corrupted 'states of affairs' are, now, very close to coming to an end...*

"An example of: *'coming to an end'*, is the dismantling of the 'soul trap' that has been undertaken, and is still ongoing, and has been for a long time – in Earth years - by higher inter-dimensional beings, and there are now many gaps in it. This is allowing many souls – *but still mainly only the enlightened souls whom are aware of it, and know how to get through it,* to either go beyond, *or to voluntarily return –* but this time with their full memories intact. And also for other souls, coming here for the first time from much higher dimensions on other planets – *to help humanity* - to pass through the gaps in it and come here.

"Some of those in the modern era, in fact they are ever increasing now, whom have chosen to re-incarnate here, from other, enlightened higher realms, are called 'Star Children'...as I have mentioned to you before…And I believe you all to be the third wave of those that have done so, in recent decades…

"So that is some of the good news, and just some of the endeavours of...some of the others...'on your side'...that yesterday evening I promised you all I would reveal as well...

"The 'less than good news' is that the parasites are well aware of all this of course, and one method of counter-attack they are using against the incoming, enlightened souls incarnating here now, is that they have tasked their manipulative institutions and elite minions with increasing the insidiously deceitful programmes of extremely harmful, often deadly, vaccinations.

"This was a response actually predicted by an 'old soul' philosopher called Rudolf Steiner, back in the nineteen twenties - but perhaps if you, Anders, would comment on what he said in relation to this?…As you had far more contact with him than I did…"

"*Yes, yes of course, gladly!* Really excellent chap, knew him well, his writings and lectures were very important, very helpful – *still are of course.* He said on this subject…one...moment...please...everyone - I'm just recalling it...ah yes - that was it!….He said, during one of his series of lectures called: 'The Fall Of The Spirits Of Darkness', and I think it was in...was in...lecture thirteen, yes that was it! - he said about this:

'*...A way will finally be found to vaccinate bodies so that they will not allow the inclination towards spiritual ideas to develop, and all their lives people will believe only in the physical world they perceive with their five senses...*'

"...Somewhat tragically prophetic, those words, in light of what is happening now. He believed, *and quite rightly so*, that there were *no limits* to the knowledge and understanding that humans could attain. He was a philosopher – yes, but he also had a deep knowledge and understanding of esoterica, which is that knowledge understood by those initiated into the hidden, inner mysteries and secrets of the True Reality...

"He asked me to read through his first draft manuscript and then to help him edit it, as well as translate it into English from German, of his quite brilliant work: 'The Philosophy Of Freedom', or as he preferred to call it in the translation: 'The Philosophy Of Spiritual Activity', which was published a couple of years later, in eighteen ninety three. We have a signed first edition of it in our library, along with all of his other works, which you are all most welcome to read sometime!" He then sat back to let Magda continue.

"Thank you Anders. Yes, his writings and lectures illumined many pathways to knowledge and understanding, for so many people, that, *the opposition*, would have preferred to have remained in darkness and unknown about to them, and, as you said, his legacy continues today...thank you again for telling us all of that Anders.

"What Rudolf was predicting is an example of the sophistry of the so called 'Global Vaccination Programme', which is figure-headed by some very prominent wealthy elites, particularly the Gates' Foundation, and many other bought-and-paid-for 'celebrity' lackeys, and of course all of them are sycophantically praised for their 'efforts' by the mainstream corporate media. In many countries the injections are now compulsory, and has as its manifest agenda the prevention of illnesses – *'because we are so very concerned about your health...and we really do want to help you...!'*

"However, for just one example of many like it: in a region of India recently, the evidence was quite different to those benign claims. The polio vaccine imposed upon the populace there resulted in causing over *forty-five thousand* cases of polio and associated debilitating illnesses – when *prior* to the vaccinations there had been...only *twelve!* - not twelve *thousand* – just *twelve...!*

"Bill Gates, *who is basically a eugenicist* – that is someone who believes that the only way to 'improve' the human race is done by excluding certain 'inferior' genetic or ethnic groups from continuing to reproduce, which will eliminate them, as they are less desirable, and other types are far 'superior'...which will engineer a 'better' human stock and social order, which was at the core of the Nazi's philosophy of course – he is all that - *at best!* - *and at worst* - he is a callous and cold hearted psychopathic proponent of systematically murdering over six million-million men women and children as part of the elites de-population programme...

"He is Head of the Gates Foundation with his wife, Melinda, and has commented publicly on TED TV – which stands for: Technology, Entertainment, Design, when giving a specious presentation about the 'formula' he has devised to avoid over-population, and I will paraphrase: *'well that (the vaccine programme) should help to take care of the population problem...part of the formula'*

"What was I saying yesterday about psychopathy and the *'ends justifying the means'...?!* And normal, good people would just say: *'oh they wouldn't do that...!'*?

"Our good friend the late, great, Jim Marrs, who was a wonderful speaker and lecturer, and who gave so much insightful clarity and knowledge to the surface world, helping millions to see through the dark illusions, and a lot of his talks are still on-line, said this about *'the population problem'* the elites such as Gates and co. continually wring their hands over:

'...well, every human being currently on the planet would fit into the state of Texas, although that's not an invitation! - they might get in the way of those of us that already live there...!'

"He too had a wonderful sense of dry humour, and we miss him..." She gave a sad half-smile to Anders who returned it to her with a slow and deep nodding of his head. Exhaling a long breath Magda continued her talk.

"But...moving on...part of the latent, or hidden agenda, of the vaccines is, of course, the systematic barrage against a human body in its youngest and most vulnerable years with a series of highly toxic cocktails of chemicals including mercury, aluminium, nano-technology, and virally corrupted and genetically modified bio-matter, which are all flooded into that extremely young, and undeveloped body's natural immune system - *which is unable-to-counter them...*

"The long-term permanent damage, change and disruptive effects to a young body - and its mind's - true functioning are

250

incalculable...and of course, the vaccinations enable exactly the *'condition of being'* that Anders has just quoted to you from Rudolph's prophetic vision...

"Incidentally, Australia has recently passed Laws which will imprison any health official – for even remotely expressing *any doubt* let alone *disputing* any of the official benefits of vaccinations – to ten years in jail, and anyone else who dares dispute them– *even with evidence* – will face long prison sentences as well...

"There are now armed, black balaclava'd, black combat clothing attired 'Vaccine Enforcement' Police Squads set up there...When I saw them recently, on a trip I had to make, they, and the whole situation reminded me vividly of the days when the Nazi S.S. and their Einsatzgruppen paramilitary death squads were stomping all over Europe in their jackboots...

"The elite, female politician and Health Minister, Jill Hennessy who was strongly behind this draconian, psychopathic legislation...has no time for parents who believe vaccine safety requires: *'any further study in order to ensure they are safe for their children...'*, which is not surprising as the whole corrupt Government has been bought and paid for by 'Big Pharma", and she further considers vaccine skeptics as:

'people who dispute the benefits of vaccines are just 'brain-dead sheep'...'

"Nice Lady...

"But I think she made a slip of the tongue though when she said 'brain-dead', *she was probably too excited by it...*because varying degrees of that condition are more or less guaranteed from the vaccinations she so strongly promotes...

"Think along the lines of the biblical story of King Herod who ordered the killing of all the first-born male infants in the land, in an attempt to eradicate the threat he perceived was contained in the stories of an infant Saviour called Jesus whom had recently been born...

"I am not saying that the vaccinations have such an immediate and brutal effect as that! - because if they did, *even unawakened people*

251

would openly rebel against them and refuse them en masse! No, they are designed to be far more subtle and longer-term-damaging than that. Although tragically, many young, little ones do suffer terribly very soon after being injected.

"Girls approaching the ages of puberty and fertility are another target group, and as they already have severely compromised immune systems from the vaccine injections in their earlier years – when they are then given further injections designed to counter *'potential'* health problems that may occur, from, for example, cervical cancer, what happens instead, in so many cases, is that they often exacerbate those grave problems, and cause many more often atrociously debilitating illnesses of the body and mind...

"In third world countries with even less so-called 'stringent' monitoring, female fertility has plummeted from what it was prior to having vaccine injections...*what was I saying earlier about preventing the reproduction of those considered 'less desirable'...?*

"For different reasons those at the opposite end of their lives, the elderly, are also targeted by vaccination injection programs, particularly the "flu jab', and it is free! - *Of course it is...* Because in their evil, perverted way of thinking the elites running this program regard the aged masses as simply a burden on resources and they will be of little further value...so they reduce the time they remain being 'a burden'...before being re-cycled...

"Actually taking high doses of Ascorbic Acid – vitamin C, several times a day in its pure powdered form with purified water, and coupled with zinc supplements against the 'flu is far more effective – and far safer...

"In fact many doctors whom have researched the wonderful, natural and wide ranging curative benefits of vitamin C – even against cancerous tumours - and put their findings out to the world, have suffered some terrible retributions from the pharmaceutical industry – because of the threat to the billions they make peddling their products...but there is much proof of its tremendous benefits put out by brave doctors and researchers online still though."

252

Magda noticed Jake's prompt, shocked reaction to this, and paused for him to say or ask something, but he then sat back, shaking his head and putting his hands out for her to continue.

"Another part of the longer-term latent agenda of the vaccine programme is behaviour modification – and chemical patents for this technology in America go back to the seventies – and these days also by activating the microscopic nano-technology in the vaccines and the 'smart-dust' inhaled from the chem'-trails' - with the new 'Five G' electro-magnetic-frequency radiations, soon to be rolled out across the planet...but not in Israel...I will explain why not there another time...

"However, *there is 'Good News!'* - which is that the 'de-handicapping' of your DNA, and the reconnecting of all, or most, of its twelve strands, will be fully achieved - without the constant interferences to prevent that happening - once your race has thrown off its shackles and has elevated to the fifth dimension once again as its default state of being.

"Once there you will no longer be just prey to be harvested by the parasites and their elite minions...But they are desperately working to prevent your elevation, your ascension, from happening of course...

"So, they are some reasons as well – although I admit I may have gone off-track slightly here and there! - but that info was all relevant - why our lifespans are very, very long when compared to those of the surface humans.

"*'Just How long?!' I can hear you thinking!* Well, for now let me just say that the very minimum life span here in Aghartha is usually around *five to ten or so times longer* than that of an average human life span on the surface World...For myself, and all my dear sisters, and Anders, they have, so far, though, been *considerably more...*"

"*Oh My God!*" Sophie exclaimed, breathing rapidly, "*I knew it*...Well, I mean I didn't *know* it, I just sort of picked up on what *I thought were hints about it* when you, Anders, spoke in the Trocadero, and I pointed it out to you Jake at the time didn't I?! - and again when we sat talking with you afterwards Magda...*but I'd no idea you were all so...oh I'm sorry I sound really rude, but that you all were so, so...*"

253

"...Old?!" Magda said for her, with a wide smile, then she laughed softly and said, "I do not think you are being rude at all Sophie! Your reaction is to be expected and is quite natural. Yes, we did drop the occasional hints in conversation, then quickly gloss over them, because they helped to subliminally prepare you for the truth as, when, *and if,* we decided to reveal it to you at a later date. So yes, we are quite old! – Even *'ancient' you might say!"*

Anders chuckled as well, and said, *"...Not quite ready to be fossils yet though!"*

Magda smiled at him, which then turned into a chuckle as she said, *"talking about fossils!* - I remember your frustrated incredulity Anders, back in sixteen fifty, when you told me that you had come across the recent publications of that Christian Archbishop and Primate of All Ireland, James Ussher. He had apparently traced back all the generational lineages in the bible, made various calculations, and then publicly asserted that the Earth was no older than four thousand or so years – and he stated that fossils must have been deliberately created by God, but purely as decorative and curious oddities...I think that was what he claimed, am I right Anders?!"

"Mmmm, yes, yes you are! and he did! Quite ridiculous it goes without saying, but I remember it well...*Although I try not to!* He actually claimed that the World was quite obviously created on October the twenty third, four thousand and four B.C.! Anyway – despite all his fervent and ludicrous assertions – which must, obviously, have had the Vatican's sanction prior to their publication, I do find it rather hard to imagine myself as eventually being called: *just a fossilized 'decorative and curious oddity!"* He muttered, shaking his head and rolling his eyes.

They all laughed, partly due to Magda's brief tale, and partly due to Ander's comical expressions and further comments on it. Composing herself, and pleased at the again lightened atmosphere Anders had just created after them talking about the latent agendas of the vaccines, Magda continued talking.

"Here in Aghartha great age is venerated, it is regarded with deep respect, because with it comes so much experience, wisdom and understanding. Tribal societies on the surface world have a similar respect for their elders, but sadly, western industrialised societies hold it in contempt. When – if - you reach a certain age up there you are 'retired' – as you are considered to be of little further, or of no more use or value, in your workaday production capabilities.

"And so, after a 'lifetime' of work, many of those whom are forcibly retired – particularly men, often, and very sadly, die soon afterwards, and statistics prove this to be quite true."

"Aye...sadly me Uncle Jack did, Magda." Jake said wistfully.

"Forty-odd years in a steel wire works, then told he 'ad to retire, an' less than six months later he just passed away. It were like he'd lost his reason for livin', he weren't bein' 'charged up' any more like, from goin' to work, an' so 'is battery just went flat and, well, that were it..."

"I am sorry to hear that Jake. But you are right, it is as if their whole 'raison d'etre' has been taken from them, and sadly as so many of them know of no other way of living with the same fulfilment and purpose...so then they just...shut down...

"Societally, in the industrialised countries, the cult of callow youth, fresh from upto two decades in the propaganda programming warehouses of 'education', is held in much higher regard. Because, cynically, more future ongoing production and consumption value can be had from them. They are also more malleable and unquestioning of whatever demands 'the system' makes of them.

"With age and experience though, many people start to see through all the programming, all the 'smoke and mirrors', all the non-sense, and really question what it is all about, and why they are doing what they are doing, so it is preferable to remove – retire – and by other means I have just mentioned - those potentially dissenting and seditious – to 'the system' - voices from the workplace and the wider society..."

She sighed, saying, "as we have often said, 'the surface societies have *deliberately inverted values...*"

Sophie was nodding at her in agreement, and said, "yes...I know

255

exactly what you mean Magda. Two older staff were 'given' – *or more accurately - forced into* - early retirement from the company I work for last year.

"They'd been constantly at loggerheads with the new, much younger management team, from the National company that had bought out the old family run business, and they were always criticising all the nonsense compliances, changes to well established routines, and the bureaucratic hoops the new management kept implementing for them all to jump through...A lot of what they said – the two that were retired - *was just plain old common-sense*, but the new management wasn't having any of it...So they were forced out...and a few weeks later *three* much younger people were recruited...all keen and willing to do whatever they were told without question – and on much less a pay-grade...of course!"

"Yes, I imagine they would have been Sophie. Thank you for that, it underlines what I was saying...It sounds like it was as well a classic example of 'Parkinson's Second Law', which states: *'All officials will seek to increase their subordinates – all those of whom – will find work for each other...'*"

Anders quietly 'harrumphed', before adding, "Yes, nice chap, Professor Cyril, ahead of his time of course. I met him in Singapore in 'fifty eight, he'd just published his most famous work, 'Parkinson's Law', satirising Government Bureaucracies. He'd found out in his scholarly researches that the British Empire, just a few years after the war officially ended back in 'forty-five, *was approximately ten times smaller then* than it had been before the war started - *but it had over five times as many bureaucrats administering it!*

"His First Law was, is: *'Work expands to fill the time allocated to it...!'*"

"Thank you Anders – I had forgotten you met him, thank you for that. So...moving on...yet again!

"Our diet includes vegetables and plants that we grow naturally, in nutrient rich soils. We also consume highly nutritious, and energising bio-compounds that we have created, and we also consume certain other compounds that were known about and used in ancient times. They are known as 'orbitally rearranged monatomic elements' – or 'Ormus'.

"In the times of the Egyptian Pharaohs it was call 'Mfkzt', and it is the transmuted white powder of gold, which their alchemists created, as an aid, amongst its many other, super-conductivity attributes, to longevity. -

"The author and artist, Sir Lawrence Gardner, a Fellow of the Society of Antiquaries, Knight Templar, Historian and an Associate of the Institute of Nanotechnology, although his full ceremonial title was: 'Chevalier Labhran de Saint Germain' and 'Presidential Attaché to the European Council of Princes', wrote extensively on the subject. However, *more as well on all of that another time!*

"And of course we have no deadly toxins, poisonous chemicals or nano-technologies deliberately put into our food, water, or the air we breathe, to cause us physical and mental damage…All of which are deliberately used in the manufacturing processes by the surface food production corporations, and by other agencies, as we have talked about before.

"Those of us whom spend a lot of time on the surface world frequently return here to go through processes which de-toxify our bodies of all those poisons before returning to continue our works… During the past half to three quarters of a century we have had to do that *much more frequently* than we used to have to do…

"The types of pure and natural foods we eat here more than satisfy all the physical body's and mind's regenerative energy needs.

"We do not ritually kill other sentient beings to eat their bodies. A human being is not a natural meat eater, the lower intestine is a long one, designed for a vegetarian diet. Predatory meat eaters have strong, sharp teeth and claws, and a completely different digestive system, to process raw meat and other body parts. None of those, and the other necessary attributes a true carnivore possesses, are present in humans.

"So our diet does not include the meat and other body parts from

257

dead animals. Another reason is, and it is really one of the most important – because it is on an energy level – which everything is...when you consume the body parts of an animal that has been killed by experiencing what amounts to torture, and died in terror, pain and suffering, you are consuming and absorbing all of those energies which permeated throughout every cell of its body as it experienced those very powerful negative emotions – *and they go directly into your body.*"

Dave quickly said, *"Ah! – oh dear!* – when you put it all like that – which I have to admit, I obviously hadn't considered before, well, there goes the BBQ we had planned for next week! Well, I suppose we could do it without...dead animals' body parts!"

" - Of course we can!" Mel said, "it's been increasingly on my mind to stop eating meat for a while – and what Magda's just said has made me absolutely determined to! We'll just have to apply ourselves and find alternative diets!"

Jake was thinking that he would too – but he'd still allow himself one of Big Sammy's Breakfast Baps as a treat on a Saturday morning! - *He'd keep that thought to himself though!*

"Now...let us explore some areas of the hidden history and relevant contemporary events of both this inner World and the surface World – and please continue inputting your comments and insights about anything I mention.

"Or if you want something I mention clarifying please just jump in and ask me to! - Asking questions is the only way to get the answers to help you sort things out in your own minds, and start to understand them!

"Just back tracking slightly - I mentioned 'tunnels' from the surface to here...well, the two largest ones connect from under the polar ice caps, and there are others also from beneath the largest pyramid in Egypt at Giza, some of the other pyramids in Bosnia, Peru, Brazil, China, North America and many other locations, and many of them which are, as yet, undiscovered by the surface races, as some of them are now under the seas – like the ones off Japan, which the authorities

258

studiously deny, or in very remote areas on the surface.

"Even when they are discovered, such as the recent Bosnian pyramids and the temple ruins at Gobekli Tepe, in Southern Turkey, mainstream archaeologists and their various associations of 'professional bodies' – *aka: Manipulative Institutions* - and the mainstream media *immediately go into overdrive to attempt to do everything they can to ridicule and discredit such finds - and those who made them* – particularly the very early dates - tens of thousands of years ago - when they were constructed.

"Yes, Cognitive Dissonance is part of the reason why they do, of course it is, but the main reasons by far are that the truths of them would call into question the veracity of the whole story of human history that has been peddled by them to the masses.

"And all the careers of those mainstream archaeologists would then be at risk, having spent years building them up for themselves – all based on limited perception theories but they have presented them as fact – but are error riddled and mostly false conjecture by them, but is promoted by them as being true and factual…which is in accord as well of course with the parasites' agenda…

"At Gobekli Tepe they have had no choice but to retreat snarling and with their tails between their legs! And also in Bosnia, although there they are still fighting a desperate rearguard action! *Even though it was recently realised that the energy emissions from them were still provably functioning – after thirty four thousand years since it was built…the great age proven by vegetation found inside it and carbon dated…!*

"There are tunnel entrance *branches* as well in several mountain ranges, remote forested and jungle regions and even in some major cities. To modern day surface dwelling mainstream archaeologists these tunnels – at least those they have discovered, are an enigma, a puzzle, to which they have put forward various explanations, but none of those have, so far, been correct.

"The closest explanation of the truth of them in fairly recent times was revealed by Jules Verne, he was a guest here with us on several

259

occasions, and he wrote the book: 'Journey To The Centre Of The Earth', in eighteen sixty four.

"He purposely used the technique of wrapping a dramatic, adventure fiction story around a kernel of truth. These days that technique of introducing truths into the subconscious of a population is called 'predictive programming', particularly by Hollywood. It is preparing people for the time when that truth – whatever it is - will eventually be openly acknowledged, and people are then more likely to accept it, as they have been 'warmed up' to it already.

"Jules - along with many authors since - was very successful in doing that, his story has since become a classic work of literature and known to millions. But the *vast majority* of the masses at the time of its first publication – and the low percentage within those masses who could actually read, or even afford to buy books - were much more susceptible to be conditioned and programmed to believe that everything related to fiction *was obviously just that* – purely an entertaining fictional story of 'made-up' imaginative fantasy. So it was not taken too seriously, as it *'obviously'* couldn't possibly be true.

"The social conditioning and programming of the masses was powerfully, and continually reinforced by the severely limited 'Three D', five-senses-only perceptions of the world around them – a world which was all too often just a dull, dim, harsh and depressing, enforced 'reality' most of them, so, so sadly, lived their entire lives enmeshed within, never knowing of anything else but that. Not *too* dissimilar to today, I have to say, but...as we have explained before, that entrapping paradigm of limited perception – which leads to limited belief - is now gradually breaking down as human consciousness expands, which will change...everything...

"But even today, the visible, physical, 'material' realm - *let alone the invisible 'spiritual' realms* - is not, currently, to any really significant degree, understood properly at all by the surface World's 'experts' and 'intellectuals' in the mainstream sciences' philosophies, with their very limited tools of 'Three D' five-senses-only rigid systems of analysis. Because humans have to open all their eyes,

outer and inner, to see beyond all the illusions...*sorry – yes Anders?"*
Anders had discretely indicated to her he had a comment to make.

"Thank you, yes, well, hesitant as I am to interrupt you! - I just want to add a thought, as a comment, of mine, it's very relevant and flows quite smoothly and appropriately into what you've been saying Magda, and which I'm sure you will concur with me on when you hear it…

"You will all perhaps recall what I said to you in The Trocadero Cafe last Monday evening about the allegorical tale of Plato's Cave...?...well, I didn't mention then, that there was a small, 'select group' amongst all those people in the cave, a group that had decided to set themselves apart from the others. Though they were still on their knees, and still in chains, like everyone else was, and just staring at the shadows on the cave wall in front of them...like everyone else was...

"...But...*eventually they claimed they knew just about everything there was to know about those shadows!* – not who or what deliberately made them, or even *why* or *how* they did, or why they were on their knees in chains in a cave - *in the first place!*

"But they claimed they did know all about every flickering nuance and behaviour of the shadows, because they had been studying them for so long in that position. This 'select group' argued constantly and often quite vehemently between themselves in their self-important and self-appointed little coterie, as to who was right and who was wrong - about all their observations and theories…and regularly shouted them out to all the others around them - who weren't in their little select group...

"Well, eventually, all that little select group merely achieved was contributing heavily towards creating the stereotypes of, and indeed they actually became, what we now call...*'mainstream experts and intellectuals'…!"*

It only took a second or two - but then all the others laughed long and loud at Ander's humorously scathing summation…

"Aye! y'put that brilliantly Anders!" Jake said, still chuckling, "it's

261

like what me Dad said about 'em once: *'they know more an' more – about less an' less…'!"*

"Exactly!" Anders replied, his eyes twinkling.

Magda grinned at Anders, thanking him for his humorously tailored, calumnic extrapolation from the allegorical tale of Plato's Cave. She then moved on to comment briefly and more specifically again about where they all were now.

"Here in Aghartha – which…I suppose you would be technically correct if you were to say that this is a 'cave' as well - but a planetary sized one! - but it is obviously a very different 'cave' to that alluded to by Plato! One in which we have, also very obviously, evolved very differently, in the more stable, physical and philosophical climate here, inside, within, planet Earth, over many, many *many thousands* of years…

"That evolving has been an achievement which hopefully, will commence to be replicated during, or towards the final stages – and then continue beyond - this historic period of elevation and transition for the surface races. That elevation will have as part of it as well many disclosures which will…well, basically shatter…the beliefs of all those stereotypical groups of whom Anders has just so eruditely and accurately described.

"Amongst those eventual disclosures will be, *eventually,* the fact of our inner World here of Aghartha, and what we have knowledge of and understand, because everyone who has successfully gone through the period of full awakening on the surface world, and naturally elevated to the fifth dimension, hand-in-hand with the planet, deserves to know and to understand the full truth of what they, and the Earth, really are…and their true history...

"Let us now go back in time to the surface world for a while – not literally just yet though! I mentioned Egypt before, as it is called now, long ago it was called 'The Land Of Al Khem'. Al Khem means 'One Point' – which I will explain the *meaning of* shortly. They are the root words for *'alchemy'* and then later for the more 'mainstream acceptable' science of *'chemistry'.*

"The pyramids there are a legacy inherited by the much later Egyptian civilization, they did not build them, nor the Sphinx, which incidentally originally had a lion's head. The Pharaonic styled human head was carved from it in a much later millennium, hence it being out of proportion – smaller - to the body it rests on. The Sphinx is much older than the pyramids, whose construction also pre-dated the covert invasion of humanity on the planet by the parasites.

"There is one obvious observation that the pyramids and the Sphinx well pre-date the last inter-glacial period or 'ice-age' as they are more popularly known now - in fact the theory of 'ice-ages' existing at all, and displaying approximately twenty two thousand year cycles, was only accepted internationally by mainstream scientists since the mid eighteen seventies…!

"That 'obvious observation' has only in recent decades been proven beyond any doubt, but mainstream Egyptologists still refuse to acknowledge it, and the mainstream media ridicule or ignore it of course! Which are the *all-too-predictable* responses of the parasites' and their elites' agenda to keep hidden any knowledge of the true history of humanity that is at variance to their desired version for the masses to believe in, of what has really occurred on the planet...

"*It is the evidence of water erosion of the Sphinx and particularly of its base, which is typical of rain falling on it regularly over many centuries.* But the last time that whole region was not a desert as it is now, with hardly any rainfall, but was a verdant – green - landscape with a great variety of flora and fauna...*all watered by regular rain fall* - was before the start of the last ice age, over twenty thousand years ago...

"In fact it is doubtful that humans could build the pyramids even today. It was actually tried by a large Japanese team sponsored by the Nissan company in the late nineteen seventies, and their attempt was to only construct a one fifth scale model, some eighteen metres high.

"They failed to do it, even when they had to resort to using modern power tools, bulldozers and even large helicopters to transport and position some of the stones!

"When they first started the project, using only the types of hand tools – hammers and chisels and the supposed techniques which the mainstream Egyptologists claim would have been used by the early Egyptian builders, it soon became clear that it was impossible for them to quarry, cut and transport the initial large stones that were required. They were also unable to get those big stones they had finally used modern power tools to eventually make, across the river Nile, and had to return home somewhat dejected.

"So to transport *over seven million* – mainstream Egyptologists claim *'only' just over two and a quarter million* - large blocks of granite, quarried and cut using hand tools, *for just one pyramid* five times larger, some weighing many scores of tons from up to five hundred miles away, crossing the Nile with them, and then raising and very accurately siting and positioning them, all done by a supposedly technologically primitive civilization, was obviously just not possible...it was totally unfeasible...

"The pyramids were not sited or positioned haphazardly either. Extending outwards and for way, way below the pyramids is a granite 'mountain', which acts as a – hah! - a good pun! - *'a rock-solid'* foundation to support their weight. How would 'a primitive society' have known about it being there? They were also accurately positioned and sized in accord with the Earth's dimensions and astrological alignments - that have only in recent centuries, or even decades, been known about to modern humanity's mainstream sciences...

"Mainstream Egyptologists and their fellow archaeological historians claim that it took about five thousand slaves twenty years to build them – but just 'the simple' logistics of that are a nonsense, as that explanation would also mean that they would have had to find, quarry, shape, transport, raise and position a multi ton stone block *very precisely - every three minutes or so...day and night...!*

"To say nothing of the more mundane logistics of feeding and housing such a large workforce...and no scrolled texts or other records of any other type have ever been discovered even remotely pertaining to such a momentous endeavour. Many other, lesser constructional endeavours had been – *so why not the pyramids...?!*

"And I say again, the pyramids have *within* and *without* them highly complex mathematical and astrological information in their design and layout - much of which has only been vaguely known about by mainstream sciences in recent times, and they still have many complex mysteries yet to be discovered and understood.

"The main pyramid is actually eight sided not four, because the subtle shadowing that is created in its sides – or it did when it was clad in smooth, highly polished – *to a modern day optical lens quality* - twenty feet by five feet limestone slabs – which were designed to clearly illustrate the equinoxes. The highly polished cladding was removed to be used as building materials for decorative parts of some of the palaces and civic buildings in and around Cairo!

"Interestingly the name 'Cairo' originally stems from the Arabic: 'al-Qahirah', which means literally: 'Place or Camp of Mars', as well as: 'the Victorious'...

"So what you see of the pyramids now is nothing like the magnificent sight they once were. They are still very impressive of course, and still capture the imaginations of millions, but imagine how much more of their imaginations they would 'capture' - if the deliberate vandalism of stripping away the glass lens smooth, shiny outer layer had not been done!

"Of course at the time the parasites wanted them to be entirely demolished – eradicating all trace of them, but the logistics of doing that were actually beyond their elites then to achieve.

"The current location of the golden capstone, which sat on top of the pyramid, was, is, an ancient object of great power, is known to us, it is hidden away in the possession of...of one of the elites' secret societies in another country...

"So who did build them – and how? Well they were built by two collaborating non-terrestrial races. The technology of sonic severance to quarry and shape the building stones and cladding, and acoustic resonance levitation technology to raise them were the basic techniques they used....those races were the Mantids who collaborated in creating the overall design, and the second race was more involved in overseeing their construction. Their name, or as close as the human pronunciation is capable of saying it, was shortened to the 'Kilrotti'.

"They have a matriarchal society from at least the sixth dimension, but the more advanced of their race are ninth dimensional, and are light beings whose primary works are to clear away the lower, negative energies in the lesser dimensions.

"When they manifest for short periods of time in the denser third dimension, within the humanly visible – or 'de-codeable' - light spectrum, they appear as mostly taller than humans and have a feline appearance. They can be seen represented in ancient art and statuary, sometimes showing them to have human female bodies and cat like, or leonine heads, or just totally feline as later works show them mostly as cats. Bast and Sekhmet are the two named sister Goddesses mainly represented in the discovered statuary.

"They also constructed many other buildings and edifices in remote, almost inaccessible – to surface bound humans - areas of the world where massive, intricately shaped rocks weighing many tons – some nearly a thousand tons, were used as part of those complex constructions, and which are all far, far older than they are said to be by the mainstream archaeologists of course.

"The ridiculous assertion that the Egyptian pyramids were simply large tombs made to put dead Pharaohs in is also nonsensical, it is a cover story, and taught in schools to keep people in ignorance of their true functions. However, they were decommissioned, like so many of the ancient sites were, at the instigation of the parasites...

"Prior to that decommissioning they were one of the major, transmitting nodal points of an energy grid over the surface World - as well as - for the main pyramid at Giza, a 'Stargate Soul Portal', primarily, but not exclusively, to the Orion constellation...

"Before and after the era of constructing the pyramids, other huge edifices and gigantic statues were also constructed and created all around that region, and in many other locations on the Earth. Some of that statuary, created by human civilisations, using technology long forgotten to today's civilisations, represented ancient Hyperborean 'Gods' – beings who were thought to have come from the far North, but most of them were actually emissaries from here, Aghartha, who went to the surface world.

"They went up to, and all over the surface world to warn, and help humanity to devise counter measures against the parasites, when they, we, *finally realised that the parasites had more than just started to gain a foothold there...*

"There are many surviving structural legacies from their time up there, for example, some of the stone circles, and standing stones *that all interlink* along the planet's major Ley lines, which as well as being used as ancient track-ways for accurate navigation, are also arteries along which the earth's magnetism and its other natural energies flow, and they can be tapped into and amplified...

"Regrettably though only a fraction of all the original stone circles and standing stones have survived to recent times, having been deliberately destroyed and scattered, some by clearing the land areas for agricultural, then later, for industrial usage, by the money wealthy elites who came to *'own' the land*, and often by the Church to discourage 'pagan' and 'heretical' practices of worship.

"I just emphasised *'own' the land*, well, one morning, at sunrise, out in the wilderness deserts of Northern Australia many years ago, I was talking with the shaman of an Aboriginal tribe - I actually spent several months with them - and have returned to re-visit him and the tribe for a few weeks, every two or three years or so, the Shaman said: *'I liken the concept of 'owning' the land as being like two fleas on a dog's back – arguing over who owns the dog!'"*

Mel chuckled and said, *"that's clever!* What an insightful way to put it! And when you think about it, how silly it really is to say: *'I own that land! It's all mine, mine, all mine!'* But how can you?! *Its always been there and it always will be! –* long after *'you'* have gone...! - In fact it probably gives a sigh of relief when you have! It doesn't go around wailing, *'oh woe is me! My Owner and Master has gone, what am I going to do...!'"*

Magda and the others were all amused at her commentary, and chuckled loudly.

"*Exactly* Melanie, that concept of *'ownership'* – therefore being able to exclude, then divide and rule, is a core element of the parasites' and their elites' stratagem...

"Churches, which came to - *'own the land'* - were mostly sited on ley lines, particularly on their intersections, for many reasons, prominent amongst them being the deliberate tapping into the energies *for their own purposes*, or to block their flow - like poisoned and un-natural foods clog up an artery in a human body...with severe, and often fatal results over time...

"Associated with the Ley lines are subterranean waterways, which have pure flowing waters running through them which are highly sensitive to absorbing the emotive or psychic climate of those living on the Earth above. *And not just the people living on it – but every living organism.*

"Imagine what now distorted and imbalanced energies all the sub surface – and sometimes they mingle with those *on the surface* waterways conduit, transport and spread on their journeys into the oceans, from: the sites of nuclear explosions, major battles - or even minor ones...or the killing of thousands, millions, of trees and the same amounts of acres of interdependent plant life – *the world wide wood web!* - when deforestation takes place over vast areas – often to tarmac them with millions of miles of mostly unnecessary roads – unnecessary due to the long known about but hidden, anti-gravitic technology, or build huge industrial cities which are basically generators spewing out concentrated, imbalanced and unnaturally negative, harmful energies...

"The Earth is a complex, sensitive, living, inter-dependent organism, and she has suffered greatly...but the time has eventually come when she says: *'That's Quite Enough! I will stop this! I will rid myself of these annoying, harmful fleas!'* And that is happening now...

"Do you remember me explaining to you how the whales help to

268

clear away all these imbalanced energies that eventually find their way to, and concentrate in, the oceans' depths…?

"Well, after the parasites invaded the negative energies they had humans unwittingly create for them rapidly increased, more and more of them were corrupting and imbalancing everything, often overburdening the whales, so our emissaries showed the spiritual leaders of human communities – the Shamans and the Druids for example, how the stone constructs can be created to help diminish and filter them away and re-balance the energy flows, all over the Earth's sub-surface and surface areas. That was one of the primary methods of the counter measures they instigated that I mentioned. But, in later centuries, the parasites had their elites organised to decommission many, nearly all, of of them,

"All around the planet the subterranean waterways, and the Ley line grids, are being particularly targeted in these more modern times by the rise of the industrial technique of 'fracking', to extract the energy from fossil fuels, by breaking deep into the sub-surface, and then injecting under high pressure many specifically toxic chemicals. *'Much Needed Energy Sourcing',* is the slogan of the manifest agenda for this.

"The latent agenda, i.e: *the real reason,* is that doing this is designed to destroy the efficacy of the function of the Earth's subterranean arterial waterways and the Ley grids…

"It is particularly sickening when you now realise that there *is absolutely no need* to source and mine buried fossil fuels to supply a global energy system, in this destructive – *or in any other manner.*

"Abundant, pollution-free energy generation and the almost cost free transmission of it for everyone, everywhere, to make use of it, has been known about, and the technology to do just that has been available, but hidden away, by the elites, for over a hundred years, as we have explained to you before...

"...and we told you whom the specific, elite individuals were who were responsible for deciding to hide it all away so they could continue to profit from the other means of energy production they

269

have a monopoly over, and so deny humanity...

"Actually, just briefly going back to stone constructs, near to Scarborough – and Filey, where you all live, there is a small village called Rudston, its name stems from 'Red Stone', where the largest megalith or standing stone in the whole country can be seen.

"It is approximately six thousand years old, *according to mainstream archaeologists,* weighs over forty tons, is over twenty five feet high above ground, and the same dimensions are believed to be below ground. It is gritstone, the nearest source for that type of stone is ten miles away. The local church was built intentionally alongside it. Curious how so called *'primitive peoples'* from the Neolithic age, but I say a much earlier age, could quarry, craft, move and erect such an immense object, is it not...and why would they...?! And what did they know that has now been forgotten? *Well, you all know now!*

"Aye it is curious! - Well it was! - Until y' just explained the reason for 'em Magda! Often thought along sorta similar lines meself! *Ha! - Pun unintended!* A lot o'the blokes I went UFO spottin' with when I were a lad used to talk about 'em.

"Anyway - I've bin there! – to the church yard at Rudston, quite a few times an'all Magda! Good country lanes all around it for a relaxin' ride out on't bike all round there. Usually stop off an' 'ave a coffee from me flask and visit it – y'can walk right up to it an' touch it. Amazin' thing it is!

"I were talkin' to a bloke there once an' he told me it lines up wi' the mound at Willy Howe, a mile or so away, an' then in a line upto them standing stones called 'The Devil's Arrows' near to Boroughbridge, which're nearly as tall. Keep meanin' to 'ave a ride out to them an'all. An' he also told me them three are all part of a fifty mile line at least, line o' similar stones! Allus fascinated me 'ow an' why they did it!"

Sophie said, *"In all the years I've lived in Scarborough that's the first time I've ever heard of it!* The one at Rudston – and the others!- *and it's the biggest in the country...!?"* Jake promised her they'd have a ride out to see it on her day off next week – and have a picnic next to it!

270

Magda then said they also line up with many similar stones and other constructs she'd visited many years ago in France, and they were, are, all part of the global network.

"Moving on...'non-constructional' legacies which those earlier Agharthans were instrumental in the formation of, and some still exist to this day, are various groups and organisations of Seekers and Disseminators of Knowledge and Understanding. One of which, just for example, evolved into Druidism, which flourished in those far away days, particularly amongst the Celtic race - and it is still widely, if covertly, practised today.

"Those emissaries from Aghartha who travelled extensively over the surface world for many, many years, were comprised of some of the descendants of the lost continent of Lemuria, which was first colonized around nine hundred thousand years ago. Tragically, the continent was sunk over twenty five thousand years ago by forces unleashed on it by an unprovoked attack from Atlantis, where a coterie of the Higher Adepts had degenerated and turned away from the Path Of Light...

"For various reasons a lot of even our records of that time are hazy, and many were later found to have been destroyed, but from the records that do remain we strongly suspect that this degeneration in Atlantis, which ultimately lead to its destruction as well as that of Lemuria, coincided closely with the arrival of the parasites...whom either played their part in instigating it, or, more likely, perhaps, they came very soon afterwards, having sensed, across the dimensions, all the powerful negative energies emanating from the planet at that time.

"Millions and millions were killed, over a relatively short period of time, due to those devastating, Earth changing - literally changing the appearance of the Earth's surface – cataclysmic events.

"It would have been like a powerful negative beacon to them, or like a predatory hunter that pounced after scenting its vastly weakened prey...

"Whichever was the case, the lengthy primary mission of those early emissaries was to help the surface races not only to be aware of the arrival of the parasites, but also to attempt to counter the grave future threat and great danger to humanity that they posed.

"Sadly, despite all their efforts, over all that time, they were not totally successful in doing so, as the parasites, having sensed the great potential of subverting the *'creator-race'* of humanity, in order to supply them with their sustenance, had quickly infested them too deeply, gaining too deep a foothold...And the rest, as the expression goes: *'is history...'*

"Our remaining records do tell us that they eventually returned here, to evade the massive forces that had been tasked to hunt for them all and then kill them. Also they wanted to ensure the security of Aghartha, which, admittedly would never truly have been under threat as it was, and is, fifth and sixth dimensional, where the parasites cannot infiltrate. Had the surface races been able to maintain their fifth dimensional status, the parasites would not have been able to linger there. But the surface races had been too weakened by the cataclysms, and were rapidly dropping down to the third dimension – the hunting grounds of the predatory parasites...

"Since then we have all had to continue to operate much more covertly against the parasites, and avoiding their elite's Hunter Forces, in an ongoing, secret war. Hence our obsession with trade craft that you have all witnessed! I have to say, we have done so with considerable successes, but our greatest success – with surface humanity and the Earth ready this time to elevate to the fifth, and with the alliance of extra-terrestrial and higher inter-dimensional beings – our greatest success is yet to come – *but it will come...because in the future time line we are, we are all, creating - It Awaits Us!"*

Magda paused then from her narrative and suggested a well deserved break, and she would bring some refreshments out for everyone. Anders insisted on doing that for her and so the five of them wandered over again to the balcony as she answered the many questions they all poured out to her. Anders soon reappeared carrying a silver tray and tall glasses of water, which he placed on the round table for them to collect, and then wander back to the balcony's edge.

Chapter 16: The High Balcony (iii)

As they all stood standing close to the balcony's far edge, looking out at the incredible vista and sipped at their invigorating, pure, fresh water, Anders and Magda continued to answer the flow of their almost non-stop questions.

Mel then asked her about her Gypsy – Romany – origins and how they tied in with being from Aghartha...

"Well, when I first said, earlier, *'we are from Aghartha'*, yes, that was quite true of course, but my particular family...has...different, but nonetheless, interesting antecedents. It will take me a few minutes to touch upon some of the main points – are you sure you would like me to...to talk briefly...about it?"

"Oh yes please Magda – I'd love to know! – We all would! – wouldn't we...?" Mel looked at the others who all agreed with the same enthusiasm.

"Very well, but there will be a lot of unfamiliar, unknown and confusing names and events that will crop up as I do!

"My sisters and I, are originally from a very ancient tribe of peoples called, the Athingani, a word derived from the early Grecian scribes which means, 'The Untouchables'. They were widely known for their knowledge and abilities in the practice of all forms of magic, particularly though of divination and fortune telling. In the more modern era we became known for doing it by using the crystals, the Tarot cards and palmistry...*but we have many more abilities of course!*

"Our parents lived in Phrygia, which is now part of Asian Turkey. Before they were...killed, in an invasion against our kind, just after my youngest sister Sinda was born, they were High Priests in a sect of Melchizedek, which was of the same order that the Epistle to the Hebrews, one of the older books in the New Testament, identified Jesus as being a High Priest of as well...

"Melchizedec is also mentioned in the fourteenth book of Genesis, and he was associated with a deity called Sydyk, now often called Zedec, who was, we now know, a higher inter-dimensional entity actually known as Enki, or Ea, in the extinct for at least seven millennia, Akkadian language.

"He was the Patron God of Eridu, a vast city in Mesopotamia which is now mostly Southern Iraq, Kuwait, Syria and other divisive countries created by the European Colonial and Industrial Powers – who then had claimed they: 'owned the lands!' Today's mainstream scholars argue that the ruins of Eridu are the oldest city and man made structure on Earth, and was founded fifty four centuries before Christ…

"But there were, are, many *more that are considerably older...*for example, the construction, in stages, of the temple and calendar complex at Gobekli Tepe stretches over a period of two hundred and fifty thousand years – *two thousand five hundred centuries,* and there are many more which are far, far older, which are yet to be discovered. *Mainstream media and archeologists world never consider these expansions of the horizons of ancient history to be revealed to the masses of course.*

"At Gobekli the chronostratigraphy – which is the study of ground layers, clearly indicates its great age, and also because it was rebuilt and reoriented after each crustal and magnetic pole displacement. I was there recently – but I will resist digressing and talking about it too much now - but we will talk about it and the true ages of other ancient constructs another time! So...back to what I was saying before...

"Mythology from the time claims he, Enki, lived in Abzu, which is the primeval fresh water sea of what they then called the underworld...but was actually part of Aghartha. That water has a fertilising, life giving, enhancing and...sustaining...quality – which is the source of the very water you are drinking now! Rituals still exist today in the modern religions of washing and baptising in fresh water, such as in the pools of Islamic mosques and the baptismal fonts of Christianity, which were formerly performed in the river waterways...

"He was there, way, way before the first 'modern' humans were created, by him and his half-sister Nin-Khirsag. He also had a half-brother, called Enlil, who was actually the wrathful God of the Old Testament. *I did warn you about some confusing names and events! Another time I will go into more details about it all for you.*

"Anyway...back to *our* story...it was in the middle of the night when we seven sisters were roused from our beds by our parents. They told us that we had to be as quiet as possible, and we were now going to go on a journey, and we would be away from home for many days, because we were in great danger if we stayed at home, as an invasion by another tribe was expected within a few days.

"Our parents explained to us that they feared the expected invaders would abscond with us, as seven sisters of High Priests of the Athingani in the Sect of Melchizedec would have been a very valuable prize for them...Indeed, it may have been the real reason for their coming invasion that all the rumours were circulating about in the city...So then `we all quietly left our home to travel on our donkeys, lead by our parents who were on their horses.

"Our parents had wrapped all the animals hooves in thick felts to help prevent any noise of our departure from the city being heard...Our parents had also already packed and loaded the donkeys and their horses up with enough food, water and other essentials, for all of us, for many days.

"A few hours later, in the early hours of the morning, it was still very dark, we arrived at our destination, a hidden entrance to the safety of a deep cave, high up in the nearby mountains.

"Our...tearful and very distressed parents kept assuring us all again and again that a group of their friends were already on their way to come and look after us whilst we were hiding away in the cave, and would be with us all later in the day.

"They said they had to return, because their duties and positions as High Priests meant that they would be needed by the whole populace if - *when* – the invasion and its predictable barbarities happened...

"So, *after heart rending farewells,* and our parents' promise to come back for us as soon as it was safe to do so, taking all the donkeys back

275

with them, they left.

"*But...they never did return for us...and we never saw them again...*

"It was actually after *two days and nights* of us being alone had passed, that we all – *my sisters and I...we all...sensed, that our parents, they had...they...both...had...just died...*In later years we found out that they had been...tortured, and finally killed by the invaders - *for refusing to reveal our whereabouts...and so keeping us, all their children...safe...*

"*They were so brave, so caring and so loving...I still miss them even after all these, all these, almost countless years now...we, we all do...*"

Magda's voice had quietened to just a distraught whisper as she said that, her head drooped, and she wiped away some tears that had run down her cheeks as she had recalled these desperately sorrowful memories.

The tears on Sophie's and Mel's cheeks just ran down un-wiped away, they were both immobile in their shock and empathy for her, and for all her sisters...

Magda then blinked rapidly and quickly raised her head up, her red hair flying, as she inhaled deeply.

"Half a day after we had...we had *sensed...*about our *dear parents...*we were spirited away from the hidden cave by the friends they had told us were coming to look after us.

"They were a group of one man and three women who came for us that day. They were emissaries from here, in Aghartha, who told us that they had been searching for us, but it had taken them much longer as there were many enemy patrols out all over the countryside searching for us...and then, because of...what had happened...to our dear parents, we were all brought here by them, on a flying craft they summoned, *then we were all cared for and raised up by them throughout all our young, formative years...*"

She paused, and slowly looked sideways at Anders, the sadness that had been in her eyes before had suddenly, mostly gone, and in its place they were now filled with a great, *an immense, filial love for him that shone from them into his,* and she reached out to gently touch his upper arm, where it lingered for a few moments.

Ander's adam's apple bobbed up and down, his jaw clenched tightly, as he smiled back at her, his eyes matching and reflecting back the same great love and affection he had for her...then Magda slowly withdrew her hand and entwined her fingers in front of her and looked back again to the two, now utterly spell-bound, young couples.

"Time - *a lot of time,* so many years...then passed...and during all of it we continually had so much love, care, help, gentle teaching, learning and instruction - but always with plenty of time for fun and play – *and not just when we were very young!* It all, inevitably, lead to great knowledge and great *understanding*...of, *of many things*...

"My sisters and I all lived together here. Well, here mainly, but in twos and threes we also went, at first just for a few days, then eventually for months at a time, to live in a secret monastery hidden in the snow and ice mountains of Tibet. There we were so privileged to study under the guidance of Ascended Masters and Maters, and many High Adepts; again, furthering our knowledge and understanding of, of...incredible things...

"Eventually...we all agreed and decided, after meeting with the King and our Tribal Council, to return to the surface world for long periods at a time, and use all our knowledge, understanding and the many abilities and natural gifts we all possessed and had refined over so many years...We devoted ourselves to work for The Great Cause, The Great Commission, against the despicable tyranny of the parasites and their corrupt elite minions there.

"So we went back to the surface world and successfully infiltrated and joined with those whom eventually became generally known, collectively, as 'The Romani'.

"We chose them because, well, *there were many reasons*...but not the least of them was because if we had gone and established ourselves into a more 'statically-based-society' we would have had serious problems every twenty or thirty years.

"Because it would have been all too obvious that we had not aged as all the others in that society had...I mentioned earlier we experienced that problem, when I was telling you about the Amsterdam Antiques business...So being part of a nomadic community, helps to overcome that difficulty. But, as I said, there were other important reasons as well...

"The Romani originally came from tribes that migrated from Northern India, in the early eleventh century, and as time passed they split into many other nomadic, tribal and societal groups...as Wanderers over many lands…

"Our cultural identity from living so long in Aghartha and for long periods as well in Tibet, was already totally bound up with the ideals of *freedom, wisdom and understanding* - and by having no ties to any one particular country, which was in tune with theirs.

"At least, not having any ties to the illusory and formed to be Deliberately Divisive - as we have talked about on other occasions - elites' designated, colonial boundaries found on the surface world...that divide it up into illusory countries and territories...when it is really *just one,* beautiful planet..." She smiled enigmatically.

"Some of the very early, popular folklore on the surface world about us, about The Romani, was that we were a restless, wandering peoples who were searching for the way to return to some mythical, ancestral home.

"Well, technically that folklore came about from reasonably true observations, as some of us were often observed going to the more remote areas of the earth - but we always went in a very roundabout and wandering manner to avoid being followed – particularly as we neared those places where we could go into the hidden tunnel branch systems, to access our flying crafts.

"Hence the origin of *some of the folklore* that developed, long ago, of an un-usual, and nomadic wandering race.

"Once we were safely in the tunnel branches we would get on-board our silver crafts, to return here for a while, for various reasons...to recuperate...to study...and plan our next forays - *not that any of that was known about to the originators of the folklore about us of course...!"* A light laughter tumbled from her lips..

"Some of that folklore all came about as well, due to, in the very early, long ago times, a dispute which resulted in several other races having to leave this inner world, and their memories of the locations of the hidden tunnel branches were erased. But they continually searched for them to try and return. Most of them had also enjoined on the surface world with The Romani by that time as well.

"That aspect of the folklore is now not true of course, as long, long ago we all reconciled all our differences and we all now live as one people, in harmony, wherever we are....and we can all come and go from here as and when we need to!

"But the old folklore was true in the sense that some of us did – *and still do of course* - spend a lot of time, to all outward appearances, to be just wandering on the Earth's surface. *But we deliberately chose to do so, and to be there - to covertly help and guide humanity, in many, many ways, and in conjunction with many others* – as I spoke about earlier, when I explained about us having various 'legends' so we are accepted as having many different roles and positions, in many different cultures and societies.

"For a long time now we have had, because we embarked on many projects to create them, all the necessary 'Earthly' material resources and credibility indicators valued by those living on the surface world, and all the skill sets and all the legends to operate in all levels of the cultures and the societies we can move in.

"But we can now return more frequently and much more rapidly and much easier to Aghartha, our true homeland, through the mobile portals.

"Eventually we enhanced the portal technology even further, from being simply static ones in various hidden locations at first; then to them being mobile; then so they also gave us the benefit of *an optional time-dilation* as well, which means that if we activate that option, and anyone had, *however unlikely that would have been,* observed us going into a portal, they would then see us come out of it more or less straight away - *but we may have been back here, or somewhere else...for many months...*Just as you have all experienced - the first time of course was when you all returned back to Fair a few seconds after you left it – but you had been in the Trocadero Cafe with Anders, and then our main room with me, for several hours...

"I hope all of that helps to make our story, our history, a little clearer for you all...? *Although I suspect it may have raised even more buckets full of questions from the Well of Questions!*" She laughed lightly.

Mel and Sophie were once again quite unable to contain their emotions having listened to what this *remarkable*, this *amazing being*, this *wonder-full lady* had just revealed to them, and they quickly stepped to her to hug and thank her – for all of that and for everything else…

Sophie said, her teary voice quivering,

"Ohhh Magda...thank you...and I'm so, so very sorry if you had to, had to remember some terrible and such sad, sad things...But I, I could just listen to you all night! – but you don't have nights here – so, so – for ever…!"

Jake and Dave were no less deeply impacted by everything Magda had just entrusted them with, by her being so open, and telling them so much. The implications of it all were...were...well, almost too much for them to grasp…

Jake could only shake his head and falling back on his usual humour he commented,

"Aye, thank you Magda, thank you, very, very much...*'S all incredible...all of it...Wow!* - An' y'right about 'avin buckets full o' questions! *Me arms are achin' from windin' all the buckets up from that Well...It just keeps gettin' deeper an' deeper!*"

Magda beamed at him, and then at them all, and said, "well my dears, *thank you!* And Sophie - please do not be *sorry-full, such memories, to me, are as precious as a purseful of silver pennies! Sometimes it is good to open it up, and then with gratitude...to count all your blessings* - to coin a phrase – *oh! that is a good pun!*

280

"So...well...then - whilst we are 'on this page', so to speak, I think we will turn over a few more of them to take it all a little further for you...But shall we go back to the sofas and sit down first before I do?! They may only be a few pages, but there is much, that both Anders and I need to reveal for you in them...and you may be more comfortable sitting down as we do!"

Chapter 17: The High Balcony (iv)

As they all walked slowly back over to the sofas, Magda and Anders answered many questions, and continued to do so for a while after they had sat back down.

Magda then continued speaking about relevant things from 'the pages' she mentioned earlier...

"All the different races here have, long ago, all learned from tragic, first hand experience, the ultimate lessons of the futilities of obsessing with and engaging in conflicts and wars, especially after Atlantis *destroyed itself by the abuse and catastrophic mishandling of the immense powers it had weaponised*, over fifteen thousand years ago, it was a devastating event which now, once again, has its parallel in the potential for it to happen again on the surface World today…

"However...ever since the aftermath of that...we have all lived in harmony together, and by embracing an existence dedicated to the attainment of ever more understanding and enlightened minds, knowing only peace, understanding, study, Good Works and the beneficent applications *for all*, of the true realities of material and spiritual existence...and without the suffering, or the misery of negative emotion driven conflicts…

"*It is our choice* to cultivate these positive lifestyles and philosophies because we are very aware of the benefits for *each individual – and therefore collectively for all of us, and for the planet, in doing so.* Consequently we Agharthans have made incredible spiritual and technological advances over all of that time.

"For example, just as an overview, we are now familiar with, understand and use, the powers and energy forces of *external* materials, of their *outer nature*, and of their relationships and quantum linkages and entanglements to the *inner, energetic spiritual nature, or singularity – which was, is, the meaning of 'Al Khem' – 'One Point' - the 'oneness' of universal consciousness,* and its manifestation in each and everyone of all the myriads of sentient beings' psyches in the

Multiverse.

"I am not being boastful when I say that we are now more highly evolved than our Atlantean ancestors were in these respects - and have surpassed even their immense technological achievements...

"So...all our spiritual and technological developments have *obviously not* just been made over the last few hundred years or so, that *the current* surface human 'civilizations' have made in their mainly warfare, industry, trade, money and power motivated technology developments. A significant part of their technology was only discovered due to the motivation and emphasis on research to primarily weaponise whatever they could for use in warfare.

"Wars to plunder and then protect all the resources necessary for those industries, and it also enabled the parasite controlled elites with the means to be able to kill ever larger numbers of other humans ever more efficiently, and over greater and greater distances...

"As an example of that, after the surface scientists discovered how to access the power of nuclear energy, they then immediately weaponised it, and used two bombs to destroy two large cities in Japan which immediately killed hundreds of thousands of unsuspecting people, and caused desperate misery for many generations there afterwards. Those bombs were dropped on them despite secret overtures having been made from elements within the government of Japan to America's, to commence peace talks, and achieve an end to the war...

"But the opportunities for the parasites to immediately benefit from the foul, vast, negative energies that would be released from such wholesale murder, and in the longer term, for their elite minions to have greater economic and other controls, which would further benefit the parasites, were far too great for them to even fleetingly consider peace...

"Concerned emissaries from Aghartha, and many other non-terrestrial civilizations - also using flying crafts - started observing and monitoring *the thousands of nuclear bomb explosions* that were then test fired in many other surface and sub-surface locations, over the following decades. Many were exploded underground, which we know were deliberately orchestrated by the parasites *against us.*

"But fortunately the surface humans have yet to penetrate much further than fifteen to twenty miles or so directly beneath the earth's surface. But, nevertheless, such explosions do have severely damaging effects on the Earth's interior - and not just its interior of course…The immensely powerful energy released *impacts heavily and destructively on many other dimensions,* and on those positive entities whom exist there…

"We have already talked about how some, well, most, of the tremendously important technological developments that have been deliberately suppressed - because of how revealing them would *totally change and transform* global societies, economics, politics - and ultimately lead to the dismantling of the ruling elites' cabal of power….

"Changes and transformations all to the betterment and benefit of the surface masses of humanity. Benefits and revelations that could - *would – will!* - result in the complete loss of power and control over those masses by the parasites and their human puppet-like psychopathic elites.

"Well, a lot of that technology was acquired by the shooting down, retrieval, and reverse engineering of those flying crafts monitoring the nuclear explosions. Unidentified flying craft were reported being seen by many hundreds, thousands, of people all over the world, and increasingly so ever since then.

"Discounting the man-made reverse engineered ones, in more recent times, the other crafts, as I have said, were not only from Aghartha but also came with other beings from other planets who came here as concerned observers as well, and often they prevented the nuclear explosions by using their technology to disrupt the functioning of the bombs. Instances of that inexplicable non-functioning occurring on both sides are well documented during the period of the so called 'Cold-War', when Communist Soviet Russia was the Western Alliance's designated enemy…

284

"...which was all a wickedly crafted illusion in the first place...as the so called 'Communists' were all originally organised, trained and funded with the money they received from the New York Banking House of Kuhn Loeb and Company, which still exists, and from many others of their elite associates, particularly the Rothschild dynasty. They all assisted in its creation and development, to benefit from the future conflicts that were then to be orchestrated and played out.

"The obscene, shocking barbarities, and the sheer magnitude of the wholesale murder that the series of Communist elites, since their inception, inflicted upon the normal citizens of Russia - and in many other countries as well of course - far outweigh even those of the Inquisition...But more of all the carefully hidden specifics of that period of history, will have to be for another time...

"The observers from here, and...*other places*, were all too aware that the powerful war-like, or more accurately: *war-obsessed*, elites, who were, and still are, utterly infested and controlled by the parasites, had finally developed the means, once again, to potentially destroy this planet...And if left unchecked they could be soon moving, along with the parasites, to other planets much further afield than the moon, and eventually be able to occupy - or threaten to do the same to other planets out there...

"So, in addition to disrupting many of the explosions, they then 'fenced off' the Earth a few decades ago, with an energy grid that prevented the larger, astronaut carrying rocket type of fossil fuel burning technology craft used in those times, from venturing out to other planets, effectively preventing any further, major excursions into the far realms of the Multiverse...

"Now this had the effect as well of the elites having to cease any further – at least any further that would be open to the public's gaze – manned, large space rockets to the moon, or anywhere else. Yes they had hidden technology craft that could do so, *and were doing so*, but they could hardly use them openly, as then they would be admitting that they had them...!

"That is the reason the overt space programme was wound down.

The covert, or secret, space programme continued of course, with even more billions and trillions of dollars poured into this unacknowledged project.

"However, we are aware that the elites' unacknowledged secret agencies now have at least one operative Stargate portal to Mars, a planet that is completely different to the heavily edited images of its environment that are put out by NASA.

"The technology for creating that portal mostly came from the highly technologically developed Draco-Reptilian race that has an alliance with certain factions of the elites, or rather it started off, long ago, by being allied, but they gradually gained a dominance over those factions, which suited the parasites' agenda...But all of that is something else I, or another of us, will talk about with you in more detail another time, I just want to cover some of the background, and the main, salient points for you now.

"There is some dispute as to whether the three extra-terrestrial observer craft were actually shot down at the White Sands Missile Proving Grounds of the Roswell Army Air Field in July, nineteen forty seven, by a, a recently developed at that time as well, longitudinal scalar energy beam weapon, first designed by Nikolai Tesla.

"He had not designed it for use as a weapon of course – that was done by...others...in unacknowledged, secret underground locations of the American military industrial corporations, who based their research and development on the papers and working models that were all confiscated, after Nikolai's death. Confiscated initially, by the American FBI, but then they all went to certain shadowy agencies within the American military industrial complex...

"Or, instead of being shot down, whether the craft were deliberately crashed by their occupants, so as to give the elites, the opportunity to reverse-engineer their technology.

"Deliberately doing such an act most definitely contravenes Multiversal Law, and would have provoked a severely punitive response against them from other, infinitely more advanced, non-terrestrial, and higher inter-dimensional entities, whom oversee and police the Inter-Planetary Federation. Because an advanced race cannot be allowed to deliberately just present a much less developed one with their superior technology. By staging a crash – even if 'shots' were fired at them – just to satisfy any such investigation - they could claim it was not deliberate...they were forced down, and so that's why they crashed..

"There were no altruistic motivations at work by 'the Greys' who were operating the craft, to present such technology to humans. No, quite the opposite, in return their race had been permitted, after negotiating with the top levels of the overt American Government, and the covert Deep State where the real power lies – and which President Eisenhower broadcast his fearful concerns about to the American public towards the end of his office...they were permitted to continue with their ongoing abductions of people, of both genders and ages, on an ongoing basis.

"Current estimates are that approximately one million women, men and children disappear globally every year now, due to them being taken by them. I will not today burden you with the details of what happens to them, or where they go.

"That shooting down, or deliberate crash, was near to America's - and in fact the world's, first and only one at the time, nuclear bomber squadron airfield at White Sands in northern Mexico. Those retrieved extra-terrestrial craft – one was totally obliterated - and the surviving beings, along with those that were killed, were quickly taken away by the American military.

"However it happened, whatever the truth of it was, it did result in some of their technology being reverse engineered and added to the ongoing development of propulsion energy technology, crystal based miniature electronic circuitry applications, fibre optics, light emitting diodes – LEDs, kevlar type ballistic impact resisting compounds, and many other materials and technologies which were also developed from what was discovered in those salvaged crafts...

"Very soon afterwards, as you would expect, human technology made a great leap forwards from the large, heavy valve operated

287

electronic devices, with slow and limited functions, to light weight miniaturised crystal circuitry devices capable of immensely high speed concurrent multi functioning, which, apart from being immediately weaponised, also opened up soon afterwards all the routes to the Technotronic Era...as envisioned by Brzezinski, about whom, and what, he envisaged that to be, we have both – and Jake has! - quoted to you what he actually said about it.

"I suppose from a 'psyops' – psychological operations, point of view, that is weaponising them as well, particularly by creating all the modern weapons of - *Mass Distraction*...

"...Whilst we are on this theme of technology, let me briefly go further back in time again, to long, long ago, when the inter-dimensional, predatory, vampiric parasites covertly invaded and began their infestation of the human race...

"Ever since that happened – Anders has called it: 'the ambush of a weakened and unsuspecting race,' others have called it: 'The Fall Of Man', a Fall...into the coveting and obsessing over material wealth, money, power and control, all symptomatic of a Dualistic Consciousness, that creates so many negative energies, essential to the parasites' survival.

"As their infestation spread rapidly across the surface world in those long ago days, the humans' previously higher, default state of living with an enlightened awareness, and a higher, benevolence creating Unity Consciousness, *and a higher, greater sense and perception of the possible,* were all, as we have previously talked to you about – were all deliberately and persistently whittled down over the generations from the masses' awareness.

"Looking around, even briefly, on the surface world, it is all too often distressingly clear to see how entrenched now those heavily diminished, and barely recognisable products - the distorted results of all that 'whittling down' have become in the mass cultural mainstream.

"As the parasites, working through their elite human agents were gradually achieving all of that, at the same time it was crucial for them to - just about literally - 'piece by piece', securely hide away 'from the sight', and so from the awareness, of the human masses, *almost all* of the remaining traces of specific ancient artifacts and technologies which used to be there, because if they were openly revealed and exhibited and their functions explained to, and understood by, the masses, that could possibly commence a remembrance of the realities of what life was really like before...and definitely would call into question the mainstream narrative of human history. So an ever darkening veil was drawn over them as well.

"Same subject - but jumping forward with it now to more recent times, just one example of an elites' deliberately created organisation to achieve that, *despite all their propaganda claims to the opposite*, but it is, in reality just another of those 'manipulative institutions'.

"This one was cynically corrupted after its creation to be in the very forefront of drawing a dark veil over them – *and literally – and physically*, 'piece by piece' - hiding such artifacts away from the public's, the masses' sight – and it is called the Smithsonian Institute, administered by the American Government. Its main museum is based in Washington, but it has over two hundred other sites in forty five states as well, including affiliate organisations in other countries.

"They stored, and continue to store, in many secret locations, all well out of public sight or access, thousands upon thousands of artifacts and other proofs, *that would absolutely not just call into question the accepted mainstream's dogmatic and limited narrative that is taught of human history and achievements – but completely turn it all on its head! And not just of the 'human' history and achievements...!*

"They have managed to hide away or destroy, *oh so many artifacts and objects* that would utterly transform the masses' understanding of their real and true historical time-line of human life *on* the planet...true explanations and true understandings of the greatness they once had as their default condition – *and still have, but it is all unknown about,* hidden away, under the veils, in that dark, shadowy room...whilst a false and deceptive narrative of it all is peddled to them instead...

"Yes, of course, the Smithsonian and other similar organisations have for public viewing many, many interesting things in their museum displays, *but there is nothing at all really contentious to the parasite's and their elites' desired, false narrative for the masses consumption…*

"Just for one example: they were a party to the organising of the cover up, from public awareness, of the discoveries of hundreds of extremely large humanoid type skeletons, and many others with the elongated skulls typical of some of the early Egyptian Pharaohs - whom were non-terrestrial, and their later human-hybrids, and they have not just been excavated from that country, but from all over the world.

"All those remains, or most of them, and so many, many more similar remains, were transported to the Smithsonian, who then secretly had them taken aboard Naval vessels and dumped into the sea...or hidden away..."

Dave jumped in to exclaim and ask, *"Wwhat?! They, they just dumped them…?!* And you mean, well, you're saying that if there were *giant skeletons,* well, *obviously there must've been giant...people…?!"*

"Yes, David, there really were...to quote Hamlet: *'there are more things, Horatio, betwixt heaven and earth than are dreamt of in your philosophy…!'* Although in the original first folio, written in sixteen twenty three, it actually read *'...our...'* not *"your' philosophy…'.* Hamlet was actually speaking in general terms - about the limitations of human thought and knowledge at that time...but 'our' was later edited out by others – *'can't be dropping too many clues to 'the great unwashed' can we...?!'* I can imagine those responsible for that editing saying..."

"*Wow!* We weren't told that in English Lit. at school! But, I'm still stunned that, crikey me!..*They just dumped them in the sea! – with God knows what else…?!* That's unforgivable!...the *basta...*ahem! - sorry! - expletive deleted!"

"Yes...David, I'm afraid most of them were dumped into the oceanic depths, and some were hidden away in their vast storage facilities, to be unseen and unknown about – to the masses - like so many things they got their hands on...

"In fact in America, where many of them have been, *and still are being found*, it is now illegal to excavate, announce the discovery of, or to publicly display the large skeletons...But various Masonic, and private museums have some on display in glass exhibits, in fact I have seen black and white photographs of the current Queen of England when she was much younger, looking at one towering over her at well over twice her height in just such a place, and having the truth of them explained to her...

"...During and since the Iraq and other wars, and the permanent American military presence in that whole region, the well organised elite officials' sanctioned and planned the initial looting of specific sites of their ancient artifacts – and many ancient texts, mostly on clay tablets, recording the true history of humanity, were removed. Including the so-called 'Baghdad Battery' – a device over two thousand years old which could still produce electricity...from the museum in Baghdad and items from many other cities. This looting was performed by elements of the American military, and it has swelled all their hidden coffers considerably...

"I am sure you remember that previously – last Monday - when you were all in The Trocadero, Anders likened some of what we are talking about now to: *'the placing of dark veils over a bright lamp in a lovely room so that its positive and radiant light became dimmer and dimmer...so that now 'the room' is so dark and shadow infested that such things as were there before are unseen and unknown about - to the vast masses of the Earth's surface humans...'*

"Well, one reason that can be achieved is because: *'History is always written by the Victors'*, how true that is...and if you dig deeper – to use an archaeological pun! – into that statement, it logically implies that if there is a 'Victor' there must, therefore, be a 'Vanquished', which then logically implies there has been a war, or a conflict, and as the global elites have used and aided America to be their 'Victor' in over two hundred and forty of those wars since it was

291

founded...one can imagine that those 'Victors' employed to - *'write the history'* - have become rather good at it by now…!"

"So those - throughout the ages – *'whom were 'doing the writing of history',* and so placing many of the dark veils, achieved exactly that, by reinforcing the perceptions and beliefs that: *'there's nothing to see here...nothing going on, never was, this is how it has always been, and this is all normal...'*

"A major result of such malefic machinations, and so many, many more – *and not just over a few hundred years, but thousands* - and all the sophistry allied to them of course, is that most of humanity, became, and still is, so locked into, completely distracted and preoccupied by, the very limited perceptions of 'reality' from their materialistic 'five-senses-only-left-brain's-perception'. And that state is further reinforced by all the outpourings from those stereotypes who claim to know all about the shadows on the cave wall...of the immediate, three dimensional, physical only, 'scientifically explicable' world that they can see with their two eyes.

"They are what we call 'Three-D persons' – *because 'they believe only in the physical world they 'perceive with their five senses'* – to quote Rudolph again...

"So...the masses are easily lead to believe only in what they are told is – *historically* - 'realistic' and 'possible', and to what is only very close *and immediately in front of them in their experience.* They have become so disconnected that they can only perceive, and so only believe, the only things that are *'true and real'* are the things that they have been told about are *'true and real'* by all the manipulative institutions. Things they can see, touch…and so on...*and anything else that they can't do any of that to is just: 'fantasy, fiction and fairy tales'!*"

Sophie couldn't help herself from interjecting again and she said, *"Yes! That's so right!* - Well...it's not *'right', it's desperately tragic!* I know because over the years I've felt like I've been more and more drawn into being like that. *Sort of like a relentless pressure to just accept everything as it is, and certainly don't keep questioning it, but just get on with it...!*

"But like Labi Siffre sang in that wonderful song he wrote: *'Something Inside So Strong'* – I love all the lyrics in it, especially:

'The higher you build your barriers – the taller I become...My light will shine so brightly It will blind you, Cos there's Something inside so strong...and we're gonna do it anyway...!'

"That song has always inspired me! I know it was about the evils of Apartheid in South Africa, but it now applies to the whole world of today, because it more than *just seems* that the battle lines are drawn – *but they really are* - between all of 'Us' the people – and the parasites and all their 'elites'...

"*I've always* resisted *'it'*, but never knew exactly what that *'it'* really was – until now...thanks to meeting you and Anders...I've been like that ever since my childhood ended and my teenage years started, and I started to question things.

"But school, then work, and all the usual draining hassles you face, all those, well, *'deliberate pre-occupations'* – like you've said, just sort of, well, dampened it down – Ha! - It's like you get more and more 'dampened' until you're wet through, then when you're eventually soaked in it you then just end up *'going with the flow!'* - in that river everyone else's struggling and slowly drowning in!

"*Huh!* - it was the poet Florence Smith - but she was known as *Stevie* Smith - who summed it up brilliantly for me as well in her poem: *'Not Waving but Drowning...* Sounds comical when you first read or hear those words I know, but they, and the whole poem hide a much darker meaning..."

Magda and Anders were nodding in agreement and sympathy as they listened to her heartfelt exposition. He was particularly impressed with her visually powerful and analogous way of speaking to communicate how she felt. That analogy of 'dampening – soaking – flow – river - drowning' is something else I can weave into my presentations he thought!

"...But when I'd listened to you talk, Anders, in the marquee at the Fair that first time, it was during and after that, that I felt like, well,

293

like I realised *I wasn't alone in thinking like that, it wasn't 'just me'!*

"Because, before, I hadn't come across anyone else who thought about things like that, or even at least talked – *or even tried to* – about them. When *I tried* to talk to people I knew, know, about anything other than, well - *flippant trivialities* – such as last night's T.V., a Facebook photo-message or something like that, well, their eyes just glazed over and I could actually see them just *switching off...!*

"Towards the end of your talk, I felt like it was as if I was starting to take off a heavy full-face motorbike helmet with a very narrow, dim and dirty visor – *and then, later that night* – well, *it was in the early hours of the next day - when I finally 'got it off' - I could hold my head up and, and I was aware of, and saw much bigger, brighter and further away horizons all around me...!* I hadn't seen them before or even realised they existed!...and, and, oh, *so much, much more...!*

"...Like being able *to really think* so much clearer and better, and I had feelings and senses that I really was much, much more capable of...of, well...*doing anything!*" Her voice finally cracked and she had to take some deep gulps of air to settle herself, Jake's arm tightened around her shoulders, holding her closer to him.

Anders smiled at her and said, "I'm truly delighted that my words helped you so much, and clearly had such a positive, beneficial and very prompt effect on you Sophie! *Thank you for saying so.* But the credit must really go to you because you were so obviously *ready and willing* to, to hatch out of your 'egg shell!', throwing away the restraining chains of illusion...

"The old adage of: *'when the student is ready the teacher will appear'*, certainly proved to be true for you - and for all of you...! *And If you don't mind me doing so Sophie*, I'll incorporate those analogies you've just used of the: *'heavy, dim and dirty, narrow visored full face helmet', and the 'dampening until you're soaked and going with the flow – Not Waving but Drowning'* - into my speeches in future! They are very powerful yet easily-identified-with images.

"And you are absolutely right about dear Florence's poem! Her words, together with yours, do perfectly describe the...mmmm, yes,

294

yes I will...! Thank you Sophie!" His voice quietly petered out as he appeared to be deep in thought about Sophie's recounting of her experiences and her *'awareness analogies'*

Magda smiled at them both, and then to the others, "it really is a wonderful thing to have the opportunities, and be able to, to openly, and spontaneously, share ones deeper thoughts, insights, experiences and perceptions with others on the same wavelengths, and yours Sophie will now be added to Ander's – *and my* - future talks to help introduce many others to, and aspire them to...those wavelengths as well...!

"And thank you as well Sophie for reminding me of Stevie - she was always such great fun! I must revisit her works. *Actually...*these words of hers, they are so especially relevant now as well - have just come to mind:

'And they were brave.

For although Fear knocked loud

Upon the door, and said he must come in,

They did not let him in.'"

Dave's head jerked up on hearing that, " *- that's what you said mate, more or less...!"* he looked at Jake with an astonished expression on his face, *"...when we were stood at the end of Filey Brigg yesterday afternoon!"*

*"Oh aye!...*yeah I did, it were an'all! Well, more or less like y'say– I said...*'time's come fer us to stop bein' afraid...'cos that's how they want us to be...'*, summat like that...it's not quite as poetically put – but 'Ey! - *Mebbe I'm a poet – an' I didn't know it...!"*

Amidst more groans...Magda smiled at him saying, "well, whether they were poetically put or not, they were still fine, strong and brave words you spoke then as well Jake..."

"Oh! Right...Thanks...Magda..." he replied, looking a little embarrassed at her praise!

"Soooo...these are momentously exciting - but they are still precarious times! - Even with the new cycle and tide of positive,

295

uplifting cosmic energies starting to flood over the Earth, aiding the rise of human consciousness, and with the readiness this time of the Earth to synchronise with this. Plus, there is the voluntary incarnating of many more, much older and fully enlightened souls onto the Earth to help and assist – which, indeed, they have always done, but many, many more have done so in recent decades."

She chuckled gaily, *"they are actually lining up to come here now! -* they desire to be part of, and help, *in these exciting times…!* Because the human race is once again making so many epoch changing, enlightening and spiritual advancements now.

"Also, this is one of the major reasons why we, and the extra-terrestrial race, acting as Ambassadors for the many others, who all live predominantly in the fifth and sixth dimensions, and higher ones of course, are so keen now to make direct contact and establish mutually beneficial relationships with you now.

"We all have a huge, vested interest in your elevation, and *'they'* are now, most emphatically, coming 'off the fence', to assist as well - *because there is every chance that you will soon be in their world!* Ha ha! – you could say – *that you will be their new 'neighbours', because you will be sharing parts of the same dimensional places with them!*

"*We* have *always been* 'off the fence' and a Resistance…Ha! - literally an: 'Underground Resistance', operating covertly over the millenniums with many selected individuals and groups of humanity working against the parasites and all their elite minions. Universal and Multiversal Law permits our interventions – to a degree - *because we are of this planet*, we are not from outside of it, just coming in and interfering.

"When human…*'ascension'*… a word some people are using for it - although it does have some unfortunate overtly Judeau -Christian religious connotations, occurs, you, and the Earth, will…*'Elevate'…the word we prefer*…from the third dimension directly into the fifth dimension, effectively bypassing the fourth.

"Why will you 'bypass' it? – Well, because you will have already, by then, have overcome the dark energy which resides in the fourth, despite having been..."

She then smiled and nodded briefly to Sophie before saying..."having been: *'soaked in it, and in the flow of it',* for thousands of years...*and you will have overcome it!*...no longer drowning...but waving – waving to greet a new future - *and be more than ready to go beyond it...!*

"You will have managed to climb out of that Stygian river of the nether regions, and cast off those sodden garments and 'dried out'! The parasites exist only in the lower fourth dimensions, and as humanity has for eons been under the control of their fourth dimensional dark energy, and ascended over it, so you will have no need to go from the third, then to the fourth, before you enter the fifth.

"*Oh...we have been discretely involved in such a lot of other...works and occurrences...for such a long time to get to this stage!* And *now* there are the endeavours we have been involved in, liaising with the extra-terrestrial, and higher inter-dimensional beings, and establishing contact protocols for one race to act as Ambassadors for all of them, as I explained to you yesterday.

"You now all know that they also have great concern for the current precarious situation that the Earth and humanity is now in, and why, and they are also implementing strategies to directly hinder the parasites.

"Just one of which is to initially make their presence known to more and more surface humans. These off-planetary beings are contacting people just like you, to assist in the full disclosure that humanity is *certainly not alone in the Universe,* and when that fact is fully realised – *you remember 'the hundredth monkey syndrome...? -* so too will all the facts and realities of that gradually but surely follow *- just as the bright light of day follows the darkness of the night.*

"The light of all the alternative, higher technologies and energy systems – which will ultimately lead you to 'new' philosophies and paradigms for humanity to live peacefully all together with on the planet, all of which will come from that 'Pandora's Box' of implications that we talked about last night...

297

"More and more surface humans will soon fully wake up, de-trance, and so once again realise their true nature, potential and reality...*and they are more than just starting to do so*, because there is just so much encouraging evidence that people are starting to remove, one by one, those light dimming veils...

"...and, like you have just told us Sophie, *'take off those awareness and perception obscuring helmets'*...and once the planetary and human morphogenetic, positive, vibrational frequencies are sufficiently raised, the parasites will have no other choice or option but to either choose to evolve spiritually themselves towards The True Light - and so abandon their agenda here, or, if they choose not to do that...they will be eliminated naturally and become extinct.

"Because *they cannot now* - thanks to those hindering strategies and the many other works of extra-terrestrial and much higher inter-dimensional beings, and of enlightened, awakening groups of humans whom many of the old souls re-incarnated into - *they cannot now* just safely retreat, abandon the Earth, and move onto another planet – or summon any reinforcements from where they come from - in the lower to mid levels of the fourth dimension.

"They will *not be able to survive* within the future Earth's higher, positively raised frequencies. They have managed to be so devastatingly influential and active, primarily engaged upon vampirically feeding off you, and so lowering, for so long now, the Earth's and it's populations into the much lower levels of consciousness and energy frequencies.

" But as these are raised they will also raise and positively affect, and clear out the negative frequencies in some of the lower levels of the fourth as well, which is their natural habitat...and that endeavour of clearing out negative energies in the lower dimensions is also being undertaken synchronistically by those much higher feline looking entities that I mentioned earlier...

"...so if the parasites choose not to evolve they will have nowhere to go, the expression: *'between a rock and a hard place'*, accurately sums up their current position. This is the reason they are now so desperate and tasking their elite human agents to throw everything they can at humanity to drastically reduce the population, and demoralise and dis-empower those who survive that. Because they know that they themselves face elimination if they fail - like a vampire who is trapped outdoors just before the new day's sun comes up - and knows it cannot tolerate it when it does, and will be burnt into a pile of ashes by the exposure to the light of that rising sun's rays..."

Magda paused for a few moments, to sip at her water, and let all of this be absorbed by the two young couples. Dave, churning it all over in his mind said, "so it looks like there really is some *'light at the end of the tunnel'* then from what you're saying – and if I understand it right, by raising the frequency levels of the third dimension which we currently live in - it will blend into the lower levels of the fourth where they exist and raise it there as well?

"...Sort of like brightening all the subtle hues that spread between the main colours in the rainbow – that you showed us when you focused in on it for us the other night...when you showed us how the dimensions are layered and blend into each other...? But it's still just, well, *all so incredible,* and it still amazes me how much, huh, just about *everything* we've been and *still are being told – or programmed with* - starting with what's taught in schools...*just isn't true or correct...there's no wonder we've gotten into the state we're in!"*

"Yes David, sadly, all that which you say you are – *and quite understandably so* - still amazed about, is correct, *but it really is changing.* So please do try not be too disheartened or overwhelmed by it - you, *all of you* - and everyday countless numbers of others on the surface world are becoming more and more aware of all the manufactured deceptions. And even by just being aware of them, and wanting to do something about them, you are transmitting positive energies *that help...*

"And the four of you are doing, and will do, so much more than: *'just being aware of - and wanting to do something about it',* as your 'Pandora Quest', as you very cleverly named it Melanie, unfolds...!"

Jake, now resting back against the sofa, and having topped up his and Sophie's water glasses, said to Magda, "you said they – the parasites - 'have a choice to positively evolve'...", then with a casual shrug he asked her: "...so what d'you think then - are the likely chances of 'em doin' that?!"

Magda sighed, "Personally...I consider it unlikely...but I am always prepared to be pleasantly surprised. But they have to be given the chance, to have the choice, because Source, the creative energy of all, decreed a Multiversal Law that grants all sentient life-forms Free Will, so if they choose not to...well, that will be their own choice, and then their inevitable elimination will be a direct result of that very choice they made themselves from their own Free Will.

"If they do choose not to, so it will not then negatively affect the karmas of all the many others who were instrumental in raising the consciousness frequencies – resulting in their demise..."

"Right, I think I understand...it's like, as if, I 'ad some sorta 'magic machine gun' wi' an unlimited amount o' bullets, an' I hosed 'em all down wi' it - aye they'd be eliminated! – But I'd 'ave a lot o' bad karma then meself to repay over many lifetimes *because I personally decided I did all that – eliminatin' - to 'em?!"*

"Yes, that is correct Jake, it was a good way to put it. If you did that you would certainly incur a lot of 'bad karma', just like one does with any deliberate action one takes in the realisation that it will cause harm or distress to another. Acting purely spontaneously in self-defence of yourself or others is another matter entirely though, in those cases the negative Karmic Law is not so rigorously invoked."

A few moments of silence passed again as they all thought about this, and then Magda continued,

"...Moving on...Let me give you one very interesting and very encouraging example that you might want to do your own research into as well - of this awareness change, this 'veil removing awakening'…

"This is the current work being done - that I observed by remote viewing recently - by parasite *untainted* scientists and associated study groups who are making bold preliminary steps forward by openly studying in some academic institutions - the 'Noetic Sciences' - which are the actual mechanics of the influence and effect that mind and consciousness – the 'oneness of consciousness' that I have mentioned, have on physical matter.

"'Matter' is, after all, just how we perceive, or de-code a denser, lower vibrational energy – and these study groups are now, once again, 'on the right track' - after a few, shall we say – '*pointers*' - from others of us, in this right direction...and they are making steady, and very encouraging progress...along with other insightful research into the closely related field of the physics of 'quantum entanglement' – which is the actual interdependency, weaving and relationships between conscious thought and 'matter' - despite many of those involved in this work in the wider community being marginalised by the parasite infected, career maintaining, corporate mainstream scientific community and their media lackeys who will always attempt to vitiate their, and any others', similar works and studies of these realities...."

Mel leaned forward slightly to speak, "I for one certainly will Magda! – That sounds fascinating! Thank you! - Never heard anything about it before! But I really get the feeling, and sense that it is somehow more than relevant and connected with the work I do in my own time when I am creating jewellery, yes, for decorative and 'glamorous' purposes, but also for healing purposes using specific crystals and rare and precious metals – not that I can afford many of those! I sense, as well, that it will take what I'm doing, or trying to do, to another level.

" - Actually Lucia said she is going to start to share her knowledge with me about the, the more esoteric properties of crystals – which I have really only been slightly aware of upto now and really want to discover more about ! – Ha! *There we go!* - I just recognised another of those '*coincidences - that aren't*' Anders!"

He smiled at her as he inclined his head and raised his palms up as if to say: '*Yes – indeed! – There you go...!*'

301

She smiled back to him and then followed quickly on with, "Soooo...Magda - am I right if I'm understanding it all properly, from what you're saying, that there is *only one consciousness - that 'Al Khem'* – *'One Point' - was it?* in the Universe?   Not zillions of different types coming from every different separate single living thing in it...?

"And if that's so, here on Earth – well, *up there on Earth!* - How come then that we don't naturally act all together from that 'oneness consciousness' – but, yeah...of course...I suppose it's because we've obviously been dimmed and dumbed down so much...?

"But then, surely the parasites must also share that *'one consciousness'* as well as us - but they are just pure evil and totally negative! – So how can *they be like that* when *we're not!* – If we're all sharing that same...*consciousness*? Well, *deep down we're not - bad*, I think, I believe...I really believe that *'normal'* human beings, well, that we're essentially, innately inclined...*to want to do good and feel positive...*?!

"Excellent   Questions   and   Very   Insightful   Comments Melanie!...Anders replied to her. Magda smiled and said,

"Yes, they are, absolutely, perhaps if you would be so kind to answer them Anders, it would make a change for everyone to listen to you for a while - rather than risk tiring you all out by just listening to my voice!"

Chapter 18: The High Balcony (v)

A nders nodded, and then he turned his head towards Magda, smiling widely as he replied with his olde worlde charm, and a twinkle in his eyes,

"Of course, yes, I will, gladly! Thank you - although *I sincerely doubt* that anyone would *ever tire of listening to your enchanting voice Magda!"*

"Such charming flattery Anders!" She replied with an amused smile towards him, then she leaned towards Mel and Sophie and said to them in a loud but supposedly surreptitious whisper, with one hand at the side of her mouth in a mock attempt to prevent Anders from hearing, "but we Ladies *will never tire* of such charming and pleasing flattery - *will we my dears?!"* Both Mel and Sophie giggled as they shook their heads in agreement

Jake then rapidly commented, back with his usual deadpan humour, *"Errr...'ang on then, please, just need to mek me a note o' that..."* He looked down and pretended to be writing very quickly, muttering to himself as he did so: *"...keep...on...charmin'...an' flatterin'...never tires...from it!"* He then looked up from his studious pretence of rapid note taking.

*"S*orry! – Just pickin' up some tips to add to my, my er, *existin' 'relationship skills'...!"*

Sophie, struggling to keep a straight face, wryly commented with mock surprise, *"Oh!? – Really?! - What 'existing skills' are they then...?!"*

"Owwwwh! - Ouch!" He responded, but was visibly mollified with a big kiss on his cheek and a hug of his arm from her, and he laughed along with everyone else.

Anders, chuckling, said, "Well then...*Ha ha!* Very amusing! Indeed, yes...y'know, it's my, *it's our,* firm belief that playfulness and abundant humour are excellent indicators of high intelligence...and believe it or not *laughter is your greatest and ultimately your most effective weapon, as laughter dispels the fearsome...the more serious you become - the more substantial your fears will manifestly become...Love, Laughter, Lightness, Lucidity, and Life! will be your Five Guardian Companions as you start to travel onwards on your 'Pandora Quest',* and it is quite clear that they are all well known and familiar companions to you all, so well done all of you.

"Oh – and another indicator of high intelligence is the ability to ask deep and insightful questions like you have just done Melanie - and none of what I've just said has been *'flattery'* from me – *it was merely the simple stating of facts!*

"Soooo...to, to start to answer your question Melanie...yes consciousness is indeed a universal constant – all living sentient beings possess it, whether they are living in a physical body in the third dimensions, or in a non-physical light body in the higher dimensions.

"Magda told me that when you all sat with her, after my talk in the Trocadero Cafe, last Monday evening, that she showed you a 'thought form' rainbow - and you mentioned it earlier David - which reminded me - and then she zoomed into it to reveal all the subtle hues of all the colours to illustrate how the dimensions blend and layer. Well, 'consciousness' is not at all dissimilar, as within 'it' there are many hues, levels or layers as well...so, hold onto that thought for a moment and let's take it further with some live examples:

"...imagine a large, and very hungry, predatory carnivore, let's say it's a Tiger, it's in a jungle on Earth, and it's stalking its smaller prey - *then the Tiger suddenly pounces, kills it, and eats it!*

"Now, if you were somehow close by and watching all of that as it happened you would probably be very disturbed at those sights and even consider that creature to be evil for inflicting such fear, pain and then killing and eating its victim!

"Well, it isn't really, it is just behaving instinctively and naturally according to the current, low stage of its own individual level of consciousness. Yes, there is added nourishment for it in the blood of its victim due to the secretion of adrenal compounds and other rare chemical energies generated from the terror its victim experiences just prior to its traumatic death; but primarily, it is just the bulk of its meat content it sees as food, that the Tiger is after to survive and satisfy its hunger.

"It is only the parasites, using their infected, psychopathic humans whom, having a higher level of consciousness, consciously and *deliberately choose to inflict* prolonged, intense suffering and terror on their victims prior to eventually killing them.

"For example, as part of their satanic ritual sacrifices - *to deliberately consume and benefit from the rare energies from their terrorised victim that are briefly amplified within the altered blood chemistry...particularly one rare chemical called 'adrenochrome', and also from the traumatised energies emitted from their lower chakras, when they obscenely abuse those body parts, which are all especially potent for them when the victim is very, very young...*

"Which is one of, if not the main reason why paedophilia has always been so prevalent amongst all the ruling elites...*and is why hundreds of thousands of children 'disappear' every year across the globe...*most ending up, and for most of them, tragically, their lives literally 'ending' in those - *despicably evil* – paedophile networks...

"I don't want to seem to be indicating *even in the slightest way whatsoever* that I am favourably comparing that hungry, hunting Tiger's instinctive, lower consciousness actions to those deliberate, vile and foul acts of, mainly, the 'elite' humans, or attempting *to rationalise* the parasites and the elites' obscene and sickening behaviour, no, I'm not – *and I don't do 'rationalising' anyway* because: *'at the end of the road of 'rationality'...lies the silence of the mass grave...'*

"No, what I'm trying to get across to you is that the Tiger did what he did without the higher levels or layers of conscious abstract thought, it was just pure instinctual behaviour to just survive by hunting and eating.

"But the parasites working through their human agents' have much higher levels and layers of consciousness than that Tiger has, which

305

enables them of course to make *deliberate, abstract, conscious choices to do what they do...regardless of the negative karma that they incur in doing so.* And they are the exact opposites to the choices that we in Aghartha made...aeons ago...that Magda has talked about as well."

Mel said, "yes, I see what you're saying. That does help to...well, help me to get my head round it all! And all that about the paedophilia...my God...all those poor, poor children...that's just so sickeningly evil, unforgivable...*No wonder the elites' authorities always try to deny it and cover it all up!*"

Anders nodded sympathetically. "Yes, *yes they certainly do.* Official, so called 'enquiries' are just designed to constantly stall and whitewash over what is really happening. The revelations a few years ago about the English 'celebrity' Jimmy Saville – who was connected right up to the very 'highest elites' in the country, and he was protected by the elites' controlling it's various State Security agencies for over fifty years, mainly because he was a procurer of children for those elites, being a horrific case in point...

"But...I'm glad my attempt to answer your question was helpful to you. These are momentous subjects, and I, we, are just attempting to introduce you, all of you, to them. I could obviously talk at much greater length and in much more detail about them, but for now I think it's more important, and more appropriate for you to just: *'get your head round them'* as you said, so you understand the basic concepts.

"Perhaps now, you will research further into it, and I, or Magda, or others of us here, whom we can introduce you to, would be more than happy to discuss things in greater depth with you – with you all – at a later date."

"I will, and thank you Anders!"

"Well, perhaps if I now veer away slightly, but relevantly, for a few minutes, I can link some other issues to all this – assuming you're not all overburdened by all the wide ranging info' dropping from us both so far this evening...?!"

The four of them were quite emphatic in their agreeing for him to

306

continue.   Assuring him that they were in no way being 'overburdened'! Jake summed up how they all felt when he said, *"I feel like that Tiger, Anders! - I've got a ragin' 'unger! But not for food - for once!   For, well, for knowin'...an' understandin'...more an' more...'cause the more we know an' understand o' what we're up against – the more, well, the better chance we 'ave of o' bein' effective against it...!"*

"Thank you Jake, thank you all! And you are absolutely right! Ah! *The appetite for knowledge and understanding!* What a wonderful craving it is! And how good it feels when it's satiated – only ever temporarily though – until you have to go out and hunt for more! *So...let's do that now...*

"The parasites have had many opportunities, over the aeons, to choose to renounce and evolve upwards away from depraved, low level, negative energy infested consciousness – that we call 'evil'. But they have always, deliberately, chosen not to...and as a consequence of doing so they have effectively sealed their own fate, because they are now trapped *within* the lower levels of the fourth dimension due to the intervention – not 'interference' - as that is not permitted by Multiversal Law, of other positive, higher beings - other galactic entities who have worked to effectively quarantine or 'fence off' the Earth – which Magda has already mentioned, with spacial and dimensional blocking, energy grids.

"Which, incidentally, is one other reason for so many sightings of their crafts in recent decades in the stratosphere and way beyond that into space.   After all, quarantining an entire planet is no small undertaking.   And another reason why many of those crafts, involved in that operation, have been shot down with the scalar energy beam weapons, and other advanced and hidden technologies, that were weaponised a long time ago now, by the elites' secret agencies.

"The 'fencing off' or 'quarantining grids' are to prevent the parasites, either in their current human hosts' forms of natural human bodies - *or their more preferably desired future hosts of 'trans-human' cybernetic, advanced technology implanted humans, with artificial intelligence*

307

operating their re-structured neural programs. Such humans already exist – they have been nearly perfected at a secret underground military research base in the wilds of Australia called 'Pine Gap'.

"The various heavy metals, other compounds and nanites in the chem-trails, all regularly ingested by humanity, and the Five G and other activating radiations are major components of this trans-human restructuring of the natural human neural programs...

"They intend for the trans-human, and artificial-intelligence technologies to be operated by transmissions from a central source, thus creating and inflicting on humanity 'a cloud mind' or 'hive mind' to subsume their truly natural and individual minds. *Which is exactly what their latent 'Trans-Humanism' agenda intends to trans-form humans into.* Just listen to the recent statements from Elon Musk - who is just one of the 'public faces' of those whom control much of the research and development of this - when he describes his vision of it.

"His vision, and that of others like him, *speciously* – which is the art of convincingly presenting a false and misleading argument, similarly to sophistry - expounds all the supposed benefits – of technology enhanced humans. How much 'better', how much 'smarter', you will be - than being 'simply human'...!

"There is so much evidence of this already being well underway and it can be clearly seen, despite the deliberate obfuscations – and outright lies - about it from the mainstream media. For example, join all the ever increasing dots of the ways their *manifest agenda* of so called 'Smart' technologies are so forcefully promoted *'as being of such great benefit to humans'...*

"I often walk, deliberately observing, in the busy cities of Western civilizations, and I see, distressingly all too often, evidence of the trans-human neural programming changes already well underway. It is the robotic and almost unthinking way so many of the masses function and behave...*but...I don't want to get too drawn into all that today...!*

"What people just don't seem to realise though, of course they don't, is that once they are all intrinsically, step by step,   lead inexorably towards trans-humanism, and then linked up and 'switched on', into, the new generation of RNA processor quantum super-computers, oh - RNA is the artificially created cousin to your natural DNA - one cubic centimetre of which *can contain the entirety of human knowledge since humans first appeared on the planet...*so they can then be directly programmed with exactly what to think, and exactly how to behave...*and they can also, it goes without saying - be just as easily...switched off...*

"The most obvious dots that can be seen in the implementation of this *latent agenda* are those which are occurring in three carefully planned stages of the manifest agenda:

"the *First Stage* is *portable* technology – *you physically carry them* - like your mobile 'Smart phones', or 'Smart tablets'.

"The *Second Stage* comes when they become *wearable,* like the so called 'Smart e-watches', then eventually...

"The *Third Stage* of course is when it all will just be *'Smart implants'* into the human body...and its brain...shortly after birth...*in addition to the nanites and associated components from the chem-trails* - which are already happening! So I can't emphasise it strongly enough: *Beware Of Anything Labelled – 'Smart'!"*

"Bloody 'ell! - Oh! Sorry - *'scuse mi French!"* Jake expostulated.

"But when y'put it like that an' point out an' then join all the dots to see the bigger picture, it - it's so flamin' obvious innit?! - An' 'ow about this...as bein' dead relevant to what y've just said Anders!:

"A mate o'mine came round to see me t'other day, Wednesday it were, an' he were showin' off his new *'Smart e-watch'!* Sayin' 'ow much easier it is to Facebook stuff an' do email an' all that. Especially when he gets the 'heads-up' display glasses he's ordered, that work on 'gesture recognition' instructions! An' like y'say Anders he thinks it's great! He'll be one o'first int' queue for an implant upgrade when they're all fully rolled out...!

"Crikey me! - *I 'ave to admit though I were a bit impressed with it meself!* - But it'd be no good to me as I'd 'ave to keep tekin' the watch off when I'm workin' so it didn't get damaged! - I don't even wear a

309

normal watch when I'm workin' - *'cos I've bust that many by snaggin' 'em on bits of engine or whatever!"*

"Yes, well, there you are Jake...you've recently witnessed at first hand exactly what I'm saying...he would be easily convinced to have access to the entirety of the internet by simply having it implanted and installed – directly into his own brain...the technology components to do that are now miniscule...in the eighties they were about the size of a grain of rice, but now an injection, like a vaccine, can introduce them...

"Someone with those or similar practical concerns to yours, and not knowing anything at all about the hidden, latent agenda to all of this, might well be more easily convinced by all the cleverly marketed benefits of having an implant instead...! After all – wouldn't that be: *'the Smart thing to do?'* - and who doesn't want to appear as being *'un-Smart'*?!

"They have chosen the word 'Smart' with insidious cleverness...In fact I read a lengthy article on a mainstream news-online site recently about a family in America who had 'volunteered' to have some basic implants so they could activate their domestic *'internet of things'* - 'Smart appliances' - in a similar way – *I think they'd obviously been well paid to extol its benefits though!*

"Some features of those implants, which the article emphasised, were that the Mother was ecstatic about knowing – in her mind!- - exactly where her children were at all times, when that feature was activated or turned on automatically by tapping an 'app' on her 'smart-watch'! She said about that feature, *'our family pet, our dog Rex, had been implanted a couple of years ago - and it gave us such peace of mind in case he wandered off!...and now I know where all my young children are all of the time - so I'm not afraid anything bad might happen to them because if they start to wander off I'll know straight away...!'*

"She had also expressed similar delight at being able to turn the house's lights – and the Christmas tree's - on and off – oh...the article came out prior to Christmas, which was cleverly done as that is a time when the consumer-programming is in an even higher gear - on and off by waving her hand at them, and the husband was similarly delighted at being able to lock and unlock the front and back doors, open the garage and start the car in a similar manner – *'we all feel so much safer and in control now'*, was one of their predictably inane comments - that the article repeated several times…!

"So why am I decrying and obviously being so against all of that…? What's wrong with 'feeling safe and in control' as a result of it…?!

"Well, sadly, it is people just like them who could've written: 'The Letters Sent Back Home From A Christmas Turkey', the gist of which said: *'…Having a great time!...All's fine here! Nothing to worry about! Lots of friends with me as well, and we all get fed loads and loads of different things! My accommodation is warm, safe, comfy, clean and very nice, I really like it here…So glad I came…!'*

"…Then…for some inexplicable reason - *no further letters were received, back home, after the 15th of December…!"*

The black humour of that caused a ripple of uneasy mirth amongst the two couples, and Mel said, *"Oooh…that poor turkey!* Listening to that Anders makes me even more determined about becoming a vegetarian…!"

Dave gently took hold of her hand and said quietly and consolingly to her, "Don't worry luv, it was just a story - *real turkey's can't actually write letters like that – I know, because the ones I've read were just gobble-gobble-gobblydegook…!"*

She gave him a humorously withering look and said, *"That's terrible Dave!* - Well, if they could that's what they'd write, *poor things…!* Sorry Anders! Dave's just being silly, please go on!" Her withering look had changed to a barely suppressed smirk and wide eyed glare at him. Anders had actually lowered his head to mask a smile at Dave's comment to her, he then looked over to Jake and said,

"Jake - you just mentioned what I think is the most dreaded of words that has recently permeated your language! and it is: *'Upgrade!'.* My heart sinks when I hear it! *Swear as much as you like! – But please don't say the 'U' word!*

"Have you all noticed how all these devices are constantly being *'Upgraded'*? People have become hooked and addicted to them by deliberate social programming...and now they accept without question, and are so keen and excited for the constant *'Upgrades'* to the latest device? They will queue round the block from the early hours of the morning – even camp out on the street the night before! - just waiting for the shop to open, and get in first to buy them!

"And it's not just mobile phones that the concept of *'Upgrading'* has been applied to – it's all technology consumables! - As if being *'Upgraded'* is just a normal, acceptable, sensible – *'and very 'Smart' thing to do'*...? The use of the very word *'Smart'* is so insidiously, wickedly clever.

" - Because: *who wants to be seen by their peers in the desperately-seeking-status illusory world of 'conspicuous consumption' - as not being – 'Smart'...?!*

"The Truth, hidden behind all those illusions, is that all the *'Up-grading'* of these technology devices *is an inversely proportional phenomena,* which means as one thing 'goes up' – another thing automatically 'goes down'. So of course it is leading inexorably to the *'Down-grading'* of all that it means to be *truly human...*

"Do you all see now how people are so easily persuaded and become so addicted - by all the cleverly marketed, apparent benefits - *when they have no idea of, and are deliberately blinded to - the real reasons behind it all...?!*

"Sadly though, when we are talking about the general masses, still locked into a lower level of unawakened, and materialistically preoccupied consciousness, *convincing them that they've been fooled, even if it's in the most dangerous way possible for them, is always going to be immensely more difficult than fooling them was in the first place...*To paraphrase what Samuel – whose nom de plume was Mark Twain said.

"Y're Dead Right Anders!" Jake sighed loudly, "I just know if I said 'owt now against me mate's 'Smart e-watch' to 'im, and told 'im

anythin' about all o' this, there's no way he'd listen - *and he'd say 'I'd gone off me rocker'...an' accuse me o' becomin' a 'conspiracy theorist'! - As if that were a bad thing!"*

"Quite possibly Jake, quite possibly, and just like *'Smart Technology'*, 'conspiracy theorist' is another insidious and wickedly clever description – it was actually created by the CIA after the Kennedy assassinations in the nineteen sixties, as a response to the growing questions and evidences that the 'official story' of the 'lone crazed gunman' and everything else about those evil acts were totally false.

"So then, to counter them, the corporate mainstream media were instructed to use it to repeatedly scoff at and discredit as *'being off their rockers'* as you put it, those who were disputing – even with proof - all the evil lies of the official narratives of those tragic events...*and all the other, countless events and states of affairs that have followed*...Curiously they never use the opposite description of: *'Coincidence* Theorist' though..." He said wryly.

"But, back to your friend, and perhaps others like him as well, you never know, you can always try...you could 'bundle up' your trying by saying as well that it's not just 'stage two wearable smart e-watches', it's payment for goods using debit or credit cards as well!

"Because not so long ago you inserted your card into a machine and pressed code buttons to activate a payment, now it's been *'Upgraded'* so you can just place it over the machine, and it is now being promoted, and will soon be marketed, as being *so much easier for you* if you just had an *'Upgrade'* of a miniscule implant in your hand or elsewhere in your body, activated automatically by a checkout till - *instead of the terrible inconvenience and obvious risks of actually having to carry all those cards and remember all those PIN numbers!*

"And if, or when, cash is finally done away with, which they are indefatigably working towards, and all transactions are electronic, well, by then it will be too late...as awakened people like yourselves – who will be labelled as 'conspiracy theorists', 'extremists', 'dissidents', 'hate speakers' or 'radicalised', and all the other propaganda buzz

313

words and phrases, you will be at the top of their list to deny you from being able to make transactions to buy food, pay bills and so on, and on...and then what can you do...?

"However! Let's Not Despair Just Yet! I'm just telling you what they are desperately planning, not what will actually happen. And certainly will not happen if what we, all of us, are planning, comes to fruition...

Let's go back now to, where was I? - Ah yes! The quarantining of the planet...

"Soooo...the quarantining of the planet has prevented them from eventually spreading out into and potentially contaminating and imbalancing this entire section of the Multiverse – and beyond, should this new opportunity for the current human renaissance fail. Those extra-terrestrials and higher beings who have been instrumental in the quarantining have not interfered *directly* in human affairs, that is not how these things work. They have 'simply' taken the necessary steps to quarantine the risk to them...

"They consider that it is now upto the humans on the Earth to seize this opportunity to ascend by becoming their own 'Cavalry', almost like a rite of passage, so to speak, to do so. And if – or when - they do and it all goes to plan, the parasites will then, fairly quickly, become extinct as they cannot survive on a higher positive planetary frequency coupled with the raising of the level of human consciousness...And the parasites cannot, now, *escape away from it*...If humans fail to ascend to a Level One civilization all the aspects of the evil, dark agenda of the parasites will come to fruition of course.

"But...eventually, and it would be inevitable, that they would, in time, *destroy themselves*, and most likely the planet's surface as well, even possibly the entire planet, as that has happened in this solar system before, eons ago, *and as we share this planet we are justified to be doing what we are doing – directly now - to help you and all the others to counter them...*

"I must just take a slight detour for a moment and tell you a little more about another reason why they can't now flee from the planet –

about their recently thwarted alternative escape plan and, or, future plans to expand further out into the Multiverse...

"...they tried to set up a route by having a gateway from three dimensional Earth into the fourth dimension, created for them by the elites' few scientists who knew the real purpose of the large Hedron Collider at Cern. But that failed on its day of being put into full operation due in great part to the focused positive energy of a mass meditation by many tens of thousands of good and enlightened humans all over the Planet connecting all their individual consciousnesses, to adversely affect the device...

"And the Planet, the Gaia, was part of it as well by causing electrical storms and other ground energy phenomena that helped to prevent it from working...A truly admirable achievement by the many thousands of humans, amongst you and unknown to you, who are also 'on your side'..."

Mel gasped and said, "*I knew - I know - one who did it! Who was part of that!* - My friend at work!...I remember that she, she mentioned something about it to me, but she didn't go into any great detail about it, even though she was *incredibly pleased and on 'cloud nine' about it for days* - but I didn't know then what she was talking about really...*Oh my God!*"

Anders smiled at her, and then at the others, "You are all going to find yourselves attracting and bringing into your orbits more and more people who are waking up and re-tuning in to their higher awarenesses and *unlimited* consciousnesses, as time goes by. This will not be by 'coincidence', as I have explained at length before - but by you actually creating such circumstances and happenings, *and then recognising them...*

"So! Excellent...! You now have some knowledge Melanie of what she did, what she was part of, and later at some stage perhaps you will be able to add to her knowledge, and the local Support and Resistance group she must have worked with as well...

"So, to go back to what I was saying just before I mentioned the Hedron failure...and the fact that the parasites are now locked into a quarantined planet and only the contiguous dimensional layers to it...Trapped...and now facing exposure to higher positive energies...

"What they now are facing is a process that will be similar to the lighting of an 'anti-pest-smoke-fogger' in a heavily flea infested room where all the doors and all the windows have just been firmly closed to prevent them from being able to flee – ha! Pun intended! - from the room before lighting it, so none of them will escape the deadly – to them – fumes that will gradually fill that room.

"Once the process is over, the windows and doors can be opened again to let the fresh air back in and circulate in and out freely, and their remains can be hoovered up and disposed of, leaving the room to be fully used and enjoyed without hindrance once more...*All assuming of course that 'the anti-pest smoke device' is successfully set off in the first place...*"

"*Aye! An' I know exactly what y'mean by that an'all Anders!*" Jake said, "...as we 'ad to do the entire 'ouse, not just one room, a few years back when I offered to look after a mate's two cats for a fortnight when he went off on 'oliday! – *Well I didn't know they'd got fleas did I!* An' they spread everywhere an'all, quick as a flash, *right job sortin' 'em it were!* We 'ad to use them smoke bombs in every room - an' in each shed an'all! Me Mum an' Dad weren't right pleased with me about it I can tell y'...they said me mate'd ' 'ave to tek 'em both to local cattery next time he went off on 'is 'olidays!'"

Anders smiled at him and said, "Oh dear Jake...! But like all parasites it just shows you *how easy it is for them to get in and quickly infest - if at first – and not just at first, but as time goes on, they're just not suspected of being there!*...And how they have to be dealt with by a concerted, well planned and time consuming effort by everyone affected and involved – *once they do realise...*!

"My analogy wasn't the most elegant or accurate in all respects I must admit, but it gets the point across, and it certainly illustrates how to eradicate them...

"I need to add though that the actual core or source of the 'pure evil' negative energy that is concentrated in the parasites will not be destroyed, as energy cannot be, it can only be transformed into something else, somewhere else, but it will no longer have dominion by symbiosis – which means a living together, in intimate relation, *mainly* for the purpose of nutrition, of dissimilar life forms, which is the essence of parasitism...and the conscious host life forms – which are the parasites and their human agents, who are the primary hosts for that pure evil energy, which, when those two are...removed, that evil energy will no longer have its dominion, through them, over the masses on this planet..."

Jake interrupted again, "So...if all goes to plan...there's goin' to be quite a day o' reckonin' an' *'hooverin' up'* then, at some stage, against all these 'elite human agents' that have been, and are, directly responsible for so much, well, *ongoing misery* – although that isn't the best or anything like the strongest word for it I suppose – but you know what I mean...?"

Dave then added, "And as you've both explained Anders – you and Magda, the elites have a depopulation agenda – but it seems to me that if, like Jake says, *'it all goes to plan and there's a day of reckoning'* - against the elite human agents, and all the rest of 'em lower down the totem pole, and the comparison you made of destroying masses of fleas infesting a room, well, will that cause quite a, quite a depopulation anyway when all of it happens...?!"

"Yes...and...No!" Anders said, "...*Yes*, there will be *'a day of reckoning'*, well, many years of it I predict, but right upto one second before midnight of the day before it those humans who choose to renounce everything they have been part of must be given the opportunity to do so...And a lot of them will have 'only' been in the lower to middle levels.

"Of course many will say that those who do so are just trying to worm their way out of facing whatever retribution is decided at that time to be appropriate for them. Which may be true in some cases, but as time goes by *they* will gradually...*'dis-incarnate'*...because their consciousness will be incompatible to the new energy environment of the planet.

317

"But the point is that it wouldn't *just be them personally* who would be revealed, as they are given the opportunity to 'confess', and everything about their involvement becoming known about – by losing their anonymity - which was one of their greatest assets, *but the names of many others in the levels much higher up who were involved that they were aware of. Plus, the sheer scale of all the deceptions they had been engaged upon, and what they were doing to the detriment of humanity. All of that will also be revealed and become known about.* The names of some of those in very high level positions who deceived them, will, of course, be a great shock for the masses to come to terms with.

"Such colossal revelations, as part of a process of 'Truth and Reconciliation' from those who do come forward and confess would also...well...*hopefully*...they would also help to go even further to convincing the remaining hardcore sceptically programmed nay-saying habitual disbelievers amongst the masses, and the sneering and ridicule motivated mainstream 'talking-head journalists' still trapped in their cognitive dissonance, to come to terms with, and face upto those facts...

"For example, if you had managed to totally convince a group of people for all of their lives that eggs do not exist, they are just a fantasy, a silly theory that only the gullible could possibly believe in, and then one day you suddenly put *a full basket of egg*s in front of them all and tell them: *'actually – they do exist - these are eggs!'* – some of them would still not believe you or believe what their own eyes were seeing. *Their cognitive dissonance just could not accept the fact.*

"They would probably say: *'they are...er, they are - 'miss-shapen fragile balls of something or other you've just made to trick us...!'* and then scuttle off...like the man did in Churchill's comment about most people who: *'when they stumble over the uncomfortable truth about something - they quickly pick themselves up, dust themselves down and scuttle away...!'*

"But in this case those that scuttled away would be leaving those who *are capable of open mindedly* putting aside their long held programmed belief that eggs didn't exist, in the light of this new fact in front of them, to realise exactly what they are - *and of course to enjoy then a greater portion of the lovely omelette they can now make from them...when they are shown how to!*"

Subdued chuckling at his words rippled amongst the two young couples, and they remembered as well how Anders had comically scuttled off a few paces in the Trocadero cafe last Monday evening when he'd told them Churchill's quote previously.

Jake said, "that Spanish omelette you made t'other day were better than them I 'ad in Spain Soph'! An' it's true that: *'y'can't mek an omelette wi'out breakin' a few eggs...'* - who was it who said that first...it's a well known sayin innit?!"

"Yes, it's very true - the saying has been attributed to Benito Mussolini the Italian Fascist Dictator of Italy in the second world war who used it a lot in his speeches, although he was implying much darker overtones in his recipes for social changes...However, let's set aside our culinary analogies for the moment – *even though they do give us much food for thought...!*"

A not so subdued groaning rippled between them all this time on hearing that!

"Oh - a final but very relevant quote to us from Mussolini – he also said about Fascism:

'Fascism should more appropriately be called Corporatism, because it is the merger of Corporate and State Power'.

"And this is *exactly* what we are witnessing now on a global scale and it spells a very frightening and dangerous scenario if the situation is ignored and such – *Fascistic* - Corporate Power is allowed to continue...

"Just going back now to what I was saying before about *'days of reckoning'* - many of the elites and their minions will have 'jumped ship' well before then, before that one second to midnight, and they are doing so even now, they are some of the 'whistle blowers' and the revealers of the truths of what they have been involved in so far. They are doing so because their conscience and consciousness is no longer able to live with the realisations of what they are doing. It is true to say that: *'a rising tide raises all boats'*, but those that remain anchored, determinedly clinging onto the bottom, will be swamped by it - and just disappear without a trace...

"I also said *'No'* in my reply to you David. I meant 'no' in the sense that at the end of the day, the 'day', actually will be years, probably a whole generation, 'of reckoning'...of 'Truth and Reconciliation', and during that time it will be realised *just how few of them controlling all of humanity's affairs there really were...at its core, or in its top echelons of the pyramid of the elitist power structure they had created.*

"There are only thirteen or so mega-wealthy and powerful family blood lines at the very pinnacle who direct their policies downwards to their many thousands, millions, of minions to implement – some of those whom know what is happening and what part of the latent agenda they are implementing, but the *vast majority* in the lower levels of the pyramid certainly don't.

"I'll tell you the family names now, they are: Rothschild (Bauer or Bower), Bruce, Cavendish (Kennedy), De Medici, Hanover, Hapsburg, Krupp, Plantagenet, Rockefeller, Romanov, Sinclair (St. Clair), Warburg (del Banco), and the Windsors (Saxe-Coburg-Gothe).

"The Rothschilds dynasty is unquestionably the most visibly and financially powerful, with accurately estimated assets of Five Hundred Trillion…! *That's five hundred million – million millions…!* Basically - *they 'own' everything!*

"Just compare their, and many, many other, of the elites' lifestyles within the financial and control system they have created that has stealthily enslaved humanity - to just use them as wage and currency debt slaves – and unwitting creators of the required negative energies:

"*...the great mass of the people* starting at around the age of four have to spend upto the next fifteen years or so being left-brain entrained repeaters of the limiting programming of 'education' – and research proves that creativity and critical thinking significantly diminishes at around the ages of ten to twelve after being exposed to all of this programming, of course it does because the aim of it is to produce compliant worker drones to enter the 'world of work.' – Usually amongst older people initially, whom have all gone through the same limiting programming. They then have to do tedious, mind-numbing and repetitive work from nine to five, five days out of seven, which is seventy percent plus of their week, just to pay to live, and become good, obedient consumers.

"The late, great comedian George Carlin said: *'some people see things that are and ask, Why? Some people dream of things that never were and ask, Why not? Some people have to go to work - and they don't have the time or energy for all that...'*

"Work is often done in boring and depressing environments, where people are not stimulated by anything really creative or really constructive...and as Henry Thoreau, the essayist, poet and philosopher said, *'...the mass of people lead lives of quiet desperation, as their resignation to it is confirmed as a desperation...'* Which all, I say, predictably and inexorably, drains their souls...

"Then, eventually, they have children and the process is repeated over again...and as that constant drip, drip, drip of draining continues, week after week, year after year, the subconscious mind's thoughts, perceptions and beliefs tend to take on the default position of frustration, stress, dis-content and so many other similar *un-natural* states – overall it's a dominance of negativity. And so, because humans are a 'creator race', the subconscious, *charged with and focused on* the prevalence of all those negative emotions will then create more of them, more negative energy, *especially* – and most particularly - *Fear.*

"*All of which, of course, are the parasites' required sustenance.*

"In most cases, the sole motivation for going *'to work'*, is simply to receive the next pay-check — *and the Fear of not getting one.* But no matter how hard they work, they will never seem to have enough money, and always seem to struggle.

"Have you ever wondered why the mega-corporations reaping

321

billions a year in profits pay dozens of millions to their CEOs, Chief Executive Officers, and as close as possible to the minimum wage to the majority of its employees…? "Well, this has been carefully designed, because it goes without saying that a person who is constantly stressed and worried about money, who is fearful, 'on the edge', always struggling, and 'drained', will, as George was implying, never have the time, energy or inclination for independent thought, self-education, introspection and — eventually — spiritual awakening…

"And, of course, all those constant and very intense, negative emotional energies just create and physically manifest more and more of those outward circumstances in their lives...and cause many illnesses within their inner-selves...It is a vicious circle…

"So...how does all that compare to the lifestyles of the elites? Well, once again, I'll quote George to sum it up for us:

'...Hey - they own this place. It's their Big Club, and you ain't in it. You and I are not in the Big Club. And by the way, it's the same Big Club they use to beat you over the head with all day long when they tell you what to believe...'"

"Aye, he were a brilliant comedian!" Jake said, "but he were so spot on with a lot o' what he came out wi'. I've watched a lot of 'is shows on Youtube, he always meks me crack up laughin'! But he really meks y'think an'all about what he's sayin'!"

Anders smiled, nodding his head. "Yes he was Jake, as I've said before, using humour is a very powerful way to get a serious message across...and he was a master of it...So, moving on...to continue...

"The top elites also created four individual States, which operate under their own Laws, so there is no Court of Law on Earth that could ever prosecute them, those States are: *The City of London*, for finance, controlled by the Rothschilds – NOT part of the UK, the *US Federal Reserve*, also finance and a private bank, ultimately owned by the Rothschilds – NOT part of the USA, *The Vatican City*, for indoctrination, deception and scare tactics – NOT part of Italy, and *Washington DC*, for the military, mind programming, brainwashing and depopulation – NOT part of the USA.

"- *And in terms of their numbers that is going to be one of the shocking realisations for the newly re-awakened humanity* - just how such a tiny, infinitesimal minority compared to the nearly seven billions of humans on the Planet, managed to control nearly all of them...and that they had despicably, callously, planned and were ready to implement the killing of eighty to ninety percent of those billions of unsuspecting men, women and children to reduce the population on the planet.

"That despicable but characteristic, parasite infected mindset of those elites was clearly illustrated when the husband of the present Windsor, Saxe-Coburg-Gothe, Queen of England was quoted as saying that after his death; *'I'd like to come back as a virus to destroy all the useless eaters...'*

"So yes, it is quite possible that there will be direct and prompt retributions against some of those core elites - *and particularly against all the satanic paedophiles that are already known about...*

"And in the early days of turmoil and terrible shock at the extent of what has been done, what was really going on, and what they had planned to happen, on so many fronts, humanity's emotions will be running high with their desires for justice, retribution and revenge...

"But 'the tide' of humanity's consciousness will be ever rising and the desire for violent retribution and revenge will diminish, as those emotional energies will be incompatible with the enlightened state of a higher consciousness.

"What happens once 'the tide is high', 'the dust has settled', and all those types of comparative sayings, is then, of course, upto humanity, but *'Truth and Reconciliation'*, and an effective and realisable *'Transition Plan'* - which has already been mostly worked out - will really be the only way forwards then to avoid much more bloodshed and further misery. Because those remaining, hard-core elites will by then have their backs well and truly against the wall, and like cornered rats they will fight back with desperation, but unlike a cornered rodent those elites will still have their devastating armaments and a lot of their mercenary manpower at their disposal…for a while anyway...

"So, I, we, think that a minimum of twenty years plus, a generation or so, will pass before the entire planetary organisation of its social structures, its – new - energy resources, and whatever forms of trade or barter, or non-monied economic new infrastructures that are implemented under a Transition Plan, *start to take real effect.*

"It will be rather like push starting a stalled car, it takes a lot of concentrated effort and determination at first, *as there is so much inertia to overcome*, and progress is slow initially, but soon it will start rolling forwards faster and faster until it fires up and takes off on its own..."

"Aye! - *We know all about an' are good at 'avin' to push start cars aren't we Dave!?*" Jake chuckled at him, recalling his, Simmo's and Reg's heaving and pushing of Dave's car along the road when it stalled on the way home from the Fair last night!

Anders leaned back into the sofa and crossing his arms over his chest he rested his chin on a raised hand, his head looking down in thought. After a few moments he sat up straight again with his hands on his knees and continued talking.

"Let's just go forward in time now to that period of the Truth and Reconciliation revelations and the *coming together again of humanity*...with the implementation of The Transition Plan...

"There is an aphorism – and I like using aphorisms as well because they're very useful concise phrases that describe major principles – so...there is an aphorism that will very effectively reveal what had been their – indisputably – *major, fundamental principle at work on the planet before*, and it was called: *'Divide And Rule'.*

"What does that *really mean*? - Well, surface humanity had, for thousands of years, been purposefully lead to believe they are all individually completely separate, different, and unconnected with each other. That they were purely physical entities, nothing more, 'simply human', with just a few basic operating senses. Beings that were: *'here once just for today and gone forever tomorrow'.*

"And they were further divided by differences of race, nationality, gender, religion, politics, status and so on and on and on...and we can now see as we look back – from our view point in the future – how those false perceptions of separateness were heavily promoted by the rise in the corporate mainstream media of so called 'identity politics' - based on all of those falsely perceived divisions.

"Actually - just as a quick but very relevant aside allow me to illustrate, quite graphically, one of these major 'falsely perceived divisions':

"When the first astronauts returned to the Earth's surface, having seen it for the first time from far away in space, they generally said, and I'll paraphrase, that: *'as we looked down on it, it was at first strange to see that there were no lines drawn all over it marking out all the different countries that we all had, for all our lives, been used to seeing on maps of the Earth.*

' – Maps that are hung up on the walls of every school's geography room! But we saw and realised that the real Earth wasn't like that at all! – It was, instead, all just one surface mass, and all the people down there on it were all living within artificially created boundaries, borders, or divisions - but they, WE, really are just one humanity living all together on this truly beautiful planet we call Earth...!'

"Such comments from them were quickly suppressed by the corporate mainstream media of course, and many of those early astronauts lived out the remainder of their lives completely changed by that awareness, that true perception of reality...

"In fact it was the astronaut Edgar Mitchell who later established the Noetic Sciences Institute that Magda was telling you about earlier...

"...But some of the lives of the more publicly vocal of that profound truth - which lead them then onto other enlightened perceptions, and were informing the public about them, were, *quite unusually, of a much shorter duration than young, fit and healthy people could've normally expected them to be...*"

Dave let out a gasp, shaking his head, and said, "*Of course!* Wow! I never, ever thought about that Anders! Of course there're no big

325

black border lines drawn over the Earth! When you put it like that it's so painfully obvious! Upto now when *I've* thought about the Earth, or parts of it, I must admit - I've automatically pictured all those black border lines superimposed on it! *Wow!* That's so, well, *so simple – so powerful and obvious - when you realise….!*"

"Yes, yes it is David, well said, and once you start to, to simply remove such binding chains of perception illusion, it allows your true perceptions to expand greatly! So...*back to the future…!* - To get a few glimpses of some of the realisations *that will become known to all*...and which will temper the forging of the new realities for everyone's future lives on Earth…

"Humanity will have by then, eventually realised just how much they had been contemptuously deceived, cynically manipulated and deliberately programmed by the parasites and their elite human agents to be convinced of their individual total separateness from each other, then, once divided, and further manipulated, using *fear* mainly, to reinforce a sense of helpless dependency – on the 'pay-check' for just one example, as I was saying before – and how they were willingly bundled into affiliation groups for their so called 'safety and security', but firmly divided along all of those lines I've just mentioned.

"So, as the generations passed by, all those divisive perceptions of one's self, and one's immediate society, and its culture became automatically absorbed into the programmed belief system of each individual…

"*But...but, but but…! It will be realised that by far the biggest divisive perception the elites created was: 'Organised Religion'…*

Anders then 'harrumphed', as he cleared his throat, took a deep breath and altered his voice to sound exactly like a loud T.V. Evangelist as he continued:

"*'We are the Chosen Ones, we are white, educated, superior Caucasian males and we say, 'Our Religion is The Only Truth and The Only One that offers you the chance of Salvation, because only we Priests, chosen by God, can intercede and communicate on your behalf to our Lord - The Almighty God! You are all sinners here on*

Earth, and you all have to suffer and come to Him on your knees because you are all sinners, born into sin, and who will face Judgement before Our God for your sins, unless, and only through us - who are chosen by God - you regularly confess your sins to Him and beg His Forgiveness! -

"So Our Religion is far superior to any other of your primitive beliefs! – So it is our God given duty To Save You by converting you! - But if we can't because you won't disclaim your primitive beliefs to believe in us, and regularly go to our Church and worship only as we tell you how to, to worship 'Our One And Only True God', then when 'The Day Of Judgement' comes, without our help, you will be Damned For All Eternity in The Fires of Hell!

"And if you persist, as well as encouraging others to practice other forms of belief and worship other Gods, and not to believe what we are telling you - we will seek you out – and kill you...!'"

He breathed deeply again, and reverted back to his normal, quiet, cultured voice before continuing.

"And exactly that kind of sick, psychopathic mindset, still exists today, *particularly within the Jesuits Military Religious Order of the Catholic Church.* You may have noticed the initials INRI displayed at the top of their staffs, on clothing, badges of office, paintings et cetera? Well INRI are the initials for 'Iustum Necar Reges Impious', which is latin for: *'it is just to exterminate impious or heretical Kings, Governments or Rulers'.*

"Part of their liturgy in the ritual of promotion to a command position in it is – *oh, and they have to repeat it on their knees whilst a dagger is held over their heart* - I'll paraphrase it for you: 'you have been taught your duty as a spy to ingratiate yourself and insidiously plant the seeds of jealousy and hatred between communities, provinces and states that were at peace, and incite them to deeds of blood, involving them at war with each other, to create revolutions and civil wars...only that the Church might be the gainer in the end...*and that the end justifies the means*...none can command here who has not consecrated his labours with the blood of the heretic, for without the

327

shedding of blood no man can be saved...'

"Then later, 'The Extreme Oath of the Jesuits' is a lengthy repetition they have to repeat, parts of it are: '...The Pope is Christ's vice-Regent and is the true and only head of the Catholic or Universal Church throughout the earth...he hath the power to depose heretical kings, princes, states commonwealths and governments all being illegal without his sacred confirmation and they may be safely destroyed...'

"So they are authorising priests to go out, conspire, kill and destroy – *for Jesus!* Surely religion is about worshipping God, a God of Love...?! How many people have suffered and died because of the poisonous religious doctrine from the minds of these insane psychopaths...?

"Their Oath goes on to have them state: '...I will have no opinion of my own...but will unhesitatingly obey each and every command that I may receive from my superiors in the Militia of the Pope and of Jesus Christ!'

"Towards the end of their Oath they then agree to: '...I furthermore promise and declare that I will, when opportunity presents, make and wage relentless war, secretly or openly, against all heretics, as I am directed to...to exterminate them from the face of the whole earth; and that I will spare neither age, sex or condition; and that I will hang, waste, boil, flay, strangle and bury alive these infamous heretics, rip up the stomachs and wombs of their women and crush their infants heads against the walls, in order to annihilate forever this execrable race...at any time I may be directed so to do by any agent of the Pope or Superior of the Brotherhood of the Holy Faith, of the Society of Jesus...'

"*How dare they mention Jesus's name in this sickening, insane Oath!?*...But all religions do the same thing...they all say my God is correct and yours is wrong...and so you have to die...! It's just sickening pathological insanity!

"I remember talking to The Marquis de LaFayette, who was serving under General George Washington at the time, he said of them: '...beware the subtlety of the Roman Catholic priests, for they are the

328

most crafty, dangerous enemies to civil and religious liberty, and they have instigated most of the wars of Europe...'

"And during the middle ages, their pathological, insane doctrine resulted in well over four million women and girls being tortured, hung and burnt to death by the Catholic Church's Inquisition. Because it classed and accused them of being witches, or 'wise women'; or with beliefs and practices contrary to their male murderers' pathologically fanatical religious dogma.

"For being classed as *'Heretics'*, millions more, of men, women, children and even their babies were also condemned to dreadful, horrendous deaths.

"'Heretic literally means: *'a free thinker'...*

"All over the Languedoc region of Southern France, there were independent, flourishing, benign and very enlightened societies, *originally founded by Mary the Magda-lean*, societies that knew, and were vociferous in saying that you don't need an intermediary – a Priest – or some other religious official from a vertical male hierarchy - to communicate for you on your behalf to the Divine, and to do so whilst you are on your knees in a richly decorated and elaborate building.

"*Because you are all capable of communing with the Divine on your own – because it is within yourselves...*

"In one of their villages called Albi...*over thirty thousand men, women, children and babies were horrifically slaughtered in a single day...*for having these so called 'heretical beliefs', and that was just one of many days and many other villages that suffered similar fates in that particular crusade, named the 'Albigensian Crusade', and in many other crusades, which in their totals lasted for hundreds of years, all on the direct orders of - *a 'Holy' Papal Edict...*

"And that office of Inquisition where such Edicts or Orders and Commands come from still exists to this day...under the name of: The Congregation for the Doctrine of the Faith...

"The full truth of all the barbarous acts of the Papal Armies - and of the Many Other *Deliberately Divisive* religions of course – who all did

329

more or less exactly the same thing over the centuries – will, in the future, be revealed and made known to all…

"And then the obvious question of why 'The Church' – *or any of the other divisive religious organisations* – which supposedly should all have been preaching and practising doctrines of Love, of Light, of Care and Compassion – *why did they need armies in the first place to torture and brutally kill men, women and children en masse…?!*

"The answer to that question will be realised by then of course - that it was the dark, latent agenda at work...And on a very well organised, global basis it was very effectively and constantly generating vast outpourings of negative energies from all those savage actions – actions which were, yes, obviously at the very pinnacle of that mountainous, heinous scale of atrocities – but there were countless other execrable actions and deeds also, performed all the way down its flanks, every step of the way, to the 'lesser' levels of that heinous mountainous scale...

"But they all created the highly desired and savoured sustenance of negative energies on an ongoing basis for the evil-embodied parasites. Their willing human elites, who planned and commanded the carrying out of all those vile acts, with their easily programmed minions, were richly rewarded for doing so.

"They were also given the dark knowledge of how to maintain and grow all the different branches of this divisive institution – *and many more* – by enslaving and programming human minds, to generate for them more and more power and material wealth, from which they could then continue to create even more…

"It's more than highly likely that the whole false concept of 'Organised Religions', of which just Christianity alone currently has well over twenty-five thousand different, divisive sects and creeds! - with their patriarchal hegemonies, their brain-washed, mind controlled ranks filled with all those stereotypes who know all about the shadows on the cave wall…!

"They had vast wealth and powers to *Divide and Rule* over humanity, and they deliberately suppressed so many spiritual truths –

330

and the fact they all very effectively *hijacked spirituality for their own despicable agendas*...all of these revelations, as part of 'The Truth And Reconciliation' and 'Transition Plan' process, will result in them all being, more than highly likely, *to have absolutely no place in the future enlightened world of humanity's raised consciousness* when such truths about how shockingly *Divisive Of Humanity* they all were, are finally, and fully revealed.

"They will, by then, be just obsolete, foul concepts of the dark past, and been replaced by a growing and ever deeper spiritual knowledge, and *understanding* of the true practices of Universal Oneness, Love, Compassion *and a Unity Consciousness.*

"An understanding that each and every human is Divine within themselves, *that the kingdom of – so called – 'Heaven'- if we use that word as an adjective and not a noun - is already within you...And that 'Heaven and Hell',* as nouns, were just *Divisive* mythical locations, just parts of their whole false doctrines and teachings to create great fear and willing, obedient compliance, so there will of course then be no need to crawl on your knees in supplication before a human intermediary in a Church, Mosque, Temple or whatever...

"...And so, in the future, humanity will finally have arrived at the realisation of how they became far easier to be controlled and harvested, once they were *Divided and Ruled over* by the hidden hands of small, centralised and very powerful elite groups, and as well, that at the very pinnacle, most of those groups were all interlinked on familial bloodlines.

"But in the near future - their institutions and edifices of power and all they stood for will be in the final stages of being fully and finally decommissioned and dismantled, and all their occupants known...

"*So...why did I just go through all of that? – when I've already talked about most of it to you before...?!*

"Well, because this time of hearing it, from your new, higher viewpoint and so broader and wider perspective based on your now increased knowledge and understanding, I wanted to point out, with a few more details, *for you all to really see,* how organised religion fully

331

exploits the *'Divide and Rule'* tactic.

"It can be said so quickly, almost flippantly: *'Divide and Rule!'* – but its effects are utterly devastating..."

He smiled sadly then, and said, "one of the main focuses of Magda's ire is politics and politicians – as you now all know! Mine is, you might've guessed...! - Organised Religion! Anyway...let's leave it there now for the time being...and move on!

"Also to become known about in that now bright future...will be...Us...and this inner World of Aghartha...Humanity at large, in that near future, will have finally woken up and become aware, and they will all be sharing in the abundant resources all around them, *and within them.* All helping each other to understand that each of them, yes, is a separate biological, *physical* entity, *but they are all part of just one – energetic singularity of consciousness.*

"Just like a drop of water is in an ocean, each individual soul or 'drop of consciousness' forms that ocean's vastness of consciousness, and the inherent power of that true reality...

"...and when a soul chooses to manifest and incarnate into a physical body that is born into the third dimensional physical realm here, or anywhere else, it is with the intention to have *the experience* of a life in a physical body, to enable not just its own spiritual growth in the natural ascension of the upward spiral of spiritual evolution, *but also to help others,* in many ways, not least by sharing those *experiences* back into the group consciousness of beings it incarnated into..."

He paused again, to smile at them.

"Imagine all that...!

"It is not fanciful or dreamily unrealistic – because all of that – and much more - *is what we have achieved here in Aghartha...!*

"Whilst I am briefly wielding the broad brush strokes of spirituality in the future that awaits humanity, I must say as well that it will become widely known that there have been so many accounts over the ages, which the power elites deliberately suppressed and hid away of course, accounts from psychics, visionaries, shamans, mystics, artists poets and authors...whom all had actually seen the true spiritual energetic form of humans as ovoid, droplet or egg shaped beings of light...

"You'll remember me saying on a previous occasion that such gifted people were always targeted by the elites for having such knowledge and perception...? Well, just one example of them was the author Carlos Castenada who wrote about the teachings of Don Juan, a Yaqui Indian sorcerer he met with, and Don Juan eventually allowed him to study under his tutelage and guidance. Carlos described how Don Juan explained to him that these luminous spheres were our true spiritual form or nature, *and that we are all connected by a myriad web of light fibres*, known to many Eastern traditions as 'The Hairs of Shiva'.

Don Juan also described to Carlos how, by learning to change his position in these interconnecting light clusters he could, during lucid dreaming – which is when you are dreaming but you are fully awake and not asleep - visit other realms and realities..."

Sophie then said, "*I've got that book!* I haven't read it yet though – *and how I got it was really weird!* I was in my friend Michelle's charity shop last Thursday morning, it was when I was looking for a 'Home Sweet Home' sign - like you've got Magda' in your caravan! - for Mel and Dave's new caravan home!

"Well, when I was in there looking through all the piles of books as well, I reached up to get one that was about the poems by Keats, who I really like, but that book almost literally jumped out when I did and it fell down and landed right on top of my bag! So I thought *'okaaay – it's obviously intended that I have this one as well!'* I shall read it now as soon as I can! Wow! - It's amazing that you've just mentioned it as well Anders!"

Anders smiled at her and said, "Well done Sophie – you recognised an event creation you made in direct response to an unconscious desire to learn something! How many people who are unaware would have just 'tutted', picked it up, and put it back on the shelf?!

333

"I'm sure you will enjoy and get much out of your reading of it! We have signed first editions of all Carlos's books – and of John's – Keats, books and manuscripts of poems in our library that you are welcome to read as well…! I too love John's poems especially 'Endymion', the first line is: *'A thing of Beauty is a Joy Forever…'*

"I know that he was a favourite of yours too Magda?" He looked across to her with a knowing smile on his lips.

Magda nodded her head slowly in reply, her eyes far away in obvious fond reminiscence, and she quietly said, "Yes, yes he was, dear John's work was – is – so…so beautifully thoughtful, insightful…and…outsightful" She then breathed deeply, as she came out of her memories, and said to him, "But do please go on Anders, what you were saying is very important; perhaps we can talk of the works of the great poets we knew - and know, another time…"

"Indeed, yes, yes of course we can, it'd be a great pleasure to do that. Sooo…back to where I was…Ah yes, well, just to briefly round up what I was saying…to the shaman, wise woman, the mystic…the artist, author - *and the poet*, and many others, they all have the ability to see the essential true reality all around them appearing as *energy and consciousness, not just separate 'physical matter'*. They have the desire to go beyond the everyday habitual perceptions of their environment, within which they consider, and rightly so as well, that people have been entrapped by them.

"All those visionaries could – can – see that humanity was – is – almost hopelessly entrapped within a habitual energy field which is supported and maintained by the whole society and its perceptions and beliefs. The world is seen in that way by the masses of humanity because they have all been programmed by the same 'software', you could say, to believe it really is that way; and the habitual mould that their view of the universe fits into effectively prevents them from seeing it in any other way, and cognitive dissonance reinforces it.

"So the visionaries broke out of the mould, and as escapees from limited perception they sought out and saw new worlds of realities, potentialities and all their differences - *and that the multiverse is founded upon consciousness and energy alone...*

"The artist William Blake said that: *'Energy is Delight'*. And it is only the moulded conditioning to be good materialistic consumers that makes people ascribe *the significance and importance of material 'Things' and 'Objects' to that 'Energy Of Delight'...*because people were psychically manipulated to create false perceptions of nature which in its turn created the false nature of their perceptions then their beliefs – or to put it another way – they perceived and so *believed* - only what they had been *deliberately moulded to learn to perceive and believe...*"

"*Wow!*" Dave commented, "As an artist I've studied Blake's work quite a lot, and I remember reading about some of that in his writings, but I found it hard going then I must admit, *but now you've sort of put it into context,* and joined so many of the dots for me I can see and make more sense of what he was saying – *I think!* I must revisit his work now, I'm sure I'll see it all with new eyes – *and new perceptions!*"

"Excellent David! I thought you must have been more than vaguely aware of his work when Magda and Ruth described your paintings to me, and I'm really looking forward to our meeting tomorrow morning at the gallery and talking a lot more with you about it all.

"In fact it might be worth you considering writing in depth, to explain all about your works as well, especially as your perceptions are now expanding so much, but we'll go somewhere for a coffee and chat about that tomorrow after you've taken the digital camera back to Sophie who is kindly lending it to you..."

"Great, yes, of course! What a brilliant idea! I've never really written anything before about my work, well, I've made a few notes, now and then, nothing at length or in any real depth though, it never really occurred to me...!

"But I can see now how doing that would add another dimension to my work...to help get *'the message'* across...to help people *understand* a bit more about the concepts and the motivation for what I'm doing...and why...!"

"Ah! Well, there you go! You will be 'adding another string to your bow' - and joining the august ranks of those who write! And you will have all the exciting challenges of learning how to do it and use it!

"As I said before - one of the true joys of Life is the love of constant learning! *In fact...I love it so much that I still don't know exactly what I'm going to do when I grow up...!"*

He said that with such self-deprecating humour, whilst shaking his head in mock dismay – that it caused loud spontaneous laughter amongst them all!

Sophie thought to herself, with further amusement, well, if he didn't know – *at his obvious great age and incredible wisdom* - I don't feel too bad about myself not really knowing either...!

Mel joined in by saying, when she had stopped laughing – and thinking similar thoughts to Sophie's as well,

"I can get what you write printed at work in my own time, after hours, with pictures of your paintings to illustrate it as well Dave! Sort of like brochures or pamphlets, given out at your exhibitions, we'd just have to pay for the materials only, and that wouldn't be much at all! - In fact, thinking about it, the company might even be willing to sponsor them! – after all it'd be advertising their services as well! I'll have a word about it with the manager tomorrow afternoon!"

She smiled widely at him in great excitement, and he expressed his thanks and gratitude to her for such a great idea as well, deeply touched once again by the willingness to help from all these wonderful people sat around him, and then in an emotion cracked voice he told them all...exactly that!

After they had all settled again Anders resumed his talk, "...both Magda and I have touched on the following before, but it is worth repeating again now...

"When that particular, unique vessel of a physical body ceases to function, the soul, the eternal consciousness, normally – when there is

336

no soul-trap to prevent it from doing so - returns to Source. That ocean of *vastly higher, infinite and divine creative consciousness,* and shares all those experiences of that life in a physical body into it. All that knowledge is stored within what is called 'The Akashic Records.'

"Your soul does not die like the temporary body does, in your truest form, you, we, are all immortal, spiritual beings...who repeatedly incarnate to *experience* 'life' in physical bodies, and not just on the Earth, until that developing soul attains fully enlightened awareness through the experiences of many lifetimes, and then has no need to constantly reincarnate to learn the many lessons it needs to free it from the cycle of Karma.

"That soul then ascends in its upward spiral into the much higher non-physical, spiritual dimensional realms which are the true domains of Light Beings, and finally it attains unity with the Divine Infinity, which some traditions have called 'Nirvanas'.

"And as Magda said, a few minutes ago, about all of this... *'some of those very old enlightened souls have always 'volunteered' for rebirth on Earth to aid humanity – working from within...and onto other planets as well to aid the indigenous beings there - but particularly more so on Earth over the past few decades'.* I'm sure you can all now think of many people in many walks of life, some prominent, some not, who were and are – somehow very 'special', and incredibly gifted in myriads of ways, who have done and are doing just that...?!"

Four, much, *much* younger heads all nodded as they each thought about that. Jake immediately thought about his Dad, and a series of connections, almost volubly, suddenly clicked into place in his mind, he was tempted to verbalise them straight away but he thought he'd wait, until he had a clearer idea of what they were connecting up to make. But he sensed that whatever it was, it was so huge that he was going to have to step right back to see even a part of it...and for the moment he was too fascinated about what Anders was saying to break into his flow.

So he decided to let his unconscious mind work away at it whilst his conscious mind listened to Anders. - Huh! It's true what Soph had

337

said about, *'now being able to think loads better – like it's in a much higher gear!'* – As even a week ago such concepts about unconscious and conscious minds - and how to use 'em - wouldn't have occurred to me…!

He refocused his attention back to Anders, but he noticed Magda looking and smiling at him, as if she had read his thoughts…

"Souls are 'memory wiped' of their previous life's memories with a burst of radiation very similar in a way to that of an E.M.P.W. - Electro Magnetic Pulse Weapon – that is a device which will, for example, if it's deployed over a targeted city, cause all the electrical devices in it to stop functioning, but without destroying all the buildings in it…

"So there is no period of evaluation, recuperation or of guidance to decide where to incarnate next for that soul. Consequently the majority of them, as their physical lives unfold once again in the dark milieu of the parasite infested and dominated world, they soon become a repeating generator of all the negative energies the parasites need for their sustenance, for their very survival, it's like a prison farm where there is an endless supply of docile livestock…

"However, there have been many souls, over the millenniums, that did manage to evade the soul trap, and now, mercifully, that soul entrapping energetic grid net is starting to fail and it will, in the near future be eventually fully dismantled by those of us whom are working constantly, with others... now to achieve that."

Sophie was amazed, again, at how she was now able to take in of all of this 'very heavy' esoteric, occult – hidden - information from Anders and Magda, and she realised that Anders was deliberately repeating some of the things Magda had said earlier, just to further reinforce them, she supposed.

And she was taking it all in whilst calmly sitting here in a World *she never even knew existed less than an hour or so ago!*

She had a sudden flashback again to when she was sitting on one of her favourite benches at the harbour in Scarborough during her lunchtime nearly a week ago now – and what a week it had been since!

Then she had been sitting in a World that was, on the surface of it, totally familiar, but she'd just started to learn the night before that it had so much more going on in it, and it was all so wickedly, craftily hidden away from most of the people living on it...

It was just before Jake had approached her to say 'Hi', and she had been enjoying and reflecting on her 'new' mind's awarenesses and thought processes that had seemed to sigh with relief when they had been unlocked and allowed to stretch and expand to cope with the revelations she'd heard from Anders the first time she'd heard him speak. And all that 'unlocking' had happened just the night before...and so she proceeded to share those thoughts again with everyone now.

She finished verbalising her thoughts to everyone by saying,

"Soooo, I think, really, why I've just told all of you all of that – is well, I'm worried, no not worried, but I am a bit anxious, at just how I'll cope sitting back at my desk in the morning facing another normal – *and it'll seem a very normal humdrum day - having experienced and seen and now knowing all of...well, about everything tonight..!*

"There's just been so much you, Magda and Anders, have opened my eyes and my mind to! The same for all of us as well! So much, so very, very much...Especially the 'soul-trap' which is just mind boggling! Well, boggling to my old mind – *not to my 'new' one!*

"And I don't want to sound like it's all about *me, me, me!* But I suppose I am just a bit worried that tomorrow...and on from then...is going to be, well...*oh I dunno* – 'difficult' isn't the right word – d'y'know what I mean? - *Any ideas anyone...?!*"

Mel said, "I'm glad you said and asked that Sophie *'cause I was thinking pretty much the same too!* I'm at the printers doing an afternoon shift tomorrow, and yes, I'm going to negotiate a deal with them for Dave's printing, which is important, but, well, I just feel, sort of...that I should be doing a lot more as well...*I just feel that I want to sort of 'hit the ground running'...!*"

Magda then smiled at them both and said in a calmly reassuring voice, "Let me try and offer *you all* some help and guidance to come to terms with it all, in order to balance, ground and gradually 're-purpose' and transition yourselves my dears.

"What you are feeling is totally natural, it shows you have great empathy and compassion which fill you with the desire to be pro-active. Sometimes when people wake up, when they become spiritually aware, when they re-become enlightened, well, actually, *everybody already is,* you don't have to actually *'look for'* or *'to seek'* enlightenment – because it is already within you! – *you just have to recognise it and then allow it...*

"...and when momentous truths are revealed to them and they finally see what is really going on and why, it can cause them to forsake and remove themselves away from what they then consider to be the false, constraining, humdrum, slumbering normality of their previous lives and change their lifestyles completely.

"Sometimes that can be a good and a necessary thing to do, it all depends on each individual's circumstances of course. In all of your cases though, perhaps you could try to put everything in its place and balance it all by realising that the routines *of your individual lives are still just as important, and actually even more so now.*

"Why? Because they will help to keep you grounded, and involved in your society and give you a sense of perspective. By perspective I mean that the works, the jobs that you all do are not just important because they enable you to currently survive economically on the surface world, but they also help to amplify your involvement in helping to change the world around you…

"...otherwise, to give you just one tiny example of that - how could you have been pro-active and helped to do just that by helping David tomorrow Sophie - by lending him one of your company's new and expensive cameras to start to really promote his art? And the great support and intuitive help you will be giving to Jake in his, new, future work...

"David, you are soon going to become very well known as an artist, your paintings – and writings – inspiring thousands! Particularly the

340

young students you will teach in the part-time lecturing job you will almost certainly be offered now!

"And Melanie, you are involved with a printing company that is going to help by creating information to give to hundreds, *thousands* of people to read and digest at David's exhibitions all over the world in the future...I also foresee great possibilities for you with your creative works with jewellery, as you learn more and more about their healing and the many other powers they have, which Lucia is going to reveal to you...and I see the possibility of you recycling that wisdom to benefit many others, in workshops you will conduct in the future to do so...

"...and you Jake have a wide circle of friends and colleagues who respect and admire you – and not just for the skilful and creative work you do. You said you are going to 'lay the groundwork' for them to become aware of what you know now. And...of course...there is the crucial future work you are going to be doing with our engineers, who will also coordinate it with others, now working all over the planet doing the same or similar. The results of which will ultimately change your world almost unrecognisably...

"So for all of you, in essence, you are giving *'service to others'*, it is the opposite of *'service to self'*, which is all about acquisition, stepping over or on others - just to get what you want *for yourself.* All that *involvement with people* you all have in your current lives is really, *really important.* *In fact you will all be 'hitting the ground running!'*

"And I haven't even mentioned the further contact *you will all be having soon with the, the 'off-planet' visitors that have already made their initial contact with one of you...! And the implications that will reveal to you all...!"*

"As I have said, we have seen it many times before when people have become...awakened...that sometimes they disassociate from their previous lives, and become isolated. Now, for some individuals that retreat into a life of lonely contemplation it can be a good thing for them individually, but at this stage of humanity's awakening it needs more and more people like yourselves who are *involved, meeting and interacting* with many others in your World.

"You will all be drawing towards you, like magnets, increasing numbers of others who are awakening, and encouraging those about to. You can all be of service to others by helping them - because you have all already experienced going through the shock, bewilderment and 'mind-boggling', awesomeness of seeing a great part of the true picture beyond the veils and chains of illusion. You will all help many others to *change their direction of travel and to discover...*even if they stumble a bit at first – *but remember that is a good sign - because they cannot stumble if they are still on their knees...!*

"So then, with your help, they will soon find their balance, to stand properly and learn to walk, and then to jog, then to run faster and faster along the same or similar paths you are already on – all of which lead away from that dark road to nowhere that they were all on before, and go instead towards the sunlit mountains - just like you illustrated so well in your painting David…

"It is all crucial work, all part of The Great Cause, and now, at this stage of what is happening on planet Earth, there really is no higher calling that you can all be involved in and play your parts in…"

Magda looked at each of them, seeing in their expressions that they were now all well on the way to transitioning from the *'little me what can I possibly do?'* stage, to knowing some of the answers to that, and realising the powers they had within them to create the outcomes they desired. She smiled inwardly at the truth of the words Melanie introduced into their talk the other day: *'there's no fate but what we make...'.*

"Oh my God!" Sophie then blurted out, tears welling in her eyes, *"I'm sorry Magda!…You must think I've been really...silly...and self-absorbed!* Of course, *you're so right again...*when you put it all like that of course how could I ever've thought any different…?! *I, I'm sorry, I wasn't thinking straight, everything just..."*

She had to stop talking then as her voice had been getting croakier with emotion and the tears were now running freely down her cheeks, her hands were so tightly clenched together they were shaking on her lap.

"Oh no, no no of course I don't Sophie! I would never think that of you - because it is not true - it is just not in your make up - please do not be upset and berate yourself so Sophie." Magda replied to her, reaching over to her and gently separating then taking her hands to hold them in hers.

"I admire you, I admire you all, for you are all doing so incredibly well, you really are...and I am sure the sort of concern you voiced Sophie has been felt by you all, it is only natural...quite natural!...and in addition to all of that you then you have your group's 'Pandora Quest' - which brings it all together – but specifically it is being part of a vast global network of many others working on the production, and eventual revelation of an entirely different energy system...

"When the time is right the knowledge of it, and working examples of it that millions will see and witness and have free access to will all be released simultaneously onto a global computer network that is beyond the current internet, but will at first harness it, then take over it, because the elites can simply switch off or firewall the traditional internet – like the elites in China do to prevent their population from accessing vast parts of it they do not want them to see..

"It has to be done like that, it is the safety in numbers syndrome, for all the reasons we have spoken to you about before, of the terrible dangers of attempting to do it as individuals, or small groups in just one location or just one country.

"Ruth and I have introduced you to 'trade craft', by talking about it and demonstrating it, well, it is an art with which you will all become very proficient in because now you are really going to be living two lives - the first is the one you have been living upto now, *and will continue to do so* - and the second is the new, secret one that you will live in parallel harmony with the first one.

"The second is, of course, where you know the truth about where you are now, about us, and extra-terrestrial and inter-dimensional beings...*and everything else you all now understand.* You all know what is really happening on your world from the talks we have had, and your own, ongoing, further researches into it all…

"In trade-craft parlance all that is called 'The Intelligence Cycle'. It is when you are exposed to, then seek out and research more and more raw information, then gather it altogether and sift through it to translate it all into meaningful patterns of Intelligence – of Knowledge - by joining the dots - that you can act upon. *'Knowledge is power'*, yes! - *But only if you act upon it…!*

"The only thing I ask you *not to do* at this stage, is to reveal, to anyone, who we really are, or to reveal the existence of this inner World of Aghartha. Those facts must be kept secret by you all, *at least for the time being*, but eventually as the work you do in your secret second life of The Pandora Quest bears fruit there will be those within your social circles we can reveal ourselves to...and perhaps even bring here.

"There will come a time, when, by various means, we will eventually make the fact *about us* known to the world at large. The timing for doing that will be crucial, as it will have to be calculated carefully to interject without too much turmoil with the aeon changing events for humanity such as the Truth and Reconciliation period, and the implementing of The Transition Plan.

"At that time, and prior to it, you will all have important roles in, and participate in, that revelation. So another of your roles, before then, is to work secretly on our behalf just by doing everything you are going to be doing, which will all help to pave the way for that revelation – *and many others* - within your expanding social spheres and your communities, because everything you do individually and as a group – *will bring that time forward...*

"I say *'on our behalf'* but really I mean *'on all our behalfs'* of course, and there are many, many other...'cells' of people like yourselves, to use the 'trade craft jargon', doing the same Great Works in The Great Cause, all over the World. *So, all in all, I think it is true to say that you are certainly not going back to 'humdrum work-a-day-worlds' when you all return to them...!"*

Dave quickly added, "And as Magda said you've kindly offered to loan me one of your company's professional digital cameras and email me all the super-quality photos I can take with it of my paintings when I meet Anders at the gallery in the morning – *and that's going to be a brilliant help only you could've done Sophie!"*

Sophie smiled back at him realising that he was trying to buoy her up as well with his gratitude at her offer of help. Jake put an arm around her and hugged her to him, and said to Magda, "'s funny y'said that about talking to others an' pavin' the way, sorta layin' the groundworks an' all that – I were just sayin' to Soph last night as we were leavin' the Fair with all me mates we met up with after we left you, that I wanted to start to tell 'em about all these things an' all. Well, just bit by bit at first like, like you an' Anders 'ave done wi' us...I know they'd be up for it, we were wonderin' then, last night, if, at some stage, if we could...some'ow introduce you or Anders to 'em and y'might talk to 'em – *after I, we, 'ad sort o' laid a bit o' the groundwork like...?"*

"Of course we will Jake – and there you go! – You have already been thinking and planning along all the lines I have just spoken about!"

Anders joined in again, "Excellent! I look forward to meeting your friends with you one day Jake! - I might even be tempted to have a ride on a motorbike as a pillion passenger - if I was offered one!

"Must admit though that I haven't been on one since Thomas used to whizz us around the country lanes on his!"

He then sighed with a note of great sadness, "you may remember Thomas as 'Lawrence of Arabia'...he had a crash whilst riding his Ariel Square Four and died of his injuries six days later, down in Dorset, back in 'thirty-nine.

"We found out later that it was more than conceivable that 'the accident' was actually either arranged on the orders from MI6, and had been intended to be fatal, or they got to him whilst he was in hospital afterwards...because of what he was then still achieving off his own bat, so to speak – and was directly against, and might have even de-railed, or at least have been a great embarrassment to the British

345

Establishment if he had made public his knowledge of the elites' Deep State long-term agenda for the Middle East..."

Jake thanked Magda and Anders, and assured Anders that he'd be more than happy to give him a ride out on his bike any time he wanted! Thanking him back, Anders said he'd definitely take him up on his offer one day soon, he then continued,

"...and if I may underline and concur with what Magda has just said and I'll say it myself - *I too think you are all doing – much more than 'remarkably well' like I said earlier – but you are all in fact doing 'incredibly well', taking on so much wide ranging, and deep, but essential to know, 'non-compartmentalization-ed' information in such a short space of time...and making commitments and plans based upon it - it all takes some doing...and so I too greatly admire you all for doing that...*

"Well...I think for today all that remains talking-wise – or of 'wise-talking' – and I hope it hasn't all been too burdensome 'a wise-talking' for you all so far! - Is for me to mention a couple more facts about Aghartha that you could possibly do some further research into in your own time.

"Then Magda has arranged a surprise for you all which we think you might just enjoy...!

"...I mentioned earlier - 'previous visitors' who have been here before, well, for now I just want to talk very briefly about three of them whom we have brought in. Two of them were American military officers called Admiral Byrd and Admiral Forester. They had been making reconnaissance flights over the polar regions as part of what their military called 'Operation High Jump' in nineteen forty six to forty seven.

"Interestingly, ever since then *no aeroplanes – and certainly not civilian traffic ones* - have ever been allowed to fly over either of the Arctic poles, in case those on board saw below them that parts of the landscape were not quite as they had always been lead to believe they were. Passengers might as well have seen obvious traces of the tunnel entrances which are quite large at the poles...

346

"The global mapping websites for public consumption are all heavily edited before release of course. And it's not just the images of the earth, other planets, particularly the Moon and Mars, that have vast areas 'photo-shopped' out. There are many enterprising websites now though run by people whom painstakingly scrutinise all of these official images, pointing out the areas that have been obscured...and what they might be deliberately hiding...

"When the two Naval officers were returned to the surface world they were ordered by the American government to keep quiet about everything that they had experienced, seen and spoken with us about.

"Admiral Byrd passed away in nineteen fifty seven, but his secret diaries of his time here meeting with us were eventually published in secret in the nineteen seventies. Needless to say, under orders, the mainstream media immediately launched a campaign to discredit them and claim they were untrue forgeries, just as you would expect. They are excellent reading, now available online, and give detailed accounts of his meetings with us...

"There was a publication prior to the diaries, which alluded to some of the content of our talks together, and that was in an article in The National Geographic magazine, in the early 'fifties, when they interviewed him. But he revealed a little too much information for the Government's Intelligence Agencies to be happy about, so they clamped down on it, threatened the magazine's editorial staff and most of the copies were withdrawn and destroyed just prior to their release...the remaining ones already out on the sales stands were frantically bought up en mass by the same agencies! However, a few copies did actually manage to survive in the public domain and we have one in our library – as well as his diaries.

"After that episode, government officials warned them both again, in no uncertain terms, to keep absolute secrecy from then on about all he truths of what they had seen and what we had spoken to them about on their visit here.

"But despite the threats, Admiral Forester's conscience and concerns got the better of him, and as a result he was killed on May

347

the twenty second, nineteen forty-nine. The official version, of course, surprise, surprise, was that he committed suicide - by jumping out of a window at the Bethesda Naval Hospital, sixteen storeys up – where, incidentally, he was being held against his will. Curiously though, for someone intending suicide he left deep nail scratches all around the window frame - which looked more typical of someone desperately trying to cling on to it...Also that date was *just the day before* he had bravely decided he was going to publicly reveal the secrets of what he had seen here in a Press conference, and of the refusal of his government to cease the exploding of nuclear bombs, which had been the main reason we brought them here - to broker a cessation of those highly dangerous and damaging activities.

"Tragically, the parasite infected elites who control all those government agencies not only ignored our request, but they actually increased the bombings, above and below ground...*and to this date there have now been well over two thousand...!*

"The murder of Admiral Forester was officially classed, as I said, as, 'a suicide', as that is the standard operating procedure in these actions by the Deep State, and other agencies drawn into any investigation of it are quickly ordered to toe-the-line and come to the same conclusion...and the mainstream corporate media was ordered to back it up totally deny and ridicule any stories or 'wild rumours' that he was about to make any revelations...

"Interestingly in the David Bowie film: 'The Man Who Fell To Earth', there is a scene where two American agents burst into a hotel room wearing American football helmets and kill a man about to reveal secrets, secrets their 'superiors' desperately wanted to keep hidden, by throwing him through a large window many storeys up...

"That was a bravely done scene for its day, in fact the whole film was, *as just one of the things it planted in the viewing public's mind* was that these things are done to its – well meaning – citizens, by their own government's agencies...

"Going a little further back in time, Edmund, an English scientist, who later became *Sir* Edmund Halley, first proposed in sixteen ninety

348

two, the 'Hollow Earth' as a theory, he knew it wasn't just a theory as we had approached him a long time before that and had helped him with various of his researches and scientific discoveries. You probably know about a comet he discovered which was named after him…'Halley's Comet'?

"We became good friends over the years…and we brought him here several times…it was only in his later years, when he had carefully and successfully built up a very respectable reputation as a scientist that he presented 'his theory', as we jointly agreed and decided as the best way at the time for him to approach and explain it, just to put the knowledge and the possibility out into the public domain – similar, in a way, despite his many imaginative exaggerations, to what Jules Verne did, and others of course, who later used the growing mass medium of popular fictional writing.

"Anyway…Edmund gave his presentation to his fellow scientists at the Royal Society, and amongst all the details he expounded upon then he explained the Aurora Borealis as escaping vapours that were lit up by the inner luminescence from here, but his 'theory' was not widely promoted or considered too seriously by his establishment peers, and despite his great reputation he suffered all the predictable clamorous scepticisms and baying ridicule from them as a result.

"But, nevertheless, through his efforts, that knowledge found its way onto the surface world, even if it was only in a small way – due to the fairly limited means of communications in those days, but even so, it was still a very valuable contribution he bravely made…

"Well…I could go on a lot more, but, I imagine, with everything we've told you about so far it's probably *more than enough* for you all today! No doubt we could spend *at least another hour* or so answering questions – which I'm sure you all have plenty of!

"But could I suggest instead…that you perhaps digest everything over the next few days, do some research, and then we can all meet up again to have a question and answer session then? - Unless you have any burning questions right now that we can help you with…?!"

He looked expectantly around at the faces of the four young people, who were all obviously deep in their own thoughts. Mel then looked at Dave and said to him, "I think that's probably best don't you Dave? My head's *so full it's all stodged up!*" He smiled back at her, "*Yeah – mine too!* You're right. I need some time to sort it all out as well!"

Sophie said, "*Mmm, same here! There's just so much!* I think a few days to let it all settle before coming back to you is a good idea too!

"Oh! *But actually though...if you don't mind* - there was one question I, I've wanted to ask but never got round to asking you Magda – you might think it's a bit silly now, and it's not actually about tonight, well not specifically, but, well, I, we, Jake and I, never got round to asking you before, because the last times we've been with you there was just so much happening and everything you talked about was just so, well, *involved and amazing,* I suppose I forgot...so could I...just ask you now - *how did you know my and Jake's names when we first saw you - when you came out of your caravan at the Fair? - And it was if you knew we were coming...?!*"

Magda smiled at her, "*Of course you can my dear, and I'm happy to tell you!* In fact now is probably a better time for you to ask me as before you might not have, may I say, fully understood the answer to that question. *But you, and all of you, know so much more now, so I am sure you will!*"

She paused to take a deep breath before continuing, "I have talked at length before about seeing auras *and that everything is energy,* and earlier this evening Anders talked about how psychics, mystics and others with similar gifts describe how they can see the so called 'material world' all around them, including all the living, sentient beings in it, in terms of auras of energy, and that they can see people – just as Carlos described, as 'egg shaped globular forms of intense clusters of energy' which emanate as light from which filaments of pure consciousness extend and interact with the other forms of energies all around them...

"...Well, Lucia had advised me earlier that evening, when we first met, that she had seen in her crystal gazing that two people, a young lady and a young man, would be coming later, both together, and they didn't yet realise it but they were both going to be very important in everything we are doing...and she also warned me that others, 'the opposition', were also going to be present.

"So, I was waiting in my little caravan with her, and watching out for you both. I had put a glamour on the steps to the caravan to dissuade any others from coming in until you had arrived - they would have simply thought they had changed their minds and decided not to bother coming in.

"As I was watching and seeing every-'thing' and every-'body' around us in that same way Carlos described, in terms of pure energy and light, I saw you both coming when you were some distance away.

"I knew immediately it was you two both together because your auras and filaments were so much brighter and more prominent than all of the others in the vicinity. I then reached out with part of my consciousness to you - *and that is how I learned your names.*

"The Multiversal Laws we adhere to would not have permitted me to simply reach deeper and force you to come to me, *because it always has to be from your own free will.* But I thought that a little, well, intriguing surprise for you would be permissible and appropriate, so I came out and spoke to you, *inviting* you to see me later - which you both did, from your own free will!

"I had been communicating with Anders throughout all of this, and he had suggested that you both first went to him to listen to him, so that Jake could be 'brought upto speed' about the general background to everything, as you already were Sophie - because you had visited him the previous evening...So that is why I told you someone else wanted to see you both first and I also warned you of *'others'*, *'not from here'*, being present, and for you to be careful.

"And unknown to you I placed a psychic protection over you both to dispel any attempts upon you that we knew they might try before then, as they would be able to see you as I had seen you of course. I also let the twins at the merry-go-round know about you, so they were expecting you. So, all in all, there was a lot of 'trade craft' going on that evening that you knew nothing about – *but you do now!*"

Sophie's mouth had formed a perfect 'O' as Magda had been speaking, and her eyes were by now almost as wide. She turned her head slowly to look at Jake *"Wowww…!"* Was all she could manage to say to him, Jake could only add a long loudly whispered *"Yeahhh – Wowww!"*

"Thank you for everything you did Magda!" She quietly replied a few seconds later when coherent speech had returned to her. "Thank you! It's incredible! – it's just like Mel said to me this afternoon: *'The Truth is always stranger than any fiction…!'*"

"You are most welcome Sophie! And yes, I agree, it is a good saying; because humanity, over hundreds and hundreds of generations has been falsely lead to believe all the fictions served upto them as being 'The Truth' and how, therefore, they should perceive the world…and so they have done exactly that upto now *with such habitual expectancies based on how they see and perceive it that they, well, most of them, cannot do so in any other way* - because they have been programmed to collectively believe that the world is made up of 'separate solid objects' - *and not as it really is – which is an infinite web of interacting energy patterns…"*

Chapter 19: A Spy in the camp...

Jake blew his cheeks out with a big sigh, reached up to rub the back of his neck, then wiped his jaw with his hand before letting it drop into his lap with a slap and then said, "Well...I definitely feel like that I've gone – in the past week or so – *from being at infant school to now being a Professor - with everything I've learned! -* But compared to you and Anders, Magda - *I'm obviously still 'a babe in arms'!"*

Magda laughed, *"Oh I don't know Jake!* – I think you are going to be an excellent Professor! And anyway if you were still 'a babe in arms' - *those arms would have to be as strong as Tarzan's or Samson's – just to pick you up!"* She laughed again, Jake and the others joining in with her.

"Well, *ahem,* speakin' now as a Professor then...! *I do 'ave a burnin' question!...*It was sort o' triggered off, I think, when you mentioned, *'old souls reincarnating to help'* Anders...I mean, *I might be right off track 'ere,* but it got me wonderin'...wonderin' about me Dad, an' all his inventions. *But really the one he was workin' on in secret* – I've told Soph' all about it, well, what little I knew about it then, *but now I think I know a lot more than just the little I did* – an' what I think is that he was gettin' pretty close to comin' up with some device that made or tapped into that 'free energy' all around us like you've talked about Anders.

"But then he got that bloody Alzheimer dementia, and that put a stop to it o' course. So, d'y'think that if he was, gettin' close to crackin' it, that, well, *mebbe this illness he's got might not 'ave been just 'by chance'...Could that be possible...?!"*

Anders slowly sat back looking intensely at Jake with deep sympathy, he then turned his head to look at Magda, and they both seemed to have a few seconds of non verbal communication again between them before he looked back to Jake and very quietly said, "yes, I'm afraid it is possible Jake. Varying degrees of severity of that debilitating illness, and many others like it, *can be, and, indeed are, deliberately induced.*

"Often in individual cases it is a despicable pre-emptive action the 'Wreckers' are tasked do to - *to effectively neutralise someone who has been flagged as a 'most-likely-threat' in the near future.* It is more subtle than...well, waiting to discover that they have become *'definitely-an-immediate-threat'* - and then having to throw them out of a high window as soon as possible, or take other, drastic, preventative action...which will then be officially classed as a suicide...

"...I won't go into *too much detail* about the actual energy transmission process and the psycho-physiological mechanics of how they induce it right now, but I will say that *it is just one part* of the reason for the chem-trails being sprayed from aeroplanes all over the world, and *the global proliferation of all the different vaccines now being so forcefully promoted* – particularly for the very young, the ageing, and those approaching 'retirement' Magda talked about earlier.

"As we said before, in some countries vaccines have become mandatory so that people, one way or another, unavoidably ingest many damaging chemicals including mercury and the malignant derivatives of aluminium, viruses and also the specific nano-technologies, all designed to, to damage human synaptic and neural functions in the brain and in the general nervous and immune systems...*by disrupting the body's and the mind's natural electro-magnetic harmonious functioning when the nano-techs are activated* by directed micro-wave energy beams.

"Patents in America for these types of *'individual and mass behaviour modification technologies'* go back at least forty years – the energy beams are mainly from the H.A.A.R.P – High Altitude Aural Activation Research Project - transmission grids and now, as well, from certain built in frequencies contained within the global spread of the new 'fifth generation' of the more powerful, military grade, 'Smart', 'Wi-Fi' transmission grids, and from transmissions emanating from geosynchronous satellites that are already in place...all those 'delivery

354

systems' are more for *mass area coverage and targeting whole populations...*

"*But...*The Wreckers also have hand-held devices which amplify and transmit the activation frequencies to *specific individuals at close range.*

"...I know it happened fairly quickly in your Father's case because your memories of it all were shared by you to Magda during your partial mind fuse together, then you kindly agreed for her to share them with me. We both think that he was probably close to a breakthrough, a discovery, before...before the illness struck him.

"But we decided to wait, to give you the time to arrive at a similar conclusion about all of this *on your own*, which we knew you soon would, and we didn't want to cause you any further distress until then by us saying *it was deliberate* and then suggest your re-igniting of what he was working on - *until you knew, and understood more - and were ready to do so...*"

Jake had been nodding silently at Anders as he spoke, then with a determined sigh he said, "Yeah, I am now Anders, like I said before, an' I'm goin' to go through everythin' of 'is like a dose o' salts now, I know where he kept a lot of his notes an' other stuff like small experimental models an' all that well hidden, he didn't keep everythin' in 't'Bletchley Huts' as he called 'em.

"*Oh Bloody 'Ell! Of Course! - Listen to this! - There's Three Things! Well, Three 'Dots' as in 'connectin' The Dots an' seein' what the line they make points to!'*

"*Dot 'One'* - shortly before he started to...*change*...he'd 'ad a 'flu jab' at his annual check up at the new Doctors' mega-surgery that's now in town. He'd never 'ad one before at his old Doctors little surgery, but that'd got closed down. Apparently them at the new one 'ad more or less insisted it'd be a good idea for 'im, when he 'ad to go an' register there, so he did, but it put 'im right out o' sorts for about a couple o' weeks after! So me Mum an' I said, *'we weren't goin' to have one o' them if they made y'feel that rough! – When the winter comes we'd just stick to paracetamol an' moanin' if we got it'*, we both said!

355

"Dot Two - I remember 'im sayin', durin' that time he was ill from it, when he surprised me by tellin' me where he'd *'idden all his 'secret stuff'* as he called it, that he was: *'tellin' me in case 'owt 'appened to 'im!'* I s'pose I didn't tek what he said that serious then, as I thought he just 'ad a dose o' *'serious man-flu'* like, I mean y'don't do you when y're still in that *'infant school'* an' y'don't know anythin' about what's really goin' on...d'you?! I couldn't imagine *'owt serious 'appenin'* to him like he was hinting at – *just shows you how wrong y'can be...!*

"An' Dot Three - we'd 'ad an attempted break in t'sheds a few days before he first started to feel dead rough from his jab, an' then really come down with it. But the sheds an' the house are well locked up an' secured, an' ages back he 'ad rigged up bloomin' good security alarms, motion detectors, with flood light systems, an' they were all on separate circuits, so 'ooever it was who tried to get in couldn't 'cause the alarms went off an' back garden were all lit up wi' all security lights. Early hours o' mornin' it was. Police just reckoned whoever it was might've been after the motorbikes or any tools we 'ad layin' around, as they said there'd been a recent spate o' shed-breakins in the area.

"They might o' been right...*but I don't think so now*...Anyway...me Mum an' I are goin' to see him on Tuesday evenin', so I can try and talk to him about what he were workin' on, that's if he's, if he's...well, *able to...*"

"Well done Jake, and I agree with you about those 'three dot connections'...they all point and line up towards a bigger, hidden agenda at work in the picture they indicate...I know it's not going to be easy for you, *when you re-ignite his work* – but you will be having all our help as well of course.

"What is more than likely to have occurred as well, as an ongoing chain of events, over time, is that your Father, having 'a track record' of being involved in 'Ufological Societies' and also being a successful, independent innovator and inventor, was flagged as *'a person of interest'* long ago to keep a watchful eye on, and from everything you've told me about him he was astute enough to realise that, *hence all the precautions he took to secure the properties...*

"You see, *he is one of the types they fear most* – someone who has gained knowledge and insight, and who has a proven track record of being more than capable of making the mental leap to go from theories to discovering and creating functional and working concepts – and someone who has sufficient financial resources of his own, and, most worrying for them - someone who is just working quietly away and quite independently from the oversight of any institution they have infiltrated...

"It's likely, and obviously I'm only guessing, because I don't know yet, but for example - had he recently ordered any unusual or 'specialised components' – *because that would have, without any doubt at all, really started all their alarm bells and warning lights ringing and flashing...?*"

"*Oh crikey me! Yeah that's right Anders he 'ad!* For the last, well, it'd be a good few months or so, he'd 'ad little packages bein' delivered two or three times a week. Before that usually it'd been much bigger stuff just two or three times *a month*, an' as I say recently none of it were big stuff though, mainly smallish packages - he just said, *'they were specialised magnets an' electronic bits an' pieces...'*"

"*...And presumably he had ordered all of them on-line...?*"

"Oh aye! - Well most of 'em anyway, sometimes he were on 'is mobile doin' it, a*n' they were from all over t'world!* - China, Germany, America – an' England as well...*Ohhh No...! - They were tracking him 'on-line' an' on 'is mobile weren't they?!...*He's got all the usual – an' a bit more - internet security stuff on his computer, *but he wouldn't o' known, he'd've 'ad no idea* - like I didn't then – *but I do now,* that they can get into any computer or mobile at any time and see what y're up to...*he'd've just thought that ordering stuff from so many different places all over t'world wouldn't leave any trails for anyone to make sense o' what he was doin' I suppose...*"

Anders sighed deeply, "*Yessss,* it's all much clearer to me now Jake. *That is exactly what will have happened to trigger their responses.* It also explains more as to why you were being followed and were then

357

targeted by Wreckers last Monday night when you went to the Fair. *And targeted just as you were approaching the merry-go-round portal...*

"They had found out that we were there - or at least they had detected the general area of one of out portals which would've given you safe access to us...as I explained in The Trocadero. They probably suspected that you knew much more about what your Father was doing, than in reality you actually did, and they would've thought you somehow knew about us - and had secretly arranged to meet us for advice and help, *with the intention of taking his work further...*

"So they attempted there and then, to target you as well. Fortunately, you Sophie – and I remember you saying – that you saw them before they could do anything – and - I remember you saying as well that you had sensed a dread, and a headache coming on, but Jake had chased them off and any effects of their attempt were obviously dispelled by the immediate, *ahem*, positive energies of Love and Affection that you shared between you...straight away..."

Sophie drew a breath in loudly at this, and said, *"Oh My God! So if I hadn't seen them...?!"*

Anders replied with a grim smile and nodded his head at the implications of her unfinished question. Mel looked quickly at Dave before saying, "I know we too were, were targeted as well, because I sensed that same *'dready headache'* starting as well! But, like you said in The Trocadero Anders, too many people got between us and them...so...they, those Wreckers were after Dave as well then – it couldn't've been me – because *what threat was I to them - then...?!"*

"Yes Melanie, I'm afraid that is most probably correct. The, procedure, they use to do this, from a reasonable distance, is not like a laser that pin points its focus on one target, on one mind, but it would also affect someone who was standing very close to their intended target.

"None of you had had any recent vaccinations, so they couldn't have activated the nano-tech' in them – remember what happens with a micro-wave cooker and metallic particles...? So I think the device they were using would have, would have, I'm sorry to even say this to you, most likely have caused something similar to, to a heavy stroke...To put it crudely its rapid application, in a crowded scenario, like you were in, is more like that of a shotgun than a rifle...

"No doubt David your exhibition of paintings and the initial local press article about it had been seen by...someone...and that had prompted their response. If your paintings had just been amateurish ones of *'boats in the harbour and local scenes'*, well, there'd've been no threat for them there, so you were marked as a 'person of interest'...and again, they would have thought that you may have been deliberately coming to meet us as well, because they know we have had much involvement, *over many years*, in promoting the works of artists just like you David - enlightened artists whose works can make greater and greater numbers of people start to think anew, re-assessing their belief paradigms, which can, *and does*, cause great changes in perceptions...

"So between the two of you at the Fair that evening – David and Jake, you were both, completely unaware that you were two people they would definitely have tasked their local Wreckers to, to interfere with..."

Sophie then said, *"Oh my God! We all came that close...?!* Since then though none of us have seen, or felt, them again...but from what you're saying they won't just have given up! *So, do you mean they'll be trying to do it again...?!"*

Magda now replied saying, "No they certainly will not have given up. I think it is likely they already have, or, I should say, that at the very least they have had to change their tactics and put into motion the means of discovering more – gathering more Intelligence - about you both – Jake and David, and specifically about *what you are actually doing now*, and what you particularly are perhaps planning and *intend to do Jake...*

"They know you all 'disappeared' after riding on the merry-go-round, and they had discovered we had a...what we call a 'general usage' time portal there...*somewhere*...but definitely in the area of the merry-go-round...The portable one in my caravan is very different, and it is heavily cloaked with powerful wardings, and is not detectable by them.

"Also before then you had psychic protections I put in place over you, whether you knew about those or not, *but they will have detected them around you*...and also that your auras are of much 'greater intensities' than...well...'normal folks'!

"So they will have had to assume you were all on your way – and then did - actually meet with us, which then significantly changed the complexity of the problem for them.

"By that I mean, before, you could have been targeted as merely unsponsored or unsupported individuals and that would have made their problem one they could solve easily and quickly...but now, they know that *we must know,* and so *we must be sponsoring and be 'onside' with you,* and as far as they can know *perhaps many others are now as well*, because they will have thought that the first thing we advised you to do would have been to share everything you know – *with us* - and with others we may have introduced you to – so that in future 'merely' targeting you especially Jake, would no longer guarantee the solving of their problem…

"I say *'you especially Jake'* because the danger, the threat, to them of you being someone with a high probability of being another key figure - instrumental in trying to release to the world the practical reality of how to generate and apply free energy – and all that implies that we have talked about at length – that has a more immediate threat to them than the longer term effects of perception changing that your artwork – and, now, your future writings will achieve David.

"Your works are of course just as valid and just as important but they will, by now be considered to be a lower concern in their prioritising of the immediate risks to them..."

Magda had considered mentioning that William Colby, a former Director of the CIA had been found floating in the Potomac river, over twenty years ago, just days before he was about to give the full operational details of such an energy device, and many millions of dollars to fund its promotion into the world, to a group working on its disclosure to humanity.

But she decided that at the moment the fear created by knowing that would cause them would be detrimental to them implementing the delicate but powerful strategies they needed to do to handle this situation.

So she stopped talking for a few moments to reconsider the best way for her, and her young friends, to proceed.

The two young couples kept their rapt attention on her as she paused in her analysis of all these events, her phenomenal mind working at warp speed to assess and consider the myriads of options and likely consequences, and then how best to present those she settled upon as being practical and workable by her young friends. It was just a few seconds later when she asked them all,

"Now...I don't want you all to descend into paranoia, but has someone, anyone, recently – as in over the past week or so since your visit to the Fair, been and becoming, perhaps quite unexpectedly involved with you? Someone who visited, or is, or will from now on be – for apparently innocuous reasons – be continually coming into contact with you repeatedly for the most plausible of reasons in the near future...?...Particularly someone you have known long enough to trust - or at least not to consider having even the slightest suspicions about...?"

The four of them slumped back into the sofas as they immediately started to search through and replay in their minds all the interactions with others they had had over the past week.

After a few minutes Jake, with what seemed like great reluctance raised his head, and was about to say something when Magda discretely touched her lips with her forefinger so that he remained quiet whilst the others were still thinking.

The look on his face though told her that someone he knew had fitted the profile she had outlined...

A minute or so later, and almost together, both Dave and Mel looked up with similar expressions of shock and dismay on their

361

faces.

Only Sophie was still looking down, thinking and slowly shaking her head, but when she looked up and saw the dismayed expression on Jake's face, then similar ones on Mel's and Dave's faces she said, *"Oh! What?! - Who? Who Jake…?"*

Jake had his teeth clamped over his bottom lip as he shook his head, as if trying to shake off the awful truth he'd just realised, but he couldn't, and he said, with great resignation in his voice, "The only person I can think of who fits the bill is...*Reg...*"

"That's who we...came up with as well mate, *I'm real sorry...*" Dave said.

"Jeeeesus wept…! *Reg! He's been me mate for years! I can't believe it…!* But, but now when I look at how he's suddenly right in me orbit – out the blue...*but he must'a bin got at! Surely, a, a mate, even though I 'aven't 'ad that much contact with 'im for a good few months, he wouldn't just...spy...an' betray me...me Dad – an' everyone - would he…?!"*

"I am very sorry Jake." Magda said, "I know it is painful, especially so when it is someone close, who, who does this...but please, talk me through why you have come to that conclusion about that person – and then - why you two have as well Melanie and David."

So Jake detailed for her where, when and how, early yesterday morning at Big Sammy's, Reg had told him about his finding of an old Norton motorbike in bits, which, Jake said, "...is a bit unusual I suppose but it does happen" – he then said: "*an' anyway summat similar 'appened to me recently with two old bikes - so it never occurred to me to think twice about it – bikes I'd come across – well, in truth it was me mate from the garage who 'ad an' he told me about 'em - two second world war bikes left in a barn in Bridlington, a few weeks back now."*

He told her that Reg had asked him to do up the one he'd found – an' make him a cafe racer out of it, which would take a fair bit of work over a few weeks, and of his suggesting that he could drop it off first

thing the next morning – which had been this morning - at his shed –
"*Oh Crikey Me!*" He then interrupted himself,

"After we'd got his bike an' all the bits he 'ad for it in me shed this mornin', he 'ad a good look round, and he then said, well, he suggested that: *'if I were ever thinkin' o' 'avin' a bit of a clear out o' the sheds, he'd offer me a good price like for owt I wanted out to make some more room!'*

"Well, I 'adn't considered it before, but there is a lot o' stuff in at least two o' the sheds that 'asn't been touched for years, an' so well, I thought that if I 'ad a bit more space I could mek good use of it now me business seems to be pickin' up. *So I showed him round 'em all!*

"We went in all the sheds an' he 'ad a good look at everythin'! *I didn't think owt of it!* He's a mate, an' that's his business – buyin' an' sellin' stuff from house an' garage clearances an' all that. He goes all over the North East doin' it, which is 'ow he came across the old Norton last Thursday – *or so he says* - an' he did offer me some decent cash for some o't stuff in't sheds, an' he offered to 'elp me free gratis – at no cost - to spend a mornin' clearin' stuff out I didn't want an' he didn't either an' then tekin' it to tip in 'is van.

"But I said: 'I'd 'ave to run it past me Mum, *although I expect she'd be glad of a big clear out!'* But I couldn't ask her right there an' then 'cause she'd gone out for the day to see an ol' friend who's been ill an' she 'adn't seen her for ages, so I didn't want to interrupt or bother her right then, by ringin' 'er, y'know!'

"Anyway, after he'd 'ad a good look round we left it at that as he was goin' off then to meet you and Mel, Dave, to move all your stuff from your flat to the charity shop an' your caravan an' all that…

"But I did get a text from 'im later this afternoon asking me: *'if I'd 'ad a word wi' me Mum an' was she ok to have the clear out?'*…I replied sayin', *'yeah, me Mum's ok with it, an' I could use the space! But gimme a week or so to finish off the chopper I'm doin' an' then I've gotta couple o' biggish jobs for Ol'Billy I've promised to do for him, an' then I'll get back to you on it mate, cheers!'* So that's where we're at right now…"

"Good...very good Jake, your reply – true as it obviously was, will have given you a slight respite." Magda said.

"So...let us look more closely at, and analyse the events you have just described Jake, *so we can start to see the full picture 'those event dots' make,* despite being hidden behind some very effective: *'role camouflaging'.*

"I think we should start with the attempted break-in you had. No doubt if it had been successful some things would have been stolen - *to make it appear 'as just a break-in', and not as a reconnaissance mission* of where your Father was, and you still are, working...Particularly as you said the Police had told you there had been a sudden spate of other break-ins of garden sheds recently in the area, *so it was not a surprising or unusual event in the area at that time…it was not just your sheds that had been targeted…*

"In fact it is obvious now to me that the other break-ins were 'stage-crafted' to create that impression. However your break-in was unsuccessful – *but soon after that 'someone' appeared* – as you said, *'in your orbit',* who managed, without much prior warning at all to you, to gain legitimate entry *and have a good look around inside all of them!*

"That person you met yesterday morning found out from you that you were busy doing things in other places for the rest of the day and evening, so the only opportunity for you personally to remove anything before he came the next morning – this morning - would have been in the middle of the night after you returned home, and they will have covered that possibility by having the sheds under observation from well before your arrival home to the arrival of their agent, your 'friend', with his conveniently found motorbike the following morning.

"You obviously made no mobile calls to someone to quickly go in and remove anything whilst you were out, as any calls you made would have been monitored, and so they would consider it reasonable to assume that if anything was in there somewhere, it would still be there…

"I know all this might sound overly complicated, convoluted and a paranoid way of thinking to you all, but it is an introduction to how you will have to think to really see the most accurate picture or scenario of a recent, or actually unfolding event within the milieu of all the known facts or 'dots' you already have – and those that you do not yet have, but are likely to have, or will, occur…

"To put it much simpler – it is like doing a jig-saw – you have just properly identified this 'piece' and you have now worked out and realised how it fits or connects into the bigger picture…

"…I have no doubt that it would have been – *others* – looking around inside your sheds as well Jake, seeing through this Reg's eyes, and instantly assessing and recording what he was seeing...

"Fortunately though you have said your Father had the foresight to previously remove anything immediately obvious or 'incriminating' that he was working on, so seeing nothing 'obvious' may have seemed *slightly unusual* to them, based on their suspicions...but in case anything *was actually there* but stashed away out of sight, or made to look like something else – something quite innocent and innocuous, that person then suggested and planted the idea in you of having a thorough clear out – *and some generous cash and free help to do it as an incentive…!*

"Yes, of course you could remove anything 'incriminating' beforehand but they will now have the sheds under observation in case you do that. Does that interpretation of the events – by joining the 'dots' in a different way – or fitting in those likely pieces of the jigsaw help you to see a different picture Jake…?"

"Aye, aye it does right enough, an' with the *'twenty-twenty vision of hindsight'* now, when y'put it all like that Magda, it certainly does! Huh! I never even thought about 'avin' a look at 'im to try an' see his aura like you showed us 'ow to...an' I've been practisin' everyday an' all!

"Never thought to do it on 'im as he's a mate...or I thought he was...Anyway...for me it's good you broke down your thought processes like you 'ave, it all 'elps me – an' rest of us! But me p'ticly,

365

as I've always been at me best when sussin' out *mechanical things* rather than, well, *people*!

"But I were good at chess! – Me Dad taught me an' we used to play some good long games a couple times a week, he always said, *'it's the best way to learn 'ow to concentrate an' think strategically Jake…'*, so I suppose what you're on about is a very similar way o'thinkin'…?

"…an' it's like y'say about *'perceptions'*, I was played and made to look the wrong way, whilst summat else – *what was really goin' on* – just passed me by, *an' I never saw it…didn't even look for it!* But you said that the sheds'll *'be under observation now'* – in case I start movin' any stuff out - *'ow'll they be doin' that Magda?"*

"I must say that the more I know about your Father, Jake, the more impressed I am by him, and by his foresight. Teaching and playing chess with you regularly when you were younger was a marvellous thing he did to develop your concentration and your critical, strategic and analytical thinking skills.

"In fact Anders and I are embroiled in a game at the moment – we started it four days ago – and it is his move next, but I have told him I am now twenty eight moves ahead – *despite what moves he makes* - to a checkmate, and he has admitted to knowing twenty six of them, but needs the missing two to achieve a stalemate!"

She looked at him with amused half hooded eyes and an expression of gleeful, but friendly competitiveness, placing a hand on his forearm as she spoke. Anders shook his head with an exasperated sigh and mock dismay on his face, then shook his finger-spread hands in front of him and said in a shaky but dramatically panicky voice, *"only one move you could make is missing now! I found the other one! But the remaining one you could make is, I'm certain, between your moves eighteen and twenty one – but I've only got until three tomorrow morning to find it before my timer runs out and I have to make my move…!"*

Sophie, Mel and Dave, not fully knowing the tactical intricacies of the game of chess were more amused by Ander's acting than impressed by the content of what he was saying.

Jake was both – and he admitted it saying, *"Woww!* The most I could ever plan ahead was three moves – an' they didn't always work out either...! *But twenty eight moves ahead to checkmate – ot a stalemate - regardless of what the other player does...?! That's more than world class! – It's Superhuman stuff!"*

"Oh she is believe me!" Anders said resignedly, *"The last time I actually won a game was back in the nineties...seventeen nineties... and that was really only because she was distracted by her heavy involvement in the huge revolutionary events in France at the time...!"* he added wryly. Magda waved her hand and shook her head in dismissive modesty as she started to speak again.

"...Back now to what you were saying Jake, and to your last question - most likely there will be at least two optical and acoustic devices – watching and listening, and a covert, well hidden, 'mobile response team' monitoring them, somewhere in the vicinity.

"The devices – sound recording cameras basically – although there is nothing at all 'basic' about them – they will most likely be the size of and look and fly exactly like...for example - 'dragon flies', or similar flying insects.

"So from now on you must not even glance around you when you approach the sheds in the future. Because it will be interpreted as you trying to see if you can spot them – that will immediately alert the response team that you are now what is called *'third party aware',* which a normal, innocent, or unsuspecting person never is...

"But, having said that, fortunately you were an exception to the rule, Sophie, when you became aware of being followed by the Wreckers at the Fair.

"Someone who is third-party aware, always has - *unless* they have the experience and *considerable skills* to mask the *'tell-tale give-away mannerisms and furtive behaviours',* which in trade craft are called *'Tells'.* They indicate, to those who know what to look for, that their target now realises they are being watched or followed...and it is these 'tells' or *'give-away indicators'* that will be the first things they will be looking out for...because they will then validate their suspicions that

367

you are...*'upto something!'*

"So...you now need to exploit the opportunity you have to turn their devices against them! You can do that by feeding them visual and acoustic data that you are not upto anything at all, you are just carrying on working normally! – and so create an observable persona that most likely knows little or nothing of what your Father was working on...and you are certainly not carrying on with his *research and work...!*"

"*Bloody 'Ell!* - Oh – s'cuse me! But, so - instead o' fairies in't bottom o' mi garden – *I've got some 'super-techno-spies' down there then?!*"

"...I have to say that I do not know about the presence of any members of the Faerie realm in your garden Jake..." Magda replied with a tongue in cheek expression, "*...but that is quite possible as well...!* But I do know - *with an almost absolute certainty* - that there will now be present some *'super-techno -spies'* as you have just called them!

"It was, and is, all a very well executed example of the 'trade craft' we have often talked about and demonstrated Jake, and these..'.people'...are masters of it. *But so are we!*...And now you, all of you...with practice and ongoing guidance from us, are going to become, from real necessity, *just as skilful and capable of using it...!* All of you because you are all obviously involved, so, let me propose, *in general outline* to you what I think your next moves, just like those in a complex game of chess, should be…

"*The actual 'nitty-gritty' details* you will have to act out and skilfully implement on your own though, with each of you using your own skills, personalities and unique ways to do so. But you will not be alone, or isolated as you do so because as you now know – *I and all of us - are only a thought away from you...*

"...So...First of all, from now on, your personas, your normal selves that everyone knows you by, *must not change in the slightest.* Especially not to the heightened perceptions of those who now have you under surveillance.

"You must continue to appear, and to behave in everything you do and say as if everything is carrying on quite normally - just as it always has done, *this is the crucial fundament because it will definitely help to allay any definite suspicions about you – especially of being third party-aware – which by implication would clearly signal that you have 'something to hide'.*

"And as I have just said to you Jake doing that will give you the opportunity to further feed them false data via their surveillance devices. It will not be easy, especially when you come into contact with Reg again Jake, knowing about him what you do now – that he is now one of their 'Watchers', their 'HumInt' agents, which means a 'Human Intelligence' agent, and sometimes called a 'C.H.I.S'. - a 'Covert Human Intelligence Agent'.

"The surveillance devices are called 'TechInt' which means 'Technical Intelligence', and monitoring your communications they call 'SigInt' or 'Signals Intelligence' - so you must, *absolutely must not, give him, or 'the others', any reason at all to be suspicious.*

"Remember, Reg is just a conduit *and ultimately* it is the parasites and everything they stand for looking and listening through his eyes and ears...and through the eyes and ears of others unknown to you – the Humints – C.H.I.S.'s – *The Watchers* - who will be involved now and in the future, and it is all of them, but initially through Reg, that you have to creatively use your trade-craft skills to ultimately deceive the parasites. But I think at the moment it is only their host person Reg that *you will see*, interact with, and have to convince in the first place – and so you must continually maintain your usual, normal persona that he is familiar with, for him to interact with.

"Actually this might help you – all of you – to do that, you remember your first attempts to create your own psychic protective diamonds? - Well, imagine from now on you are surrounded as well by a thick spongy layer that is made from a distillation of your personas, your characters, your mannerisms, it is a duplicate 'you'. And you must deliberately use this 'layer' to interact with him - and any others you suspect with.

369

"It can be probed, and poked at, but it just absorbs all those attempts, because what they see and interact with on the surface they will soon realise is just the same all the way through it...allaying suspicion...*and so it protects the real: 'everything-you-really-are-and-know'* - that is hidden and secure deep down in the middle of it...Does that make sense to you all…?!"

"Yeah, it does an' I hear what y're sayin' Magda, an' I, as I'm sure we all do, really appreciate these tips and advice like you're givin' us, I think we'd all abin lost up that proverbial creek wi'out 'em as paddles! An' that idea of 'avin like a *'persona buffer'* around you is a great 'advice tip' – I can already see it as being like the soft rubbery laminate the archery targets I use are made of, as nowt gets through them! *But it ain't gonna be easy for me wi' Reg*, but...then again, *nothin' really worth doin' ever is, is it?!"*

"No, it will not be easy Jake, and no, 'nothing really worth doing ever is'...*Oh My Goodness!* That is far too many *nasty negative 'no's'* we've both just said together about this! Let me put some positive *'Yes's'* in to outweigh them!

"*Yes!* – You can do it!

"*Yes!* - You all can!

"*Yes!* – You know how incredibly important this is!

"*Yes!* You all now know what is really going on in your world and the crucially important parts you all have to play in helping to change it! - and these new actions are an important part of that.

"*Yes!* – You know about those of us *in* our world and *on* yours who on your side helping you!

"*Yes!* - You – We – all of us – all of humanity - *will get through all of this!*

"*Yes!* – The time has finally come for us to achieve that!

"*So Yes We Will!*

"*There! That is much better! The 'Yes' word has so much more power! And 'Yes's' are so much nicer anyway!…"*

The two young couples couldn't help themselves from grinning at her, she had lightened their moods with her positive exuberance but maintained the seriousness of everything at the same time.

Jake then added his own brand of deadpan humour into the mix by saying, "Well, from now on, as I'm goin' to 'ave another, like - 'double personality' – wrapped around me to work with and use to interact with Reg - and any others I suspect o' bein' like 'im - *it shouldn't really be too 'ard for me* – as I used to be schizophrenic – *But We're All Right Now…!*"

This caused more groans and *'that's terribles'* from everyone just like Ander's culinary analogy puns had done earlier.

Having contributed to his share of amused groaning, Anders then leaned forward slightly saying,

"All Excellent Advice Magda, you have shone a positive and uplifting light on all of this. You mentioned, as well, 'ongoing guidance'...So perhaps I may add a very brief little story that is also positive, and humorous in a way - but I think it will offer some very sound guidance as well to self-insight and one's possible perception bias when observing and then analysing people - and events - that happen in real-time right in front of you…?"

"Please do Anders! I am sure I am speaking for everyone if I say that *your little story sounds most intriguing!*" Magda smiled at him, then looked to the others for confirmation and getting it from their nodding heads and expectant expressions, she, as much as they all did, thoroughly enjoyed listening to Ander's unique way of telling entertaining, but very pertinent stories that always had deeply insightful meanings and messages layered within them.

"Thank you, well then...now...imagine a car with three businessmen in it that has just stopped at some traffic lights which control a pedestrian crossing in a suburban area very early one morning. Then, to their amazement, right in front of them a young lady slowly strolls across the road - and she is completely naked…! The driver of the car, a staunchly religious, highly moralistic person, and a pillar of the community, is shocked and immediately annoyed at such a brazen display of what he perceives as obviously a deliberate and

371

promiscuous act by the young lady!

"The first passenger in the car is a bit of a 'Jack the Lad' with a lascivious eye for the ladies and ogles her lustfully as she slowly walks in front of them, and he wishes he had been alone in the car - as he thinks she is obviously giving out a clear and wanton signal that she is available!

"The second passenger looks at her for a moment - then quickly gets out of the car grabbing his coat and dashes upto her and covers her with it. As he does so she suddenly wakes up! Mortified and highly embarrassed at the situation she is in!...But effusively grateful to the man for helping her!

"You see, he had noticed that her eyes were closed and she was walking slowly – not provocatively – *because she was sleep walking!*

"...So...the same event...seen by three different men...all at the same time...*but interpreted in three totally different ways due to their perception biases!*

"Sooo...is there anything else we can learn, take out, and put to good use in future from what that little story is telling us? - Could there be any *'trade-craft-user-guidance'* in there for you? Well, yes, there is – and it is this: if, or most likely when, something unusual or unexpected happens, try not to immediately and unquestionably accept *what you are actually seeing, hearing and experiencing based purely upon your immediate perception and emotional responses to it.*

"Take a moment, or two, or more...as long as you need...to really see, question, analyse and so *understand* the implications and the possible - even quite abstracted consequences - *of what is really happening* – just as the third man did, *unlike the other two men who just rushed in judgementally and so they falsely interpreted what was really happening because of their immediate, emotionally driven and programmed-perception-responses to it.* Which all resulted in them totally missing and ignoring the one crucial fact – *that her eyes were closed!* - and the consequence it implied…and so as a consequence of that it was highly probable that she Asleep *And* Walking at the same time...!"

There was a moment or two of quiet stillness as the two couples thought about all this, then they spontaneously applauded, and Mel, as they quietened down, with a lopsided grin, asked Dave: *"...which man would you have been then Dave...?!"*

" - Oh the second passenger without a doubt! *As I wouldn't dream of looking at any other girl and having naughty thoughts about her – all of those I have are only for you and you alone of course...!"* He promptly and honestly replied, but doing so with his own style of dry humour. Mel blushed slightly, hiding a giggle behind her hand.

Sophie, grinning as well, then asked Jake the same teasing question and he more or less repeated what Dave had just said, but then added, *"I'd also be the first man, the driver, as well..."*

Sophie's eyebrows shot up in surprise at this, despite her realising, from the tone of his voice, that his obvious humour was still in play....*"because Anders said: 'he was a, a 'pillock' of the community...!'"*

She pushed him back into the sofa as everyone groaned and laughed again. "What was that Mel you were saying about *'men and sensible answers'* earlier...?!"

After several minutes of energetic discussion between them all, Magda said, "Well everyone, we could go on and on discussing all of this – and it would be enjoyable to do so - but I think we have *more than covered* the essentials *and much more* for this evening, so I think it is time now to have a well deserved break – *and have that surprise for you all that was mentioned earlier!"*

Despite the seriousness of all the topics they had been intensely discussing, the four young people all suddenly sat up in excited anticipation.

"Oooh! That sounds good Magda! What is it?!" Mel asked her.

"Aha!" She replied, raising an extended forefinger in front of her. *"Watch This!"*

Chapter 20: The Amazing Journey

Magda gracefully got to her bare feet, turned around, and looked up into the sky above her. Within seconds one of the larger silvery crafts silently glided down to hover just inches above the wider section of the patio floor twenty or so paces away from where they were sitting, and a wide doorway aperture shimmered open in it.

"*Our transport awaits! -* Oh! That is – of course – only if I am right in assuming that you would all like a ride around in it...to see a few places – and then *to go and have some supper...?!*" She asked them ingenuously, turning her head towards the two seated and now mesmerised couples, her eyebrows raised and a wide smile on her face.

The sudden appearance of the large oval shaped silver craft which was about twice the size of a single deck bus kept them in a stunned silence for a few seconds only - and then Jake surged to his feet exclaiming, "*Wowww!* OH YEAH! *Oh Yeah! Awesome!*" He pulled Sophie up and hugged her tightly, "Look at that! *Just look at that!*"

Sophie's face was a picture of excited delight as well as she stared at it wide eyed hugging Jake, as were Mel's and Dave's who had both now jumped to their feet in total surprise and excitement as well.

"Well I think that is a definite *'YES'* from everyone Anders!" Magda said to him, laughter in her voice.

"*Yes I think it most certainly was! Without a doubt! – There are definitely no erroneous perceptions from Us about that!*" he replied, with the same laughter in his voice, as he got to his feet, "after you my dear! Please do lead the way!" He stepped aside courteously for her to precede them.

For a moment or two the young couples seemed rooted to where they stood as they continued to stare in total amazement at it. Dave and Mel being the nearest first managed to overcome their involuntary paralysis and take some initial hesitant steps to follow Magda. Jake and Sophie quickly caught up with them, Jake was laughing and shaking his head as he stared wide eyed at it as they followed Magda. He kept repeating *"...it's incredible...it's incredible...!"*

Dave said, *"It's just like a bigger version of that craft in the recent X Files film innit mate?!"*

"Aye! That's right! It is...an' we're...oh crikey me! *We're goin' to go in it...bloody 'ellll!"*

Magda stepped lightly through the circular doorway and moved to one side turning to face them, her hands clasped lightly in front of her, smiling at them.

"Please come in, have a look around and take a seat when you are ready!"

Dave and Mel went inside first, and as Jake approached the entrance he reached out to touch the craft and felt a faint tingle from it. The surface was warm, smooth and shiny like glass or a highly polished metal but he sensed that it wasn't made from either of those materials. There were no sharp edges, seams or joins in it anywhere on the outside that he could see. Sophie, hanging onto his other arm, giggled as she looked at him and said, *"if you shake your head anymore it'll fall off!"*

"I...I know! It's just...just..." He was interrupted by shouts and exclamations of astonishment from both Dave and Mel who were already inside. Dave reappeared at the entrance with a massive grin on his face, "You won't believe this! Come in – I won't say anything – *just come and see for yourselves...!"*

Magda said, "I will just reset the electro-chromatic filters first to give you the full effect..."

She then gestured for them to enter as well.

When Jake and Sophie went inside the softly but brightly lit interior they saw that the inside was the same silvery chrome like material as the outside; even the comfortable looking dozen or so moulded seats set in an outward facing circle right in the middle of it, and a round desktop or table surface they surrounded were as well.

375

Then the internal light dimmed slightly and at the same time the walls, floor and ceiling – which all smoothly curved and flowed into each other suddenly all became totally transparent letting the warm, bright natural light from outside in, so it was like looking through a non-distorting glass shell. Only the ring of seats, the round table top and a circular area of the floor beneath them remained opaque.

Magda said, "Anyone looking at the craft from the outside will still see it just as you saw it before, but now, from the inside of course *we can see through it*...the reason there is an opaque area below the seats is because that is where the energy converter and the propulsion system are housed.

"As this is one of the larger crafts, down there is a bathroom, kitchen, dormitory and a storage area." She pointed to one end of the internal area. "They are cloaked behind the transparent wall – come on I'll show you!"

As they followed Magda to the far end another doorway shimmered open and amazingly they could see through into a corridor that wasn't transparent, it looked as if it was jutting out of 'the rear' of the craft into mid air! "We keep these more private areas obscured, but we still have all round vision in flight..." Magda explained.

They looked into the kitchen – which looked nothing like any kitchen they had seen before, the only familiar item was a sink basin with a tall chrome looking tap. Magda explained that if necessary it was possible to prepare meals here for upto twelve passengers on longer flights, the two bathrooms had showers and toilets, next to them was a large storage room with stacked chrome shiny containers lining the walls leaving a sizeable space in the middle, and the last room had low divans in it for resting on.

The two couples had been awestruck during their brief tour but once back again in the main interior of the craft their questions about it all erupted, then Jake asked the one he'd been dying to ask:

"*So...How...how...is it made?* An' *how...does it actually fly...?* An' *how...oh Crikey Me! I've got about 'alf a day's questions about it already Magda...!*" He blurted out as he paced around the starkly minimalist interior.

Magda smiled at him and then at all of them, enjoying and sharing in the childlike thrill and amazement which was radiating tangibly from them. Before she could answer him Anders came inside and the entry doorway closed silently behind him. Nothing actually moved to close - instead the opening just seemed to shimmer slightly for a couple of seconds – like the doorway to the corridor had, and then it wasn't there any more, it was a 'solid' continuous wall again blending in with the now transparent glassy walls around it.

"Make that a full day's questions now!" Jake said as he stared at the curved wall where the door had been just behind Anders..and back to the now 'disappeared' corridor doorway they'd all just exited from.

"Sorry about that! – I just had something to do quickly before joining you!" Anders then nodded to Magda as if confirming something private between them.

"Wellll...", he said, "to answer you Jake...technically speaking *we* didn't *'make it'...we just modified, amplified and then amalgamated the relevant matrices of the various energies we required using thought and conscious intent interfacing with some technology we have for this purpose – and so we caused it to appear, to manifest...*

"You've no doubt heard of 'Three D' – Three Dimensional - Printing? Well this is created by Sixth Dimensional Printing...now the way Three D Printing essentially works is that you need to have a supply of raw materials – *most of which* have basically been dug up – originally mined from the ground in various locations, then transported to be worked on in other locations to change them into the various substances required, then they are all transported again to a 'print location' where the new object you want to make is then made from them by the 'printer' - which I suppose you could say 'clones' a prototype model you made previously and you want to reproduce – although some of the latest printers now work directly from a computer designed model, but don't forget - that computer originally went through the same material supply processes *to make it...!*

"Quite a lengthy process all in all! – Especially with the Three D printed housing projects the Chinese are currently working on that I looked at recently…

"However, with 'Six D' printing the process is much simpler – *but slightly more complicated* – because we…er, let's say…we access all the necessary 'raw materials' directly from *their specific energy sources at their quantum level*…'matter' as you now all know is energy vibrating at different frequencies regardless of its appearance - whether it is a seemingly 'solid rock' or a drop of liquid water or the smoke from a fire.

"So…instead of digging all that 'raw matter' up, then transporting, and heating, cutting, banging and bending it all and then fastening it all together…instead we access the purer 'source' of the *higher* sixth dimensional reality of the *energy-matter* we need where we can then…manipulate, amalgamate and reconfigure it 'at source' to form the energy profiles and layout of the 'matter' form we require.

"We do have some assisting technology which helps us to then hold those isolated energies in stasis, during the crafts design in the final stages of that whole process – *and to create many other things of course* – we can then influence those specific energies of the matter we need with the combined power of one of our 'engineer groups" meditative *conscious intent. S*o there is no need to make either a 'physical' prototype to clone, or use a computer to design it first. And then we just move it or…*re-manifest it*…to have the lower, physical object properties here within the mid-fifth dimension…*Simples!*"

"When we use them on the surface world they have two modes of operation. The first mode is when they retain their fifth dimensional…'physical reality', but they are invisible in the third dimensional frequency of the surface world. But we can switch them to a third dimensional frequency to make them suddenly appear to anyone looking at them.

"It is an advanced form of 'stealth cloaking'. Visitors from beyond the planet use the same technique, which is why when they go in and out of the dimensions people observing them on the surface world often say, *'they just appeared! – then disappeared!'*

"Aaaa*ah!* Aa*Ha!*" Jake stuttered, "*Well...I did ask!* - Better make that a week of more questions now!"

He then looked down at the opaque silvery circle on the floor, which spread just beyond the seating and circular table arrangement.

"And you said Magda, that this is the, the, well, *it's the engine...?!*"

"Yes, that is correct Jake, it is a slightly more advanced form of – *engine* – that Anders explained has been known about since at least the nineteen forties on your world. Functional craft that use a more basic form of this technology have been made on your world by the secret, unacknowledged agencies, well, not actually *'made on'* but rather *'made in'* their hidden, underground military bases, since the early nineteen fifties.

"One of the *many differences* ours have though, as well as their method of creation, that Ander's has just explained, is that we interface or interact – guide and direct them – by using our conscious thought, which is...'tuned in'...to their artificial consciousness, as I mentioned earlier..."

"Oh, *oh wowwww!* It's obviously working now as I can just hear a very faint hum from it...?!" Jake said.

"Yes, it is more or less constantly operating as it draws the required energy to do so from the zero point energy fields all around us..."

"*Wow!* Well...*I did ask...! Zero point energy fields' to run an engine indefinitely'?! An' control it all wi'y'mind...! Well That's another week at least o' questions now!* - I think I need to sit down – *it's all just, just too incredible...!*"

"Please do – wherever you like! Then we will have a little excursion so that you can see a little more of our world – and perhaps we can even meet some...*others*...that live here as well...", Magda said, quickly giving Anders a fleetingly conspiratorial smile..."before we have our supper!"

Once they were all sitting in the surprisingly soft and comfortable moulded seats Mel said, "Oh I've just realised! - T*here's no seat belts!* Er, so...*we obviously don't need them...?!*"

379

Anders replied, "No, no seat belts necessary Melanie! The anti-gravitic force field the craft automatically generates around itself once it's in flight, absorbs inertia and so eliminates all the effects of 'G Forces' – Gravitational Forces – that come from acceleration, turning and stopping – otherwise, well...we wouldn't survive in it *for very long...!*

"Also, because of the inertial absorption it means we don't have to 'go up the gears' to accelerate and gain speed, we can move immediately at whatever velocity we...literally...decide upon...!

"But for today, as it's your first time, we will set off nice and gently for you!" He then looked over to Magda, "Shall I sit down and take control Magda – so you're free to point out and comment to everyone on what we're going to see when we're airborne...?"

"Yes, please do Anders, thank you. Well, everyone, a belated 'Welcome Aboard!' *Are we all ready now for the: 'Ander's and Magda's Marvellous Magical Mystery Tour'?!*"

A chorus of loud and excited *'YES'S!'* came from the two young couples. Sophie was feeling the same sort of stomach fluttering excited anticipation she'd felt the very first time when she'd sat in a carriage waiting to set off on the Big Dipper at Blackpool – but this was a hundred times more intense! She gripped Jake's hands tightly with both of hers, her teeth clenched, and was grinning wider than she ever had before!

Anders was sitting down as well now, and had placed his right hand palm down over a circular pad that all the seats had on one of the arms.

Magda had remained standing and she moved to stand a few feet away in front of them.

As she looked down into their excited faces she felt a wave of joy and great affection for them all at their bewildered, innocent excitement, yet at the same time it was tinged with a deep sadness as well, because none of this should be new to them, they should have been born into their world where such realities as all this had been in commonplace usage there for decades...

But they had been deliberately denied of it all...and her eyes watered slightly...*'Oh Bless them'*, she thought, *'...and all the countless others that for so long have been so wickedly denied so much of what really could have been for them...but it will come...!'*

"I'm ready now my dear..." Anders said very quietly to her, he had picked up on her thoughts and his ancient eyes told her he totally sympathised with them as he smiled at her. Magda sniffed delicately and flicked away some loose strands of her long hair that had slipped over her face.

"Thank you Anders – well, without further ado – *off we go then...!*"

From a stationary start there was no perceptible feeling of movement or acceleration as they rose vertically. The only way they could tell they were moving was that the colourful patio floor beneath them quickly became smaller and smaller and the ivory coloured crystalline tower rapidly skimmed past them.

Sophie thought that...*it's like when you're sitting in a still train and there's another one right next to you that's still as well – and you can see it through the window – then suddenly the other one starts to move away but you think it's you that's moving!*

The craft – which was just like sitting in a large clear glass, long oval bubble, then changed direction at what seemed like a right angle and moved away from the massive tower, and all the scores of others which quickly receded away and disappeared behind them.

It's nothing like you feel when you're accelerating on a bike Jake thought, suddenly recalling and comparing it to the sense of speed he'd had on the chopper as he had put it through its paces on the Whitby road early yesterday morning, *but I reckon we're goin' a lot faster now than the 'undred an' twenty I did then! - More like it's a thousand an' twenty – an' more!'*

Lots of other shiny crafts of different sizes flashed past them sometimes coming disconcertingly close before they rapidly disappeared as well as they flew away in all directions, like the tracer fire – but *much* faster – that you see in war films!

They were passing now over a very different and vast landscape

381

way, way below them, looking down on it like you do when you can see right down into the far depths of a clear sea from a glass bottomed boat on holiday trips in the Med'. It now looked like an undulating green carpet, with curling shiny lines like veins of silver making random patterns in it. Mel, feeling a touch of vertigo again as she stared down at it, said,

"Look! It...down there...*it looks like it's a jungle!* It's just like some of the photos' we printed in a magazine article at work last year of the Amazon jungle that were taken from way up in a special new design of hot air balloon!"

"Yes it does – *and it is* Melanie!", Magda said, "We are passing over The Great Forest and the many rivers that run through it..."

She then spoke quietly to Anders asking him to take them lower down and fly closer over the tree tops. *What happened next really was incredible! It was like rapidly zooming in on a photo on Google Earth!* There was no angled descent like you have in an aeroplane coming in to land, but instead there was an immediate cessation of the sense of moving forwards and then a rapid plummeting straight down as the ground below seemed to zoom in to clearer and clearer focus as they got closer and closer to it – then it all just stopped!

They were now right above the verdant canopy of the huge trees that they could see stretched down hundreds of feet to the ground. The lush greenery below them extended all the way to the far off horizons.

"Please feel free to stand up and walk around to have a better view!" Magda said, "I only suggested you sat down before we set off as sitting down whilst in transport is perhaps more familiar to you! - Unless of course you are on one of the overcrowded trains that always seem to be running these days! We only really use the craft's seats when we know a journey will take quite a while...or when it is a meal time in-flight..."

Getting to their feet, a little shakily, the two young couples moved over to one of the curved side walls, huddling together and pointing out to each other, with surprise and delight at the flocks of large brightly coloured birds that had suddenly flown out of the trees and were now swirling all around them. Some landed on the roof gazing down at the occupants as if they were inspecting them before they flew off to rejoin the others circling effortlessly around the craft.

"I've enabled the external transparency chromatics so they can see who we are." Anders said as he walked over to join them.

"*Corrrr!*" Dave said as he watched them, "*I've never seen any birds like these before! - Their colours! They're incredible!* – They're like, like all the bright iridescent colours you see on an insect's wing!"

"My auntie's got a parrot." Mel said, "*...but these are like a sort of cross between that - a parrot, a, a flamingo, and, er, an albatross!* – not that I've ever seen an albatross *for real* though!" She laughed, and looked over to Magda, "these birds look almost tame and friendly! – *It's like they've just come to have a look at us and say 'Hello'! -*

"They don't seem like my auntie's parrot though – if he didn't know you and you got too close to him *he'd peck and bite you straight away* and then *swear loudly at you!* My teenage boy cousins have taught it just about all the swear words they know between them, so now it's like it's got 'tourettes syndrome', it's funny sometimes - *but my Auntie gets really cross with them for doing it!*"

"*Huh!* Don't mention *that bloomin' parrot!*" Dave muttered, "*..first time I went up to say 'Hello' to it, all nice and polite like, it bit two buttons off my best shirt in less than a second and then screamed at me to 'F...' OFF!'*"

Jake burst out laughing - as everyone else did, between his guffaws he said, "*Blimey mate! -* You'd not want one o' these 'avin' a peck at you – *they must be twenty times the size of a parrot!*"

Magda, chuckling said, "Oh deary me David! And Melanie - *I can quite understand your Auntie getting very cross about that!* But these birds would not 'peck at' you – I assure you all that your buttons and everything else *would be quite safe with them!*

"Yes - they are 'tame and friendly' as you said, they are quite capable of defending themselves of course, should the need ever arise for them to do so, but they have no natural predators here to threaten

383

them, and they are all herbivores - they eat the berries from the trees, so they in turn are no threat to any other birds or smaller animals here...*and as far as I know - no mischievous young boys have taught them any bad language!*"

Sophie was, as they all were, whilst Magda was speaking, avidly watching them, her face upturned with obvious delight at their graceful, welcoming displays, looking up and twisting her head round and round to follow their effortless swooping and soaring above them. She said, almost breathlessly, "I came across some fantastic music the other day by, by..." She screwed her eyes shut for a second to recall who it was..."Oh yeah...*'Yann Tiersen'*, he's called – and *it* was called – *oh what was it...?!* Oh that's it!: *'La Valse Des Monstres'*, I think it would be *the perfect soundtrack* to watching them!"

"Oh - *Splendid!*" Anders said. "You like Yann's music as well?! *So do we!* That particular track is so hauntingly romantic yet *so full of energetic life*...I think you're quite right my dear, *it would be perfect! -* Just a moment now, *let me see what I can do...*" He strolled back to his seat, sat down and placed his palm over the circular pad again, a second or two later the perfect sound, almost as if it was being played live in the craft, of the instrumental playing of the enchanting music filled the craft.

"*Oooooh* Wowww*! This is it! Thank you Anders!*" She beamed at him, her eyes filling as she swayed listening to the music, watching the amazing birds flying around them.

"Mmmm, *I wonder if they'd like to hear it as well...?!*" Anders said quietly. Then, within seconds the random individual patterns of movement from the birds started to change subtly, then quite noticeably, morphing into more complex, yet somehow organised patterns of intermingling movement from them all together, and at the same time they flew faster and faster around them.

"Yes...you know...*I rather think they do!*" He commented as he rejoined them, looking skywards.

"Oooooh LoooooK! They're – they're - *it's like they're all flying a dance to it...!*" Sophie's eyes now overfilled and tears of joy and delight ran down her cheeks as she clapped to them in tune with the happy, vibrant music.

Magda had a faraway look in her eyes and she said, "When I listen to the way Yann plays his music...*I sometimes think that all the Multiverses could dance together to this tune...because it is not where you go to on the dance floor...but the joy of each step you take to get there...*"

"*Ahem...*" Anders coughed politely, causing Magda to turn around expectantly with a swirl of her long, filmy yellow dress. He had approached her with one arm behind his back and his other extended towards to her with his palm uppermost, his upper body leaning forwards slightly in a stiff bow, and in a perfect French accent he said, "*If Madame...she would like...ze floor of ze Multiverse is ours...!*"

With a beatific smile Magda slowly and gracefully extended her arm to place her hand on top of his with exaggerated elegance, and then after a few slow, measured, deft, ballerina like paces which Anders matched as he stepped lightly backwards he suddenly pulled her closer to him - to poise themselves in a still, formal ballroom pose together, just for a second...*and then...they danced!*

Oh their dancing was so sublime! It was like an amalgamation of a Tango, a quick step, and sometimes a waltz...then, after a few minutes, as the spirited fast paced jig started to fade it suddenly started again from the beginning and Anders swirled Magda round and round both locked together by the crooks of their elbows as she laughed joyously, her eyes sparkling, her head back, and her long reddish auburn hair whisked and floated behind her along with her billowing, gossamer like yellow sari dress, her bare feet hardly touching the floor as she moved with such elegantly sinuous, feline grace...

To Sophie's eyes, blurry from happily ecstatic tears, it looked as if the two of them were actually dancing along the branches and broad leaves of the treetops amongst the growing crowd of rainbow hued, flying, yet dancing birds, whom seemed to be mirroring all their joyous movements...

"*Come on! Come and join us all!*" Magda called to the two young couples standing mesmerised at this exquisitely surreal scene of dancing from them and the now hundreds of vibrantly coloured birds…

Sophie grinned up into Jake's face and reaching for his hands she pulled him onto the floor to dance with her, Mel was doing the same with Dave - and then the six of them were flowing in movement together.

As the fourth or fifth repetition of the music faded away for the final time, their dancing had become almost like a vigorous, innovative, galloping barn dance as they'd frequently interchanged their partners, whooping and shouting, taken over by the sheer, surreal, and energetic fun of it all.

Mel flopped onto a seat and applauded, her hands high above her head, breathing rapidly after her exertions and she laughed loudly crying out *"Woooo! - Ww*ooowww*W!"* Magda and Sophie joined her, laughing as well as they flapped their hands in front of their faces to fan the air. Jake and Dave, hands on their knees, stooped over, and out of breath, grinning at them.

Only Anders seemed totally unruffled by all his exertions, and he stood waving goodbye to the birds, which everyone else then did, as most of them gradually dispersed back into the trees.

They talked excitedly amongst themselves for a while, then Anders suggested that they resume their tour, so he went back to his seat and the craft started to move again, but at a very sedate walking pace, just above the highest branches. The few birds that had remained gracefully glided aside in formation as it passed amongst them. After a few minutes they came to a natural break in the forest where a wide river flowed.

"Crikey me!" Jake said, "It's almost as wide as Filey Bay innit Dave!"

"Woww, yeh, it is mate. Now that's what I'd call *a proper river!"* The two girls, with Magda, stood up and walked over to them. Looking out at the view Magda said, "when you look at the surface of the world from space it looks as if most of it is covered in water, in

fact some other, *non-worldly* beings do actually call it: *'The Water World'*...and in fact there is far, far more water below the surface.

"I am sure you remember me telling you all about the whales' songs? - Well, water conduits vital, coded energetic information as I explained then, it is all a crucial part of the Gaia for the well being of the whole planet...and there certainly never has been nor ever will there be any so called 'Fracking' here - injecting toxic chemicals under high pressure into and damaging the shallower sub surface arterial Leys' waterways, designed to disrupt and corrupt them...the manifest agenda of gas and oil mining is just a profitable – in many ways to them – deception of course..."

Once it had passed the tree-line at the edge of the river's bank the craft descended slowly to roughly a house's height, the giant trees towering above them on one side. It then continued moving slowly above and along the very tall reeds that filled the bank's width, which varied roughly between three to five or six car lengths or so, before they petered out some distance into the river.

The two girls were leaning their hands and foreheads against the clear walls as they looked down and across at the serene and peaceful vista as they passed slowly along it. Sophie then thought she'd seen some movement in the reeds just on the periphery of her vision, so she glanced back and down at the river's edge that flowed amongst the furthest reeds and did an almost cartoon like double take – then with a sharp inhalation of breath she grabbed Jake's arm and exclaimed,

"Oh! Oh! *Oh!* W,W*what – who – is that down there...?!"*

They all quickly looked down at where she was now pointing. Jake said, *"What y'seen Soph'?"*

She was pointing at an area of the reeds whose upper lengths now seemed to be moving unnaturally on their own.

"Summat big's movin' below 'em!" Jake said, then he exclaimed: *"Whaaat?! What's that...?!"*

A large, very hairy, almost human but more ape or bearish like form had emerged and was parting the reeds with its massive hands to stare curiously up at them. River water dripped off its brown and russet coloured long furry hair, as if it had just been swimming.

Magda said, *"Oh Good! There they are!"* and she walked away from the two young couples, a little further down the clear wall and the craft moved slowly down and closer to the creature so that it could see her clearly. It moved its large shaggy head to follow her movement and then astonishingly it smiled as if in recognition of her, revealing large tombstone like teeth in its simian features, and raised a furred hand, its long dark fingers spread wide.

Magda smiled back at it and copied the movement with her right hand. It then rose up getting bigger and bigger as it stood to its full height and the two young couples realised that it had been partly crouching before, mostly hidden in the reeds.

Seeing it at its full height now it was about ten or twelve feet tall...*"Bloooody 'elllll!"* Jake gasped in shock, his mouth and eyes wide open – and they stayed wide open, the same as the other three's were now.

"It looks a bit like, like...'Chewbacca' - from StarWars...!"

"Oh-My-God!" Dave said, "I, I think I know what it is...! - *It's a BigFoot! A Yeti! 'S'godda be! - Can it?!...Oh My God..!"*

"Well done David!" Magda said, still smiling as she turned her head towards them, *"You are quite right*! On the surface world they have been called BigFoot, Yeti, Sasquatch, Bun Manchi - and many other names in the local languages of the old tribes that lived, and some still do, in the more remote regions...

"These are distant relations to some of the – *giants* - we talked about earlier..."

"I know about...well, only what I've read and heard about them – *I suppose we all do, we all have* – but they've always been just a sort of, sort of...*part of mystery folklore* – like, like - the *Loch Ness Monster...!"*

"Oh she is *quite 'real' as well David!"* Magda said, very matter-of-factly, "...she and many of her kind use the hidden and vastly deeper underground waterways to move around the planet, and like salmon do they always return to their own spawning grounds, which is why she and others are occasionally seen in that particular Loch - *and lots of other places*, before they go...elsewhere...*often coming back here of course...*"

"*Blimey O'Reilly...!*" Jake muttered, "A coupla weeks back if y'd told me that Unicorns, Giants, Dancin' Birds, Yetis, an' now Ol' Nessie an'all – *as well as everythin' else – 'were-all-actually-real'*...I'd've said...well...*no prize fer guessin' what...!*"

Then he grinned and added, "I thought at first that it were ol' Simmo messin' about down there! - *I said he could pass for a bald yeti when we were at Magda's that first time!*"

"Come over, come closer - *let him see you - then he'll know you in future.* I've known him and all the others for a long, long time...He is the great-great- grandson of the first one I, we - my sisters and I, first met.

"When my sisters and I were all *very young,* we used to come here a lot to play in the forest, climbing the trees and swimming in the rivers with all of them. Sometimes we, and the much younger ones of the tribes, would sit on the backs of the bigger, older ones as they swam along exploring the rivers...

"...we loved having piggy-back rides as well from the older, stronger ones - *after we and their children had all climbed up as high as we possibly could into the trees* - and then we travelled for miles and miles through the dense forest like that!"

" - *Our Guardians often got quite concerned about us though - when we just went off for days with them...*but they always brought us back safe and sound – apart from the odd grazed knee, scratches from the branches...and our clothing all damp and dirty...!"

"*Mmmmmmm...*" Anders said in mock admonishment, slowly shaking his head, "*What a tribe of seven, headstrong little girls you all were then!...*And still are! - *I'm delighted to say!*" He grinned at her. "*My Goodness Me...! – You all more than 'often'! - caused me and the others many fretting palpitations as you all screamed like wild and excited little banshees - clinging onto their backs, hundreds of*

389

feet up in the air – or way out in the rivers - and then went off and disappeared...for days at a time...!"

Magda scrunched her shoulders up, in mock contrition, and with a *'little-girl's-caught-out-for-being-naughty-grin'* on her face, she fluttered her eyelashes under raised eyebrows, and rolled her eyes at him. Anders couldn't help himself from continuing to grin even wider back at her, as they then quickly mind-fused to share some very old and very fond memories...

She then looked to Sophie, Jake, Mel and Dave, saying, *"...Our excuses were the exciting impetuosities and exuberances of playful youth! But - I can now quite understand* just how concerned Anders and the others must have been at times...but we had a lovely childhood here...after leaving...*Anyway...*

"We were hoping some of them would be around here today... which is why Anders was delayed getting into the craft at first – *he, sent a message to them -* to let them know we were coming if they were in the vicinity!"

Despite being slightly lower now, but still fifteen or twenty feet or so up in the air above the reeds inside a hovering flying craft the four of them still walked a little warily over to where Magda was standing and now looking down. As they did so Magda had been staring intently at the large hairy creature, and it had been doing the same to her.

She blinked rapidly a few times to break off her gaze, and turned to look at them as they all clustered around her, and she said, "they are all highly telepathic, it is an attribute they developed from the times when they lived - more often then than they do now, on the surface world. It was essential as a survival aid as some humans they encountered were, and still are, intent on hunting and killing or capturing them...

"...so by using telepathy they could immediately warn their families and others of danger – even over the immense distances of the wilderness regions which are their natural habitats...and of course, like I just said, for more pleasant purposes - *such as arranging for their families – and us today - to meet up...!"*

"Their...*families...you mentioned their 'children' before...?!"* Sophie asked her, staring intently down at him.

"Oh yes, they are very family and tribally oriented, and they are monogamous, mating for life, which is reasonably long, two to three hundred years at least here, slightly less on the surface world due to all the modern day pollution up there...the main reason they are there less and less now...and because of the hunters of course.

"They are very intelligent, gentle giants and very spiritually aware beings, highly attuned to all of the planet's subtle energies. He was just telling me that his family is here with him as well – *and they have all been fishing together in the river for their supper!"*

As soon as she had finished saying this the reeds all around the immense creature slowly moved aside as well...and others appeared, standing up to look at them. One was obviously female, with a very young one held in her arms, suckling at a breast, she was smaller and of slighter stature than the first, now clearly male creature, and there were three others, two males larger than her but not as tall as the first one, who was obviously their Father, and a much younger looking, smaller female standing partly obscured behind her Mother, shyly peeking upwards from around her hip like a little girl would do.

The first, huge male they had seen reached down amongst the reeds in front of him and then straightened up holding a massive silvery fish by its gills in one hand. He held it up high towards the hovering craft, offering it to them.

"Oh Bless Him!" Magda said, "...he is telling me that they have had a successful fishing trip and would like to share their catch with us...*so we can eat a good supper later too!"*

By now Anders had quietly joined them, unnoticed by the two couples, and he was holding a package about the size of a deep A3 box file wrapped in several large green leaves which he handed to Magda saying, "here you are my dear, just as you asked!"

He then grinned at Jake, "...you're not the only one with a penchant for good chocolate ol'chap! They love it too! Magda suggested we bring some for them - hoping that we'd meet, so I think it's an excellent exchange! - *Not that he would've expected anything at all in return for his gift of a fish*, that is quite a, *touchingly spontaneous and very generous offer he's just made to us!"*

"Thank you Anders!" Magda said, taking the heavy package from him and partly unfolding a leaf to reveal shiny dark chocolate slabs, and held it towards the family group below for them to see it, in the same gesture of offering a gift.

Broad smiles, nodding heads and jerky, bouncy movements of their bodies with much arm waving as if they were punching the air clearly expressed their pleasure at seeing what Magda was showing them.

Sophie, having observed the exuberant responses from the group below them, then looked up into Jake's face, hers was a picture of wide eyed, calculated innocence, like Magda's had been a few seconds earlier, and trying desperately now not to smile, she said to him, "Well – *that explains a lot Jake!"*

"Huh? W,what's that? - *Explains what Soph?!"*

"Well...all *what they're doing now is exactly what you do when you've got a whole chocolate cake in front of you! Who knows - maybe – maybe y're related?!* – 'Cause I mean, it's pretty clear that – *that the resemblance is definitely there!"*

She could then no longer hold back her gush of laughter and attempted to smother it by burying her face into his leather clad arm and hugging it tightly.

"*Mmmm*...sorry about that folks...!" He sighed loudly with mock, and patronising toleration. "Soph's obviously halloocin'...hallucent – *seein' things that aren't there...!"* He turned his head, nose in the air, away from the mirth quivering girl hugging his arm, but a grin which then stayed on his face ruined his act of affronted but tolerant composure.

"I keep seeing clear evidence that your excellent humour is more than *just rubbing off a little bit* onto Sophie now Jake!" Magda said to him, grinning widely as well, "...*but watch closely now,* all of you, otherwise you might all think you are all: *'seeing things...!'"*

She then moved closer towards the clear glassy like wall, paused, and a circular doorway shimmered open, she then stepped or more accurately – *she glided* - through it...! *'How does she do that?!'* Sophie thought to herself, *again*, watching in fascination.

Loud gasps of alarm and astonishment at what happened next erupted from the four of them as Magda, who was now levitating in mid air, glided a few feet forwards, away from the craft and then slowly floated down to the reeds to 'stand', eye to eye, in front of the more than twice as tall hairy male creature who'd quickly pushed aside the tall reeds in front of him for her to do so.

She nodded rapidly to him now they were in a close proximity greeting, and she held out her gift to him. He nodded rapidly back again to her, still with a huge smile on his face, and reaching out with his free hand, with Magda helping him, he carefully removed some of the large leaves that were covering it, and then wrapped them tightly around the big fish's head - so she could carry it without letting it slip from her hands - before holding it out to her - and then they exchanged their gifts.

The others of his family had moved excitedly closer to him in anticipation, and from the top slab he quickly broke off large thick chunks of the richly dark chocolate, handing one to each of them.

Before they put the chocolate into their grinning mouths to eat them, they first rapidly nodded, their eyes showing their gratitude to Magda, then, after sniffing it with the same pleasurable intensity of a wine connoisseur, they sucked and chewed at the sweet confection, their eyes screwed shut in unmistakeable pleasure.

Their treats were soon eaten and then the large male plucked up a long reed and wrapped it tightly around all the remaining slabs, deftly tying a knot into a carrying handle for their precious gift.

Magda remained with the family for a good few minutes, communicating telepathically with each of them, and then smiling with delight, she glided slowly towards the Mother and her baby, holding the huge and obviously very heavy fish with apparent ease in one hand away to her side, and she reached out to gently caress the little ones furry head, who then actually ceased his intense suckling to stare wide-eyed up into her eyes, and squeeked happily to her.

Just before she rose up to return back to the craft, with a wide smile she raised the large fish up high with both her hands now clasped around the leaves, and nodded her head in gratitude again to them all. The huge male mirrored her actions with their gift.

As she floated upwards but remained facing them, all the family raised their hands in farewell to her, then to the others in the craft, who all returned the gesture. Then they lowered themselves to disappear again amongst the reeds, and the only sign of their presence as they moved away towards the trees was an occasional movement of the reeds' tips as they passed stealthily below them.

Once back inside the craft, the doorway shimmered as it closed, and Magda, now walking, held up the huge fish for everyone to see. She held its leaf covered head at her chest height, the widest part of its body was almost as wide as hers, and its broad tail was dangling just off the floor.

"Crikey Me!" Jake said, *"...that's a fish an' a half! Must weigh a ton! What is it?!"*

"It is called a 'Zander', sometimes a 'Steel-Head' it is a cross between a salmon and a trout, they can live in either fresh or salt water, and they are found as well on the surface world, but mainly in Canada and further North – *though not usually quite so large as this one!"*

"Let me take it my dear, and I'll go and disappear into the kitchen to prepare our supper!...*I did have something else in mind for us...*" Anders was saying as he took the big fish from Magda with the same apparent lack of any straining to hold it.

"...*but this certainly trumps that!* I won't be long! And whilst I do perhaps you would take us to where we can enjoy it with a view as well! Actually – *I think I've got a pretty good idea of where you might be thinking of going to...!*" His eyes twinkled at her, then he said to the others, all still gazing awestruck at the huge fish he was now holding,

"– I hope you are all hungry! - *It's steamed fish for supper!*"

"Aye! *I am! – But, er...what's everyone else 'avin'?!*" Jake replied with deadpan concern.

Chapter 21: The In-Flight Meal

"Wow! *Thank you very much* Anders! That was definitely *the best, the finest,* the *tastiest* fish supper *I've ever had!*" Sophie said, putting her silver cutlery down and daintily dabbing at her lips with a dark blue linen napkin.

Mel said, "*Absolutely!* It was su*perb!* You are *a chef extrordinaire!* Thank you!

Dave verbosely agreed with both of them as well as he finished clearing his plate, and then complimented him further. Jake was still munching away, having had a large second portion of the steamed fish and subtly piquant sauce that Anders had made to accompany it, and, as Magda had said earlier, 'there was still plenty left for Lucia and Ruth to enjoy later!'

"*Oh you are all being far too kind!*" Anders modestly replied. - "It's just something I managed to cobble together at the last minute! *It was rather a surprise* - a nice surprise, when I saw him hold it up for us I must say! We were going to have something quite different! *So I'm very pleased you all enjoyed it!*"

"*Blimey!* If that were summat y'just '*cobbled together at the last minute*', me mind boggles at what y'can do in the kitchen Anders! *It were brilliant, best I've ever 'ad too! Thank you!*" Jake said. He sighed contentedly, and leant back, putting an arm around Sophie's shoulders to give her a quick hug.

Magda grinned and said, "*I can tell you that he is being far too modest!* - Do please tell everyone about the times you had with some of the chefs that are now '*household names*' Anders!"

Anders smiled at her, a look of reminiscence coming into his eyes as he leant back contentedly as well before starting to talk. "Well...in *fairly* recent times...I first met Georges – Georges Escoffier in Cannes, early in...it would be...ohhh...eighteen seventy nine...Tuesday of the second week in February, now that I remember! - Magda and her sisters were just too busy in Paris at the time to go, so they asked me if

I would go down to Cannes on the train with two trunks full of paintings to meet with an art dealer who had expressed a lot of interest in promoting and exhibiting some of the artworks of the painters we were all involved with...and so off I went, and a very pleasant and successful trip it turned out to be as well – in more ways than one!

"The art dealer had suggested by letter, that on the evening of my arrival, after I'd settled in and rested after my journey at the hotel he'd recommended, and kindly booked a room there for me, that we meet at his friend Georges's restaurant which he'd recently opened called, *'Le Faison d'Or'* – 'The Golden Pheasant', which, like the hotel, turned out to be a truly delightful place.

"Tonight's supper was a sort of homage to the wonderful things Georges used to do there – and other places in later years – particularly with the fresh sea bass, although I had to use finely chopped dates rubbed in orange zest tonight - as I didn't have any crushed Muscat grapes marinated for days in a very dry, vintage Picpoul de Pinet wine, to add to the thick, creamy, fermented goat's cheese sauce base like he usually did - and Georges kindly showed me how to - when he took me into his kitchen during some of the many evenings I dined there! -

"But I think I got away with it for us all tonight! Georges and I met up again a few years later when he had moved from Cannes to Monte Carlo for a while, and then onto London. He was partnered with Cesar by that time – Cesar Ritz, at The Savoy, and I spent quite a fair bit of time there with both of them, not only enjoying the produce of their gastronomic talents, but also learning some of the rudiments of their art from them.

"You'll've all heard of 'The Ritz Hotels'? - Well, in London, basically that's where they all got started, named after Cesar of course. Magda and I helped out with most of the initial financing for his enterprise, and over the years that investment proved to be quite fruitful, enabling us to use the profits from it to help with many other worthwhile enterprises we came across...

"Which is what we normally do with all the profits from the

multifarious business ventures we have established over the years – all were run by us and our friends under our various 'legends' of the times of course! And a lot of the older, more established ones, are now continued to be successfully run by others of us...In many countries!

"Then, in later years, when I was back in Paris again, I picked up a few tips from Adolphe, Adolphe Duglere, a true genius of a chef at the 'Cafe Anglais', which by then we had a small interest in as well...I first started going there – *well we all did 'on and off' didn't* we...?" He said looking at Magda who nodded affirmatively, "...because as well as the excellent cuisine we all enjoyed the company of the actors and singers from the Opera House just around the corner who usually dined there after a performance, and were often with some of their influential Patrons who were dining there as well...

"I'm not name dropping, but Magda and I were invited one evening to a private dinner hosted at the Cafe Anglais for the Tsar Alexander. He was a very pleasant chap, and we got to know him and his family quite well after that, and of course you'll recall, Magda, our lengthy stay – he insisted that all your sisters came with us as well - at his invitation at one of his winter palaces just outside St. Petersburg a couple of months later....and everything that happened there of course...?!

"- Ha ha! *I think he was quite taken with Lucia don't you?! –* And I'll *certainly never forget* the look on her face just prior to our departure when he presented her with that large gilded chest full of rare crystals and gem stones from his Siberian mines! - Took two of his more burly servants to carry it out and load it into our horse drawn carriage!

"Lucia's look and reactions when she'd seen what was in it weren't at all dissimilar to those of our friends at the riverbank when you showed them the slabs of chocolate!"

He chuckled with Magda, who had a faraway wistful look in her eyes as she said, *"Ohhh yes!* - I do remember as well...that I had to quickly and discretely put a restraining hand on her arm as she was so excited, then when she saw those two poor men staggering and slipping over the snow and ice with the heavy chest, out of concern for them *she was just about to levitate it to save them from struggling! – Which might have been just a teeny bit too much for those two chaps, Alexander and his family, the Troop of mounted cossacks he'd ordered to escort us, and all the high ranking dignitaries that were present to have witnessed...!*

"...despite everything we had demonstrated to them and talked about during our lengthy stay there!"

Anders laughed at the memory of the scene. *"Yes, indeed!* Quite right, *I rather think that display stemming from her distracted - but well meaning concern just might've been!* Fortunately that exquisite Fabergé egg he gave to you was somewhat more easily transportable in your hand luggage!"

Mel gasped, saying, *"Lucia mentioned it yesterday to me in your caravan Magda! It - I mean the crystals and gems – but she just...she just, sort of casually said they were from Russia, from a friend she had there...not, not...the actual...Tsar...of Russia...!"* Her eyes almost as wide as her dinner plate.

Magda chuckled at that as well and gave them a brief accounting of the exciting journey they had all made then in the luxurious State Carriage, pulled along by six magnificent Don horses from the Imperial Stables, and escorted by a dozen fierce looking, armed and mounted Cossack troops, through the snow and wintry conditions of Northern Russia.

She laughed as well as she recounted, *the looks of extreme consternation,* on the Cossack Commander's face, and on all of his mens', when she had stopped the carriage and they all proceeded to disembark into the deep snows alongside a narrow track in the middle of a deep and gloomy forest later that evening, to thank him and his men for accompanying them, but they had now arrived at where they wanted to be...

"He, and his men *were quite understandably not at all happy* about just leaving seven ladies and Anders in the middle of a snow packed, darkening forest in the middle of nowhere with the night falling so rapidly! We actually heard a pack of wolves howling not too far away...! I had to use a gentle glamour to persuade him and his men that everything was fine!

"On their return they would only remember and report that they had safely escorted us to the train station, which had a rail link to the port where our ferry would depart from!

"Unknown to all those gallant men of course was that a tunnel branch was then less than a mile away, well hidden in the foothills, which we all quickly levitated to with all our belongings and gifts once they had departed...!'"

Sophie was absolutely enchanted with the brief tale Magda had just told them, shaking her head slowly in wonderment, as she told her so!...Anders then took up his culinary tales again,

"...Actually, amongst the many things Alexander generously gave to me - including all the silver cutlery we're using now - was that gold fish serving ladle with the ruby and diamond encrusted Romanov Imperial coat of arms..." He pointed to it resting on the now greatly diminished fish on the massive and highly ornate silver platter in the centre of the round dining table.

"...yes...it's the very one he gave me then - *much better to use it for what it was designed to do instead of having it sitting in one of our museums I think – we don't hide things away...!*

"*...and I'm quite sure that if he were sat here with us today he'd quite agree!*

"In fact if he was sat here today - *there probably wouldn't' be any fish left! – Quite an appetite Alex' had!..*Anyway...Sadly, the Cafe Anglais eventually closed, for various reasons, in nineteen thirteen, but, we've lots of good, fine memories of the times we dined there with such varied and interesting people!

"So...I am very grateful *to all* our now absent, dear friends, who were so kind to take the time and teach me so much about their culinary arts - *not that I would ever consider myself capable of holding a candle upto what they could create in their kitchens of course...!"*

Sophie was totally enthralled, and looking at Jake, Dave and Mel she saw that they obviously were too. She thought that the brief glimpses that Anders and Magda had revealed, once again, just now, into their unnaturally long lives were truly enchanting, and awe inspiring, *and so, just so romantic and so exciting!* In her mind question after question was now vying for attention to be asked, but she chose to ask Magda the one that she'd had for a long time first.

"Magda...I, I really hope you don't mind me asking...but, when...Lucia...when she was going to levitate the heavy chest full of crystals and gems - just before you stopped her, and when you – *glide* – and when you all levitated through that snow filled Russian forest at night, and when you went out and floated down to the, to the family in the reeds...*how...how do you do that...?!"* Her voice ending in almost a whisper.

Magda smiled at her, and then tilted her head down, looking downwards in deep thought for a moment, then she leaned forwards, her head now up and her hands flat on the table top, her long slim fingers splayed out, a pose not dissimilar to a card player 'putting all their cards on the table -' for all to see...

"I do not mind you asking me at all Sophie, it is a question I imagine that you all probably would like to hear...something... of how it is done...

"Sooo, as well as the ancient knowledge of acoustic levitation – using complex resonances of sound to reconfigure the natural wavelength force and effect of gravity and so raise or move large heavy objects such as stone building blocks – and to demolish walls such as those of Jericho! - The art and ability to immediately levitate *oneself* and *objects at will*, is closely related to telekinesis - the art of focusing the mind's innate power to harness – forces – to then move 'objects'.

"I said 'related' – imagine acoustic levitation and telekinesis as being the very young great grand-daughters, and what I will now try and explain is the *Great Grand-Mother* to them. And those great grand-*daughters* are *just two* of her vast progeny...of her offspring...

401

"But, be warned, it does all tend to defy a precise 'modern-day' scientifically mainstream empirically simple, or brief explanation or interpretation, mainly because it is a process of *'Gnosis'*. That is a higher spiritual wisdom coupled with pure, true, advanced knowledge - *and understanding.*

"Then, once attained – *or, more accurately I should say* – once one has been made aware of it in the first place, and then guided to and then shown how to climb up several rungs of 'The Ladder of Gnosis' that extends upwards - perhaps *ad infinitum* – like 'Jacob's Ladder', mentioned in many ancient religious texts, and was, in part, an analogy for one's spiritual ascent to the heavenly realms...It is then a process of just...*Knowing,* in the full lumination as well *of Truly Believing You Can, By Eradicating The Resistance To That Of The Habitual Lower Consciousness, and then...the key is: Allowing...*

"As I've mentioned to you all before about other esoteric, psychic abilities such as telepathy, intuition and deliberate creation, this is also something *that you all are quite capable of doing.*

"I know Anders explained some of this, in his first talk to you in the Trocadero Cafe, about your creative ability that is *innate* – and he told you that the word stems from the old Latin word *'natus'* which means 'born' - *within all of you.*

"However, as both Anders and I have also explained, the conscious, Light Filled Awareness of your capabilities to utilise these – and many more abilities - has been deliberately dimmed and rendered almost dormant by the parasites – at least within the general masses of humanity.

"There are many individual adepts and those who still live in isolated meditative communities on the surface world who can levitate their bodies at will quite naturally...*plus do many other things of course which would seem quite 'Magical' at first sight!* - And then there are those as well *who can perform true 'Magic' of course* – both black and white...*not that 'Magic' itself is either* – that depends entirely on the intention and purpose to which it is utilised by the practitioner of it...

"All my six sisters and I – and Anders - *not all of us at the same time though!* - Have cumulatively spent many, many years over many, many visits, living with and learning such occult – which simply means *hidden* – knowledge and abilities from Ascended Masters and Maters at one such remote, isolated monastic community. And I really do mean *a very remote, isolated and very secret community* in a high, totally inhospitable, mountainous region of Northern Tibet. I did mention it, but just briefly, earlier, when I explained to you all somethings of my family's' ancestry.

"Our initial sojourns there were many, *many centuries* before the Chinese invaded and occupied that country in the nineteen fifties, not that that has, in fact, disrupted those particular Masters and Maters, and all the others who live there, very much at all, as they too can obviously utilize glamours and wardings of course to hide their location from prying and hostile eyes - even if a spy or seeker could get anywhere close to it physically. It is also energetically shrouded and so unknown about to remote viewers who are constantly seeking it, along with all the modern satellite imaging devices.

"There were many other similar, offshoot communities living quite openly within the general populace, for many decades prior to the invasion, which have since dispersed across the surface world, at least...those who survived it did...

"Where we were, and we still return to, now just every few years for several months or so, is connected to here by a branch tunnel, and now for a long time, it has had a portal to it in Shamballah, at the King's residence.

"Learning how to levitate ourselves and objects at will was just one of the basic abilities we were enlightened to there and instructed in. I remember towards the end of one of my early visits to 'The Secret Monastery' as a neophyte, a student, a long, long, *long time ago*, we - myself and an 'Ascended Mater', which is Latin for 'Mother', deliberately trecked on foot for half a day to a nearby high peak, through the deep snow, ice and freezing wind to where there was a secret, hidden, small cave.

403

"When we finally got there the sky was quite dark but the mountains all around us were subtly illumined by all the starlight and a huge full moon. I had to sit, cross legged, just inside the cave's entrance, overlooking a world of immensely high, snow covered mountain ranges that just seemed to go on and on forever in front of me – actually, it was that view, many centuries later, which inspired the design of the tapestry you all admired so much in my caravan!

"Before sitting though I had had to remove all my 'warm' robes *until I was wearing only my birthday suit!* The Ascended Mater – *then similarly un-attired* - sat down next to me and in moments she was radiating heat from her body until she had melted all the snow around us cocooning us both in warmth, and made us impervious to the ferociously bitter, sub-zero wind.

"She gradually reduced *her warm cocoon away from me* as I initially struggled and then finally managed to create and maintain my own, which she had spent the previous weeks instructing me how to in preparation for this – but that had been whilst we were out of the strong freezing wind and inside the relative warmth of the cliff top monastery. Although I say *'warmth'* - the ambient temperature in there is only ever just above freezing to one's 'normal' senses…

"When she was satisfied that I had managed to create and maintain my own protective cocoon of warmth, and was transcending into a state of consciousness where the *illusory mental de-coding perception* of 'cold' did not exist in, and my body was regulating its own comfortable temperature despite being in that savagely freezing environment, we levitated ourselves a few inches above the now wet, snow and ice melted ground.

"We stayed there like that for nearly two days - although it only seemed to me, at the end of it, to have been a couple of hours at the most, as time is only linear in the third dimension. We had left our physical bodies in the safety of the cave and surrounded by our protective cocoons as she guided me on my first forays into the astral realms…and then many higher dimensions beyond...

"On my next stay there - at The Secret Monastery – not the cave! - I learned to walk barefoot over the glowing embers in a fire trench with no damage or pain to my bare feet.

"So I had learned by then *to understand,* and so, how to overcome and *'de-code' and 'dis-mantle' from me* the lower consciousness's habitual perceptions *of what it regarded as 'reality'* – such as intense cold, and intense heat...As well, of course, as part of all that, how to levitate at will.

"All such things are, basically, all dependent on knowledge, understanding and then applying it by learning to transcend your consciousness to *'de-code', 'dis-mantle' and so nullify* what your everyday, conscious, and habitual mind is perceiving and telling your body how to respond - to what it *'thinks'* is real...as I mentioned just now, it is all about *'eradicating the resistance of the habitual lower consciousness's perceptions'*...

"Essentially, one starts with meditation, quietening the 'everyday' mind, thus eventually connecting and fusing with the true nature of higher consciousness, and de-fusing from the lower mind and the habitual perceptions it has of the so called *'material reality of the world of 'things' ',* until *'every-thing'* – your -*'self'* included - appears as interconnected luminous vibrations of energy, which you can then learn to interact with and manipulate, *using the attention of your higher conscious intent,* levitating if that is your intention; with much practice and careful guidance of course, until eventually you can do it at will, instantaneously...almost like a habit..."

Magda then looked around at their faces, seeing various expressions on them that clearly showed their intense attempts to process what she had just said.

"Oh dear, I hope you are all not too bemused by all of that! It is, I must admit, hardly the stuff of relaxing *'after-supper-talk'!* So...as an introduction, perhaps we will leave it at that for now and come back to it another time...? Let us stretch our legs shall we and have a look at the view again now?!"

Their seats, around the circumference of the round table they'd used to dine on, swivelled round smoothly for them to stand up and walk over to the 'front' transparent side of the craft. They all stood close to the transparent wall looking out over the fabulously idyllic view of the tropical beach scene that Magda had guided the craft to whilst Anders had prepared their fish supper.

They could hear the watery sussuration of frothy waves, fifteen to twenty feet below them, from the cerulean blue and turquoise freshwater sea as they raced up the pinky white coralline beach sands before rolling over and spreading their glinting foamy rivulets over the beach, before flowing back to do it all over again and again. Tall, broad palm like trees edged the wide beach as far as their eyes could see in both directions.

"It, it's all so, so absolutely gorgeous..." Sophie whispered reverently, her eyes watering again with sheer joy from looking out over the exquisite, natural, peaceful beauty of the scene in front of her.

"Yes...yes it is indeed. It is one of our favourite places..." Magda replied just as quietly.

Anders then said, rather more loudly, *"Absolutely it is!* It's a lovely place to have supper...and then enjoy a gentle stroll afterwards along the beach! But before *we do* have that stroll - *I do hope* you'll all like the musical accompaniment I've just put on that I think goes so well with being here...it is the extended version of Ralph's - Ralph Vaughan Williams – 'Fantasia On A Theme By Thomas Tallis', I think it is exquisite and spiritually uplifting music...especially when you listen to it here, it's just one of his many fine compositions…

"The next music I thought I'd play for us, before we have our stroll, is by Gustave Holst, it is 'The Choral Hymn To Vena From The Rig Veda, Set Three', and it is, I think, just as equally uplifting..."

The stirring, transcendental - but gently so, heart and soul fulfilling music at low volume allowed the whispering like sounds of the waves close by below them all to accompany it. Sophie leaned into Jake, resting her cheek, dampened again with overflowing tears of pure happiness and ecstatic joy, onto his upper arm, her arms wrapped tightly around his waist, her eyes half closed in rapture at the paradisical scene and beautiful music flowing through them.

Standing next to them Mel and Dave lovingly hugged each other too, and apart from the two couples' deep breaths emanating from this experience of pure joy they were silently and utterly transfixed with everything their senses were registering for them.

When all the beautiful music had finally faded away Magda quietly said, "Thank You Anders, that was all so lovely to hear again...thank you. Well...everyone – shall we have a gentle stroll now along the beach before we depart?"

The two couples slowly unfurled themselves whilst agreeing enthusiastically to the suggestion of a stroll along the beach, but less enthusiastically so to the prospect of ever having to leave this wondrous place...this Elysian State of Happiness...

The craft slowly moved to hover a few inches over the pinky white beach and a wide doorway shimmered open for them all to step out at once together onto it.

They walked a fair distance along the shore, whilst talking and listening intensely to the replies from Magda and Anders to their myriad questions and desires for more and more details about everything they'd heard and seen so far that evening.

After a long while they came across some fallen palm trees and sat on the broad trunks, to continue their talking and to share their thoughts, for a few hours more, and to gaze over the surreally beautiful sea and sandy landscape all around them.

When they were ready, not that they wanted to be in the slightest, to leave, the craft, now way down the sands of the beach behind them, was summoned by Anders and it moved silently towards them, then hovered close by, and so, reluctantly, they re-embarked, for their flight back to Shamballah...and then to return to their world...

...Like pilgrims journeying back home from a sacred place...*having left only their footprints in the sand, and having taken...only their memories...*

To be continued...

Please read on to the following pages: 'About The Author...'

ABOUT THE AUTHOR

Made in Sheffield.

'Child of the sixties, teenager of the seventies, man of The World'.

Gave up on the mainstream's scholarly pursuits because they were just limiting his *real life* education, but those he had were:

Fulwood Infants, Oakwood Preparatory, Nether Green Juniors, King Edward V11 schools. Granville College, Sheffield Polytechnic, Middlesex Polytechnic, Sheffield University, Carnegie College Leeds, all Fine Arts or investigative social studies courses.

Employed and self-employed experiences, during and after the above include: paper rounds, supermarket shelf stacking, security guard, dustbin man, insurance salesman, nightclub bouncer in Sheffield and later in London. A pit machinery manufacturing factory labourer, Royal Marine Commando recruit, in the mid seventies, for a

409

month, University Officer Training Corps for 2 years, forestry worker, Friern Barnet mental hospital laundry worker, supervisor in a remand and assessment centre.

Full-time tournament tennis player for 2 years in France and England. Care staff member in a childrens' home. Renovated a large house in Leeds for student accommodation as a live-in landlord. Sandhurst Graduate, Territorial Army, then an Infantry Platoon Commander, retired (due to moving abroad) after several years just before promotion to Captain. A security business, and then an architectural antiques business in the Lake District; also ran 'Survival & Adventure Training Weekends' for the 5th and 6th formers at a public boarding school twice a month during term times. Whilst living there he also doubled for Ben Cross in the 1986 TV film 'Strong Medicine'.

Moved to a village, with his lady partner, in central Mallorca, at the foothills of the mountains, where they bought and renovated an old house, and single-handedly built another smaller one (illegally – but got away with it) in the grounds; then decided to buy a ruin just outside the village to transform it into a bar/cafe, and run it; he also worked for a Mallorquian demolition/excavations company, picked olives, coached tennis at two very prestigious clubs, established a small coaching school in the village, painted and sometimes sold his artworks.

He had two Alsatians he regularly walked with up in the forested mountains, and one winter he drove a nineteen fifties Willys jeep from Carlisle to Mallorca, keeping it for several years, for road transport as well as for lengthy, exploratory excursions up in the same mountains.

Rotherham bus station site refurb' labourer. Marlborough College's summer school tennis coach, then the coach at a nearby top public boarding school for girls, then Batchwood Hall, St. Albans, as a coach and veteran UK competitor.

Then to Salisbury as a motorcycle riding instructor. Bespoke office furniture design, manufacturing and installation company as a general help. Moved to Scarborough to open his own work's art gallery/studio. Bar stock-taker for a nationwide hotel chain, (and in later years in Scarborough he occasionally did the same for the Royal British Legion.) Property renovation/project management/sales, own business, and established his own property portfolio of over a dozen rental properties all over the North of England, but nearly went bankrupt.

Now he just lives alone with his two cats: 'Big Floyd' and 'Little Harry'...does voluntary work for the local Age UK charity shop one day a week, paints, prefers classical music these days, doesn't have a TV, reads voraciously and researches, rides a motorbike and has started writing...

Some experiences mixed in with the above: he lived in a caravan during school holidays to compete in tennis tournaments all over the UK. At Granville College he lived in the YMCA Sheffield, but was thrown out due to the management discovering he was regularly having his girlfriend stay overnight. Homeless - so he lived in an air-raid shelter in the woods for that spring and summer, then found various lodgings. Enjoyed the Rock n' Roll scene in Sheffield. Met Patricia Crowther, the white witch and High Priestess of the Wiccan coven at a lecture she gave in Sheffield. When living in London he attended the Society for Psychical Research, and the Theosophical Society.

Travelled on the secondary route trains to Morocco, including the Marrakesh Express. Got ripped off in the bazaar. Had an incredible kundalini awakening experience whilst alone one warm, rainy afternoon on an old train slowly rattling through France.

Travelled throughout Europe, and when in Greece on a motorbike, again, mainly 'rough camping' – stayed awhile in an isolated village high up in the northern mountains where he was the first Englishman that the elderly Headman had met since leading the Resistance in the second world war! He had worked with British paratroopers and the S.O.E.; on being told that the author was in the Officer Training Corps attached to London University he was very hospitable - having tables immediately set up for a day and night long feast, music and

411

celebration in the village's main street!

Lived in the woods near the beach on the island of Santorini for a while, in later years he travelled all over France and Spain on his motorbike, rough camping again, exploring Crusader castles and ancient ruins. Met 'El Rey de los Gitanos' – the 'King of the Gypsies' in an ancient mountain village deep in Southern Spain, where they stabled their horses in the houses' downstairs rooms, and the families lived upstairs....

Competed for the army as a long distance runner and crewman in the 3 Peaks Yacht Race – the yacht was almost wrecked in a ferocious storm out at sea and he nearly drowned; shot pistol and rifle at Bisley in the shooting team – runner-up North of England Pistol shot. Drove a tank once across Salisbury Plain. In later years he lived near to Stonehenge, previously lodging near to Silbury Hill. Saw many strange things in the skies, and also later, whilst living in the Scarborough area as well. He was Chairman of the Scarborough Lawn Tennis Club and a Team Captain.

Sailed a small wooden boat with a friend across the Med, spoke briefly with a dolphin who often swam alongside at sunrise.

- *Apparently he's still not really sure what he's going to do when he grows up...!*

The author is also an artist, some of his works can be seen on his website:

www.fineartandfurnishings.co.uk

Made in the USA
Middletown, DE
15 March 2021

35578819R00230